Taking Chances

A *WeHo* Story

Sherryl D. Hancock

Published by Vulpine Press in the United Kingdom in 2018

ISBN: 978-1-83919-014-8

Cover by Claire Wood
Cover photo credit: Tirzah D. Hancock

www.vulpine-press.com

Also in the WeHo series:

Chapter 1

"Alright, *Palani*," Kana said, her tone stern on the smaller woman's first name. "What can I do for you?"

They were standing in the parking garage adjacent to the San Diego Police Department. Kana had met Palani Ryker the day before, when she and her partner in homicide had questioned Mrs. Ryker about a murder. Now, Palani had turned up, lingering near Kana's Lincoln Navigator. Kana had been quite shocked to see the beautiful woman seemingly stalking her, and it showed in her reactions.

Palani smiled inexplicably, biting her bottom lip. Kana was dumbfounded.

"What?" Kana asked in spite of herself.

"It's the first time you've said my first name," Palani said, sounding awed.

"And?" Kana was still bewildered at the young woman's obvious exaltation.

"And you pronounced it right, with the emphasis on the last syllable. Most people get it wrong the first time," Palani explained, still smiling like a kid at Christmas.

Kana shook her head, then glanced at her watch. "First of all, Mrs. Ryker, you told me your name yesterday, pronouncing it, assumedly, correctly. Secondly, had I not been paying attention then, I also had seventeen years on Oahu to learn how to pronounce Hawaiian names properly."

Palani didn't seem daunted by Kana's tone in the slightest. Her eyes still sparkled with excitement, even as she purposefully wiped the grin off her lips.

"What is it you want, Mrs. Ryker?" Kana asked. It was not the first time that morning, and she was getting agitated.

"Are you in a hurry?"

"Rather," Kana replied, blinking twice. *Is she ever going to get to her point?*

Palani hesitated, not wanting to irritate Kana but wanting to talk to her all the same.

Kana looked back at her for a long moment, then sighed. "Get in," she said, unlocking the passenger door with the remote.

Palani smiled and walked around to the passenger side of the Navigator. Kana got in on the driver's side and started the vehicle up with a rumble. Palani looked around curiously. The interior of the Navigator was black leather, and it smelled good. She noticed the beaded crystals that hung on the rear-view mirror. It was a combination of carnelian and black onyx, the crystals for passion and inner calm. Both hung on silver rope chains that intertwined.

Kana nodded at the officer at the gate to the parking garage as she drove by him, putting on her sunglasses and pulling onto the road. This was an unexpected turn of events, and it was throwing a normally unperturbable Kana off a bit.

"So what is it you want?" she asked.

"To talk to you."

"Is it something else you remembered about the case?" Kana prompted, desperate for that to be the case.

"Well… no. I told you and your partner, Officer Ako, everything I knew yesterday."

"Then I'm not sure what we're doing here."

"Well… I just…" Palani grimaced, suddenly feeling foolish.

She'd had a hunch about Sergeant Kana Sorbinno of San Diego PD Homicide Division, but now she wasn't so sure. But it was too late to turn back. "I just wanted to talk to you… in a less official capacity," she added in a rush when she saw Kana's dark eyes narrow.

"So talk," Kana said, her tone all cop, throwing an unconcerned shrug.

Palani looked back at her, biting her lip. Kana Sorbinno was a lot more intimidating than she'd really realized. What if Kana told her she was crazy? What if she laughed in her face? Was this even a good idea? What if she was wrong? All these questions swirled in her head as she tried to think of something to say.

Palani had worked with another model named Jerry Castle a number of times, and they'd become close friends. It was well known in the modeling community that Jerry was a lesbian. In getting to know her, Palani had realized that despite not understanding the gay community at all, she liked the other woman a great deal. It had been Jerry that had made Palani aware that something really was missing in her life. Palani had achieved her lifelong goal of becoming a model, and that should have made her happy, but it didn't. Jerry, who was deeply in love with her girlfriend, would frequently talk about the times she and Jane Anne would lie in bed and talk for hours. About the silly things they'd do to make each other laugh. How she couldn't wait to get done with the shoot they were working on so she could go home to her "baby."

Palani realized she'd never had that, and that she wanted it desperately. Looking back, she'd realized that even the men she'd dated before had never made her feel like Jerry said she felt when she was with Jane Anne. So Palani decided she needed to work at it. So she'd set to work trying to achieve that with Matthew, who she'd married two years before.

Matthew Ryker was her manager. He'd been there for her since the day she'd walked into his office and told him she wanted to be a model. He was a very mild man, quiet, unassuming, but when he did his job, he did it well. When he'd asked Palani to marry him, she'd been so grateful for all his support she accepted, never considering the fact that he wasn't someone she was deeply in love with. The last two years had been quiet and stable, just like Matthew.

Palani quickly found out that Matthew didn't respond well to change. She tried to do romantic little things for him, to which he simply didn't know how to respond. She tried to lie in bed and talk to him one morning after he'd haphazardly made love to her. As usual, she'd been left unsatisfied; it was something she figured was a problem with her. She knew she was able to achieve an orgasm—she'd given herself enough of them alone—but Matthew had no talent in that area. The discussion had been about something she'd thought he'd be interested in, the latest Fendi line. Matthew had grown impatient with her rather quickly and had gotten out of bed. She'd tried a few other times, in other situations, but Matthew never had the time to have "inane" conversations with her.

Then it had struck her. Did Jerry have what she had with Jane Anne because they were both women? Because women were just more capable of feeling so much more deeply? She started spending time with the couple, and found that more and more she envied Jerry.

4

Jane Anne was the classic butch type, but she was so sweet to Jerry. When Jerry would drop something, Jane Anne would lean down and pick it up. Jane Anne took charge when things were going wrong, like their reservation for a restaurant being lost or a car not arriving when it should. Palani saw that Jane Anne basically cocooned Jerry in security and love, and Palani ached for that. So her curiosity about women had started there.

She had in a small way "investigated" the alternate lifestyle, accompanying Jerry and Jane Anne to a few gay clubs. She'd been too shy to talk to anyone, and almost afraid to respond to some of the more aggressive women that approached her. Many of them had been butch, and Palani had quickly discovered that she wasn't attracted to that type of woman at all. Being so feminine, much like Jerry, she assumed she was supposed to be with a woman that was butch, like Jane Anne. She never discussed it with Jerry, feeling foolish for not knowing. The fact that she hadn't been attracted to the butch women, however, made her question her own curiosity—was she wrong?

Meeting Kana the day before, when she and her partner had come to her door to question Matthew about a famous photographer that had been murdered, had sent her curiosity into overdrive instantly. Kana had dazzled her with her dark features and proud stature, reminding Palani instantly of the goddess Pele from her homeland's folklore. At first her attraction had been on a purely physical level, seeing Kana's dark eyes and flowing black hair. Kana's size—she stood at five feet ten—rather than being imposing, actually seemed comforting to her. Then Kana's manner; she was so strong and direct. It made Palani curious about her, and somehow she'd known from the moment she met her that Kana was indeed a lesbian.

She was also sure that Kana was the one she was meant to explore her curiosity with.

As far as Palani was concerned, it had been Fate that had brought Kana Sorbinno to her door. What had been the odds of a highly attractive woman, who was also a lesbian—she thought for sure she was, anyway—walking up to her own door? When she was so curious about women anyway? To Palani it was Fate's way of saying, "Here you go, check it out." Kana's attitude had been a bit off-putting, as she'd been "all business" and far from awed by the petite model, which was what Palani was used to, but Palani was determined to at least try to pursue the matter with her. Sometimes even Fate needed a push.

Kana glanced over at Palani at the next light, pointedly. Palani knew she better start talking or Kana was likely to let her out the next time they stopped.

"I, uh," Palani stammered. "I notice you aren't wearing a wedding ring."

Kana's lips twisted in a wry grin. "That would be because I'm not married."

"Why not?" Palani asked, far too quickly.

Kana looked over at her, her eyes indicating her growing impatience with Palani's line of questioning.

"I mean," Palani began, "I… just… I looked around your car, and I didn't see…" She trailed off, not wanting to finish that thought.

"Didn't see what?" Kana asked, her lips curling in derision again.

"I, um, well…"

"Well?" Kana asked, pushing purposely.

Palani bit her lip, actually afraid to say it now.

Kana waiting, feeling irritated, and worse still, starting to feel like a real bitch for being mean in the face of the poor woman's obvious discomfit.

"Maybe a rainbow?" Kana asked finally, her tone even.

Palani nodded, her eyes showing her sudden apprehension.

Kana looked thoughtful for a moment. "I use my vehicle for law enforcement work. It wouldn't be professional to have something like that on it."

"But you are..." Palani said, again trailing off, not wanting to make a mistake here.

"Gay?"

"Yes."

"Yes."

Palani nodded, chewing at the inside of her lip nervously. "Are you seeing anyone right now?"

"I see a lot of women. Why?"

Palani shrugged helplessly. "I was just wondering if you'd be willing to see me."

"You mean romantically?" Kana asked, actually sounding a bit outraged.

"Um, yes," Palani said, noting Kana's tone.

"You're married."

"I know," Palani said. "But—"

"But what?" Kana asked sharply.

"But I want, I mean, I think I want—"

"Think?" Kana sounded even more outraged now.

Palani sighed, shaking her head and looking out the window. This wasn't going at all like she had hoped. She suddenly knew that Kana wasn't interested, and she didn't know what to do now. She felt like a total fool. She'd been so sure there was some kind of connection with this woman, but she could see clearly that she'd been wrong, very wrong.

Kana looked over at Palani. It was easy to see the woman's turmoil. She felt a pang of guilt for causing it.

"You're curious," Kana said, her voice gentling a bit.

Palani nodded, not looking at her.

Kana sighed. "And you were hoping to find someone to satisfy that curiosity."

Again Palani nodded, still not looking at her.

Kana nodded too. "Well, look, I'm sure with your looks, you won't have any problem finding someone who would kill to show you the ropes."

"I don't…" Palani began, shaking her head miserably.

"Don't what?" Kana asked. "You don't think you'll find someone to help you out? Because I assure you, you will."

"I don't want just anyone."

"And you think you want me?" Kana asked, sounding shocked.

"Yes."

Kana shook her head. "I'm sorry," she said, "I'm just not in a place in my life where I'm willing to be a hobby to a married, albeit beautiful, woman."

"You think I'm beautiful?" Palani asked, her eyes widening.

Kana gave her a deadpan look. "You trying to tell me you don't know that you're beautiful?"

"I didn't know you think I am."

"Jesus Christ, woman," Kana said, shaking her head. "I do have eyes, and they work just fine," she assured her.

Palani smiled brilliantly then, looking innately pleased.

Kana glanced over at her, then shook her head. The girl was too damned cute to be believed. She had no idea what to do with that.

They arrived at Kana's house a short time later. Palani looked over at her, a question in her eyes.

"Come on," Kana said, gesturing toward the house with her head.

Kana got out, and Palani followed her up to her house. As they walked inside, Palani noted that the place was small but nicely furnished. Nothing was overly opulent or brassy. Many of the colors were either dark or neutral. The couch and chair in her living room were black leather, the tables a deep, rich maple. The carpet was a light mocha color, with a deep blue accent rug under the coffee table.

In her kitchen, the countertop Kana tossed her keys onto was a beautiful green Corian.

Kana headed down the hallway toward her bedroom. Much to her dismay, Palani followed her; her stern glance seemed to have no effect on the waif-like model. Sighing, she continued to stride to her room.

Kana's bedroom was large, the bed a sleigh in dark oak. The other pieces of furniture in the room were the same shade. The bedding was a deep plum color. There weren't many decorations, only one framed picture hanging over the bed. It was a seascape, with dark blue and green-blue waves crashing on a rocky shore and the sun going down on the horizon.

The bathroom in the master was an open area. Palani sat down on Kana's bed, eliciting an eye roll from the tough homicide cop. Palani watched as Kana took two pills then opened the medicine cabinet again and pulled out eye drops.

"What's wrong?" Palani asked.

"Allergies."

Palani sat and watched as Kana put drops into her eyes, then closed them tight.

"Do the drops hurt?" Palani asked, noticing that Kana winced.

"Pretty much like Tabasco sauce," Kana said, still standing at her bathroom sink with her eyes shut.

"Ouch," Palani said sympathetically.

"Uh-huh."

Kana opened her eyes a few moments later, blinking repeatedly. Palani watched as she blotted her eyes with a tissue, then reached for an eyeliner pencil and started reapplying her makeup.

"If a woman isn't butch, then what is she?" Palani asked.

Kana glanced at her, perplexed. "Huh?"

"I mean, if you're a lesbian and you're not butch, then what would it be called?"

Kana looked at her for a long moment, grinning slightly. "I think you mean femme."

"Femme?"

"Yeah, the other side of butch."

Palani nodded. "So you'd be femme, right?"

Kana looked thoughtful, then shrugged as she went back to putting on her eyeliner. "I guess some might see it that way. I never really thought about it—I'm me."

Palani nodded. "So that's it then."

"What's what then?" Kana asked, lost again.

"Why you're not attracted to me at all."

Kana turned around, leaning against her sink. "Okay, tell me where your head just went," she said, her face indicating her confusion at Palani's logic.

"Well," Palani said, "femmes are interested in butch women, right?"

"Uh…" Kana started to say.

"And I'm not even sort of butch, so that's why you're not attracted to me," Palani said, sounding proud of herself for figuring that out.

Kana laughed softly, shaking her head. "What makes you think that femmes are only interested in butch women?"

"Well, there's got to be one that plays the man and one that plays the woman, right?"

Kana laughed outright then, shaking her head again. "Oh, baby-girl, who told you that one?"

Palani looked back at her. Somewhere in her head she'd caught the "babygirl" and liked it, but she didn't comment on it then. "No one, really, I just…" she said, her voice trailing off as she shrugged.

"Okay, well, you're wrong," Kana said. "It's not about being femme or butch. It's not about whether you wear makeup, high heels, or nice clothes. It's about whether or not you have deeper feelings for women than you do men. There is no 'man' in the relationship—that's the whole point."

Palani bit her lip, trying to understand. "Have you always known you wanted women?"

"No," Kana said. "It took me a long time to figure it out."

Palani nodded. "So you dated men before that?"

"Yep," Kana said. "And none of them inspired any kind of deep love or even deep feelings of attachment."

"But you feel that with women?"

"Yes. With women I feel like I can be myself and open up my heart. I'd never do that with a man."

Palani nodded, understanding what Kana meant. It was what she'd been struggling with. The problem was, she didn't know if it was just that she hadn't been with enough men to find the right one, or if she really did want to be with women.

"How do you know if it's just that you haven't met the right guy yet?" Palani asked, hoping someone could finally help her answer her own biggest question.

Kana looked back at her for a long moment. "Well, I'd say it's pretty simple, really," she said. "If you're only turned on by men, and not women, then you haven't met the right man yet."

"How would I know if I'm turned on by women if I can't ever find out?"

"Well, that's why you're looking for one, right?"

"Right."

"Well there you go," Kana said, grinning.

She stood from the counter, turning to look in the mirror and putting the eyeliner away. She started to move toward the door.

Palani stood from the bed, looking at Kana.

"So, then, what is your type?" she asked.

Kana stopped in her tracks, glancing back at her for a long moment. She grinned and shook her head.

"Never mind," she said, then proceeded out of the bedroom and back down the hall.

"Why?" Palani asked doggedly as she followed Kana.

Kana picked up her keys off the island, still grinning. "Just never mind." Turning, she walked toward the front door.

"Kana!" Palani exclaimed, moving to intercept her, literally standing in front of the door so Kana couldn't open it.

Kana stared down at her, perplexed.

"What?" Palani asked.

"Who told you my name?" Kana asked.

"What is your type?" Palani countered.

Kana grinned again, shaking her head.

"Stop that!" Palani exclaimed, laughing softly.

"Who told you my name?" Kana asked again.

"What is your type?" Palani countered again.

Kana looked thoughtful for a moment. Placing a hand on the door above and behind Palani's head, she leaned down menacingly, her eyes glittering mischievously.

"Tell me who told you."

"Tell me your type," Palani replied, putting her hands on her slim hips.

Without another word, Kana leaned in, kissing her lips softly. Then she deepened the kiss as she took a step forward when Palani moaned softly.

Palani's hands touched Kana's waist, grasping at her as every nerve in her body seemed to come alive.

Kana pulled back, looking down into Palani's eyes.

"*You* are my type."

"I am?" Palani breathed, looking shocked.

"Smart, beautiful, petite, and very feminine. Yes, you are my type."

"But you don't want to see me," Palani reminded her.

"Because you're married, Palani."

Palani stared back at her for a moment, not sure what she could say. Then, dropping her head back against the door, she sighed.

Kana stepped back, looking subdued. "I'm sorry, Palani," she said, sounding like she truly was. "I just don't want to get involved in something this complicated right now. It's not you, it's really not. It's all me here."

Palani nodded, looking very unhappy.

They went out to the car then, and Palani was very quiet for a long time. Kana looked over at her, trying to think of something she could say. It was very obvious that Palani was unhappy, and Kana didn't think there was anything she could do to change that.

"Well," Kana said, "at least now you know that a woman can turn you on, right? So that should take care of that part of your curiosity."

Palani nodded, swallowing convulsively, her head still turned toward the window. She was trying desperately to handle the overwhelming feeling of disappointment she was feeling at that moment. When Kana had kissed her, every fiber of her being had said *Yes!*, but that had come crashing down all too quickly with Kana's edict.

She wanted to cry. She'd always believed in Fate. And she thought that Fate had showed her what was right. It had been too much of a coincidence that Kana had appeared in her life like this.

But now she didn't know why she had. It didn't make sense to her at all. She wished it did, but it didn't, and it depressed her no end.

"Palani?" Kana queried, her tone worried.

Palani looked over at her. Her unhappiness was almost tangible.

"Look," Kana said, "why do you think you want me?"

Palani didn't answer for a long moment, then she sighed. "I thought Fate had been trying to tell me something. It was stupid," she said, shaking her head.

Kana looked thoughtful for a moment, then said, "Well, maybe Fate wanted me to help you figure things out as to who to be with, maybe just not the way you thought."

Palani considered that, then nodded. "Maybe."

"Do you know where Bourbon Street is?"

"New Orleans?" Palani answered with the beginnings of a grin.

Kana laughed. "No, babygirl, I meant here in San Diego."

Palani shook her head.

"It's in Hillcrest, look it up," Kana said. "My friends and I hang out there. We'll be there Friday night at ten. If you want, you can meet us there."

"Okay," Palani said, with a small smile.

"Okay," Kana said, smiling back.

As it turned out, Friday was the longest day Kana had had in a long time. It started at four o'clock in the morning with a raid. The suspect they were trying to nail made a run for it, and Kana gave chase, following the man up and over an eight-foot fence. After she'd tackled him, and had him on his stomach with her knee in his back as she cuffed him, she noted she was bleeding. Tiny, who'd caught up to her by then, pointed out that the fence she'd jumped had razor wire at the top. Kana nodded, taking it in her stride, as she always did.

She went back to her vehicle, pulled out her first aid kit, and wrapped her arm to stop the bleeding.

"You should get that looked at," Tiny commented as he walked by with her collared suspect.

"I looked at it," Kana replied, grinning.

"Joe'll scream at ya," Tiny warned.

"Only if you open your big trap," Kana replied sweetly.

"It's an injury, K. If I don't report it, it'll be my ass."

"It's a scratch, big guy, not an injury."

"It's a gash the size of Texas. Get it looked at."

Kana nodded, having no intention of wasting time at the emergency room that day. They spent the next four hours processing paperwork on the arrest. Tiny pointedly handed her the incident report for her cut; she pointedly folded it and put it in her pocket. Tiny shook his head, rolling his eyes. He was used to dealing with her stubborn attitude; nothing she did frustrated him anymore.

They'd worked together fourteen years; they'd been partners with homicide for six years. Prior to working for the homicide unit, they'd been primary members of Midnight Chevalier's gang task force. As former gang leaders in Hawaii, they had come to work with Midnight a few months apart, but had always shared a kinship due to their heritage. Both were proud Samoans from fairly traditional families, so they understood each other like others never could. Now, as partners in homicide, it proved to be a great asset to them. What one didn't think of in a case, the other did. They had a connection that let them communicate without words when interviewing suspects. Kana would know when to change tactics; Tiny would know when she was doing just that and pick up where she stopped. A number of cases had been solved with their good work. The DA loved the two. They made good cases and rarely made mistakes in gathering evidence that would cost him the case in court. He liked them so much that he'd spoken to Midnight frequently about making sure the two stayed together as partners.

Their raid turned up another lead on one of their cases, so they followed up on it. They were after a second suspect who had been thus far impossible to locate. They ended up two hours away in Los Angeles, doing what they called "banging trash cans." They turned up more information, but needed to go back down to San Diego to assimilate it and check out an address they'd gotten.

Between traffic and their information search time, they ended up back in San Diego at six that evening. Tiny called his wife, Jess, telling her he wouldn't be home for a while. Kana had no one to call, so she just kept working. They spent the next four hours reading over what they had on the case, checking the computer for records and anything that would give them another lead.

Kana finally walked into her house at 10:45 p.m. that night. She'd called her friend Terri earlier that evening, telling her there was no way she was going to meet up with their friends that night at the bar. Terri had understood, having known Kana for years and understanding the nature of what she did.

Kana sat down on her bed, taking off the bandage on her arm and looking at the wound again. She grimaced as she noted it was bleeding. Getting up, she went over to her stereo and pushed the buttons for the CD. The sound of a rain shower began in the room with piano behind it; it was soothing. She rewrapped her arm and then sat down on the bed. Her head throbbed. It had been an extremely long day, and on top of it, she hadn't managed to eat anything at all. She considered getting up to go make herself something. Sighing, she shook her head. She didn't have the energy at that point. She moved to lean back against the headboard, sitting up.

A half hour later she was half asleep when she heard a voice call out to her.

"K, you here?" It was Terri.

"Unfortunately," Kana called back, grinning.

Terri was always checking up on her. This was pretty normal for her, so Kana didn't bother to even open her eyes.

"I, uh, brought you something," Terri said, walking into the bedroom.

"Yeah?" Kana asked with a total lack of interest.

She assumed Terri had brought her food, and she didn't really feel like eating now. She just wanted to sleep.

"Yeah," Terri said, her tone holding such an odd note that Kana found it necessary to open her eyes.

Standing in front of Terri was Palani. The first thing Kana noticed was that the girl looked damned good. She was wearing all black, including a leather miniskirt, lace-up bustier top, silk stockings, and high-heeled boots. *Damn!* was all she could think.

Kana still wore blue jeans, a black Oxford-style shirt, her black hiking boots, her gun in its shoulder holster, and her badge clipped to her belt. She was the picture of a weary cop. It was the first thing Palani noticed about her.

"Well, that being said, I'm out of here," Terri said, grinning at Kana's expression.

Kana narrowed her eyes at Terri, but the other woman was already turning to leave, making a hasty exit.

"You stood me up," Palani said, her voice holding humor.

Kana breathed a deep, weary sigh. "I'm sorry, I was just dusted."

Palani nodded, walking toward the bed, her eyes on Kana. "You look very tired."

"That's because I've been up since about three this morning."

"And you just got home?" Palani asked, glancing at her watch and looking horrified.

"About a half hour ago," Kana said, checking the clock.

"My God, no wonder," Palani said, shaking her head.

Kana turned, dropping her feet to the floor and leaning down to unlace her boots. Palani watched in fascination as Kana got up, pulling her gun out and depressing the magazine release to take out the ammunition clip. She then pulled the slide back to remove the chambered round, putting the bullet back into her ammunition clip. It was Kana's standard routine, and she didn't think anything of it, but to Palani it was fascinating. Kana shrugged out of her holster, hanging it on the valet next to her dresser. Reaching down, she unclipped her badge, laying it on the dresser next to her weapon. Glancing back, she noticed that Palani was watching her.

"What?" Kana asked.

Palani shook her head. "I've just never seen that kind of thing before," she said honestly.

"Don't date too many cops, huh?" Kana asked, grinning.

Palani smiled. "Not yet."

Kana narrowed her eyes at the younger woman, but she didn't have the energy to counter that comment. Instead she went over to her walk-in closet.

"Be right back."

She went into the closet and pulled off her boots, jeans, and shirt, changing into the sweats and black tank top she usually wore when she was home.

Palani was sitting on the bed when she came back out. Kana moved to the other side of the bed, sitting back down and pulling her knees up to her chest, resting her bandaged arm on her knee gingerly.

"What happened?" Palani asked.

Kana shrugged. "Razor wire and inattention."

"Does it hurt?" Palani asked, noticing that there was blood seeping through the bandage.

Kana shrugged again. "I'm too tired to notice at this point," she said, grinning.

Palani nodded. She wondered remotely if Kana was trying to hint that she wanted her to leave, but she was determined to stay until Kana asked her directly to go. They were both silent for a while. Kana closed her eyes, leaning her head back against the wall, stretching out one leg on the bed, the other still supporting her hurt arm. Palani tuned in to the music that flowed from the speakers, hearing the sound of the rain as it sounded like it was pouring down.

"What is this?" she asked, turning to look in the direction of the stereo, actually putting her back to Kana.

Kana's eyes appreciatively perused Palani's perfect shape in the outfit she wore, even as she answered her. "Some Spring Showers thing I got a while back." She shrugged. "It's soothing."

Palani nodded, listening to the music. Closing her eyes, she could picture the rain. She sighed deeply. "It reminds me of home," she said wistfully.

"Me too," Kana said.

They both listened for a few minutes. It seemed only natural when Palani moved back on the bed, closer to Kana. Kana reached out, putting her arm around Palani's small waist. Palani leaned back against Kana's shoulder, her head in the hollow there. Kana's arm stayed around her waist. Kana grinned, noting that Palani seemed right at home. She had to admit to herself that it did feel awfully good to have Palani leaning against her.

The song changed a few minutes later. The introduction was a roll of thunder, and then pouring-down rain. It changed to the sound of rain dripping.

"This reminds me of the days when I'd sit on the lanai and listen to the rain," Kana said, her tone melancholy. A lanai was what the Hawaiians called a covered balcony.

Palani nodded. "The thing I loved most was the fact that one minute it would be pouring down rain, and the next the sun would come out and shine all over everything."

Kana laughed softly, nodding. "You never knew when it would open up and dump either."

"Nope," Palani said, grinning. "But you could guess that the minute your mom finished hanging out the washing, that's when it would rain."

"Yep, happened every time."

They were silent again for a while. Kana's fingers stroked Palani's stomach unconsciously. Palani sighed, reaching down to put her hand lightly over Kana's. She was enjoying the simple pleasure of being there, not wanting to overthink it all too much.

That night when she'd gotten to the club, she'd looked for Kana. Apparently, Kana had told Terri about her, since the tall blonde woman had come up to her and said, "Are you looking for Kana?"

Palani had answered that yes, she was. Terri then told her that Kana wasn't coming that evening, that she'd gotten held up at work. Palani's mood had fallen. She'd been looking forward to seeing Kana again, imagining that she'd at least be able to coax her into kissing her again. Hoping somehow to change Kana's mind about seeing her.

Terri had apparently noticed how unhappy she was, because she'd bought her two drinks. In no time, Palani was telling Terri her whole story, and about how she was so sure Kana was Fate's way of telling her what to do. Terri had nodded, glancing at her watch.

"Come on," she'd said, standing from her barstool.

"Where are we going?" Palani had asked, not sure what Terri was thinking.

"I'll be back," Terri told the other women at the table.

She'd taken Palani's hand then, leading her out of the bar. Palani was worried that Terri had mistaken her outpouring of whimpering as a come-on. Outside, Terri led Palani over to her car.

"Where are we going?" Palani asked again, pulling her hand from Terri's grasp and refusing to budge another inch.

"I'm taking you to Kana's house," Terri said, grinning, sure she knew what Palani had been thinking. "I'm not saying I wouldn't love a shot at you, but I also hate to see my friend miss her big chance."

Palani bit her lip in subdued excitement. "You're taking me over there?"

"Yeah," Terri said, winking at her as she got in her car. "Don't give me too much grief, or I'll change my mind and take you to my place."

Palani laughed happily, getting in on the passenger side of the vehicle. Now, here she was with Kana, and she couldn't think of anywhere she'd rather be. They just seemed to click, somehow.

Palani moved sideways, turning to lean against Kana's bent leg, looking at her. "What made you become a police officer?" she asked, wanting to know more about her.

Kana looked back at her for a long moment, reaching out to touch her waist again gently. "Midnight Chevalier."

"The Chief of Police?" Palani asked, having heard about Midnight on the news.

Kana nodded. "But she wasn't the chief back then, just a sergeant."

"How long ago was that?"

"About fourteen years ago."

Palani's eyes widened. She hadn't thought Kana was that old; she didn't look very old at all. "How old do you have to be to work as a police officer?"

Kana grinned. "Well, to be a peace officer in California, you have to be twenty-one."

"So, were you twenty-one?" Palani asked, not wanting to be rude and ask Kana how old she was.

"No," Kana said. "I was eighteen at the time I joined the department, but I wasn't a peace officer then either."

Palani did the calculation to realize Kana was actually thirty-two—not old by any means, but definitely older than she'd thought. She also found that it didn't matter in the slightest.

"So, if you weren't a peace officer, what were you?" she asked.

"I was a CI," Kana said, grinning. "A confidential informant."

"What is that?"

"Well, I worked for FORS, which was a gang task force Midnight put together. I basically used my experience as a gang leader to help Midnight and the unit take other gangs down."

"As a gang leader?" Palani echoed, looking alarmed. "You mean an actual gang?"

Kana grinned, knowing she'd just shocked the poor woman. "Yes, an actual gang. I led one in Honolulu."

"Wow…" Palani said, awed.

"It's not that impressive, hon."

"Why did you leave Honolulu?"

Again Kana grinned. "I, uh… I challenged the top gang leader in Honolulu at the time and beat her and a couple of her girls." She shrugged. "After that I basically had a contract out on me, so it was time to go."

"How old were you?" Palani asked, aghast at the thought of Kana having to leave her home because of a threat on her life.

"Seventeen," Kana said, knowing that would make it worse.

"Oh my God, Kana…"

Kana shrugged. "I did it to myself. I knew that if I beat her she'd send people after me."

"So why did you do it?"

"Because I could," Kana said simply.

Palani shook her head, unable to fathom having her life threatened, or actually fighting some other woman. Kana watched Palani, wondering if she'd managed to scare the girl enough to make her want to back off now. She knew that Palani was one of those women that couldn't conceive of the kind of life she'd led.

"But you're different now," Palani said hesitantly.

Kana looked at her for a long moment. This was her chance to disillusion the younger woman. Palani stared back at her intently. Kana could tell she was practically holding her breath, waiting for an answer.

Finally Kana dropped her head, grinning. She couldn't do it.

"Yeah, I'm different now," she said. "It's been fifteen years since then."

Palani looked relieved, and nodded, settling more comfortably against Kana's knee. Kana's hand remained at Palani's waist, even as her eyes trailed down from the younger woman's eyes and over the outfit that she wore.

"So, did you see anyone interesting at the club while you were there?" Kana asked.

"No."

"No?" Kana echoed in disbelief.

Palani shook her head.

"Was it dead in there tonight?" Kana asked, thinking it was rarely dead at Bourbon Street, especially not on a Friday.

"Oh, no, it was really crowded."

"And you didn't see anyone?" Kana asked chidingly.

"The woman I was there to see wasn't there," Palani said. "She got held up at work."

Kana nodded, narrowing her eyes at her. "Terri hit on you?" she asked knowingly.

Palani laughed softly. "No, she said she hated to see you miss your big chance."

"Oh, really now?" Kana said, shaking her head. "I think Terri needs to have her eyes examined again. Either that or she's getting softhearted in her old age."

"Oh, she said she'd love a shot at me..." Palani said, her voice trailing off as Kana's hand tightened on her waist.

A moment later Kana kissed her. This kiss was by no means timid or hesitant—it was strong and passionate. Palani found herself holding on to Kana's shoulders as wave after of wave of heat rolled through her. Kana's hands were on her back, pulling her closer, the kiss deepening further. Palani gained her bearings and slid one hand to the back of Kana's neck, her nails grazing the skin there. Kana moaned softly at the contact, and Palani shuddered at the sensations hearing that caused.

There was no time to stop and think. Palani didn't even try. Kana's lips moved over hers, and down her skin, and with expertise born of a great deal of practice, Kana had her writhing, begging for more. Kana slowly but sensually removed her clothes, laying them aside on the foot of the bed. Minutes later Kana brought her to a climax the likes of which she'd never experienced before. Palani lay across Kana, who still sat up, her head on Kana's shoulder. Kana's arms were wrapped around her, cradling her close, stroking Palani's skin.

Kana felt Palani shiver, and reached down to pull the covers up over her. Palani snuggled closer to Kana, her hand on her shoulder, her head still resting in the hollow of the opposite shoulder. Kana smiled warmly in the dim light of the bedroom. She knew she'd failed miserably at controlling this situation. Part of her worried about that, but the rest of her simply enjoyed the feel of the young woman lying against her. It did feel good—Kana couldn't deny that. Palani was incredibly beautiful, and so sweet in her innocence that Kana wasn't able to resist. Nor had she been able to ignore the taunt that Terri had wanted Palani. There was no way that was going to happen.

Kana and Terri had been friends for almost five years, almost the entire time Kana had known she preferred women to men. She'd met Terri through the woman that had introduced her to the lifestyle, Shelly. Shelly and Terri had been a couple at one point, and remained friends. Kana had liked Terri from the moment she'd met her. Terri was easygoing, and had the exact attitude about the lifestyle that Kana had adopted. It was Kana's opinion that there was nothing different about her choices than anyone else's. Some women liked men that were sweet and sensitive, some liked tough He-Man types, some didn't like sex at all.

Kana figured the fact that she preferred women shouldn't matter to anyone, other than to her. It wasn't like she was out trying to get women to change their opinion. She wasn't flamboyant about her life, proclaiming her sexuality from the rooftops. As far as she was concerned, no one she knew walked around reminding people they were heterosexual; she didn't think she needed to remind anyone she wasn't.

In this instance, however, Kana had no intention of losing Palani to Terri. She knew that Terri would have no qualms about dating a married woman, and had, in fact, told Kana she was nuts for refusing to do so. Kana also knew that Terri would happily teach Palani everything. There was nothing wrong with Terri—she was one of Kana's best friends—but Kana was damned if she was losing Palani to her. A thought flickered across her mind as she drifted to sleep, still holding Palani against her. *Why does it matter so much?* Kana didn't even try to analyze it—she didn't want to.

Palani woke a few hours later, glancing at the clock on Kana's nightstand, and then at Kana as she slept. She reflected on what had happened, and realized that she was totally comfortable with it. There hadn't been a moment of strangeness. It had seemed totally natural to have Kana touching her; it had also felt extremely right to fall asleep in her arms. Even now, watching Kana sleep, Palani felt a sense of wonder at what the other woman had made her feel.

Her eyes trailed down over Kana's shoulders, noting again how much lean muscle was there. She'd been right about Kana. The width of her was pure muscle, not an ounce of fat anywhere that she could see. Palani touched Kana's shoulder lightly, trailing her finger down her arm, noting the bandage again. She was alarmed to see that there was blood seeping through the bandage.

"Kana?" she said softly, reaching out to touch the older woman's cheek.

Kana stirred and then opened her eyes.

"Hmm?"

"Hon, your arm is bleeding," Palani said, her voice colored with worry.

Kana raised her arm, glancing at it, then shrugged.

"It's okay, babe, I'm fine," she said, her smile sleepy.

"You're bleeding."

"Uh-huh," Kana said, moving to turn over on her side, taking Palani with her as she did.

Palani gasped at the ease with which Kana lifted her and moved her over. Kana's arm was under her neck, her hand at her back, her injured arm over her waist. When Palani looked up at Kana, Kana was looking down at her with a humorous glint in her eyes.

"What?" Palani asked.

"Trying to mother me?"

"No," Palani said, biting her lip, gazing back at Kana. "I just don't like the idea of you bleeding."

Kana grinned. "I'll live, I promise."

"I know you'll live," Palani said, making a face at her. "Maybe I don't want blood all over your sheets."

Kana laughed softly. "And maybe you just want to take care of me."

"Maybe," Palani said. "Would that be bad?"

Kana looked thoughtful for a minute. "I don't know. I've never had anyone really take care of me before."

"You haven't?"

"Not really, I'm usually the one doing the care taking."

Palani sat up, looking down at Kana. "Where would I find a bandage for that?" she asked, pointing to Kana's arm.

Kana stared back at her, her face composed in a look that said, *Oh really?*

Palani narrowed her eyes. "Don't make me hurt you," she said, her voice too sweet to give the words any real gravity.

Kana laughed softly. "I'm fine, little one, just get back down here," she said, taking her hand and pulling her back down next to her.

"You need to have that wrapped again, Kana, or you're going to get it infected," Palani said, moving to sit back up.

Kana turned over on her stomach, putting her arm over Palani's stomach so she couldn't get up. "I'm fine."

"You're not fine, damnit," Palani said petulantly, grasping Kana's upper arm.

Kana looked back at her for a long moment, searching Palani's eyes. "You really want to do this, don't you?"

"I want you to be okay," Palani said softly.

Kana sighed, rolling to her side and letting Palani up. "In the middle drawer in the bathroom."

Palani got off the bed and walked over to the vanity sink. Kana couldn't help but admire the view. The woman was perfect, a tiny little perfect doll. Palani turned around and noticed Kana's eyes on her. She smiled self-consciously.

"Don't tell me you're not used to being stared at," Kana said, sitting up as Palani walked toward the bed with a roll of gauze.

"It's different when you do it," Palani said, her eyes averted shyly.

"Why?"

Palani bit her lip as she sat down on the bed, reaching for Kana's arm to unwrap the old bandage.

"Because I like when you do it," Palani said quietly.

Kana smiled. Leaning forward, she kissed Palani's cheek, then her temple, her free hand coming up to touch her gently on the neck. Palani sighed happily. This was indeed what she'd been missing. She carefully unwrapped the bandage, and gasped at the length of the gash on Kana's lower arm.

"You need stitches in this, Kana."

"I'll be fine, baby, just wrap it back up," Kana said gently.

"No, you'll scar if you don't get it stitched properly."

Kana shrugged. "Won't be my first scar, babe."

"Well, it's not going to be a scar, because you're going to go get it stitched up," Palani said hotly.

Kana looked back at her for a long moment. "I am, huh?" she asked, sounding unconvinced.

Palani gave her a narrowed look. "Do you work at being this stubborn?"

"No, it's natural," Kana replied, grinning.

Palani narrowed her eyes again. "Why do I know that's the truth?"

Kana laughed softly, her eyes twinkling mischievously.

Palani finished putting the bandage on Kana's arm and got up to throw away the old one. She walked back over to the bed and lay down next to Kana, snuggling against her. She realized again that this just seemed so right somehow. With that thought in mind, she sighed happily.

Kana gathered Palani closer, nuzzling her temple with her lips.

"This is so nice," Palani said wistfully.

"You like this?"

"Yes."

"Then you have your answer."

"My answer?" Palani echoed, confusion clear on her face.

"Yeah, you know now that you do enjoy women," Kana said. "Now you have a good starting place."

"A starting place?" Palani looked stunned.

"Yes," Kana said. "Babe, you're still married…"

"But you made love to me," Palani said plaintively.

"I showed you what it could be like, yes," Kana said gently.

"With you," Palani said, starting to look panicked.

"Palani…"

"No!" Palani cried. "No," she repeated, shaking her head. "Don't, not if you're going to say we still can't be together."

"Hon…" Kana sighed.

"Please, Kana, please," Palani said, tears in her eyes now. "Don't do this. I don't want just anyone, I want you."

Kana looked back at her for a long moment. It was easy to see the devastation in Palani's eyes.

"Listen—" she began again.

"No!" Palani cried, moving to sit up and turn her back to Kana.

Kana sat up too, reaching out to touch Palani's shoulder gently.

"Palani, it won't work, okay?" she said firmly. "It'll end up being a case of you lying to him to be with me, and eventually lying to me when you can't to keep from fighting with him."

Palani whipped around to look at her. "No," she said vehemently. "I won't ever lie to you."

"You won't have a choice, babe," Kana said calmly.

"Yes, I will!" Palani said stridently. "I won't lie to you, Kana, no matter what." She put her hand to Kana's cheek. "Please," she said, her eyes searching Kana's.

Kana looked back at her for a long moment, not sure what to say. She'd seen enough of her friends' relationships with married women; they always went badly. There always came a time for the woman to choose between her stable home life and her alternate life, and the alternate life almost always lost. Even in a society as modern as America was at that point, being gay still didn't sit well with most people. For that reason, Kana knew she was going to end up being hurt in this—she knew it without a doubt. The problem was, her heart was already begging her to give in; her body already had—it was her head that was still fighting the battle. Her heart and body were stronger, however.

Kana put her hand to Palani's neck, her expression serious. "I know you're going to be the death of me, but at this point I don't care," she said, her tone quite serious.

Kana leaned down then, taking possession of Palani's lips again, and all was forgotten for a time. Later, as they lay together, Kana thought about what she was doing. She was sure she was going to pay for this indulgence, but she just couldn't bring herself to let Palani go either. The girl was too attractive, both innocent and beautiful, intelligent and naive. It was something she couldn't seem to resist right now.

Palani lay in Kana's arms, thinking that this was where she was meant to be, that she could make this work. She wanted this to work, so it would. She was always running off to do something; Matthew would never know the difference. She could spend lots of time with Kana without him ever suspecting a thing. How hard could it be?

Palani found out how hard it could be to have an affair. She found out very quickly. What she hadn't realized was that in practicing to deceive, things somehow got very messed up very quickly. The week following her night with Kana was hectic. She had three shoots, all of which went way over schedule. Whenever she thought of a reason to run out of the house for a few hours, Kana was either at work, in the middle of a surveillance, or doing something else. She didn't even try to call her, not wanting to make things harder. Her thinking was that if she called Kana to let her know she was free for a couple of hours, and Kana was at work, it would make things more disappointing.

It didn't really occur to her that in not calling Kana at all, she was sending a message that she wasn't even trying to see her. Kana's resolve to not date a married woman hardened more every day that Palani didn't call. By the end of that week, Kana's nerves were on edge. Anytime Tiny tried to cajole her out of her bad mood, which usually worked, Kana would more or less bite his head off and go right back to whatever she'd been doing. Tiny knew that Kana had slept with Palani; he'd found out by accident. He'd called Kana that next morning, and since Kana was in the shower, she'd told Palani to pick up the phone. Palani had, and Tiny had recognized her voice immediately.

Things got worse when they went on a raid and Kana lost her temper with a suspect. The unfortunate man had made the mistake of taunting Kana about being a "dyke." Kana had come back with the taunt of "You afraid I'll fuck your girlfriend while you're in jail, honey? Or are you afraid she'll like it better with me?"

The suspect had been fool enough to take a swing at Kana, and she'd swung back, laying him out flat on the ground. Tiny had raised an eyebrow at her. Kana simply looked back at him and shook her head, walking away.

That evening, Tiny got on the phone to the Ryker home. The maid answered, and Tiny asked for Mrs. Ryker. Palani came on the line a few minutes later.

"Mrs. Ryker," Tiny said, sounding official. "This is Sergeant Ako, from homicide. Are you able to speak to me for a moment?"

Palani was surprised at hearing from Kana's partner, but understood quickly that he was asking if she could talk without being overheard.

"Yes, Sergeant, I can talk. Is everything okay?" she asked, suddenly worried that something had happened to Kana.

"Yes and no," Tiny said. "My partner's a bit on edge right now, and I think you might know why."

Palani nodded, feeling a stab of guilt. She sighed. "Yes, I do. I'm so sorry."

"Don't tell me, tell her," Tiny said simply.

"I will," Palani said, nodding. "Thank you for the call, Sergeant."

"No problem."

Palani was at Kana's house a half hour later. She'd told Matthew she had a friend that was having a crisis. She hadn't even waited for his response before leaving the house.

She knocked on Kana's door, waiting with knots in her stomach for Kana to answer. After a few long minutes, Kana opened the door. She looked tired, and unhappy. Palani stared up at her, almost afraid Kana was going to tell her to buzz off. Finally, Kana stood back from the door, allowing her to come inside.

Palani walked into the house, noticing the silence. The door closed, and when Palani glanced back, she saw that Kana was leaning against it, watching her.

"Kana," Palani said softly. "I'm sorry, I couldn't get away, and things were just crazy."

Kana nodded, still looking very subdued.

"When I could get away, I knew you were at work," Palani explained further, feeling unsettled by the fact that Kana hadn't said a word yet. "I thought calling you would make you feel worse, knowing you couldn't get away. I just..." Her voice trailed off as she shrugged, not sure if she'd done the right thing now.

"So, what did you tell him?" Kana asked calmly.

"That I had a friend who was having a crisis."

Kana nodded, seeming to accept that.

Palani wasn't sure what to do at that point. She could sense that Kana was mad, and she could see that she also had no intention of dropping her attitude. Palani walked into the kitchen, waiting to see if Kana would follow her. Kana stood leaning against her front door for a few long moments, finally pushing off it to follow Palani. When Kana walked into her kitchen, Palani was sitting on the island situated at the entry to the room, so when Kana came around the corner, she was face to face with Palani, at her eye level.

Before Kana had a chance to back up, Palani put her arms around her neck and leaned in to kiss her deeply. When their lips parted, Palani didn't look at Kana to see her reaction. She buried her face in Kana's neck, wrapping her arms around her shoulders and then wrapping her legs around her hips.

"I missed you so much," Palani whispered against her neck fervently.

Kana stood there for a long moment, doing everything she could think of to resist. Finally, she gave in, sliding her hands around Palani's waist and pulling her close. It disgusted her no end how much she'd missed the younger woman, and it did feel good to hear her say she'd missed her too.

They held each other for a long time in silence. Neither of them wanted to say anything, afraid it would be the wrong thing.

"I need to see you more than this, Palani," Kana said finally, her voice a strong whisper.

"I know, I know," Palani said, nodding. "I just need to figure things out, Kana," she added, then hurried on when she felt Kana tense. "Not with us. I know I want to be with you. I just need to figure out how to schedule things better so I can get time with you when you'll be available too."

Kana pulled back, looking down at her. "You could try calling me."

"I just thought…" Palani said, trailing off as she shook her head.

"Well, you thought wrong," Kana said seriously. "At least I would have known you'd tried to see me—that would have helped."

Palani nodded, biting her lip. "I'm sorry," she said softly, her eyes downcast.

Kana reached out, tipping her face back up to hers. "You just gotta talk to me, babe."

Palani nodded again, putting her head on Kana's shoulder, her face turned toward Kana's neck.

"Your partner called me," Palani said.

"He did?" Kana asked, surprised.

"Yes, he said you were on edge."

Kana nodded, grimacing. "I kinda lost it today, too."

"Lost it?" Palani asked, lifting her head to look at Kana.

"A suspect got mouthy—I shut him up."

Palani winced. "Bad?"

"Not good."

"Will you get into trouble?"

Kana shrugged. "Depends on whether or not he's brave enough to file charges."

"Why wouldn't he be?"

"Most guys have a problem with being flattened by a woman," Kana said, the beginnings of a grin on her lips.

"*My* woman," Palani qualified.

"Yours, huh?" Kana asked, looking down into her eyes.

"I hope so," Palani said, staring back.

Kana didn't answer. She leaned down and kissed Palani, reminding her who she belonged to. It was hours before they talked again. In the end, Palani stayed most of the night. She snuck off at one point to call Matthew and tell him she wasn't going to be home until late. Matthew just said "Fine," and that was it. Palani crawled back into bed with Kana, thinking about how different Kana and Matthew were. She had a feeling Kana would have questioned her thoroughly about the "friend." Kana would care more; Matthew didn't seem to care at all, as long as he got what he wanted out of the marriage. It was a big difference.

Kana turned over, pulling Palani back against her. Palani slid her hands over Kana's as they wrapped around her. She touched one of the rings Kana wore, looking down, then took Kana's hand to look closer at the ring. It was silver, an intricately woven heavy filigree band with a black heart in the center. Kana wore it on her pinky. She had a few other rings too, and Palani examined them as well. There was a silver ring with a ruby-red stone in the center and another silver banded ring that held deep, rich sapphires. The rings weren't delicate, but not masculine either. They were like Kana, a mixture of strong and feminine in such a combination that was so attractive, Palani couldn't imagine being without it now.

Kana leaned down, kissing her neck, looking at Palani's hand in hers.

"What is this?" Palani asked, touching the black heart. "Onyx?"

"Lava."

"Pele," Palani said, nodding.

Kana nodded, nuzzling her neck.

"I remember so many times I'd sit on the black-sand beach and listen to the haoles talking about why it was black. Then they'd be fool enough to take some sand," Palani said, shaking her head.

"Pele doesn't like that," Kana said, knowing the legend Palani was talking about.

"No, she doesn't," Palani agreed. She turned over, looking up at Kana. "We are so much the same, but so different too, aren't we?"

Kana looked back at her for a long moment, then nodded. It was true. They'd grown up in the same culture, knew the legends and the history of Hawaii. In a way it was comforting to be with someone that understood you, who knew exactly what you meant when you said something. Anyone else, even Matthew, would have questioned the word *haoles*, which was Hawaiian slang for tourists or mainlanders. Kana had known exactly what she'd meant.

"You know what I want?" Palani said, grinning mischievously.

"What?"

"Rocky road ice cream."

Kana laughed softly, shaking her head. "You really want some?"

"I don't suppose you have any?"

"I will, after I go get some," Kana said, moving to get up.

"It's late, Kana. I just… It's okay."

Kana looked back at her, leaning over to kiss her lips softly. "My girl wants something, she gets it."

She got up and pulled on her jeans. Palani got up too, pulling on her pants and reaching into Kana's drawer for a shirt, which she tied at her waist.

"Where do you think you're going?" Kana asked.

"With you," Palani said, smiling.

Kana laughed and shook her head.

At 1 a.m. they were at the local AM/PM looking for rocky road ice cream. Palani found out that Kana liked it too, but didn't eat it anymore. When they were back at Kana's house, they sat on the bed sharing a pint of ice cream, with Kana feeding her spoonfuls while Palani lay with her back against Kana's chest and side.

"So why don't you eat it anymore?" Palani asked.

Kana shrugged. "When I decided to change my eating habits, all this kind of junk was the first stuff to go."

"I really shouldn't eat it either, but I can get away with it sometimes. Was it a drastic change?" Palani asked, taking another bite of ice cream.

Kana laughed softly. "Yeah, I dropped about a hundred pounds, and added a whole lot of muscle."

Palani sat up, turning to look at her, shock evident on her face. "A hundred pounds?"

Kana nodded. "I was fat for a long time, babe."

"I don't believe it," Palani said, shaking her head.

Kana looked back at her for a minute, then nodded toward her dresser. "Top drawer there—open it."

Palani got off the bed, still wearing Kana's shirt and nothing else. She opened the drawer.

"See the envelope under the ammunition box? Open that and look at the picture there," Kana said.

Palani did as Kana told her. The picture was of the Gang from ten years before. Palani easily picked Kana out, since she was the only female in the group besides Midnight Chevalier. Kana was not lying—she looked much heavier in this picture than she did now. Palani glanced over at Kana and saw that she was watching her.

Kana shrugged. "I got tired of being fat," she said simply. "I watched Tiny change his life with getting into shape. That's when he found his wife. I wanted that too."

Palani nodded, never having had to deal with being with over-weight. She'd always been thin, and her body had just developed naturally into the way it was. She worked out, but she didn't have to be absolutely compulsive to keep it the way it was. She realized she was lucky in that respect. Looking at Kana now, compared to how she'd been ten years before, it was amazing to her how much work Kana must have had to do. She was almost a different person. The strong, proud beauty was there in the picture, but it was much less obvious than it was now. Kana's face was lean, but with the strong jawline of the Samoan people. She no longer had the rounded face from being overweight, so her cheekbones were more prominent and her dark eyes stood out. She'd also taken to getting her hair cut to better flatter her face shape, rather than the shaggy mass it had been years before. There were so many differences, and Palani was so surprised at them.

Palani put the picture back and climbed back onto the bed, her eyes on Kana. Kana watched her. Palani knelt on the bed—being on her knees put her about a head taller than Kana—and looked down at her. She took her face in her hands, kissing her softly. Kana's arms wrapped around her, pulling her closer as she deepened the kiss.

Palani pulled back, looking down at Kana again. "You have always been beautiful," she said softly. "You are more so now."

Kana looked up at her, reaching up to touch her face, her eyes searching Palani's. "You keep talking like that, and you're not going home tonight," Kana said with a twinkle in her eyes.

"Who said I was going home tonight?" Palani asked, her grin impish.

"Mmm…" Kana said, pulling her down and kissing her again.

Palani didn't go home the next day until late in the morning. Kana called Tiny and told him she was taking the morning off. They slept late, woke up, and made love before showering and dressing to go their separate ways. Palani promised Kana that they wouldn't be apart a full week again.

Chapter 2

True to her word, Palani surprised Kana by showing up at the office one early afternoon three days later.

"So this is where you go?" Palani said, leaning against the doorway.

Kana looked up from her computer, smiling broadly. "Hey," she said. "I thought you had a shoot."

"I did," Palani said, shrugging. "It got done early, so I came here."

Kana glanced behind Palani, checking to see who was around. "Come on in, and close the door."

Palani did, moving to look at the things on Kana's walls. There were posters for body armor, weapons, and police work. There was also a poster of a seascape, similar to the one Kana had in her bedroom.

"You don't go too far from home, do you?" Palani asked, gesturing to it.

"Never," Kana said, smiling. "So what are you going to do this afternoon?"

Palani shrugged, still looking at Kana's walls. She was reading the awards Kana had received and her certificates from the commission on POST.

"I didn't know you're a certified black belt instructor," Palani said, glancing back at Kana.

Kana was leaning back in her chair. She nodded. "Yeah, part of the new me," she said, winking.

Palani laughed softly. She walked over to Kana's desk then, noting the pictures there. She saw a photo of Terri and two other girls.

"Who are they?"

"That's Sandy," Kana said, pointing to a really cute blonde girl. "And that's Sue—she was with Terri."

"And Sandy was with you?" Palani asked pointedly.

Kana nodded, grinning at the jealousy in Palani's voice.

"Okay, who's this?" Palani asked, picking up a picture of a woman with big green eyes. This one was very pretty too, with long honey-blond hair.

"That's Sarah."

Palani looked at her, narrowing her eyes. "Were you with her too?"

"Uh-huh," Kana said, grinning again.

Palani shook her head, then reached for another photograph. Yet another blonde was pictured, smaller this time, with blue eyes. She gave Kana a pointed look. "Don't tell me…"

"Erica—yes, I was with her," Kana said, laughing.

"You seem to have a thing for blondes, Sergeant Sorbinno," Palani said, moving to sit on Kana's desk and looking down at her.

Kana glanced at the pictures, then looked back at Palani. "I guess I do. Hadn't ever really thought about it."

"Well, think about it," Palani countered.

Kana laughed, enjoying the way Palani was acting. It was very endearing.

"None of them were as beautiful as you," she said.

"Oh, that sounds so placating…" Palani said, shaking her head. "It may take a bit more convincing than that, babe," she added, grinning.

"Well, I'll have to take care of that when I get you alone."

"Can't kiss me here, huh?" Palani asked, moving to get off the desk.

Kana's hand on her leg stopped her. "They don't know," she said softly.

"Oh," Palani said, shocked. "But your partner…"

"Tiny probably figured it out, but he's never said anything to me directly," Kana said. "In fact, I didn't really know he knew, until he obviously told you my name and how to track me down."

Palani nodded. "Isn't that hard, though? I mean, these people are your friends, right?"

"They're much more than that," Kana said. "They're family to me."

"So they should be the first to accept your lifestyle, Kana. Have you even given them the chance?"

"Have you told your family anything?" Kana countered.

"No, but my situation is a bit different," Palani said, knowing that Kana was trying to avoid this topic. "You've been living this lifestyle for five years now, right?"

Kana nodded, looking contrite.

"It's none of my business," Palani said softly, reaching down to touch Kana's hand, which was still resting on her leg. "But I think you should give them the chance to let you be yourself."

Kana stared back at her for a long moment, and nodded. "I'll think about it, okay?"

Palani nodded. "Okay."

In the end, Kana left early that day, and she and Palani went and had an early dinner. Palani didn't have to be home right away, because Matthew was in LA and wouldn't be back until late. She left Kana's house at ten that night, beating Matthew home by a half hour. Kana warned her not to keep cutting it so close. Palani promised she'd be more careful, but things got harder and harder, because when she was with Kana she never wanted to leave.

They spent hours talking about anything and everything. Kana told her about the Gang. Palani had discovered Kana's tattoo on her chest above her heart. It was a small palm tree with the letters SOS on one frond. SOS stood for Sisters of Samoa, an extremely dangerous gang in Hawaii. Palani had been stunned—not only had Kana been a gang leader, but the leader of a gang that rivaled ones like the Bloods and the Crips. Everyone in Hawaii knew who SOS were. There was a male gang called SOS too—they were the Sons of Samoa—but the branch of Kana's gang was a fierce one as well. Kana's menacing past seemed even more so then.

They talked about growing up in Hawaii, what had been expected of them, what they'd wanted, everything. Palani found that they never ran out of things to talk about, and she loved it. So often, they'd lie in bed talking, both of them naked but nothing sexual happening. Kana's hands would constantly stroke her skin or her hair. She found that Kana made her feel much more beautiful than any photographer, and very definitely more so than Matthew ever did. Kana made her feel like she was some kind of goddess, beautiful, smart, breathtaking—anything and everything that was good to feel, Kana made her feel that way.

Palani didn't realize that she too made Kana feel better than she ever had with anyone else. Palani sought out every positive thing she could about Kana, encouraging her to be herself. Palani had also found out that Kana did bead work for necklaces. She'd discovered that one morning when she'd awoken to find Kana out of bed. When she'd found her, Kana was sitting on the floor in her extra bedroom with a plastic compartmentalized box of glass beads. Kana had explained that one of her girlfriends had gotten her into it.

"I started doing it to please her, and found out I really liked it too," Kana said, grinning.

Palani would spend hours watching Kana make things—necklaces, bracelets, whatever struck her fancy. Kana even taught her how to do it, but Palani always felt clumsy next to Kana. She was ever astounded at how nimble Kana's fingers were, to be able to handle such small beads. Palani was forever dropping her cord and losing what she'd done. Kana would grin and say something like, "Hate when that happens."

They clicked in every way possible, and Palani just knew that this was the life she was meant for. Kana filled every need she had. Things between her and Matthew had just grown farther and farther apart. He was almost a stranger to her now.

"What are you doing for Christmas?" Kana asked her one morning when, once again, Palani had turned up in the middle of the night, crawling into bed with her.

"Nothing that I know of. Why?"

"Well, I have this wedding to go to…" Kana said, her voice trailing off.

"Whose wedding?"

"Collins and O'Neil," Kana said, having told Palani about every member of what she referred to as "the Gang," the people she'd worked with in Midnight's gang task force, FORS. That information had included the latest upheavals surrounding many of the members and their relationships.

"Wow, they're getting married?" Palani asked, smiling fondly.

"Yeah, guess they figured it out," Kana said. Christian Collins and Stevie O'Neil were two people who were truly fiery in their passion and just as fiery in their fights.

"And you want me to go to the wedding with you?" Palani asked, her eyes questioning.

"Yes," Kana said, leaning down to kiss her. "I want my girlfriend to go to the wedding with me."

Palani smiled warmly, her eyes lighting up. For some reason she always loved being referred to as her "girlfriend" or her "woman" or her "baby." She knew it was silly, but she loved it anyway.

"So you're going to tell them?" Palani asked.

"Yeah."

"When? How?" Palani asked, starting to worry a bit.

"On Christmas night, by taking you to the wedding."

Palani's eyes widened. "Are you sure that's how you want to do this?"

Kana sighed. "Either they're going to accept it or they're not. Warning them isn't going to change anything. And it's not my style to ask for permission, you know?"

"I know, but..." Palani said, trailing off as she shook her head. "I just don't want them to hurt you," she said softly.

Kana looked down at her for a long moment, leaning in to kiss her lips softly. "They won't hurt me, they just might be uncomfortable—I can't imagine any of them actually being rude."

Palani nodded, still a bit worried.

"You'll be by my side," Kana said. "I don't care what anyone thinks."

They both knew that was only partially true. Kana didn't care what anyone in the department thought—or the world, for that matter—but the Gang was her family, and it was their respect and acceptance that she needed the most. Palani knew this was a huge step for Kana, and she felt very privileged to be the one she took that step with.

Kana and Palani spent as much time together as they could. One evening when Matthew was out of town, they decided to go out and have dinner. It was something they didn't do often. Kana didn't want anyone seeing Palani who would report to Matthew that she'd been out with someone else. On this night, however, Kana decided to basically throw caution to the wind.

"So, what do you feel like?" Kana asked Palani as they got into the Navigator.

They'd spent the entire day together; Kana had taken it off. They'd lain around all day, watching movies, talking, and making love. Kana had insisted that they go and get dinner on the premise that she needed to refuel from having to "take care" of Palani "so many times."

"Honestly?" Palani said, looking embarrassed.

"What?" Kana asked, giving her a narrowed look.

"I want a hamburger," Palani said, grinning mischievously.

"A hamburger?" Kana queried, giving her a look that said, *You've got to be kidding.*

"I try not to eat those much, honey."

"Oh yeah, that whole model thing," Kana said airily.

"Yeah, that," Palani said, smiling.

Kana always treated her like a regular person. She never treated her like she was a famous model. It was nice. There were never any games with Kana—what you saw was what you got.

"You want a hamburger," Kana said seriously.

Palani nodded, a slight grin on her lips still.

"What my girl wants, she gets," Kana said, sighing as she started the engine.

"Yay!" Palani exclaimed, clapping and laughing at the same time.

Kana laughed too, shaking her head. It really was very easy to make Palani happy. The girl was starved for normalcy. She always had the silliest cravings for food, like the night she'd wanted rocky road ice cream. And Kana indulged every fanciful idea Palani had.

Kana took her to a restaurant called Boll Weevil.

"They have the best burgers in town," she said.

The restaurant was rustic-looking, and had pool tables and a jukebox.

After they ordered, they sat talking. During the conversation Kana's attention strayed to the waitress serving from the bar. Palani noticed Kana's eyes trained on something behind her, so she turned to glance over her shoulder.

The waitress was a cute blonde, and Palani immediately assumed Kana was just looking at her. But then she noticed the conversation going on between the waitress and the man she was serving beer to. The man was playing pool. He wore jeans, cowboy boots, a black shirt, and a cowboy hat. He was tall and thin. As Palani watched, he reached around behind the waitress and literally grabbed her butt. The waitress jumped, and backed away from him.

"Come on," the man said, sounding slightly drunk. "Just a little kiss."

"Clyde," the waitress said, "just play your game, okay?"

"You're not gonna give me one?" Clyde asked, looking pouty.

"You know I can't do that."

"You can, and you're gonna," Clyde said, and grabbed her arm.

Palani glanced over at Kana and saw her eyes narrow. Kana reached down, pulled her badge off her belt, turned it around, and re-clipped it. Palani started to ask why she'd done that when Kana stood up.

"I'll be right back," Kana said.

Palani watched her walk over to where the two stood.

"Sir," Kana said, her tone already commanding. "Let the lady go."

"Who the fuck are you?" Clyde said, looking her up and down.

"That's not important," Kana said smoothly. "What is important is that you let the lady go, now."

"I'll let her go when I'm fuckin' ready to, bitch."

"Clyde! Stop it!" the waitress exclaimed, sensing that Kana wasn't someone he should be messing with.

51

Clyde tightened his hold on her wrist, making her cry out and try to pull it away.

Kana's hand whipped out, grasping his wrist. She applied pressure steadily, her dark eyes staring into Clyde's. Within a minute, Clyde couldn't take it anymore and let the waitress go. Kana then let him go. The waitress stepped back from him, rubbing her wrist. Clyde was doing the same.

"You bitch," Clyde said, embarrassed to have been bested by a woman.

"You say that like it's a bad thing," Kana said, her eyes glittering in amusement.

"You need a man to teach you a good lesson."

"Someone like you, Clyde?" Kana asked cynically.

"Yeah, I could teach you a thing or two," Clyde said cockily.

"Doubtful."

Two burly men walked up at that point to escort Clyde out of the restaurant. Kana went back to the table.

"Wow," Palani said, shaking her head.

"What?"

"Do you do stuff like that all the time?"

Kana shrugged. "No, but he was obviously getting out of hand. I won't sit by and watch men get abusive to women."

Palani nodded, liking that Kana was so sure of her convictions.

A few minutes later, the same blond waitress—whose tag read "Brenda"—came over with their food. She also carried a draft beer in a Pilsner glass. She set that down in front of Kana.

"This is on me, honey," Brenda said, winking at Kana. "Thank you for what you did."

"It was nothing," Kana said. "But thank you for the beer."

"He's been after me for months," Brenda said. "He doesn't get that I don't need another drunk in my life."

"Well, hopefully he'll get it now," Kana said, smiling.

"Hopefully he will," Brenda said, laughing as she set down their food. "You two need anything, you just give me a yell."

Kana and Palani ate and talked for over an hour. Finally, Kana stood, pulling her jacket off the back of her chair. Reaching into her pocket, she pulled out a ten and tossed it down on the table, then walked toward the cashier's booth to pay the bill. Palani smiled, looking at the $10 bill. It was a pretty good-sized tip for a bill that maybe totaled $20, but that's how Kana was. Always generous, especially with cute blond waitresses who bought her beer.

"That was the best hamburger I've ever had!" Palani said as they walked out.

"Then you've been missing out, honey," Kana said, chuckling.

She sensed it just a few moments before she heard him yell. Kana jumped toward Palani, turning as she did to face her assailant. Clyde missed nailing her with a tire iron by an inch at most. Kana stood with her back to Palani, blocking her from any harm. Palani stepped back and to the side so she could see what had happened.

"Oh my God!" she cried, seeing Clyde standing not three feet from them, brandishing the tire iron.

"Fucking show me up, will ya?" Clyde spat. "I'll beat the fuck out of you, you stupid cunt."

Palani was terrified. She was stunned when she saw Kana raise her hands in front of her, her fingers beckoning him.

"Bring it on, Clyde," Kana said, supremely confident.

"Kana?" Palani queried, worried.

"Don't worry, babe," Kana said over her shoulder, never taking her eyes off her assailant for a second. "Clyde's only dangerous to little blond waitresses. He doesn't know how to handle a woman that can handle herself. Isn't that right, Clyde?"

"Fuck you," Clyde said.

"Not an option," Kana replied calmly.

"I'd rather fuck her anyway," Clyde said snidely, nodding at Palani.

"Yeah, you and a million other men," Kana said, smiling sarcastically. "Too bad for you she's sleeping with me."

"What?" Clyde asked dumbly, his look confounded.

"She's fucking *me*," Kana said pointedly.

Clyde stood staring at her openmouthed for a long few moments, his alcohol-soaked mind apparently unable to conceive of the idea. Kana could see when understanding finally dawned.

Clyde shrugged, reaching down to caress his package fondly. "Maybe it's time she has a real man then, dyke."

"Maybe it's time for you to come and try to take her from me, boy," Kana replied, her eyes blazing with fury held in check.

She hated being called a dyke by anyone. It was a classic slam for any woman that didn't prefer men. It was a way of degrading a woman who had her own mind. And it irritated Kana no end. She hated being labeled by her sexual preference.

Clyde looked at her for a long moment, obviously sensing that Kana wasn't afraid of him in the slightest. She had, in fact, just insulted him by calling him a boy. It was time to teach the dyke bitch a lesson. He lifted his arm to swing the tire iron again. To his surprise,

Kana didn't move. As he brought the tire iron down toward her head, she simply reached up, snatching it out of his grasp and tossing it aside. It was the one he used for his big rig—the thing weighed a lot, and she'd tossed it like it was a toothpick.

"That all you got, little boy?"

Clyde got mad then—she was making him look stupid again! He reached behind him, pulling out the .38 pistol he had stuck in the waistband of his jeans. He started to bring the gun up. Kana heard Palani scream, but she reacted faster. Clyde had taken a step forward, putting him within two feet of her. Kana saw that he was bringing out a gun, and she was taking no chances. Bringing her foot up, she kicked him in the stomach. Stepping back, she drew her gun.

"Drop it, Clyde!" she yelled, glancing behind her to make sure she was blocking Palani.

Clyde hesitated, but didn't drop the gun. He hadn't gotten it to where he was pointing at Kana just yet. She had every right to shoot him, simply for refusing to drop the weapon, but she'd been trained better than that. She waited, her finger tense on the trigger of her Sig Sauer. He had another three inches to bring it up before the muzzle would be pointing at her. She watched for any movement.

"Kana?" Palani said, terrified.

"It's okay, babe, stay back," she said. She looked at Clyde then. "Clyde, I'm San Diego PD. Drop the gun, or I swear I'll drop you."

"You're..." Clyde said, paling significantly.

Kana nodded, her face a confident mask. "San Diego PD," she said, reaching down with one hand and pulling her badge off her belt, turning it around so he could see it.

"They let dy—"

"I don't think I'd use that word again, Clyde," Brenda said from behind him. She'd come out a few moments before to have a cigarette and had seen what was happening.

Kana grinned. She could see that Clyde had just lost all his fight. "Drop the gun, Clyde."

Clyde gave her a vile look, but did as she told him.

Kana holstered her gun, walking forward and grabbing him by the arm. She whirled him around, reaching into her jacket pocket for her handcuffs. She felt him start to resist. Sliding her hand down to his forearm, she shoved him forward, taking him to the ground on his belly. She knelt with her knee in his back as she cuffed him.

"See?" Kana said as she clicked the cuffs shut. "All you had to do was have some respect for women, Clyde. Now you're going to become some guy's woman in prison."

"Prison?" Clyde asked, his voice stricken.

"Yeah," Kana said. "That's what you get for pulling a gun on a peace officer. You're lucky you're still breathing."

Clyde swallowed convulsively, nodding. He hadn't really thought about that—he was just so mad that she'd bested him. He'd felt so stupid.

Kana stood up, hauling him to his feet. She heard a siren nearby and glanced at Brenda.

"I had the manager call the cops," Brenda explained. "That was before I realized we already had one here."

Kana nodded, grinning. She glanced over at Palani then. "You okay, babe?"

Palani nodded, looking like she was still in shock. Kana walked Clyde over to the Navigator and sat him down on the ground with his back to one of the tires. She reached out then, pulling Palani into her arms and hugging her close. She felt Palani tremble.

"What is it, babe?" she asked.

"He could have killed you," Palani said in a horrified whisper.

Kana shook her head. "It will take a lot more than some loud-mouth with a tire iron and a cheap knock-off for a gun to kill me."

"But…" Palani said, sounding tearful.

"It's okay, honey," Kana said, brushing her lips against Palani's forehead. "It's okay," she repeated, hugging her closer.

Palani nodded, but held on to Kana for a long few minutes. Kana stepped back when she heard the black-and-white turn into the parking lot, giving Palani a pointed look. Palani knew Kana was warning her to stay quiet.

Kana pulled Clyde to his feet as the uniformed officers walked up.

"Hey, Tadson, Sorenson," Kana said, nodding to the male and female officers.

"Hey, Sarg," said Tadson, the male officer.

Sorenson smiled. "Hi, Kana."

"What happened, Sarg?" Tadson asked, shooting his partner an odd look for having addressed the sergeant by her first name.

Kana went on to explain what had happened. The officers made their report and took Clyde in for booking. It took two hours to handle. By that time, Palani was sitting in the Navigator.

Kana got in on the driver's side, glancing over at her.

"Are you okay, honey?"

Palani turned toward her. "Why didn't you shoot him?" she asked plaintively.

Kana stared back at her for a long moment, obviously looking for the right way to answer her question. "Basically because I don't like to take another life if I don't have to."

"But he could have killed you."

"No, babe," Kana said, shaking her head. "I've had fourteen years of doing this job—I know when to shoot."

"How did you know? He could have shot you so fast," Palani said, her face showing her fear at that thought.

"No," Kana said gently. "He had another three inches to bring that gun up. I have excellent reaction times. If he'd even twitched like he was going to bring the muzzle of that gun up, I would have shot him."

"But what if he'd brought it up anyway?" Palani asked, struggling to understand.

"He wouldn't have, babe. I would have shot him in the hand, then in the heart. He would have been dead before he hit the ground."

Palani's eyes widened, but after a long moment she nodded. She couldn't help but accept that Kana knew her job. It had terrified her to see the man trying to attack Kana, and then for him to try to shoot her, that had just been too much.

"Jesus, I need a drink!" Kana said, grinning.

Palani looked over at her for a long moment, watching as Kana started the Navigator. Then she started to grin.

In the end, Kana stopped by a local liquor store and bought a bottle of Jack Daniels. She bought Palani a bottle of Chivas Regal, the only alcohol she would drink. They went back to Kana's house and had a number of drinks while listening to music. They talked and made love late into the night. Palani had a much deeper appreciation for Kana's abilities now. It was one thing to know that Kana was a police officer; it was another to see her act in that capacity. She couldn't help but be impressed with Kana's confidence. It did scare her a bit to realize how often Kana was in that kind of danger, that it basically meant nothing to her to have someone draw a gun on her.

Matthew wasn't due back for two more days, so Palani spent the entire night with Kana, falling asleep in her arms and waking the next morning there too. It was a very nice weekend.

Before long it was the day before Christmas. Matthew was out of town all week, so Palani stayed with Kana. That morning Kana drove them the six hours to Vegas. Palani could see that she was nervous, but doing her best not to show it. On the one hand she was extremely flattered that it was her that Kana wanted to make her announcement with, but she was also very worried that if Kana's extended family didn't accept Kana's lifestyle, it would really hurt Kana, and that it could cause a rift between them. Palani knew the deck was already stacked against her because she was married to a man, but Midnight and the rest of Kana's law enforcement family's judgment could just be the final straw in their relationship.

When they got to the hotel, the Monte Carlo Resort, they checked into their room. They were among the last to arrive and were tired from the drive, so they had a nice quiet dinner in the room and relaxed. That night, after making love, they lay together still intertwined.

"So, tomorrow…" Kana began hesitantly. Palani looked up into her dark eyes, seeing the worry already furrowing the other woman's brow.

"What is it?" Palani asked, worried that Kana was changing her mind about taking her to the wedding.

"Well, the guys kinda wanted to hang out and gamble and stuff, and I know you don't like to do that…"

Palani started to nod, concern still etched in her features.

"I just thought you might want to do some relaxing," Kana continued, "so I took the liberty of booking you a kind of a spa day."

Palani blinked a couple of times, and then her eyes lit with joy. "You did?"

Kana shrugged. "I figured it'd give you a chance to unwind and do all that girl stuff you like to do before a big night." Kana's grin was engaging, if not a little mischievous.

"Girl stuff…" Palani echoed, a soft smile lighting her face. "You mean like hair and stuff?"

"Yeah," Kana said, pressing her lips together. "I mean, unless you want me to introduce you to the guys and you can hang out watching us play cards and stuff…"

"No, no, I like the spa day thing much more!" Palani exclaimed, looking slightly alarmed, but narrowed her eyes when she saw Kana's quick grin. "Hewa'ino!" she muttered, calling Kana an evil brat in Hawaiian.

Kana chuckled, but then sobered. "So you're okay with that?"

"Of course I am. It was so sweet of you to think of that for me."

"Well, I figured it's my Christmas present to you."

"And such a perfect present too."

Kana smiled, pleased that she'd had the idea. In truth she was a bit of a nervous wreck about telling her law enforcement family about her lifestyle, not just because of how they'd feel about it, but also about how they'd make Palani feel. She wanted their first meeting to be under celebratory circumstances so it was less likely anyone would cause a scene. She had no idea how Midnight and the rest of the Gang would react; she'd never really thought past keeping things on the low key. She knew that the longer she kept her secret from them, the worse it was, but she was terrified to damage the one thing in her world that meant the most to her. The Gang was her life here, and she didn't know how she'd handle it if they started treating her differently. It was a definite concern.

Christmas morning, Kana and Palani had a late breakfast in the room, during which Palani presented Kana with her gift, a chronograph watch with a black leather band. It was the face of the watch that was unique, ringed in gold and inlaid with koa, a wood abundant in Hawaii, and finely detailed with abalone shell. It was exquisite. Kana knew the watch had probably cost a lot, and felt happy that she'd blown a bit of money on the spa day for Palani.

"Do you like it?" Palani asked meekly.

Kana stared down at the watch with her eyes shining, a wistful smile on her face. "It reminds me of home."

Palani smiled brilliantly. "That's what I thought too."

"Thank you," Kana whispered as she leaned in to kiss Palani.

Later that morning, Kana escorted her to the spa to check in. She got back to the front of the hotel in time to meet the rest of the Gang, and they were off for their day of gambling.

At the wedding later that night, Kana and Palani sat together, but Palani noted that while they were next to each other, Kana was not overtly affectionate, so Palani followed her lead and kept things very casual. After the wedding, instead of heading to the reception in the pub and brewery in the hotel, Kana made a point of leading Palani over to a completely separate bar.

"I just need to get my head right before we go in, okay?" Kana said apologetically.

"Of course," Palani said, somewhat relieved herself. She'd easily seen at the wedding how close everyone was. Tiny had greeted Kana with a hand clasp and a twinkle in his eyes when he looked at Palani. Others had smiled and nodded at Kana as they walked in, but made no comment about her companion, other than to smile at Palani or incline their heads. Palani wasn't sure if they were just used to seeing Kana with strangers or if they were just really good at hiding their curiosity. After a couple of shots and some neck rolling, Kana was finally ready. Taking Palani's hand, she headed toward the bar where the reception was taking place.

Kana immediately noted that all the women were gathered near the bar, and the men were on the other side of the room. She also noted that all talking stopped when they saw her standing there with her hand in Palani's—even the music was turned down, as if the DJ understood the tableau unfolding before him. Kana felt Palani tremble slightly beside her, and that bolstered her determination. Lifting her chin slightly, she led Palani toward where the women stood.

Kana saw Midnight lean over to talk to the bartender. He nodded and poured more shots. As Kana and Palani drew closer, Midnight walked over to meet them halfway. Palani was aware that literally every eye in the club was on them. She knew without a doubt that Midnight was the head of this family, and what she did, others would follow. Midnight stopped a foot from them, looking up at Kana, her eyes searching the other woman's, like she was looking for answers to questions she hadn't asked.

Kana's eyes were wary, but she inclined her head to the young woman next to her.

"Palani, this is Midnight Chevalier—she's the Chief of Police, my boss. Midnight, this is Palani, my girlfriend." There was no mistaking the challenge in Kana's voice.

Midnight looked at Palani and smiled warmly.

"Nice to meet you, Palani," she said, handing her a shot and giving the other to Kana. Lifting her glass, she said, "To finding happiness within oneself."

Kana looked taken aback for a moment. In fact, she was—she hadn't expected it to be that simple. She knew Midnight was an incredible person, but she'd never guessed how accepting she'd be about this. She drank the shot Midnight had handed her, feeling relief flood her veins, almost crowding out the alcohol. Kana then looked over toward Joe, and she could see that he was watching them. He raised his glass, inclining his head. Kana grinned, nodding, feeling once again overwhelmed with gratitude for the people she'd looked up to for fourteen years. They'd made this so easy. She couldn't have imagined a better outcome.

"Go hang out with the boys, Kana," Midnight said, grinning. "We girls are over there drinking our asses off. I'll take care of Palani for you."

Kana laughed, nodding.

"You want to go hang out with the girls?" she asked Palani.

When Palani hesitated, still very nervous even though she felt like things were going to be okay, Midnight put her hand out.

"Come on, we don't bite—much."

Palani laughed softly and nodded, reaching up to kiss Kana quickly on the lips. Kana stood staring after Midnight and Palani for a long moment, still completely astounded at how simple her "coming out" to her law enforcement family had been. Then she walked toward the guys, snagging a waitress on the way and ordering another shot, a double, and a beer. She caught Tiny's look and narrowed her eyes at him. He grinned, nodding in approval.

Back at the girls' bar, Midnight made introductions all around. Palani was stunned to meet Jordan Tate. "The Jordan Tate."

"Oh my God, I have both your albums—you are fantastic!" Palani said, smiling broadly.

"Well, thanks," Jordan said, smiling.

They had a few more drinks, then they all went back out to the dance floor, taking Palani with them. The women danced, while the men and Kana watched and drank. At one point a slow song came on. Christian nudged Joe as he walked out to join Stevie on the dance floor, pulling her close and kissing her. Joe nudged Rick, then walked out and took Jordan in his arms. Rick nudged Dave, and so it went until all of them were dancing with their respective spouse or loved one. Even Kana joined Palani on the floor. It was the first time they'd danced together.

Later, as other people were allowed into the club, things got a little dicey. The women of the group were dancing once again while their men watched, but other men decided to try to interject themselves. At one point Kana had to involve herself in a situation between Palani and some man intent on getting her attention. When she noticed the man dancing with Palani, Kana didn't react; she simply watched and waited. Glancing to her right, Kana noticed that Tiny was also watching. He caught her glance and canted his head to the side. He was asking if she wanted to do anything. Kana shook her head slightly, then went back to watching. Things were fine for a while, but then the man started getting too touchy. Palani glanced at Kana, alarmed—that's when Kana knew it was time to intervene.

Kana walked out to the dance floor, standing next to where Palani and the man were dancing. She tapped the man on the shoulder; he was a few inches shorter than her. He glanced back at Kana, looking up at her.

"I'm busy right now, but I'll dance with you later," he said with a wink.

Kana glanced at Palani, and Palani just shook her head.

"I don't think you understand," Kana said to the man.

"Look, babe," the guy said, turning to Kana even as she stepped closer to Palani.

"Don't call me babe," Kana said mildly.

"What is your trip?" the guy asked, reaching to grab at Palani.

Kana's hand whipped out, knocking his hand aside, even as her other arm went around Palani's waist, pulling her back against her chest.

"So it's like that?" the man said, leering. "Well, we can have a threesome," he offered.

Kana's look was pointed. "What makes you think either of us needs anything you have?"

"You don't know what I have," the guy said, oozing confidence.

"I know what you have," Kana said, her eyes black onyx and cold as stone. "I gave up a while ago, and haven't missed them since."

"Well, you just didn't have the right one," the guy said belligerently.

"You know," Kana said, her grin wintery, "that's what they all say, and none of you has impressed me yet."

"Well, I can," the man said, drawing himself up.

Kana stared at him for a full minute, then let out a harsh laugh, shaking her head. She looked down at Palani. "Babygirl, you want anything this freak has to offer?"

Palani's eyes widened at the word "freak," but she shook her head, her hands firmly on Kana's arm.

"You're missing out," the guy said, still obviously believing he was part of this equation.

"We'll take our chances," Kana said.

"Listen, bitch," the guy started, but was pulled up short by Tiny, who'd been standing close enough to listen.

Tiny snatched him up off his feet.

"I don't think you should talk to my partner like that," Tiny said menacingly.

The man's eyes widened. "She's your…?" he began, his voice strangled.

"Yeah, so why don't you just apologize so I don't have to kill you," Tiny said, his smile trite.

"Fuck that, no way!" the man said, trying to keep some shred of his dignity, even if his feet were dangling off the ground by four inches.

"What's the problem here?" Joe asked, walking up with Midnight right next to him.

"This guy thinks that Kana and Palani are missing out not going with him," Tiny said, shaking the smaller man for good measure.

Joe looked over at Kana and Palani, his eyes assessing, then glanced down at Midnight.

Midnight looked up thoughtfully at Kana. "I think we should just let Kana beat the shit out of him."

"No!" Palani cried, not wanting Kana to get into a fight over her.

"Don't worry, babe, Midnight's just making a point," Kana said, hugging Palani from behind.

"What point?" the man asked, his face showing that he was still feeling a bit brave.

"The point that you're fucking with a woman that can take you apart, little man," Midnight said.

"Fuck you," the guy spat.

Joe shook his head, knowing that was the wrong thing to say in front of Tiny. Surprisingly, it was Kana that acted. She moved Palani over to Joe, stepping forward and taking the man by a handful of his shirt. She pulled his face right up to hers, her black eyes looking into his.

"That's my chief, you little piece of shit," Kana grated out angrily. "Why don't you just take your limp little dick and get out of here, before you get yourself hurt."

"I second that," Tiny said, his tone dangerously low.

"And if they don't kill you, I will," Joe said, his arm around Palani's shoulders.

"And I'll help," Midnight said, smiling sweetly.

"You people are fucking crazy!" the man said, still dangling from where Kana held him.

Kana let go of his shirt, and he stumbled as he landed on the floor. He backed up, running into Dave and Spider, who had come up to see what was going on. They both gave him menacing looks. He glanced around, saw that a number of people were watching with interest, and realized he'd better get out of there. He headed for the door and never looked back.

"I believe this belongs to you," Joe said with a wink as he pushed Palani gently back to Kana.

Kana laughed, nodding. "You okay, babe?" she asked Palani, who looked a bit shell-shocked.

"Do you people always move in numbers?" Palani asked wondrously.

Kana laughed, as did Tiny and Joe.

"We look out for our own," Midnight said.

"And no one messes with our own," Spider said from behind Tiny.

"Nope," Dave said, winking at Kana.

"Nope," Joe echoed.

Palani shook her head. She was fairly sure Kana's little secret was now a well-accepted part of their lives. It was astounding to Palani the way that these people were able to adjust to anything, and still be as loyal as ever. It was amazing and wonderful, as far as she was concerned. Her opinion of police officers had been raised by infinite levels having been around these people just one night. They were an amazing group.

Chapter 3

In the weeks that followed the wedding, Kana and Palani stole as much time together as possible. Usually an afternoon here or there, other times a night when Matthew was out of town. One time, after a particularly hectic week at the department, Kana lay in her bed fast asleep. She and Tiny had been handling raids for other units, because many people were out sick with a flu that was spreading department-wide. She'd come home from work, taken off her holster and badge, and fallen on her bed, and was sound asleep a minute later.

Palani walked into the bedroom, noting that Kana's boots were still on. She smiled to herself, knowing exactly what Kana had done. They'd talked on the phone a few times that week, and Kana had sounded exhausted every time. Palani had known she'd be taking a chance of Kana being asleep when she got there that night, but she had found that she thoroughly enjoyed just lying with Kana as she slept too.

It was crazy, but Palani knew that Kana was the one she was meant to be with. There was no question in her mind. Kana, however, was still frequently cautious with her feelings, and Palani was half afraid to tell Kana she loved her for fear Kana would run in the other direction.

So Palani kept silent about her feelings, simply enjoying every moment she could spend with Kana. There had been no more troubles since the first time when Palani hadn't called for a week. Palani couldn't always get away for a lot of time, but she was careful to always call Kana and let her know what was happening. There were times when Palani knew that Kana was feeling irritated by their restricted relationship, but Kana didn't ever talk about it.

Walking over to the bed, Palani reached down to unlace Kana's boots, watching to see when her girlfriend moved. Kana took a lot longer to move than she normally would have; it was a testament to how tired she really was. Normally her senses were on high alert all the time—Palani knew that from experience. There'd been times when Palani had tried to surprise Kana at home, and had found that Kana was alert the moment she sensed someone near, even in the house itself.

Kana stirred, opening her eyes.

"Hey…" she said, sounding as tired as she looked.

"Hi," Palani said, smiling as she continued to unlace Kana's boots.

Kana watched as Palani slipped the boots off her feet, pulling off her socks next. Palani climbed onto the bed on all fours, leaning down to kiss Kana's lips. Kana grinned up at her.

"What're you doin' here?" she asked, still grinning.

"I came to see my girlfriend," Palani said, her eyes glittering humorously.

"And since she wasn't here, you decided to hang out with me?"

"Stop that!" Palani said, narrowing her eyes at Kana but grinning all the while.

Kana was forever telling Palani how beautiful she was. To Palani's chagrin, Kana was also frequently pointing out that Palani should be with someone better looking than herself. Palani thought that Kana was beautiful. She had a strong, proud beauty about her that lent itself to Hawaiian legends of warrior women. Kana's build and strength were something Palani could never hope to achieve, and so she was easily able to find it enviable. Kana usually just shook her head and rolled her eyes at Palani when she tried to explain how she found Kana beautiful. If pressed, however, Kana would have to admit that Palani's appreciation for her hard-won physique did make her feel good.

Kana put her hand to the back of Palani's neck, pulling her down to kiss her. When their lips parted, Palani snuggled down against Kana. She made a disgusted noise in the back of her throat as she realized Kana hadn't even taken off her "POLICE" jersey. She sat up, pulling at the offending scratchy material. Kana chuckled, leaning up to oblige Palani's need to get the jersey off. Kana wore her customary black tank top under it. She'd removed her Kevlar vest right after the raid that evening, leaving it in the back of the Navigator with the rest of her gear. The jersey sailed across the room to land on Kana's dresser next to her gun.

"Good shot, babe," Kana said, grinning.

Palani gave her a curt nod, then laughed softly.

"I should take a shower," Kana said.

"Why?"

"Because I've been hard at it all day and I would probably offend delicate senses."

"Oh, stop," Palani said, rolling her eyes. "How many times have you had to deal with me when I've just been laying under hot lights all day. Or that time after the Coppertone commercial when I stunk up your whole house with that awful orange-pineapple stink?"

Kana laughed, remembering that well. Never mind how that particular smell had gotten literally all over the house. Her look reminded Palani of that, which had her blushing hotly.

"I'm going to shower," Kana said, sitting up. "I'll be right back," she added, kissing Palani's lips softly as she got up.

Palani lay back on the bed as she listened to the shower run. Reaching over to Kana's nightstand, she picked up the remote for the stereo and turned it on, tuning in a top-forty radio station.

"Tripe," Kana called from the shower.

Palani laughed, having had this conversation with Kana a number of times. Kana considered most top-forty music "tripe," whereas Palani liked it. Kana listened to Polynesian drum music, or classic rock stuff.

"Oh my God, I almost forgot!" Palani said, jumping off the bed and walking over to where she'd dropped her bag.

"Forgot what?" Kana asked from the shower.

"I got a new CD today—Jerry gave it to me."

"Castle?"

"Yes, Castle—who else?" Palani said, grinning.

"God, I can only imagine now," Kana said, rolling her eyes.

"Stop it," Palani said, laughing. "It's really good. They're called Tatu."

"Uh-huh, and?" Kana prompted, knowing Jerry wouldn't have given it to Palani for no reason at all; Jerry always seemed to have a motive.

"And…" Palani said, poking her head in the shower, admiring the view and biting her lip. "They're Russian."

"Russian?" Kana asked, turning to look at her, confusion clear on her face.

"And lesbians," Palani supplied.

"I see," Kana said, once again rolling her eyes.

"Will you just listen?"

"You know I will."

"Yeah, I do."

Kana was always willing to listen to whatever she liked. There had been some occasions when Kana liked her music, others when she hadn't, but her comments had always been kept to a minimum. Actually, the worst thing Kana had ever said was "tripe." And even that was always said jokingly. Kana encouraged any and every creative whim Palani had—it felt really good.

Palani put the CD on, forwarding to the song she was sure Kana would like. It had a rock edge and it was called "How Soon Is Now?" Palani watched the outline of Kana's body as she stood in the shower, and true to her nature, Kana started dancing to the beat. Palani smiled to herself, having known Kana would like the music. It was upbeat enough to keep your attention, and the lyrics were really good as well.

The chorus to this particular song was close to Palani's heart, and she sang along with spirit. The line about being human and needing to be loved was so very true. No matter how a person needed to obtain love, it was something everyone needed.

After the second time she'd sung the chorus, Palani glanced up to see Kana watching her from the shower. She'd turned off the water and opened the stall door.

"Do you like it?" Palani asked as Kana climbed out.

Kana nodded, reaching for a towel and starting to dry off. "It's good," she said. "Pretty pointed."

Palani nodded. "They don't make any excuses for being gay."

"Shouldn't have to."

"No, we shouldn't," Palani said, walking over to Kana and leaning against the vanity sink.

Kana glanced up, seeing that Palani was watching her.

"I just heard today that I've got the *Sports Illustrated* shoot in Hawaii in March," Palani said.

Kana nodded. She knew it was something Palani had been hoping for. "Congratulations, but I knew they'd pick you."

"You knew, but I sure didn't," Palani said, smiling.

"My girl's the prettiest one of them all," Kana said, grinning.

Palani moved away from the counter, putting her arms around Kana's neck and standing on her tiptoes to kiss her on the lips. Kana's arms slid around her back, pulling her close to kiss her back. Palani giggled as Kana lifted her off her feet. She wrapped her legs around Kana's waist. Kana carried her over to the bed, turning to sit down with Palani on her lap, continuing to kiss her.

"How long will you be gone?" Kana asked when their lips parted for a few moments.

"Three weeks," Palani said, grimacing. "Are you sure you can't get away and come with me?"

"I'm sure, little one," Kana said. "Besides, what would you tell Matt?"

"That you're my personal bodyguard?" Palani replied, grinning devilishly.

"Uh-huh," Kana said, having had this conversation with her before. "And I'd have to guard it constantly."

"For hours on end, I hope."

"Yeah, Matt should go for that," Kana said, rolling her eyes.

Palani sighed, putting her head on Kana's shoulder. "Maybe I shouldn't take it."

"Why?" Kana said, glancing down at her.

Palani didn't answer for a long moment, shaking her head. "I'm going to miss you," she said quietly.

"Oh, babe..." Kana said. "You're taking it—this is something you said you've dreamed of for years." Kana reached over, tipping Palani's face up to hers. "You're taking it, and I don't want to hear you say you might not again. Do you understand me?"

Palani's eyes searched hers for a long moment, then she nodded, not looking too happy about it.

"Palani!" Kana said, exasperated. "You should be dancing in the streets right now, not all depressed. Jesus!"

"I know, I know," Palani said, nodding. "I just... I wish you could be there."

"Babe, you're going to be busy as hell while you're there. You wouldn't have time to do anything anyway. And besides, Matt's going with you, so you know you wouldn't be able to see me at all anyway."

"I know," Palani said, sounding petulant still. "I just wish things were different."

Kana looked down at her for a long moment, her face softening. She understood what Palani was going through, but there wasn't anything they could do about it at that point. She wasn't going to allow her to give up the cover of the *Sports Illustrated* swimsuit edition for anything, not even her.

"You'll go, you'll see your family, you'll take beautiful pictures, and three weeks will fly by like nothing."

Palani sighed, then nodded. "Okay."

Kana stared at her for a long moment, and Palani started to grin, realizing how ridiculous she sounded. She had dreamed of being on the cover of the *SI* swimsuit edition for years. Now she was finally going to do it, but she felt like she was going to miss so much time with Kana. It was crazy to be this in love with someone, but it felt really good, and she didn't want to lose it for a moment. She could also see that Kana was adamant about her going to Hawaii and not coming with her. She knew Kana was right about everything on this, but it didn't stop her from wanting things to be different.

They spent the rest of the evening enjoying each other, and talking. Kana told her she could call from Hawaii any time she wanted to talk. "Even in the middle of the night, if that's when you can get away—I don't care what time it is."

That helped to settle Palani's mind a little, but nothing would replace the feeling of Kana's arms around her. It was what got Palani thinking about the future, and what she really wanted.

The night before Palani was scheduled to leave for Hawaii, she surprised Kana by showing up at the house at 9:00. Kana was sitting in her living room, beading a necklace. She was on edge because she knew she was going to be miserable without Palani around, but she was doing her best not to let Palani feel that. Kana was constantly aware of her impact on Palani's feelings. She was trying hard not to make Palani feel bad about the situation. Kana's attitude was that she'd allowed herself to fall for a woman that she'd known full well was married; she had no right now to beleaguer Palani constantly for that fact. Kana was the type of person to take full responsibility for her own actions. She'd gotten involved with Palani, so now she had no right to whine about the situation not being perfect.

To that end, Kana had kissed Palani goodbye the night before when they'd had dinner, expecting not to hear from her again for at least a few days, until things got settled down in Hawaii. She was, of course, shocked when Palani unlocked her front door and stepped inside the small house. Kana looked up, the shock evident on her face.

"What are you doing here?" Kana asked, unable to keep the broad smile off her lips.

Palani walked over to her, then knelt down next to the table, looking at what Kana was doing. She knew Kana had been trying to distract herself. She smiled, taking solace in the fact that Kana was obviously edgy about this trip too.

"I had to see you," Palani said, reaching out to touch Kana's leg.

Kana's hand covered hers, then took it, pulling Palani up onto her lap. Kana hugged her, glad that Palani had come.

"Missed me already, huh?" Kana asked with a grin.

"You know I did," Palani said, leaning in to kiss Kana softly, then rested her head against Kana's shoulder. "I'm going to go nuts for the next three weeks, I just know it."

Kana looked down at her for a long moment. "I know, babe, me too," she said softly. "But it's only three weeks, not a year—we can handle it."

"I don't know about that," Palani said seriously. "Until I met you I didn't know what love could feel like. Now I know I'm going to feel like part of me is missing, not having you there, even if it's just for three weeks."

Kana looked thoughtful for a long moment. She leaned in, kissing Palani's lips softly, then more deeply. As she did, she reached around Palani, pulling her ring off her pinky. As she continued to kiss Palani, she took her left hand and slid the ring down onto her left index finger.

Palani pulled back, looking down at the ring in wonder. It was the silver ring with the black lava-rock heart set in it.

"Now you have part of me with you," Kana said softly.

Palani was speechless for a moment, unable to put into words how much Kana's action meant to her. She gazed down at the ring, touching it reverently, then looked back up at Kana.

"I love you," she said softly, praying silently that she wasn't making a mistake.

Kana smiled gently. "I know that, babe."

"You do?" Palani asked, surprised. "But how?"

"You show me all the time."

"I do?" Palani asked, thinking she'd made a mistake somehow.

Again Kana smiled, her eyes twinkling with subdued humor. "Yeah, in the way your voice sounds when you talk to me on the phone. In the way that you get up in the middle of the night just to watch me make necklaces when I can't sleep. The way you leave a shoot as fast as you can to run over here and be with me for two hours before you have to go home. Yeah, baby, you show me."

"Then…" Palani said hesitantly. "That would mean that you love me too…"

"Would it?" Kana asked, grinning.

"Yes, because you are always so sweet to me, you take care of me, and do all those kinds of things."

Kana was nodding. "Then I guess I love you too," she said, her eyes still showing humor.

"You guess?" Palani asked, biting her lip.

Kana gave her a mockingly stern look. "Okay, so I love you too," she said, sounding petulant.

Palani laughed softly, leaning in to kiss Kana again. They spent the next three hours together, with Kana finally making Palani go home, because she didn't want her to fight with Matt all the way to Hawaii about where she'd disappeared to in the middle of the night. Palani had already told Kana that she was sure Matt suspected something was going on. Palani was sure Matt thought it was another man—she knew he'd flip if he knew it was another woman.

It was a source of concern to Kana. She didn't want to cause Palani any extra heartache. Not to mention the fact that Matthew could probably create some waves in the press about a gay San Diego PD sergeant stealing his wife. It was always in Kana's mind not to cause Midnight any more headaches than she already dealt with on a daily basis. Kana was still extremely loyal to the woman who she felt had saved her from herself; she wouldn't hurt Midnight or her department for anything. It was a source of loyalty grounded in a deep-seated respect for the Chief of Police.

The three weeks in Hawaii were at best dreadful for both Palani and Kana. Palani was unhappy, sullen, and downright moody for the first time in her career. Fortunately, Jerry Castle was also on this shoot, and since Jerry knew all about Kana, she was at least someone that Palani could talk to. Jerry pointed out over and over again how she was blatant about her sexuality and she still got jobs, endorsements, and magazine covers.

"Guys don't mind gay women who are beautiful," Jerry said one day as she put on the next bathing suit for the shoot. "They have that whole fantasy of two women together. And besides, they all think they're the one that can turn me straight again," she said, laughing bawdily. "Idiots!"

Palani grinned at her. Jerry was a true woman with attitude. She took no crap from anyone except Jane Ann. Now Palani understood that kind of feeling. She knew Kana put up with a lot of things with her that she wouldn't have put up with from anyone else. The more she thought about her and Kana's conversation the night before she'd left, she realized she should have known that Kana loved her. After all, Kana was breaking what she considered a cardinal rule in dating a married woman.

Terri had been quick to let Palani know that Kana wasn't one to break that rule. Kana had, in fact, broken up with a woman who had lied to her about being married. According to Terri, there had been no discussion—it had been simple. Kana had told the woman, "You lied to me, we're over." From what Terri had said, the woman had been desperate to hold on to Kana, and that had been why she'd lied about being married. Kana had never spoken to her again, shutting off her feelings totally.

Palani had asked Kana about it one night, why she was so against dating married women, when women like Terri really didn't have a problem with it.

"What I do for a living is likely enough to get me hurt," Kana had explained. "I don't need to buy heartache in my love life too. Married women are nothing but heartache."

Palani had hesitated to ask then why Kana was dating her. She'd been afraid it would make Kana think twice about what she was doing. Palani didn't want Kana changing her mind at all about their relationship. So she'd kept quiet.

In hindsight, Palani realized that Kana had been telling her in her own way, then, that she loved her. That regardless of her past practices and attitudes about married women, Palani had made her change her mind in this case.

The photographer was getting frustrated because he couldn't get the shot he wanted of Palani. Palani was getting annoyed with the photographer for keeping her sitting in the hot sun for hours on end with his temperamental artist's "eye." Jerry had seen the frustration levels growing in her friend, and was trying to distract her.

"So, what's that?" Jerry asked, nodding toward the silver ring Palani still wore on her left index finger, where Kana had put it.

Palani looked down at the ring fondly, her face lighting up with a smile. She didn't hear the photographer's sharp intake of breath, or the shutter of the camera clicking away frantically. Palani looked up at Jerry, who was sitting just off to the side. Palani's face was lit by the setting sun, and she had no idea how incredibly ethereal she looked at that moment. Even Jerry knew that if the photographer could capture the look on Palani's face, it would be a moment immortalized in history. She'd never seen her friend look so beautiful, and she knew it was the light of love in her eyes that gave her that extra spark.

"Honey, that picture's gonna make you a star," Jerry said, nodding at the photographer.

"What?" Palani asked, not understanding.

Jerry shook her head, not wanting to explain at that moment. "So, K gave it to you, I take it?" she asked, nodding toward the ring.

Palani bit her lip and grinned, looking quite ingenue. Again the photographer was in heaven, taking pictures at a feverish pace. Palani paid no attention, too thrilled to be able to tell Jerry about her girlfriend giving her a ring. She finally nodded.

Jerry nodded too, aware that she was watching history being made but thrilled for Palani all the same. She'd found true love, there was no denying that.

They talked later that night at dinner. They'd chosen to hang out mostly together during the time in Hawaii, when Palani didn't have to be somewhere with Matt. They were more comfortable with each other than with any of the other models.

"This is bound to start rumors, you know," Jerry had pointed out when Palani stopped by Jerry's room to pick her up.

"And I care because…?" Palani asked, shrugging.

Jerry laughed outright. "I guess you don't."

"Nope," Palani said, shaking her head. "You're my best friend. If these people can't handle that, then they can just kiss my fine Hawaiian ass."

"You go, girl!" Jerry said, laughing.

She liked who Palani was becoming now—her own person. For so long she'd seen the beautiful girl so unhappy, but so unsure as to why. It had been something Jerry had watched her agonize over for far too long. Jerry hadn't liked Matt from day one, saying that he seemed so dull and lifeless and that a woman as beautiful as Palani deserved someone that thrilled her senses. Kana Sorbinno obviously did just that. She was also giving Palani a confidence in herself that only love could give a person. It was like watching a beautiful butterfly emerge from a cocoon. Palani had always been beautiful, but she'd never been very strong. Kana was changing that, and Jerry loved to see it happen.

Palani had been one of the few models who had never treated Jerry with a moment's uneasiness. Even coming from the solidly straight background that she did, Palani accepted Jerry's sexuality without a second thought. There hadn't been any comments about "Just don't make any passes at me," or anything like that. Palani had never treated her like she was strange, or someone who just needed to be pitied for her sexual orientation. In fact, Palani had seemed to look up to her from the moment they'd met, telling her that she'd just love to be so strong and in control of herself all the time.

Jerry's favorite saying was that she was a BITCH. "A babe in total control of herself" was how she defined the word. Palani liked that, and envied it. Now she was becoming that herself.

"You know," Jerry said that night as they relaxed over drinks, "you really could make this thing work with her, if you were willing to make the leap."

"Like what?" Palani asked, still so unsure of herself.

"Like getting a divorce, and being with Kana full time."

Palani took a deep breath and sighed, not even sure Kana would want that. Kana had never asked her to leave Matt—maybe she didn't want her to. Maybe she'd decided this was easier. Terri had told

Palani that the reason she liked married women was because at some point they'd go back to their husband and give her "space." Terri had told her that it was the best of both worlds—she got time to herself and time with a woman she wanted to be around. And since the woman was already in a committed relationship, Terri said, she got to play when the mood took her. Palani didn't understand that reasoning, but realized she'd never been on the end Terri was on, so she had no room to judge.

"What?" Jerry asked, glancing over at Palani.

Palani shook her head. "I don't know that Kana would want that," she said honestly.

"What do you want?"

"To be with her all the time."

"Are you ever going to accomplish that while married to Matt?" Jerry asked pointedly.

"No."

"Then you have half your answer," Jerry said. "Either way, Matt doesn't make you happy—why stay?"

"That's true," Palani said, seeing what Jerry was saying. "But what if Kana doesn't want me full time like I want her?"

Jerry shrugged. "There's millions of women out there who would, Palani."

Palani sighed again, and didn't reply. She didn't want just anyone, she wanted Kana. But Jerry was right—being with Matt was never going to make her happy, so why keep them both in the relationship?

Kana was having her own lousy three weeks. She and Tiny worked for what seemed like days on the same case, following leads, chasing people down. For the first week she fell into bed exhausted. Half the time she'd be awoken by her phone, Palani having stolen away and called her from the lobby of the hotel. They'd talk for a few minutes, then Kana would caution her to go back to the room. The last thing Kana wanted was for Matt to find out about them while Palani was hundreds of miles away in Hawaii. If Matt was going to throw a tirade, or even try and hurt Palani, Kana was going to be there to stop him.

After the first week, things calmed down at work, and then it was almost worse. Then she had time to miss Palani. Terri came by and dragged her out of the house frequently. Kana would sit at the bar and watch women dance. There were a number of interested glances thrown her way, but Kana ignored them all.

"Oh for God's sake!" Terri snapped. "You'd think you two were married or something! You think she's not making it with hubby down in paradise?"

Kana narrowed her eyes at Terri. Her friend tended to be blunt when it came to even the most delicate matters.

"What? You think she's not doing him anymore?" Terri asked, as if Kana was crazy if she believed that. "She's doing him, trust me on that."

"Terri..." Kana said, a note of warning in her voice.

"K, you gotta learn not to get so damn involved with these women!" Terri said vehemently. "You always get yourself stomped, and it's so not worth it!"

Kana's look changed then. "If you recall, you were the one that brought her over to my house that night."

"You were going to end up with her either way—she had you caught."

Kana sighed. There was no denying that.

"And I'm not saying don't enjoy her. Hell, I know I would," Terri said, backing up slightly at the dangerous look that got her. "Easy there, K, I know she's yours—relax. I'm just saying she's beautiful and sexy and all that, so enjoy her. But stop getting your heart so deep into her that you can't see daylight when she's not around. It's just going to make you miserable."

"Maybe I like miserable," Kana said, almost growling.

Terri stared back at her for a long moment, then sighed and shook her head. Turning to look around her, she picked out the cutest blonde she could find. Walking directly over to the other woman, Terri smiled.

"Hi," she said, all charm.

"Hi…" the younger woman said, looking up at Terri shyly.

"Oh, K would love you," Terri said, grinning.

"K?"

"Yeah," Terri said, turning to point at Kana, who was now leaning back against the bar, scanning the dance floor. "My friend Kana, she's lonely 'cause her girl's out of town."

"Oh, that's a bummer," the girl said, already smiling.

She liked the way Kana looked, with her very tough demeanor but the prettiness you don't find very often in the more dominant-type women. Sharon was definitely interested in this woman's "friend."

"So," Terri said, noting the way the girl was looking at Kana and already patting herself on the back. "Maybe you could go over there and cheer her up a bit."

"I think I could do that," Sharon said, nodding.

She walked across the room, stopping at the bar right next to Kana. Kana's very presence had an air of strength about it that was undeniable. Sharon felt it immediately. She ordered a drink, then waited as the bartender made it.

"It's crowded in here tonight," Sharon said, glancing over at Kana.

Kana nodded, glancing at the little blonde standing next to her. She'd seen her walk up; she'd also seen Terri talking to her a few moments before. Kana knew Terri's tactics well. It didn't hurt Kana's ego at all that the blonde was obviously willing to entertain whatever hairbrained scheme Terri was working up. She hadn't seen any money change hands, after all, Kana thought, grinning.

"So," Sharon said, winking at the bartender as she took her drink. "You come here a lot?"

Kana heard the line, but couldn't begin to think of a reply.

"Another Guinness, K?" asked the bartender from behind her.

Kana glanced over her shoulder and saw Sandy, one of her ex-girlfriends, watching her with a grin. "Yeah, San, thanks," she said, grinning back at her.

"The bartenders know you?" Sharon asked, looking impressed.

"Carnally," Sandy replied, giving Kana a wink.

"Oh," Sharon said, looking intrigued and shocked at the same time.

Kana laughed, shaking her head. "Make me look like a tramp, why don't ya?" she said to Sandy.

"If the shoe fits..."

"Don't go there," Kana said, grinning.

"So," Sharon said, only further intrigued by the conversation. "Do you dance?"

Sandy started to say something, only to have Kana hold up a hand to cut her off.

"I've been known to, on occasion."

"So, would you dance with me?"

Kana looked thoughtful, glancing over to where Terri was watching with a satisfied grin on her face. She narrowed her eyes at her, but then looked down at Sharon, who was waiting expectantly. Finally, Kana shook her head, gesturing for Sharon to precede her to the dance floor. Sharon walked out, and then turned to Kana. It was a slow song, so they danced close. Sharon was thrilled. Kana's arms were strong, and she smelled really good.

Kana had the air that most officers have, that presence of command that makes people pay attention to them no matter where they are. Her height and physique made her stand out even more, amongst smaller women. Sharon ran her hand up Kana's arm, feeling the strength housed there. She shivered.

Kana was feeling the alcohol she'd been drinking all night. She kept thinking over what Terri had said. It had been a couple of days since she'd heard from Palani, but she hadn't thought anything of it up until Terri's comment that night. Gritting her teeth, Kana avoided thinking about it. Even so, the image of Palani and Matt having sex flashed through her mind. Squeezing her eyes shut, she dropped her head, trying to block it out.

Sharon chose that moment to look up at her. Taking advantage of the fact that Kana's head was lowered, Sharon pressed her lips to Kana's. Kana pulled back sharply at first, but then looked down at the smaller woman. She was very pretty, the kind of woman Kana would usually date. *What the hell*, she thought, lowering her head again and kissing Sharon back, her hands sliding up the smaller woman's back.

Sharon entwined her arms around Kana's neck, pressing closer as they kissed. Kana knew she was making a spectacle of herself, and decided she needed to get out of there. Taking Sharon's hand, she led her to the door of the club. They walked outside, and Kana led her over to the Navigator. Turning and pressing Sharon against the side of the vehicle, Kana kissed her again, letting the alcohol make her reckless. They were deeply involved in the kiss when Kana's cell phone rang. Kana broke away, knowing before she even looked that it was Palani calling.

Turning away from Sharon, Kana yanked the phone off her belt and answered it.

"Yes?" she said briskly.

"Kana?" Palani said hesitantly.

"Hey, honey," Kana said, her voice gentling.

"Are you busy?"

Kana glanced at Sharon, who was leaning against the Navigator, watching her.

"No, hon, what's up?" Kana asked, walking a couple of steps away and leaning on the front of the car.

"I need to talk to you," Palani said, her tone hesitant still.

Kana felt the hesitation, and somehow just knew she wasn't going to like what Palani was about to say.

"About what?" Kana asked, her own thoughts making her tone short.

Palani hesitated, not sure where to begin, and noticing that Kana didn't seem to be in a good mood at that point.

"Maybe now isn't a good time..." she said, trailing off.

"Tell me," Kana said, more sure now of what she was thinking.

"Kana, I don't think—"

"Just fucking tell, me, Palani," Kana growled.

Palani was taken aback by Kana's tone. She'd never talked to her this way. It was like somehow she already knew what Palani was going to say.

"Kana," Palani began, "I just need you to know that I love you, no matter what—"

"Tell me," Kana snapped, getting more and more frustrated by the minute.

Palani shook her head. She'd been terrified that this would happen, and now it was. She hadn't even told Kana yet, and she was already mad.

"Tonight we went to a dinner for the SI executives," Palani began hesitantly. "Matt had a lot to drink."

Kana closed her eyes, dropping her head on the hood of the Navigator.

"When we got back to the hotel," Palani continued, "he wanted to have sex with me. I tried to tell him no, that I didn't want to, that I wasn't in the mood, but he was insistent..."

"So you fucked him."

"Kana..." Palani said, not liking the sound of Kana's voice at all.

"You fucked him, right?"

Palani didn't answer. She knew that with one word she was about to lose the woman she loved.

"Answer me!" Kana yelled, making Palani jump.

"Yes," she said, the single word filled with as much regret as was possible.

Kana nodded. "I gotta go," she said, her hand tightening on the phone.

"Kana, please…" Palani began, tears in her voice now.

"I gotta go," Kana repeated, then took the phone, and with a yell, threw it across the parking lot.

Sharon watched with wide eyes. Terri walked up then, surveying the scene. Kana was standing with her hand on the hood of the Navigator, her body bent at the waist as she leaned forward, her head down, taking deep, gasping breaths.

"K?" Terri queried, canting her head to the side.

Kana's head snapped up, and Terri could see the pain in her eyes.

"Okay then," Terri said, nodding. "You need a drink, my friend." She gestured with her head toward the bar.

"Yes, I do."

The three of them walked toward the bar. At the door, Kana stopped, yelling again and hitting the wall with her fist.

"Okay," Terri said, grimacing at Sharon as she opened the door. "Come on, K," she said, pulling at Kana's arm.

Kana went inside and headed straight for the bar. She started drinking shots. Sandy put a bowl of ice on the counter next to her.

"What's this for?" Kana asked.

"For your hand," Sandy said, giving her a worried look.

"Oh," Kana replied, feeling the effects of the alcohol.

Terri walked over and took Kana's arm, directing her hand into the bowl of ice. Kana continued to drink undaunted. Sharon stood by and watched. She had to admit she was fascinated by what she'd witnessed. Even in a drunken state, Kana was a compelling person.

Later that night, Kana accompanied Sharon home. As they walked into the house, Sharon wasn't sure what to do. Kana solved that for her, pressing her against the nearest wall and kissing her deeply. The sex that followed was the best Sharon had experienced; Kana didn't even remember it the next morning. Afterward she pulled Kana down the hall to her bedroom, wanting to get her to stay. Kana was past reasoning at that point, and allowed herself to be led. She promptly passed out, holding Sharon by the waist.

When she woke in the morning, Kana had a monster hangover. She groaned as she turned over in bed. Sharon was already up.

"Good morning," Sharon said brightly.

Kana just looked back at her. She began to get up, pausing as her head started throbbing.

"Aspirin?" Kana asked.

"Sure," Sharon said, way too cheerfully for Kana's mood.

Kana took the aspirin that Sharon handed her, then got up. Walking down the hallway, she collected her clothes, pulling them on as she did. Sharon followed, disappointed that Kana wasn't staying.

"I need a ride back to my vehicle," Kana said simply.

Sharon nodded, trying to hide the disappointment she felt. She went and got dressed quickly, then drove Kana back to the bar parking lot.

Kana was relieved to see that the Navigator was intact.

"Thanks," Kana said, reaching for the door handle.

"Wait," Sharon said, putting her hand on Kana's leg.

Kana looked over at her, as if seeing her for the first time. She blew her breath out in a sigh, shaking her head.

"I'm sorry," Kana said. "Things are just all fucked up right now."

Sharon nodded. "I understand," she said quietly.

Kana reached into her jacket pocket, pulling out a business card. She pulled out a pen and wrote her home number on the back of the card, then handed it to Sharon.

"Thanks," Sharon said, smiling now.

Kana nodded, leaning over to kiss the younger woman softly. Then she got out of the car and went to her vehicle. Sharon looked at the card, which read "Sergeant K. Sorbinno, San Diego Police Department," and her eyes widened. She glanced at Kana as she got into her truck. A cop? *Wow*, was all Sharon could think, definitely making sure she held on to that card.

Kana got home and took a shower. She called Tiny and told him she'd be in soon. She drove to the office, keeping her mind trained on work instead of what was happening to her life.

"You look like hell," Tiny said when she walked in.

"Thanks," Kana replied, going into her office and shutting the door.

She worked until 1:00, then told Tiny she was going home. He told her to get some sleep, and she nodded. At home, Kana didn't even bother to take her boots off—she just dropped herself on the bed and lay there until her mind would let her sleep again.

It was just getting dark when Kana heard movement in her room. She sat up, tensing as she reached for her weapon. Then she saw who it was. Palani stood by the bed, staring down at Kana.

"How the hell?" Kana said, shocked.

"I left Hawaii this morning," Palani said. "I needed to see you, to talk to you, to tell you." She reached out to touch Kana's face.

Kana pulled back, wary. "To tell me what?"

"I left Matt."

"You what?" Kana asked, sure she hadn't heard right.

"I left him, Kana," Palani said. "I love you. I want to be with you, if you'll just let me."

Kana stared back at Palani for a full minute, trying to assimilate what she was being told.

"You left Matt?"

"Yes," Palani said, smiling indulgently at Kana's apparent hearing problem.

Palani was shocked when Kana stood up suddenly, her hands capturing Palani's face, her lips kissing her deeply. After a moment, Palani wrapped her arms around Kana's neck, kissing her back and feeling thrilled to her very core.

"I love you, I love you," Palani said over and over again.

"I love you too, Palani."

"I brought you something." Palani reached into her pocket and handed Kana a small box.

"What is this?" Kana asked.

Palani bit her lip, smiling. "Open it."

Kana sat down on the bed. Palani did the same. Kana opened the box and found another one inside, this one black velvet. She looked at Palani, narrowing her eyes slightly. Then she opened the velvet box. The ring that lay inside was incredible. It was a platinum band, inset with black diamond baguettes. It was intricately carved with a number of Polynesian symbols.

"It's beautiful…" Kana said, shaking her head in wonder.

"You like it?"

"Those aren't lava, are they?" Kana asked, pointing to one of the baguettes.

"Um, no," Palani said, grimacing. She knew Kana would kill her for the amount of money she'd spent on the ring.

"Palani…" Kana said, her tone predictably chastising.

"Kana, I wanted you to have something to replace the ring you gave me, 'cause you're not getting it back," Palani said, smiling ingenuously.

Kana looked back at her for a long moment, narrowing her eyes. Palani gave her a cocky wink, then reached down and took the ring out of the box. She took Kana's left hand and slid it on her left ring finger.

"That's not where I wore my ring," Kana said, her eyes still narrowed.

"Well, that's where you're going to wear mine," Palani said, staring right back into Kana's eyes.

Kana was able to hold her stern look for a moment, then started to grin. She leaned forward, kissing Palani deeply, then pulled back to look her in the eyes.

"I love you. Thank you for this," Kana said.

"You're very welcome," Palani said, glad that she'd been able to resolve this trouble with Kana.

The night before, when Kana had hung up on her, she'd been frantic. She'd called Kana's cell phone over and over again. She got a busy signal every time. She'd called Kana's house repeatedly for hours. Kana never picked up. Finally, when Matt had gotten up that morning, she'd flat out told him she was leaving.

"You're leaving the shoot?" Matt had asked dumbly.

"Yes, I'm leaving the shoot," Palani had said. "And I'm leaving Hawaii, and you."

With that, she'd turned and left the room. She'd already packed her bags before he'd ever gotten up, taking the bare minimum. She had no idea if Matt knew what she meant about leaving him, but she didn't care. She was with Kana now, and she didn't want to look back.

***

A month after they'd gotten back together, Palani was living half the time with Kana. Kana had insisted that Palani be more circumspect about leaving Matt. She wanted Palani to go through the motions of a "normal divorce" so that she wouldn't lose everything to Matt because she'd been having an affair. Palani did as Kana asked, respecting that Kana wanted what was best for her.

Kana got home from work one evening to find Palani sitting on the couch, staring at a magazine.

"Hon?" Kana queried from the counter in the kitchen.

Palani looked up, surprised to see Kana standing there. She hadn't even heard her come in.

"You've got to see this," Palani said, getting up off the couch and walking over to Kana.

Palani handed Kana the magazine she'd been staring at. It was a copy of *Sports Illustrated*, and Palani was on the cover. The picture was breathtaking. Kana stared in awe. Palani was wearing a black metallic-looking bikini, her hair loose and framing her face. The sun was setting behind her—it was an incredible setting. But the most incredible thing about the picture was the expression on Palani's face—she looked absolutely ethereal.

"That is the most incredible picture I've ever seen of you," Kana said honestly, awed.

"This is the preview," Palani said. "And this," she added, pulling out a piece of paper that was at the back of the magazine, "is a release." She handed it to Kana.

Kana took the paper and looked at it, then glanced up at Palani.

"Why are you giving it to me?" Kana asked, perplexed.

"Because," Palani said softly, looking up at her, "that picture is yours. I was thinking of you when he took that shot. Jerry had just asked me about your ring on my finger, and the photographer captured my response to that question."

Kana looked at her, shaking her head. "I still don't understand, babe."

"I told the photographer that he could only publish that picture if my girlfriend signed the release, since it was her picture."

Kana stared back at Palani for a long moment, suddenly understanding the gravity of what she was telling her.

"So I could say no, and no one would ever see this picture?"

"No one but you."

Kana gazed at the picture again, her look pensive. Finally she shook her head.

"This is too incredible to keep to myself, babygirl," Kana said. "I want everyone in the world to see what a beautiful woman I have."

Palani smiled brightly, loving that Kana put it in a way that was possessive, because she wanted to be possessed by her.

"Well, in that case..." She walked back over to the couch and picked up an envelope, then returned to Kana and handed it to her. "This is yours."

Kana canted her head to the side, then opened the envelope. Inside was the second picture the photographer had taken, the one in which Palani was biting her lip.

"Holy shit..." Kana said, having a visceral reaction to the picture.

Palani looked so incredibly sexy, Kana found her pulse racing just looking at the photo.

"You're right," she said, grinning. "I wouldn't let you put this one out—you'd have every man and woman beating down my door to get to you."

Palani laughed softly. "This one is all yours."

"Thank you," Kana said, leaning down to kiss her deeply.

"You're welcome," Palani murmured against her lips.

Kana lifted her up, taking her over to the couch, where she proceeded to make slow but passionate love to her, showing her over and over again how much she desired her.

Things seemed to be heading in all the right directions at that moment, but things aren't always as they seem...

Chapter 4

A year later

So much had happened, so much that couldn't be changed... Why?

It was the question that screamed in Kana's head all the time.

She sat on the lanai of her family's home, smoking and staring out at the ocean. She ground her teeth in an effort to stop the direction of her thoughts, but that wasn't helping. Nothing helped when she'd had too much to drink. She'd had too many Mai Tais with dinner—her family was so busy celebrating her visiting that she couldn't put her glass down without it being refilled. Now the sun was going down, and the party was still going on, but Kana had escaped to the lanai, knowing her mother wouldn't bother her there, since she abhorred cigarette smoke.

Sitting there, though, Kana couldn't stop thinking. There was too much to go over in her head, too much heartache to avoid constantly. Her mind drifted over the time when she and Palani had been happy. Things had been so right, so perfect... and then they weren't.

When Palani had decided to leave Matthew, it had been Kana who'd been the voice of reason. She'd told Palani to ease out of the marriage. Kana had been sure that if her husband had found out that his very successful supermodel wife was leaving him for another woman, he'd take every penny Palani had earned. Palani did as Kana asked, continuing to live with Matthew but making plans to file for divorce, getting her finances in order.

It had been six months into that waiting period when Palani showed up at Kana's house one night. Kana had been in bed asleep, having worked all day on a case. Palani hadn't crawled into bed with her, as she normally did; she sat down on the bed, next to Kana. That had been Kana's first clue something was very wrong. Kana had awoken, moving to sit up.

"What's wrong?" she asked, seeing the look of trepidation on Palani's face.

"Kana…" Palani began, her voice shaky.

Kana sat back against her headboard, her look wary. Every sense she had told her she was not going to like this conversation.

"What is it?" Kana asked, her tone belying her apprehension.

Palani hesitated, stammering a few times.

"Damnit," Kana growled, hating the sick feeling in her stomach. "Just fucking tell me," she snapped.

"I'm pregnant," Palani blurted out, actual fear in her eyes for Kana's reaction.

Kana went completely still, staring at Palani in stony silence for a full minute. Pregnant? Palani had told her she wasn't sleeping with Matthew and hadn't been for six months. So how had she managed to get pregnant? Simple—she'd been lying.

"Get out," Kana said simply, conversationally.

"Kana…" Palani said, reaching out to touch Kana's hand.

Kana snatched her hand away, her head coming up, her look very much the gang leader she'd been years before.

"Get out," Kana repeated, her voice nearing a growl now.

"Kana, please," Palani said, tears in her eyes.

"Get the fuck out!" Kana yelled, her voice reverberating in the room.

Palani leapt off the bed, fearing that Kana would actually strike her. Kana had in fact tensed, wanting to hit Palani. She'd gritted her teeth to force herself back under control. Palani had seen the muscles twitching in Kana's jaw, and her eyes had widened in near terror.

"Go, now," Kana said, her tone low and even more dangerous than her yell.

Palani rushed out of the room, terrified of Kana's anger and not brave enough to wait to see what would happen if she defied her any longer. It was the last time Kana had seen Palani. Palani had tried to call a number of times, but Kana never answered the phone. She'd shut her heart off. She would not forgive Palani for lying to her.

Every day since then had been a struggle. Kana had done her best to harden her heart and not think about Palani. She had thrown herself into her work. She had taken and ranked number one on the lieutenant's test. Midnight had promoted her one month before, having finally gotten wind of the previous lieutenant of homicide's lazy tendencies. Kana had been doing a lot of his job for years. Midnight had also discovered that, and had told Kana in no uncertain terms that she would now be getting paid for the work she'd been doing.

Sitting staring out at the darkening skies, Kana hoped that her career would be enough to sustain her. She'd had enough of love and its decimation of her life and her heart. Getting up from the chair, she straightened her five foot, ten inch frame and walked back into the house. Heading straight to the bar, she skipped the fruit juice that went into a Mai Tai and picked up the rum instead, drinking straight from the bottle.

***

Catalina Roché was not what most people expected. She was beautiful, but tough as nails. She had an easygoing personality, but could be very intense when the moment called for it. And she was a cop—not just a cop, but an undercover narcotics officer. No drug dealer she'd ever busted had believed for a second that she had fooled them so easily, but she had, time and time again. She had proven to be one hell of an undercover cop, as part of the sheriff's office's narcotic's unit, but when she'd actually gotten the drop on a San Diego PD narc named Christian Collins, she'd really impressed. Christian, or Blue as he was known by his colleagues, was also undercover in the same high-end drug house she'd been working in. When she'd attempted to arrest him he'd identified himself and they'd closed the case together. Blue and his boss, Dave Dibbins, were very impressed with Catalina. As such, she'd been invited to become part of San Diego PD's narcotics force. She'd been put on a team called Rogue Squadron, Blue's team, consisting of three other sergeants all around her age, all good at their jobs. Cat was learning the ropes as to how they did their jobs, but she brought a lot of good expertise of her own.

Three days after Cat started with the team, they had a raid. Rogue Squadron got to the meeting sight and heard the plan from Dave. Just before they left, Kana, who was back from her vacation just that day, and Tiny drove up. Tiny told Dave that one of the people Rogue Squadron had a warrant on was someone he and Kana wanted to question for a recent drive-by. Dave nodded.

"You want to go in with us then?" Dave asked.

"Sounds like a plan," Tiny said.

"You two suited up?"

"Yep," Tiny replied, nodding, as did Kana from her vehicle.

"Then let's go. We were headed over there," Dave said, moving toward his car.

Once everyone was set, they went toward the house. Cat was carrying one of the shotguns, because Dave wanted to allow her an opportunity to do every job on the team. The shotgun was considered the point man of the entry team. So Cat was right behind Mace when he kicked in the door. The raid itself went fairly smoothly.

Kana and Tiny's suspect was indeed in the house. He was told he was being questioned under suspicion of murder as they sat him down. Cat was standing nearby, and had to jump back when the kid decided to make a run for it.

"So much for suspicion," Kana muttered, then took off after him.

The smaller man was no match for Kana's long legs, and she caught up to him easily. She snatched him up by two handfuls of his shirt and took him to the ground. Reaching behind her, she pulled out her handcuffs and cuffed the young man up.

"*Now*," she said as she turned him around to walk him to a waiting patrol car, "you're being *arrested* for evading a police officer. And we'll question you down at the jail in a nice metal room. Isn't that a bitch?" She grinned at the last.

She heard a laugh, and turned to see the blond woman she'd heard referred to as "Cat" standing near a navy blue SUV. Cat just shook her head, looking at the suspect. Kana put the suspect in the squad car and turned back around to look at the blonde, just as Cat went to pull the shotgun strap off over her head. The strap got tangled in her long hair, which had come down during the raid.

"Hold on, babygirl," Kana said as she walked over. She started to help untangle Cat's hair from the strap.

"Thanks," Cat said as she held the shotgun up and away from her body while Kana worked on freeing her hair. "Can't trust a man for this type of thing," she added, grinning.

"Not if you still want hair left when they're done," Kana replied, grinning too, just as she got the last few strands untangled.

"Ahhh…" Cat sighed, as she was able to lift the strap off her neck and put the shotgun in her vehicle.

She turned to Kana, looking up at her directly. She winked. "Thanks again."

Kana nodded, too surprised by her own reaction to speak at that moment.

The woman was very definitely attractive, with rich, straight gold-blonde hair that fell to the middle of her back and pretty sky blue eyes. She had an attractive face that was sun-kissed and smooth, and a body that could stop a Mack Truck. Kana had noticed her the moment she'd driven up to the site earlier that day. The last thing she'd expected was a surprise like she'd just been dealt.

The girl was *family*.

By the time Kana thought to say something, the girl was gone, headed back toward the house. Cat had no idea she'd just left Kana stunned into silence. Kana cussed herself a blue streak for a number of minutes afterward, then went looking for her, trying to think of a way to do that without being too obvious. She had no luck—the girl was nowhere to be found. By the time Kana thought to go back out to Cat's vehicle, it was gone.

"Smooth, K, real smooth," she muttered to herself.

She had no idea the girl actually worked for the department. She'd never seen her before, and having just come off of a couple of vacation days, she hadn't heard about anyone new. Kana assumed that the blonde worked for another department, and was just on a joint case. It happened a lot.

It was for that reason that Kana was once again shocked when she was told by Tiny that the blonde did indeed work for the department.

"She's with Rogue Squadron now," Tiny said.

"She is?"

"Yep, Collins recommended her. If you hadn't been lounging on the beach, you'd have known that," he said, grinning widely.

"Fuck you, Ako," Kana said, narrowing her eyes.

"I'm not your type, Sorbinno," Tiny replied, all sweet innocence.

Kana shook her head, laughing. It still surprised her at times, how easily her friends had accepted her sexuality.

When things had gone terribly wrong with Palani six months before, her family was there for her constantly, talking her through whatever she would share with them. It still hurt like crazy to talk about Palani, so she didn't much. But she knew that her family was there for her if she wanted to. It was a deep comfort.

Later that same day, Kana walked into Christian's cubicle, coincidentally located right across from Cat's. Christian looked up from his computer, smiling at Kana.

"Hey, K."

"Heya, Blue," Kana said, leaning against the vertical cabinets along the wall of the cubicle, glancing quickly across at Cat.

The girl was sitting typing away at her computer, her headphones on and oblivious to the fact that she was being observed.

Kana handed Christian the report she'd written for the runaway suspect. Then she glanced over at Cat again. Christian caught it and grinned, not saying anything. Kana saw Christian's expression and narrowed her eyes at him.

"You knew I'd want to meet her," she said quietly.

"You want to meet Cat?" Christian asked, doing his best imitation of surprise.

"You know, Collins…" Kana began darkly.

"I know," he said, nodding, a grin still playing at his lips. "I gotta ask though," he continued, leaning back in his chair. "How did you pick up on her so quickly?"

Christian knew that Kana had only met Cat that day at the raid.

Kana gave him a blasé look. "I have excellent gaydar."

Christian laughed out loud at that. He liked Kana a great deal—she pulled absolutely no punches.

"Hey, Cat!" he called, his voice loud so she could hear him over the music she was listening to.

Catalina glanced over at him, her eyes skipping to Kana then back to him as she took her headphones off and turned her chair to face him.

"Yeah?" she said, her eyes going back to Kana for a moment, then to Christian.

"Have you officially met Lieutenant Sorbinno?"

Cat's eyes went to Kana, and stayed on her. "Not officially, no," she said with a grin. "But she did lend me some critical assistance this morning."

Kana grinned too, stepping forward to extend her hand to Cat, her eyes meeting the other woman's.

"I think that would be considered follicle assistance," Kana put in.

Cat laughed, nodding. She took Kana's proffered hand, holding it a moment longer than necessary.

"Either way, it was greatly appreciated, Lieutenant," Cat said, her look once again direct.

"Call me Kana," she replied, her eyes narrowing ever so slightly as their hands parted.

"Then call me Cat."

"Oh yeah," Christian said. "Kana, that's Sergeant Catalina Roché. She just transferred from the SO."

Kana canted her head to the side, glanced back at Christian, then back to Cat.

"Is this the woman that got the drop on you, Blue?" she asked, slightly awed now.

Christian laughed, nodding, even as Cat rolled her eyes.

"Well, anyone that can get the drop on Blue is a friend of mine," Kana said to Cat, winking at her.

"Oh, good information to have," Cat said, grinning as she glanced at Christian and gave him a wink.

Cat's phone rang then, and she turned to check it. Her long hair dropped over her shoulder, and Kana knew the girl had no idea how sexy she looked at that moment, but she found herself a bit flustered by it.

"Excuse me a sec," Cat said, smiling at Kana again and moving to answer the phone.

Kana stepped back toward Christian's cubicle. His look was speculative.

"Don't even start," Kana said, cutting off whatever he was going to say.

Christian held his hands up in surrender. "All I was gonna say is, welcome back."

Kana narrowed her eyes at him again, but only shook her head. She got a call a few minutes later.

"I gotta go," Kana said. "Midnight's callin'."

"I'll give Cat your goodbyes," Christian said, winking at her.

"Go to hell, Collins," Kana said, even as she smiled.

"All in good time, love," Christian replied, smiling unrepentantly.

Kana glanced at Cat again, her look regretful, then headed for Midnight's office.

Later that afternoon, Kana was sitting in her office when the phone rang.

"Sorbinno," she answered.

"She's heading to The Pit for lunch," said a very familiar English-accented voice.

"Oh yeah?" Kana asked, grinning.

"Better hurry."

"I owe you," Kana replied, hanging up a moment later.

Cat had just given her order when she heard "Taking that to go?" from behind her.

She turned to look up at Kana. She smiled broadly as she nodded.

"Eating alone is bad for the digestion, you know," Kana said, grinning.

Cat shrugged. "Didn't have another option," she said, staring directly into Kana's eyes. "Now, if you're offering to stay and eat with me, then I won't have to eat alone at my desk." Her blue eyes scanned the restaurant. "Although there don't seem to be any tables open."

"There's one open," Kana said confidently. She looked over at Tom, the owner of the restaurant—she'd known him for over fifteen years. "Hey, Tom, make that last order for here, and give me my usual."

"You got it, K," Tom said, his eyes twinkling.

Tom, like many members of the gang, hadn't been totally shocked by Kana's not so subtle announcement about her sexuality a little over a year before. And like the rest of the Gang, Tom wanted Kana to be happy. He knew that the breakup with Palani had hurt her a great deal. It warmed his heart to see Kana obviously flirting with a new woman.

"Come on," Kana said, gesturing for Cat to follow her.

She led Cat back to the table permanently reserved for FORS members. It was at the back corner of the restaurant. It was a place where many members liked to be if they didn't feel like being bothered.

"Wow…" Cat said, seeing an empty table in a restaurant full of people.

She saw the little metal plaque on the side of the table. The sign was engraved, reading "FORS members only, Don't Even Dare!"

Cat laughed, and Kana grinned as they sat down.

"So you're a FORS member?" Cat asked.

"Former," Kana said, inclining her head.

"Ah, and once a member, always a member?" Cat asked, canting her head to the side.

"Pretty much," Kana said, laughing. "Everyone in the Gang is allowed at this table, as well as FORS members."

Cat nodded, narrowing her eyes. "Now this is the 'Gang' I keep hearing about, right? The best of the best?"

"Yeah, that would be us," Kana said, her tone confident without being cocky.

"So what's the story behind all that?" Cat asked, having been curious about this "Gang" since she'd heard about them.

Kana leaned back, putting one arm on the table, the other up on the back of the booth.

"Well, most of us were members in FORS when it first started up, way back when. Since we all used to be gang members or leaders, people still saw us that way. So that's apparently what they started calling us. As the years went by, people became part of the Gang by association. Like Pony, he's the sister of the woman that Joe Sinclair was married to for years. Jeanie's with Pony, so she's part of it. Blue is Joe's cousin, and Stevie became part of the Gang when Dave brought her back to the department. Kyle Masterson dated the chief years ago, before she was with Debenshire, and as the AC now, Kyle gets into the Gang by default." Kana grinned at the last.

"Okay, name them all off," Cat said. "With their ranks now."

"Well, there's Midnight, the chief. Rick Debenshire, he's the lieutenant in charge of FORS."

"Which Midnight Chevalier originally started, right?"

"Yeah," Kana said, as Tom brought their food to the table. "And Tom's the reason Midnight is still with us today," she said, winking at the older man.

"Really?" Cat asked, looking at Tom.

"Ain't all that," Tom said, shaking his head.

"Tom's the one that was there for Midnight when her world caved in," Kana said seriously.

Cat looked at Tom again, surprised.

He shrugged. "She needed someone."

"And you were there," Kana said.

Tom nodded.

"How much do I owe you?" Cat asked Tom, gesturing to her lunch.

"It's on the house," Tom said, even as Kana put in, "I'll take care of it."

Tom and Kana looked at each other with a challenge in their eyes.

"You runnin' a charity now, Ryan?" Kana asked, raising an eyebrow.

"No, I'm celebrating," Tom replied, smiling.

Kana looked perplexed. "What are you celebrating?"

111

"A friend of mine just came out of a six-month coma," Tom replied, winking at her as he walked away.

Kana gave a short laugh, dropping her head and shaking it.

Cat looked at Kana, totally lost. Kana glanced over at her and grinned.

"Don't ask," she said.

"Okay," Cat said, nodding. "So go on. You said Chevalier and Debenshire—now they're married, right?"

"Right," Kana said. "Then there's Joe Sinclair. He's a captain over vice right now."

"And he was married to Donovan Curtis' sister," Cat said, naming one of her team members, correlating what had been said before.

"Right. He's dating a rock star right now."

"Seriously?"

"Yeah, Jordan Tate."

Cat nodded, her look contemplative. "I think I heard that somewhere along the way, but I didn't know who he was at that point."

"And there's Kyle, the Assistant Chief, who's married to Rhiannon. Who's Stevie's sister."

"Wait," Cat said, holding up a hand. "Stevie O'Neil? Her sister is married to the Assistant Chief?" Stevie was another member of Rogue Squadron.

"Right," Kana said, grinning as she reached for her fork and started eating her salad.

Cat shook her head. "It's pretty complicated with you people, isn't it?"

"Oh, that's just the half of it," Kana said, laughing. "There's Spider, the LT in charge of narcotics, who's married to Tammy, former

FORS member. There's Dave, who's married to Susan, who's Joe's kids' nanny and Rick Debenshire's niece. There's my former partner, Tiny Ako, who you met this morning too. He's a sergeant in homicide who's married to Jess, who came down here from Sacramento because she had a crush on Joe. Oh, and now there's Mace, from your team, who's dating Erin, who was dating Donovan when he and Jeanie broke up."

"Holy shit," Cat said, looking shocked as she shook her head. "How do you keep it all straight?"

Kana shrugged. "It's our family history."

"So the Gang is like a family?" Cat asked, reaching for one of her french fries.

"For most of us, it's the only family we've had for years."

Cat nodded. "So were you a gang member once?"

Kana nodded. "I was the leader of a gang in Honolulu."

"What was the gang called?"

"Sisters of Samoa," Kana said. "Basically your female equivalent to the Bloods or the Crips."

"That fierce?" Cat asked, surprised.

"Pretty much," Kana said, grinning as she took another bite of salad.

"Why were you in a gang?" Cat asked, wanting to understand this woman all of a sudden.

"When I was a kid, I never looked like all the other girls. They were all these tiny little perfect dolls. I was always big, fat, and tall. So I was excluded a lot from their groups. I found out when I was about twelve that I could throw a mean punch. And that made people like those little dolls respect me."

"You mean fear you."

"That too," Kana replied, grinning. "One of the leaders of the Sisters recruited me when she saw me knock down a boy that was two years older and a foot taller than me. After that, I felt like I belonged to something," she said, shrugging.

"So how did you get into law enforcement?" Cat asked as she pulled her hamburger over and took a bite.

"I met Midnight at a gang fight."

"Was she in a gang?" Cat asked, sounding shocked.

"At that point, no. She led a gang when she was eighteen, but that's a whole other story," Kana said, waving her hand. "When she ran FORS, she'd take out gangs by any means necessary. Sometimes that meant fighting and defeating the leader. This was one such incident."

"Were you in the gang?"

"I was considering getting into the gang—I hadn't decided yet. But when I saw little five foot, five inch Midnight Chevalier beat a woman that was almost as big as me, and do it without even breaking a sweat… I knew I wanted to be in her gang."

"And her gang was FORS?"

"Yup," Kana said, nodding.

"So you became a cop then?"

"No, I was a CI for a while—I was only eighteen at that point."

"Oh, but you became a cop later, obviously," Cat said, nodding to herself.

"Right," Kana said. She canted her head then. "And how long have you been a cop?"

"Seven years."

"So that makes you…"

Cat smiled. "That makes me twenty-eight. And you're…" she said, her voice trailing off as Kana's had.

Kana grinned. "I'm thirty-three."

They ended up talking for the next hour, neither of them eating much of their lunch. Kana found that Cat was definitely an interesting woman, very up and outgoing. She was also not in any way new to the *family*. She said she'd known she was bi since she was fifteen, when she and her best friend had fooled around in bed one night. She'd loved it, and known it was for her. But when she'd started seeing men, she found she liked them too.

Kana made a comment about bis tending to be all over the map with their affections.

"I make that easy," was Cat's reply.

"Meaning?"

"I don't develop any feelings for anyone, other than friendship," Cat said, shrugging.

"No love for you?" Kana asked curiously.

"Nah. I'd rather just play and have a good time. I don't need heavy in my life—I get that here at work."

"Still," Kana said, "don't you want someone permanent in your life?"

"I have a cat for that," Catalina replied caustically.

Kana laughed and shook her head. Thinking about it, it was basically what she needed at this point. Nothing heavy, just some fun for a change.

They walked back to the office together.

"Thanks for lunch," Cat said as they got ready to part ways.

"No," Kana said, inclining her head. "Thank you."

Cat smiled, then turned down the hall, flipping Kana a wave. Going back to her desk, she glanced over at Christian, who looked up as she came by.

"Have fun?" Christian asked.

Cat looked back at him for a moment, then narrowed her eyes. "How do you know I had any fun?"

"I don't," Christian replied, straight-faced. "That's why I was asking."

"Uh-huh," Cat said, still giving him a narrowed look.

Christian chuckled, then turned back to his computer. Cat sat down in her chair and put on her headphones, getting back to work as well. She thought about Kana too.

The woman was very definitely attractive. Kana exuded a kind of power that had nothing to do with rank. It was the overall presence she had. She had confidence in what she did and said. She also had a very dominant personality—that much was evident. Cat's experiences had mostly been limited to submissive personalities. She usually clashed too much with anyone dominant.

Most of Cat's relationships had been with women who were bisexual like her, or what was called bi-curious. Which meant women who thought they might want to be with women but weren't sure. In fact, her only relationship with a woman that was a lesbian had ended badly, because the woman had become irrationally paranoid about the fact that Cat did like to sleep with men too. Cat hadn't been sleeping with anyone but the woman she was involved with, but the woman was convinced that she was. It had destroyed what relationship they had.

Cat couldn't stand not being trusted. She never lied to people about who she was, what she wanted, or what she did or felt. It just wasn't in her to lie. The woman had realized her mistake too late, and had been constantly trying to get Cat back since then. Cat knew better—the woman would never trust her, and she had no intention of spending her time reassuring her simply because of her own insecurities. She didn't care about *anyone* that much.

But Kana was definitely intriguing. She never discounted anyone that interested her simply because of their sexual preference. Just because her one relationship with a lesbian had gone badly, didn't mean all lesbians were bad. In fact, Cat had found that usually it was lesbians that would discriminate against her because she was bi. As Kana had indicated, lesbians thought that bisexuals were just too wishy-washy, that they couldn't make up their mind what sex they wanted to be with. It wasn't true. Cat simply enjoyed relationships, both sexually and companionably, with both men and women.

There were a lot of things about men that just drove her crazy, and women had their faults too. So she dated who she liked, and ended it when she got bored. It was as simple as that. The way she saw it, she was young, single, good-looking, healthy, and fairly fun to be around. She was going to enjoy what life had to offer, and if people didn't like that, then too bad.

She'd grown up in San Francisco, where people tended to be very free with their sexuality. Her mother was a lesbian, who'd gotten pregnant with her in her one attempt at marriage to a man. So growing up, Cat had seen a lot of women with her mother. Her mom had always been very careful to tell her daughter, "It's okay to be who you are. You don't have to be or do anything that isn't your thing."

While her mother was very open about her sexuality, she was also a fairly good parent. She made sure her daughter went to school, brushed her teeth, ate well, had clean clothes, did her homework, everything that a parent should do, and all on her own. Cat knew she'd gotten her strength from her mother.

She'd moved to San Diego to go to school, after a heartbreaking relationship with her best friend. She'd finished her degree and had joined the Sheriff's Department. She'd had numerous relationships over the years, with both men and women. It had been very interesting so far.

A couple of days later, Cat was working in her cubicle.

"You have lunch yet?" Kana asked from the doorway.

Cat turned around, glancing at Kana and grinning. "Not yet."

Kana just looked back at her expectantly.

Cat laughed softly, nodding.

Kana had seen that Cat was inundated with paperwork. Rogue Squadron was chasing a number of cases and doing their office time that week. Since Cat didn't have her own caseload yet, she was helping everyone with looking up information on CLETS and in any other way she could. While it was very helpful to the team, it made for long days in the office for a person that was very used to the field. Kana understood that all too well; since becoming lieutenant in charge of homicide, she'd been buried under paperwork.

Cat stood up, stretching. Kana admired the view. Cat was wearing a short denim skirt, a black tank top, and sandals that laced up just past her ankles. Her long blond hair was held back in a loose braid, although a number of tendrils had escaped, framing her face.

Kana noticed that her makeup was perfect, and as she watched, Cat pulled out lipstick and reapplied it.

Kana waited patiently, glancing over at Christian, who said nothing, working diligently on his computer. She could see, however, the grin he wore. It had, of course, spread like wildfire through the Gang that Kana was having lunch with the new girl, and it had made everyone breathe a sigh of relief. They'd never seen Kana broken-hearted, and none of them liked it at all. This was at least a step in the right direction, a step toward a healing process.

So Kana was fully aware of what Christian's grin meant—it meant it would soon be reported that Kana had taken Cat to lunch again. Kana shook her head, thinking, *I've got to get a new set of friends*, even as she grinned, knowing that would never happen. These people weren't "friends"—they were family, and you could never get away from your family.

Cat turned around, catching Kana's shake of her head.

"What?" she asked, grinning.

"Nothing," Kana said, glancing at Christian as she straightened from the doorway. "You ready?"

"Yep," Cat said, picking up her purse. "But I have a quick errand to run first. Is that okay?"

"Sure."

"I'll drive," Cat said, leading the way out of her cubicle.

"Okay." Kana smiled. This girl did take charge, didn't she?

When they got out to Cat's navy blue Blazer, Cat pulled out a small metal case. Opening it, she took out a cigarette, taking out a lighter and lighting the cigarette. Kana watched with interest.

"Does this mean you won't mind if I smoke in your car?" Kana asked.

"You smoke?" Cat asked, blowing a stream of smoke out as she started the Blazer.

"I started again recently."

"Ah," Cat said, nodding. "I don't have a problem with you smoking in here."

"Great, can we stop at my vehicle then?"

"Sure. Just tell me when to stop."

Once they got to Kana's Navigator, Kana got out and went to fetch her cigarettes. Getting back in, she glanced at Cat, who was looking at the Navigator.

Cat caught her look and grinned. "Nice," she said, nodding at the vehicle.

"Yeah," Kana said, smiling. "I like it."

Cat nodded. "I couldn't afford one, but I'd like to," she said as she put the Blazer back into gear, driving toward the parking lot exit.

"Well, I've owned my house for a few years, so my payments are low, and I don't have any other major expenses," Kana said by way of explanation.

"I rent an apartment on the beach for way too much money," Cat said, grinning. "And my credit card bills would put the national deficit to shame."

Kana laughed, shaking her head. "We all have our priorities."

"Yup," Cat said, smiling.

They were silent for a little bit. Cat was listening to the music on the radio. Christina Aguilera's "Dirty" came on, and she turned it up, singing along with the music and moving in her seat like she was dancing. Kana observed quietly. When the song ended, Cat turned the radio back down again.

"Sorry," she said, glancing over at Kana. "I love that song."

Kana nodded. "And you apparently like to dance."

"Oh, I love to dance. Do you dance?"

"Not if I can help it," Kana replied, grinning.

"So you don't go to any of the clubs?"

"I go," Kana said. "I just don't dance."

"Which do you go to?"

"Bourbon Street, usually."

Cat nodded. "My girlfriends and I go to The Flame a lot."

Kana made a face. "Too swinger for me."

Cat laughed. "Yeah, that's true. There are a lot of couples that go in there now, looking for a woman to play the third in their party."

Kana canted her head to the side, looking over at Cat. "Is that why you go there?"

Cat glanced over at her for a moment, her look contemplative.

"I go there because my friends go there," she said evenly. "But are you asking me if I go home with swingers?" Her look was pointed on the last.

Kana's head came up slightly, indicating that she'd caught the slight edge to Cat's voice.

"That's what I'm asking, yes," she said, her look direct.

Cat nodded, looking back at the road. She was silent for a few long moments, and Kana wondered if she'd made the girl mad. She didn't feel like it was an inappropriate question to ask—she'd admitted to being bisexual, meaning she had sex with both men and women. Swingers were male/female couples that liked to include a second woman or couple in the mix for fun. Kana basically wanted to know how often that kind of thing happened with Cat. It affected whether or not Kana wanted to continue in the direction her thoughts were going. Just as she hadn't been willing to be a plaything for a bored housewife with Palani, she also had no intention of ending up with a total party girl that gave it out to everyone.

"I have been with some couples," Cat said finally, her tone still even. "But I'm very particular about when I do that kind of thing."

"Particular?"

"There has to be a definite draw for me to do it, and not just with one of them."

"What kind of draw?" Kana asked, curious.

Cat glanced over at Kana then, her look measuring. Finally she sighed.

"Like a strong attraction to both of them—not just looks but personality, intelligence, all of it."

"But don't you think that it could cause problems with the couples?" Kana asked, curious rather than accusing. "I mean, men are notorious for being emotionally immature about this kind of stuff."

"Maybe," Cat said, nodding. "But I think that's their decision to make, not mine. If they want to do something like this, then they need to know what can happen." She looked at her hands on the wheel for a moment, then glanced at Kana. "I know that's probably not the best attitude to have about it, but I can't be responsible for everyone, just me. But it's for that reason that I'm almost never with couples anymore. I prefer one on one now—it's much better all the way around."

Kana nodded, satisfied with Cat's answer. She still thought it was kind of a reckless way to live her life, but Kana always held with the ideal "to each her own." She herself had interfered with a marriage, so she didn't have a whole lot of room to cast aspersions. She had only asked out of curiosity and to get an idea as to whether or not to proceed with this relationship.

Cat drove up to a local department store. Glancing over at Kana, she saw her roll her eyes.

"What?" Cat said, grinning.

"Shopping?" Kana asked, her tone belying how she felt about the activity.

"Just a couple of quick things, and then we'll leave, I promise," Cat said, laughing.

In the store, Kana followed Cat as she shopped. She looked at a few things, fairly quickly, Kana noticed.

"You bored yet?" Cat asked.

Kana smiled. "Getting there."

Cat rolled her eyes. "And now I'm going to make it worse. I want to look at shoes—is that going to push you over the edge?" she asked, her eyes widening as she grinned.

"No," Kana said, her look pointed. "But you will owe me."

"Ohhhh…" Cat said. "That does sound promising," she added with a wink.

Kana laughed and followed her to the shoe department. Standing back while two young men fell all over themselves to help Cat, Kana watched. Cat had a way of charming anyone and everyone. She flirted with the young men, and in the end, with the female cashier that rang up the shoes she'd bought. Kana shook her head in amazement.

"I doubt she was even family," Kana said, nodding back toward the cashier, who was watching them with pointed interest as they walked away.

Cat laughed, shrugging. "Doesn't matter. People like to be made to feel pretty, women especially. It never hurts to make someone feel good, right?"

Kana looked back at the younger woman for a long moment, then shook her head again.

"You're dangerous, babygirl," Kana proclaimed finally as they got back into the Blazer.

"Why's that?" Cat asked, her grin wide, her eyes sparkling mischievously.

"Because you can nail 'em all," Kana said. "And you don't even have to try."

Cat looked back at her for a moment, then canted her head to the side, her eyes searching Kana's.

"But what's it going to take to nail you?"

Kana was stunned into silence, not for the first time since meeting this girl. Finally she shook her head, grinning.

"At the rate you're going, not much," she said, her tone humorous, but with just a hint of seriousness.

Cat caught that, and smiled brilliantly.

"Let's have lunch," she said, starting the Blazer.

At lunch they talked about other things—the department, cases, whatever came to mind, but nothing in relation to them personally. Kana sensed that Cat was challenged by her now, and was seeking to build that edge. Kana wasn't sure if she should be flattered, worried, or excited by the prospect. She was all three.

It was two weeks and a number of lunches later when Cat made the next move. It took Kana by surprise, since she had become convinced that Cat just enjoyed the company of another woman that was her own kind. Kana had adjusted to the idea that Cat would be like her friend Terri. Her and Terri's relationship was and had always been strictly platonic. Kana figured Cat wanted the same thing.

Kana had also reconciled herself to the fact that it was probably for the best anyway, since Cat was far too much of a free spirit to really be in a relationship. Kana preferred relationships to casual sex, even more so since her relationship with Palani. She was craving the closeness she'd had with Palani, but dreading it at the same time, for fear it would end the same.

They were having lunch at The Pit, sitting at the table reserved for FORS.

Their food had just come when Cat looked straight at Kana and said, "I want you to take me out."

"Out where?" Kana asked, thinking Cat must mean shopping or something after lunch.

"Out, Kana, out," Cat said, her look pointed. "You know, a date?"

Kana chewed the tomato she'd just put in her mouth, her brows furrowed in confusion.

Cat sat back, looking at Kana like she couldn't believe the other woman didn't understand her.

"Look," Cat said when Kana didn't say anything. "I like having lunch with you—and I like dragging you shopping," she added with a wink. "But the fact of the matter is, I need more."

"More?" Kana asked, still trying to get her head to catch up with this conversation.

Cat gave her a frustrated look. "Yeah, more," she said, holding her hand up and ticking off her points on her fingers. "More time with you, more intimate conversation, more dark places shared together, and more kissing."

"We haven't kissed."

Cat grinned. "Hence the *more*, Kana."

Kana looked back at the younger woman, then shook her head slowly. "Okay, I've missed something somewhere along the way... Where did all of this come from?"

Cat snickered at that. "You missed the part where I said I wanted to nail you, K?" she asked, her tone so normal, as if they were talking about just anything.

"No..." Kana said, looking suspicious. "But you haven't made any moves in that arena, so I just figured..." Her voice trailed off as she shrugged.

"And here I thought you were a domme," Cat said, grinning as she winked.

"I am, but—"

"But what?" Cat asked, canting her head to the side.

Kana had to stop and think about it. Why hadn't she made any moves on Cat? Normally she would have. If she found a woman attractive, and that woman seemed open to the idea, she would usually ask her out. Hadn't she been the one to take the initiative with lunch? Yes, she had. So why hadn't she done anything else? Then it hit her as she looked at the spirited little blonde.

"Because," Kana said, blowing her breath out, "you intimidate the shit out of me."

It was Cat's turn to stare at Kana openmouthed.

"Why?" she finally managed to ask.

Kana shook her head. "I'm not sure. But I think it's because I know you can get just about anyone you want, male or female. I just don't know what to do with that."

Cat narrowed her eyes at Kana. "How about you just take me out, and stop worrying about who you think I can or can't get?"

Kana grinned. The girl didn't play any games, that was for sure.

"Alright," she said. "You got it. Tonight."

"Tonight?" Cat asked, surprised. It was Thursday.

"Tonight," Kana confirmed, her look challenging.

Cat saw the dare in Kana's eyes, and widened her eyes, grinning. "You're on."

"Good," Kana said, grinning too.

That night, Kana picked Cat up at her apartment. She was shocked and thrilled at the same time at how great Cat looked. She was dressed all in black. She had on leather pants that hugged her perfect shape, a sheer blouse with a Chinese Tang-style collar, with white embroidery over black satin running down the front of the shirt, which opened at her throat and which she'd left unbuttoned down to the curve of her breasts. Under the blouse she wore a very sexy lace bra that was on show through the blouse. She also wore high-heeled boots. At her throat she wore a choker of black crystals, suspended from which was a gothic-looking cross. Her blond hair was loose and curly. Her makeup was dark, but done in such a sultry way that Kana couldn't help but be awed by her. She was a beautiful girl, there was no doubt about that.

Kana was dressed in black slacks and a dark copper-colored silk blouse tucked in, with a black leather belt and dress boots. Her long black hair was loose as always, her makeup only slightly darker than normal.

"Wow, you look great," Cat said as she opened her door wider.

"I can say the same for you, babe."

Cat smiled brilliantly. "You ready to go?"

"Sure."

They went to dinner at a restaurant on the bay. They sat down on the balcony just in time to watch the sun go down. Cat ordered a glass of wine, as did Kana. They watched the sun set in silence. Cat turned her head, watching Kana. She could see that Kana's thoughts were far away. Cat wondered where. Kana glanced over at Cat, sensing she was being watched. She gave the girl a questioning look. Cat simply smiled.

When the waiter came to take their order, Cat looked at Kana expectantly. Kana was surprised to realize Cat expected her to order for both of them. Kana did so, noting that Cat nodded at her choices, obviously agreeing with them.

Cat was a series of contradictions, to Kana. She was both dominant in personality and submissive as well. She seemed to be capable of going with the flow no matter what came. It was an interesting quality.

"I surprised you," Cat said, having noted Kana's hesitation.

"Yes, you did."

"Why?" Cat asked, her blue eyes narrowing slightly in her curiosity.

Kana shrugged. "I'm used to women who are either dominant or submissive, rarely both."

"I deferred to your judgment. You've been here before—I haven't. I assumed you'd know what was good."

"But I have no idea what you like."

"I'm willing to try anything once," Cat said, grinning mischievously.

Kana's lips curled in a sardonic grin as she shook her head. The girl had an answer for everything, didn't she?

When their food came, they talked about trivial things. Kana found that Cat had the ability to keep the conversation light when she chose to, but she could also turn a conversation in any direction she wanted it to go. The girl definitely had a gift.

They left the restaurant and headed to Bourbon Street—Kana soundly refused to go to The Flame. Cat didn't mind Bourbon Street; she wanted to be where Kana was. Inside the bar, she found that Kana knew a lot of people. She also discovered that Kana was very definitely a hot commodity there. Women turned to look at them as they walked to the bar.

"Heya, K," said Sandy, the bartender, giving Kana a wink. "What are you drinking tonight?"

"Guinness," Kana said, glancing at Cat. "What are you drinking, hon?"

"Top Shelf Margarita," Cat said, smiling at Sandy.

Sandy nodded, her glance sliding between Kana and Cat, her curiosity obviously in overdrive.

"Sandy, this is Cat," Kana said. "Cat, this is Sandy."

"Nice to meet you," Cat said, smiling brightly.

"You too," Sandy said, her tone more perplexed.

"Just hand over the drinks," Kana said, winking at Sandy. "And don't start with twenty questions, okay?"

"Okay…" Sandy said, grinning.

Kana rolled her eyes and took the drinks.

"That's eleven fifty," Sandy said. "You want me to run your tab?"

"Yep," Kana said, even as she reached into her pocket and pulled out a ten, tossing it on the bar.

"Wow, ten?" Sandy said, picking it up and pointedly sliding it into her bra.

"Yeah, five for the drinks, and five for keeping your mouth shut, so far," Kana said, smiling tightly.

Sandy winked. "I do love ya, K."

"Yeah, yeah," Kana said, waving her hand.

Handing Cat her drink, Kana motioned to a table near the dance floor out in the open air part of the bar. They sat down. Cat looked around, taking in all the women at the bar.

"Cat?" queried a voice from behind them.

Cat turned and saw three of her friends standing there.

"Hey!" she said, getting up to hug them. "What are you guys doing here?"

"We thought we'd check out how the other half lives," said Sarah, the more outspoken of the group, her eyes already on Kana, who was watching the proceedings with interest.

Cat grinned, then looked over at Kana.

"Kana, these are my friends that I told you about," she said, gesturing to the girls. "This is Sarah, Jen, and Kareena."

Kana inclined her head to the girls, noting that Sarah was very definitely checking her out. So were they all family, or just her? Kana wasn't sure—the other two seemed fairly reserved and didn't make eye contact for long.

Sarah was a blonde, like Cat, but with dark eyes and long dark lashes set in a pretty face. She had a nice body, more on the voluptuous side than Cat's. Jen was a Latina girl, and tiny, and Kareena was a pretty, lighter-skinned black girl.

"So you're Kana…" Sarah said, trailing off as she looked directly into Kana's eyes. "It's nice to meet you."

Kana narrowed her eyes slightly, even as Cat cut in smoothly.

"Careful, Sarah," she said, grinning. "Kana outranks me."

"Is she your boss?" Sarah asked, glancing at Cat, then back to Kana.

"No," Cat said, with a grin still on her lips. "But she's with me tonight, so keep your hands to yourself."

Sarah laughed at that, shaking her head. "I can't make any guarantees on that," she said, smiling at Kana.

"Sorry, K," Cat said. "Sarah's a slut—she can't help it."

"I'm not a slut," Sarah said, giving Cat a slight shove. "Sluts aren't particular about who they sleep with. I am, I just do it a lot."

It was obvious to Kana now that this was a standing joke between the two of them.

"If you three would like to join us, you're welcome," Kana said, nodding to the table.

"Are you sure, K?" Cat asked, not wanting her friends to disrupt their date.

"No problem," Kana said, her eyes unreadable.

Cat's lips twitched, hesitating, but the girls were already grabbing chairs and sitting down. In truth, Kana knew that Cat would probably be bored if it was just the two of them, since she liked to dance. Kana preferred not to—unless it was a slow song, she was still uncomfortable in that area. Always had been.

After a little while, Jen and Kareena went to the bathroom, and they wanted Cat to go with them. Cat looked at Kana for a long moment, not wanting to abandon her at the table with Sarah. Kana gave a slight shrug and gestured with her head for Cat to go ahead. Cat got up, glancing back just as Sarah moved over to sit next to Kana. Cat rolled her eyes, thinking she'd kill Sarah if she pissed Kana off with her smartass ways.

"So," Sarah said, noting the wary look Kana was giving her. "What do you think of Cat?"

Kana didn't answer for a long moment, then raised an eyebrow at the smaller woman. "I'm on a date with her, aren't I?" she said, spreading her hands, palms up. "That should be fairly self-explanatory."

"Not necessarily. Could have seemed like a good idea at the time."

Kana narrowed her eyes at the woman. "And you're her friend?" she asked doubtfully.

"Yeah," Sarah said. "But I know Cat well enough to know she's never serious about anyone. So if someone she's dating interests me, I like to feel my way around the situation."

"Well, don't, and you'll be much safer," Kana said, her tone matter-of-fact.

Sarah's eyes widened at the hint of threat in Kana's voice. She nodded, her look measuring but a grin at her lips.

"I like you more and more," she said, chuckling.

Just then the waitress walked up. Sarah turned to her. "Two shots of tequila, and…" She glanced over her shoulder at the bottle Kana had in her hand. "Another Guinness for the officer."

The waitress nodded and walked away. Sarah turned back to Kana.

"It is officer, right?"

"Lieutenant, actually," Kana replied evenly.

"Are you always this serious?" Sarah asked, canting her head to the side.

"Usually, yes."

The waitress arrived then, putting the shots, salt, limes, and Kana's beer on the table. Sarah reached into her pocket.

"Put it on my tab, Kathy," Kana told the girl.

"You got it, K," Kathy replied, smiling brightly at Kana.

Sarah was surprised that Kana knew the waitress, and it showed. She recovered quickly, pushing one of the shots toward Kana.

"Will you at least do a shot with me?" Sarah asked, realizing she'd probably pushed Kana too much, and now she wanted to basically make up.

Kana looked at the shot for a long moment, then right into Sarah's eyes as she inclined her head. She picked up her glass, and Sarah followed suit. Kana licked the side of her hand between her thumb and forefinger, shaking salt on the spot. She licked the salt, then threw the shot back, her eyes never leaving Sarah's. Sarah did the same, coughing slightly as the alcohol burned in her throat. Kana grinned as she picked up the lime, sucked at it, and then handed it to Sarah. Sarah's eyes widened, but then she inclined her head and took the lime, sucking at it as well.

By the time Cat got back to the table, Kana and Sarah seemed to have worked out their issues. All the same, Cat eyed Sarah for a moment. Her friend merely looked back at her with a wicked grin.

Shortly after that a song came on that the four girls loved. Sarah, Jen, and Kareena got up to dance, entreating Cat and Kana to go with them.

"You go," Kana told Cat.

"You sure?" Cat asked, starting to feel like Kana was purposely pulling away from her.

"Go," Kana said, nodding toward the dance floor.

Cat got up and joined her friends on the floor, but her eyes were on Kana the entire time she danced. She noted how comfortable Kana looked, leaning back in her chair, her arm resting on the table, one leg crossed over the other. Kana watched her as she danced, and when Cat smiled, so did Kana.

Terri walked up behind where Kana was sitting, watching the same show Kana was getting from Cat.

"She's cute, K."

Kana glanced back at Terri, then at Cat on the dance floor.

"Hell yes she is," Kana said, grinning.

Terri grabbed a chair, pulling it over to sit next to Kana. Leaning back, her long legs extended in front of her, Terri watched Cat and her friends.

"So who are the other three?" she asked.

Kana grinned. Terri was always on the make—maybe she should introduce her to Sarah.

"Her friends. The one on the left is Kareena, the little Latina is Jen, and the blonde is Sarah. She's your type," she added with a wicked grin.

"Oh yeah?" Terri asked, raising a blond eyebrow. "Why's that?"

"She's a ho," Kana said, grinning.

"Bitch!" Terri swatted Kana on the arm.

"Takes one to know one."

"Don't I know it."

As the two of them watched, Sarah moved up behind Cat, sliding her hands around her waist and dancing with her, her body pressed close against Cat's back. Cat dropped her hands to Sarah's thighs, moving with her. It was the style of dancing at that point, but it was still very sexual-looking. It was also obvious they did this kind of thing a lot, since Cat hadn't missed a beat.

"Nice..." Terri murmured.

"Uh-huh," Kana said, her eyes on Cat.

"I'm tellin' ya, K, if you'd just give in and dance every now and then," Terri said, shaking her head.

"Not my thing."

"Bullshit. You can dance, you just don't ever, unless you've had a few too many." Terri nodded toward the dance floor. "You could blow these girls out of the water, and you know it."

"I don't know it."

"Bullshit," Terri said, leaning back to catch the waitress' attention.

Kathy walked over to Terri, leaning down and kissing her on the lips in greeting. Terri smiled, then whispered in her ear. Kana rolled her eyes, knowing she was getting set up yet again. It was Terri's habit to arrange things for Kana when she wanted her to do something. Within a minute, a double shot of Herradura tequila was set on the table.

"You bitch," Kana said, narrowing her eyes at Terri.

"Just drink it," Terri said, smiling sweetly.

"You'll pay for this if I'm hungover tomorrow."

Terri rolled her eyes. "Yeah, yeah."

Kana drank the shot, then chased it with her Guinness, draining the second bottle. She'd already been feeling it, but now she could *really* feel the alcohol in her system.

"Now, let's go get your girl away from Sarah," Terri said, standing up.

Kana sighed, moving to stand. They walked onto the dance floor. Cat had watched everything that had gone on between Terri and Kana. She was surprised when they walked onto the floor, just as another song came on.

Sarah's hands were still on Cat's waist. Kana went right up to Cat, looking down into her eyes as Cat glanced up at her. Kana slid her hand under Cat's hair, pulling her forward against her, loosening Sarah's hold on Cat. Cat willingly moved forward, wrapping her arms around Kana's neck, staring up into her eyes. Putting her hand to Cat's waist, Kana pulled the smaller woman's body flush with hers. Kana's body moved with the music, and there was no doubt that Kana did indeed have rhythm and could definitely move.

Cat stared up at Kana, her eyes wide with amazement.

"I thought you couldn't dance?"

"I never said I couldn't dance," Kana said with a grin. "I said I try not to."

"I see," Cat said, nodding, her eyes suspicious even as she grinned.

"So," Kana said as they continued to dance. "You and Sarah ever hook up?"

It was something she was curious about—they danced like they knew each other quite well.

Cat grinned, shaking her head. "No, she's a lesbian, and funny thing is, you lesbians have issues with us bisexual girls."

"So you never pushed it?"

Cat shook her head, making a face. "I don't beg anyone, K."

Kana touched her cheek, her thumb tilting Cat's face up to hers. "I can make you beg," she said, her tone supremely confident.

Cat felt a thrill go through her. She closed her eyes for a moment, then opened them again, looking Kana in the eyes.

"You think so?"

"I know so."

Cat continued to stare up at her, stunned to feel her breath catch in her throat when Kana leaned down toward her. She hadn't wanted a woman to kiss her this much ever! Kana's lips brushed her ear.

"I'll prove it, later," Kana whispered huskily.

Again Cat felt a thrill go through her. She was further enticed when Kana turned her around, pulling her back against her as they continued to dance. Cat rested her head against the hollow of Kana's shoulder, her hands on Kana's thighs. She closed her eyes, giving herself up to the music and the sensual feel of the way their bodies moved together.

Kana had one arm circled around her, crossing her torso, her hand on Cat's hip. Kana's other arm circled in front of her chest, her hand on the opposite shoulder. Cat felt herself melt a little more when Kana lowered her head, her lips touching Cat's neck, left wide open because of the way Cat's head rested against Kana's shoulder. Cat started thinking that Kana could probably do exactly as she said, and make her beg. She was ready to now.

Cat wasn't sure if she felt fortunate or unfortunate when the song ended. Before Kana could move away, however, Cat turned around.

"Stay here with me," she said, putting her arms up around Kana's neck.

"Is that an order, Sergeant?"

Cat grinned. "It's a request, Lieutenant."

In the end, they danced most of the night, stopping long enough to have a couple of drinks. At around midnight they walked outside. Cat had declared that she needed a cigarette. They stood smoking. Cat leaned against Kana's Navigator, Kana against the truck parked next to it.

Even standing in the parking lot, all the women walking by were saying hi to Kana.

"Jesus, do you know every gay woman in this city?" Cat asked at one point.

Kana laughed, shaking her head. "I come here a lot. So do most of the women I know. That's why it seems like I know everyone."

"Uh-huh," Cat said, unconvinced.

"Don't start with me, little one," Kana said, giving her a narrowed look.

"Or what?" Cat countered, a challenge in her eyes.

"Or I'm going to start my proof right here and now."

Cat's eyes widened, even as a smile spread across her face.

"Right here?"

"Right here."

"Right now?" Cat asked, her voice raising a bit as Kana pushed off the truck, moving to stand very close to her.

"Right now," Kana said, leaning down, her lips taking possession of Cat's hungrily.

Cat moaned against Kana's lips. There had been so much anticipation in this. On top of that, Kana's kiss was strong, confident, and so sensual, Cat felt heated instantly. She wound her arms around Kana's neck as Kana moved closer, intensifying the kiss. Cat felt every nerve in her body light up, and Kana hadn't even touched her with her hands yet. Kana's hands were on either side of Cat, up on the Navigator. Finally, Cat had to pull away, or else she was literally going to attack this woman right here in the parking lot!

"Can we leave?" Cat asked, her voice a husky whisper.

Kana grinned. "You want to go now?"

"Yes, now," Cat said, her voice stronger, even as she caressed Kana's shoulders. "Please?"

Kana smiled, not commenting on the fact that Cat was already basically begging.

"Let me go take care of the tab," Kana said. "Then we'll go."

Cat nodded, sliding her hands down Kana's arm to hold her hand with both of her smaller hands. Kana led Cat back into the club, going up to the bar.

"Sandy, cash me out, will ya?" Kana said, pulling out her credit card and tossing it on the bar.

"You got it, K," Sandy said, her eyes trailing down to where Cat's hands held Kana's.

Sandy grinned, looking back up at Kana. She knew full well how good Kana was—she'd dated her for over a year. Sandy also knew sexual tension when she saw it, and Cat was very definitely tense. Kana caught Sandy's grin and shook her head at the other woman, warning her silently not to say a word.

"Better be a good tip, is all I'm saying…" Sandy muttered as she handed Kana the credit card slip and a pen.

"You mean besides 'loose lips sink ships'?" Kana said, grinning as she added a $30 tip to the bill and signed it.

"Yeah, besides that," Sandy said, laughing.

Kana handed Sandy the slip as she pocketed her credit card. Sandy looked at the tip and smiled. Climbing on the bar in her usual wild girl manner, Sandy leaned over, taking Kana's hand in her face and kissing her on the lips.

"Thanks, honey," she said, winking when their lips parted.

Kana grinned, shaking her head. Sandy always made a point of being outrageous when she knew she could get away with it.

Kana and Cat left the bar after saying a quick goodbye to Cat's friends and Terri.

Cat suggested that she drive Kana's Navigator to Kana's house. "I didn't drink near as much as you did, just that one margarita when we got to the bar," she'd explained, holding out her hand for Kana's keys. Kana grudgingly gave them to her; the last thing she needed was to get pulled over for a DUI. As she drove, Cat looked over at Kana.

"You and Sandy were a thing once, weren't you?"

Kana glanced over at her, blowing out a stream of smoke, then nodded.

"How long ago?"

"About three years," Kana said, taking another draw of her cigarette.

"Why'd you break up?"

Kana shrugged. "She wanted more than I could give her."

"Like what?"

"She wanted the whole fairy tale thing—love, house, kids, all that stuff."

"So you didn't love her?"

"I cared about her," Kana said. "I still care about her, but it's not enough, and it's not love."

Cat nodded. "Were you ever in love?"

Kana's eyes narrowed at the question. "Once," she said simply.

Again Cat nodded, detecting instantly that it was a sore subject, and dropped it. When Kana finished her cigarette, she tossed out the butt and closed the window. She put her left hand on the center console, and that's when Cat reached over, taking Kana's hand and holding it. At a stoplight, Kana glanced over at her and saw that Cat was looking down at the silver rings on her index and middle fingers.

They made the rest of the drive in silence. Cat caressed her hand, sliding her hand up her forearm and then back down. Kana smiled at the tender action. Cat parked in Kana's driveway, getting out as Kana did the same. As Cat came around the back of the Navigator, Kana reached out her hand, pulling Cat to her, leaning down to kiss her again. Wrapping her arms around Cat, Kana held her, kissing her deeply, reigniting the fire they'd started in the parking lot at the club.

After a long while, Kana pulled away, taking Cat's hand and leading her to the front door, pulling out her keys to open it. Cat took the initiative then, moving in front of her and starting to kiss her neck. Kana groaned deep in her throat as she tried to pay attention to opening the door. Finally she gave up, dropping the keys and pressing Cat against the door, kissing her again.

Eventually, they made it inside the house. They got as far as the kitchen, and then all bets were off. Within minutes they were entangled, kissing, caressing, and basically driving each other crazy. Cat was way beyond rational thought. Kana had barely slid her hand between her thighs when she was crying out and pressing against Kana. Kana led her to her bedroom then, and they continued their first union there.

Afterward, they were both exhausted and sated. Kana had been surprised by her own reaction to Cat. Cat was very definitely an accomplished lover, but it was very obvious she wasn't used to having a partner that was as well.

"You're with a lot of bi-curious girls, aren't you?" Kana surmised as they lay together.

Cat glanced up at her. Kana lay with her head on her pillows; Cat lay sideways, her head on Kana's stomach. Kana's hand was in her hair, caressing her.

"What makes you say that?"

"Because you're not used to getting your share."

Cat was silent for a moment, then nodded. "Most of them want to, but they just…" Her voice trailed off as she shrugged.

"Inexperienced," Kana supplied.

"Yeah. I guess it's the price you pay for being with newbies."

"So why do it?"

Again Cat shrugged. "Just works out that way," she said, moving to lie next to Kana, snuggling against her. "Most bi girls are already hooked up with a man, and the ones that aren't are usually the curious ones."

Kana nodded, grimacing at the same time.

"I have to admit," Cat said, grinning, as she slid her hand over Kana's arm, which was now wrapped around her shoulders, "it is kind of cool to turn someone."

Kana rolled her eyes. "One woman at a time, huh?"

Cat laughed, nodding.

Kana shook her head. "You are definitely a wild child, aren't you?"

Cat grinned unrepentantly. Then she leaned forward, kissing Kana's lips again, pressing against her. Moving over Kana, she looked down at her.

"I also have to admit," Cat said, looking down into Kana's eyes, "that being with a woman that knows what she's doing makes me want to skip men altogether." She winked as she lowered her head, kissing Kana's neck.

Kana's hands slid through her hair, and they began once again. It was four in the morning before they fell asleep. Cat lay with her head resting against the hollow of Kana's shoulder, her upper body still against Kana's chest. Kana's hand rested on Cat's hip, the other arm holding Cat against her. She had to admit that it felt good to be with someone again. Six months alone had been way too long.

Chapter 5

Cat knocked on Kana's door a little while after they got back to the office.

"Come," Kana called, looking up from the report she was typing.

"Hi," Cat said, sticking her head in the door and smiling at her.

"Hi," Kana said, smiling back.

"You up for coffee?"

Kana glanced at her watch and raised an eyebrow at the girl. "At five thirty?"

"Well, it's obvious, Lieutenant," Cat said, walking in and perching against Kana's table across from her desk, "that you're not leaving any time soon, and I have a case tonight, so…"

"So you want to take me to coffee."

Cat smiled. "Right."

Kana clicked a few things on her computer, saving and closing out the report. Standing up, she stretched, then glanced over at Cat, who was watching her appreciatively. Kana grinned. The girl was constantly "on."

"Let's go," Kana said, gesturing toward the door.

Cat stood, preceding Kana out of the office.

They walked together down the street to the coffee shop. Kana noticed the bounce in Cat's step, and the way she moved when a car went by blasting a song she liked. Kana shook her head in amazement as they reached the door. Cat caught the movement.

"What?" she asked, grinning at Kana.

"You're damned scary, girl."

"How so?" Cat asked as they got in line to order their coffee.

"You've had two hellacious days, where I know you didn't get more than an hour of sleep each night, and you were up at the crack of dawn this morning again, but you're still energetic as hell. It's downright disgusting," she said, making a face.

Cat laughed. "Jealous?"

"Yeah," Kana said. "I want to know what you're taking, so I can get some too."

Cat laughed, shaking her head. "Sorry, babe, it's a natural high."

"That's just wrong," Kana said, wrinkling her nose up in repulsion.

"I didn't hear any complaints last night…" Cat said, trailing off as she grinned widely.

Kana scowled. "That was a low blow."

"Yep," Cat said, laughing.

They got their coffee and went to sit down. Kana gestured to Cat's frappuccino, with two shots of espresso in it.

"That stuff is what'll kill ya."

"This stuff is what'll keep me awake tonight."

"Ah, so you are tired," Kana said, narrowing her eyes.

"Oh yeah," Cat said, grinning. "But I have too much to do tonight, so I have to wait to be tired till later."

"It works that way, huh?" Kana asked, constantly amazed by the girl. Cat seemed to have unlimited stores of energy. It was like it was genetic. She really didn't seem to require too many artificial stimulants. The espresso was a rarity for her, in fact.

Cat smiled. "It has to."

"So I assume you won't be over tonight…"

"Never assume," Cat said, winking. "I fully intend to come over and crawl into your bed when I'm done for the night. If that's okay," she added.

"More than."

Kana had found that she thoroughly enjoyed Cat's company. Cat was young enough to keep her on her toes, but mature enough to understand their priorities. She never pushed Kana past her limits, whether it be not letting her get enough sleep or asking too much of her emotion-wise. They had an unspoken agreement that this was just "fun" for both of them.

Cat had found, however, that Kana required a certain level of commitment from her. She didn't expect Cat to be with her 24/7, but she did expect to know what Cat intended to do, whether it be show up in the middle of the night or not make it when she'd said she would. It was different for Cat—she was used to being a free spirit. But she'd already made the mistake of flaking on Kana one time in their short relationship. She'd gotten a touch of the ice that Kana was capable of, and she decided she didn't want to see the whole iceberg ever. After that, she was careful to make sure she didn't promise Kana anything she couldn't follow through on.

The relationship was proving to be good for both of them. It kept Kana from ruminating too much on the loss of Palani, and it was making Cat realize that maybe she did like being in an actual "relationship." It was also showing Cat what she wanted. She'd found that she wanted to know about Kana, she wanted to understand her. It was a new feeling for her; other women she'd dated had been so superficially gay that she spent more time trying to get away from their incessant chatter than she did getting to know them. The women before Kana hadn't been nearly as interesting or as intense. That was what had her so caught, Kana's intensity. There was no half-way with her—if she felt something, you knew about it. If you made her mad, she told you. By the same token, if you excited her, she told you too, and that made all the difference in their sex life.

Cat knew she was addicted to Kana and the way she did things. It was going to be difficult to lose at some point. And Cat did know she'd lose Kana at some point. They just weren't meant to be, but she was enjoying the ride while it lasted. She knew Kana was still in love with Palani, and that would never change. Cat wouldn't play second fiddle to anyone, so she would never allow herself to fall too deeply for Kana, even if she knew she could do just that. It just wasn't worth the heartache. She did still want to know the story, however, and eventually she'd get around to asking Kana about it.

Later that night, Cat crawled into bed with Kana at 3 a.m. Kana turned over, grinning as she felt Cat snuggle up to her. She glanced at the clock.

"Damn, babe…" Kana muttered.

"I'm dusted," Cat said, resting her head against Kana's shoulder.

Kana pulled her into her arms. Cat settled comfortably against her and was asleep a moment later. Kana leaned down, kissing Cat on the forehead, then went back to sleep. The next morning was thankfully Saturday. Even with the late hour she'd come to bed, Cat awoke as soon as Kana moved.

"Go back to sleep," Kana said. "I'll be back in two hours."

"Gym?"

"Yep."

Cat nodded, snuggling back under the covers.

True to her word, Kana was back in two hours.

Cat turned over in bed and watched her put her gym bag up in the closet.

"All worked out?" she asked, grinning.

"Uh-huh," Kana said, moving to sit down on the bed.

Cat sat up, kissing Kana as she did. Kana pulled her into her arms and they continued to kiss. For two hours they lay in bed, their bodies still intertwined. Cat lay on her side, against Kana's shoulder, her arm over Kana's waist. Kana lay on her back, her arm under Cat's neck, stroking Cat's shoulder.

"K?"

"Yeah?" Kana said, sounding tired and sated.

Cat glanced up at her, her look pensive. "Are you ever going to tell me about Palani?"

Kana's eyes flickered. She was surprised Cat knew Palani's name.

"Why?" she asked, her look closed off.

Cat looked back at her for a long moment, sensing once again that Kana did not want to talk about Palani.

She shrugged. "I just thought it might help, somehow."

Kana shook her head, her eyes narrowing slightly.

"K... don't be mad, please?" Cat said. "I just..." Her voice trailed off as she shook her head. "It's none of my business. I'm sorry."

Kana said nothing, silently confirming that Cat was right—it wasn't her business.

Cat moved to sit up, glancing back at Kana and seeing the closed look on her face. Cat felt a drag at her heart then. It hurt her that Kana wasn't willing to open up to her about what hurt her most. Suddenly she needed to get out of there—she felt like she didn't belong. She got up and picked up the clothes she'd dropped on the floor the night before. She walked out of the bedroom and went to Kana's guest bathroom. There she got dressed, gritting her teeth, forcing herself not to cry. Part of her was hoping Kana would come to the door and at least try to explain. Kana didn't.

Cat refused to go back into the bedroom. Fortunately, she'd tossed her keys on the kitchen counter. She picked them up and left the house. Starting her Blazer with a roar, she drove out of the court Kana's house sat on, reaching for a cigarette as she made the turn away from the house. Once her cigarette was lit, she turned up the stereo, cranking Disturbed and screaming out the lyrics with the lead singer. The song was "Bring the Violence." It allowed her to vent the anger she was feeling at that moment. The feeling of futility.

She drove home, letting herself into her apartment and tossing her keys on the kitchen table. She went to her bathroom and took two Tylenol PMs. Then she took off her clothes, dropping them on the floor and climbing into the shower. She was already beginning to feel the effects of the medicine. Getting out of the shower, she toweled her hair off but didn't bother to dry it. She climbed into bed, where she tossed and turned for a half hour before finally falling asleep. In the end she slept the whole weekend, waking up long enough to take some more sleeping meds before going back to sleep. She hated feeling rejected, and refused to look at the feeling any more than she had to.

***

A week later, Cat sat in her Blazer, watching and shaking her head as the girl walked into the house. She was watching Elizabeth Endicott, niece of Rick Debenshire and Midnight Chevalier, an heiress in her own right through her father, a very successful banker in London. *Everything and nothing at the same time*, was the thought that came to mind as she sighed, getting out of the car and tossing her cigarette on the ground, stubbing it out. Checking to make sure her gun was secure at her back, she walked toward the door. It was the house of a known dealer. The term "crack house" didn't really apply here, since that term lent itself to run-down shanties and this house was far from that. It was a mansion in a great part of town, but a dealer's house all the same.

Cat knocked, staring back at the man that opened the door and gave her the once-over.

"Wally, you know me," Cat said, giving him a narrowed look. "What you starin' at, dog?"

Wally grinned, his gold tooth glimmering in the hall light. "C'mon in, gurl!" he said, all smiles now.

Cat walked into the house, her eyes alert, even as she smacked Wally on the ass as she passed him. She spent the next half hour wandering through the sprawling mansion, talking to people as she walked through. Sure they knew her here—she was the party girl, the one with cash to spend.

She finally found what she was looking for. She was standing out on the balcony of one of the bedrooms. Cat glanced around the room, noting no one else in evidence. She walked out onto the balcony, opening the door and closing it behind her with enough force to startle the girl.

"Aren't you supposed to be somewhere else tonight?" Cat asked knowingly.

Elizabeth turned around, staring at the blond woman for a long moment. Then her eyes became as wide as saucers as she recognized her.

"Oh my God..." Liz breathed. "You work with... Oh my God..."

Cat nodded. "I'm not God, but I'm about to be your one salvation," she said succinctly.

Glancing behind her, Cat checked to see who was around, then looked back at Elizabeth.

"Have you done any yet?"

"What?" Elizabeth asked, her English accent so polished.

Cat gave her a quelling look. "Just tell me if you've done any coke yet."

Elizabeth looked shocked, but shook her head slowly.

"Good, then you're still able to attend your aunt's party," Cat said. Midnight Chevalier was having a party to announce that she was running for Attorney General. Elizabeth was expected to be there, but instead she'd come to score drugs. Not a wise move for someone whose aunt was a police chief and running for "top cop" of the state of California.

"I..." Elizabeth began, shaking her head.

"Oh, like hell," Cat said, rolling her eyes and shaking her head. "You don't show up at that party and you're going to be buying more trouble than even you can handle."

Elizabeth wisely shut up. She knew she was already in deep trouble. This woman worked with Dave, her brother-in-law—she was a narcotics officer. And here she was in a drug house. How much more trouble could she be in?

Twenty minutes later, they were in Cat's Blazer, driving toward Midnight and Rick's house. Elizabeth was shaking, she was so nervous.

Cat was smoking, blowing the smoke out the open window. She glanced over at Elizabeth. The girl was really beautiful, with her finely boned face, perfect porcelain skin, golden-blond hair and rich sapphire blue eyes. Why she wanted to ruin those looks with drugs was beyond Cat.

"I'm not going to tell them," Cat said as she tossed her cigarette out and rolled up the window.

"You're not?" Elizabeth asked, her shock apparent.

"No," Cat said, shaking her head. "But I think you'd better think seriously about what you're doing."

"Why's that?" Elizabeth asked defensively.

Cat looked back at Elizabeth for a long moment, narrowing her eyes, an indication that she didn't intend to play games.

"Your family has a lot of juice in this city. And that can be used against you, and them."

Elizabeth stared back at Cat, trying to make sense of that statement. She understood what she meant by her family's power. But how could it be used against her?

"What do you mean?" she asked finally, her curiosity getting the better of her. "Used against me how?"

Cat shrugged. "Just that if they choose to, they can put you in rehab and keep you there until the desire to cause trouble is a distant memory."

"They wouldn't do that," Liz said haughtily.

"Maybe Mummy wouldn't, sweet cheeks," Cat replied. "But you're talking about a Chief of Police now, and not one even I'd mess with."

"My aunt wouldn't do that!"

"Wanna bet on it? If she thinks it's in your best interests, I think you'd be surprised what she or your uncle might do."

Liz was silent for a moment, then looked at Cat again. "What did you mean, it could be used against them?"

Again Cat gave her a quelling look. "You think those people back there are boy scouts, little girl? They figure out who you are, and they'll use you to get to them. Is that what you want?"

Liz swallowed convulsively. She hadn't really thought of it that way. But surely this woman was being dramatic.

"They wouldn't dare."

Cat said nothing, only shrugging.

"But you're not going to tell them?" Liz asked, wanting to know before she walked into her aunt's party.

"Nope," Cat said, shaking her head.

Liz breathed a sigh of relief. She said nothing else to Cat, but continued to watch her as she drove. At Rick and Midnight's house, Cat dropped her off.

"You're not coming in?" Liz asked, surprised.

"Not my party," Cat said, smiling tightly.

Liz nodded mutely as Cat put the Blazer into gear and drove off. Liz spent the rest of the evening in a sense of unreality. She couldn't believe she'd come so close to getting caught and had managed to escape it.

Cat went back to her apartment and got ready for the raid she had scheduled for that evening. It was a minimal crew, since most of Rogue Squadron was at the party—just her, Mace, and one other guy from another team. It was a small hit, though, so she didn't expect any problems. As usual, things didn't go totally as planned.

Midnight's night went well. She announced to the media in a short press conference before the party that she was running for Attorney General. She and her friends and family then partied their asses off the rest of the night. The celebrations were interrupted momentarily at one point when Dave got a call stating that Cat had been hurt during the raid.

"Nothing major, boss," Kevin said. "I took her to emergency and she got a couple of stitches in her fairly hard head, but that's it. Just wanted you to know before it was on the news."

Dave breathed a sigh of relief, even as he grinned. "Thanks, Mace. Make sure she gets home okay."

"Will do, boss," Kevin said, nodding.

Dave hung up and noted that he had a fairly large Samoan woman watching him closely.

"Cat's hurt?" Kana asked sharply.

"She's fine," Dave said. "She took a knock on the head."

"But she's okay?" Kana asked, not caring if everyone was watching her closely.

Dave grinned. "Well, I don't know for sure," he said, his tone changing. "I was going to have to go by her place later to make sure…"

Kana narrowed her eyes at him, knowing she was being led. "I'll go."

Dave nodded. "Thanks, K. That'll save me a trip."

"Uh-huh," Kana said, giving him a sour look, even as he grinned.

Two hours later, Kana walked into Cat's apartment. She looked around, nodding to herself. She'd never been to Cat's place; they'd spent all their time at Kana's house. The apartment was nice, not exactly luxurious but pleasant enough with a decent amount of space. It was right on the water in Pacific Beach. Setting the key she'd used to get in on the counter, Kana made her way down the hallway, glancing around.

Walking into the bedroom, she saw Cat lying on her bed. She was wearing a tank top and sweats, and her blond hair was fanned out on the pillow under her head. She was asleep. Kana walked over to stand next to the bed, looking down at her.

As if sensing her there, Cat turned over, reaching up to rub her eyes. She jumped slightly when she saw Kana, then narrowed her eyes.

"How did you get in here?" Cat asked sourly.

Kana grinned. "The extra key you told me about, remember?"

Cat narrowed her eyes. "It's still trespassing," she muttered.

Kana chuckled, moving to sit down on the bed next to where Cat lay. Cat sat up, moving pointedly away from Kana. Kana's lips curled. It wasn't like Cat to be petty, so she found it amusing that she was being so now.

"Cat…" Kana said, her voice trailing off as she put her hand to Cat's cheek.

"What?" Cat replied, looking directly into Kana's eyes.

Kana's eyes searched hers, then she sighed, shaking her head. "I'm sorry," she said, her tone softening. "I wasn't ready to talk about Palani yet. I'm still not, okay? It's too painful still."

Cat pressed her lips together, narrowing her eyes at Kana.

"So why couldn't you just say that then? Instead of going all cold on me."

Kana dropped her eyes from Cat's. She had a point there. "I don't know," she said honestly. "I guess you surprised me that you even knew about Palani." She looked at Cat again, brushing her thumb over her cheek. "I'm sorry, hon, I really am. I didn't mean to hurt you."

"Well, you did," Cat said stubbornly.

"I know."

"And now I'm mad at you," Cat said, sounding even more petulant.

"I know," Kana replied, her head lowered even as she looked up at Cat, a grin starting at her lips.

"And now you have to make it up to me," Cat said, her own grin starting.

"I will."

"You better."

"I will," Kana repeated, leaning in to kiss her softly.

"Mmm…" Cat murmured. "That's a good start."

157

Kana laughed softly, hugging Cat to her. They stayed that way for a while. Cat leaned her head against Kana's shoulder, growing tired again from the Vicodin she'd taken when she'd gotten home.

"Okay, do you want me to go, so you can sleep?" Kana asked, pulling back to look down at Cat.

"No," Cat said. "I want you to stay so I can sleep."

Kana smiled. "I think I can do that."

"Good."

Kana curled up behind Cat, holding her. In that week, Kana had realized that protecting her memories of Palani wasn't going to keep her warm at night. She'd missed Cat's companionship. She knew she wasn't in love with the girl, but she did care about her. They had a good time together, balancing each other out nicely. Kana knew she'd been wrong in shutting Cat out when she'd asked about Palani, but she still wasn't ready to talk about the relationship. Cat seemed to understand that, and that was what mattered at this point.

"How do you know when it's going to be a bad night?" Cat muttered as she followed the black Porsche Carrera GT.

She was once again tracking Elizabeth, and lo and behold, Elizabeth was headed straight back to her favorite drug house. Cat shook her head. She knew the girl wouldn't listen to reason, but she had tried it the first time, hoping that maybe scaring Elizabeth with the idea that her family basically ran law enforcement in San Diego would work. It hadn't.

Cat watched as Elizabeth got out of the Porsche and walked up to the house. Cat also noticed a number of men who looked suspiciously like gang members watching Elizabeth walk in. Cat's sixth sense started tingling immediately—she knew something bad was going to happen. She gave Elizabeth ten minutes to come back out, hoping the girl intended only to purchase something and leave.

When Elizabeth didn't emerge and the four guys walked inside, Cat got out of her Blazer. Reaching back to make sure her weapon was secure at the small of her back, she walked up to the front door. She was let in, as usual, and started making the rounds, scanning the crowd for Elizabeth. Cat found out quickly that she was the topic of conversation, the "hot blonde with cash," as she was being referred to. Cat noted with increasing alarm that many of the guys intended to "tap" her. Meaning they expected to have sex with her.

Cat walked upstairs, hiding her anxiousness but aware that she had to find Elizabeth and get her the hell out of this house, fast. She checked a number of rooms to no avail. Finally she went to the dealer's master suite. Taking a deep breath, she shoved open the door. There was a chorus of "What the fuck?" and a number of other comments. Cat ignored them, spying Elizabeth already backed into a corner by two large guys. She grinned, shaking her head as if Elizabeth was just being a bad girl.

"Honey, honey, honey," Cat chided. "I told you you can't be doing this right now…" She kept talking as she walked toward Elizabeth, who looked very nervous. "Guys, trust me, you don't want to be tapping that ass right now." She winked, reaching out to take Elizabeth's hand and pulling her out of the corner.

"How the fuck do you know what we want?" said the taller of the two guys, reaching out to grab Elizabeth.

"Well," Cat said, chuckling snidely, "unless you want to get yourself a nasty case of the clap, I don't think you do."

"The what?" the other man chimed in.

"Clap, honey, clap," Cat said, pulling Elizabeth to her again, putting her arm around the smaller girl's shoulders. "My girl got herself into a mess at a party we were at in Soho last month, and the doctor said she's not supposed to play for a while, but she just can't seem to help it."

Elizabeth said nothing, burying her face against Cat's shoulder. Cat could feel her shaking. She willed the girl to keep it together.

"She's got somethin'?" the first guy said, sounding disgusted now.

"Oh yeah," Cat said, her smile knowing. "But if you really think you want her…"

"No, no, fuck no," the second guy said, stepping back as if he could get whatever Elizabeth had by proximity.

Cat glanced down at Elizabeth, her grin still in place.

"Come on, babygirl, let me take you home. Did you at least make your score?" Cat asked solicitously.

Elizabeth shook her head.

Cat looked at both men. "I need to get her down to the man—she gets really annoying when she doesn't get her stuff, ya know?"

"Yeah, yeah, go," the first guy said, gesturing for them to leave.

Cat didn't waste time. She went downstairs and walked Elizabeth right out the front door and to the Blazer. Elizabeth was shaking badly by this time. Cat put her in on the passenger side and got in on the driver's side.

"Did you take anything while you were there?" Cat asked, glancing over at the girl.

Elizabeth shook her head, her eyes downcast. Cat nodded, then started the Blazer with a roar. She drove off, heading down the hill.

Elizabeth was silent for a long while, huddling against the passenger door.

"You're going to tell them, aren't you?" she finally asked, her voice tremulous.

Cat looked over at her searchingly. "Is that what you want me to do?"

Elizabeth looked back at her for a long moment, then shook her head slowly.

"Are you sure about that?" Cat asked.

"What do you mean?"

"I mean, you knew I had you nailed, yet you went back—Why?"

"I…" Elizabeth started, then shook her head. "I can't stop," she said simply.

"Do you want to?"

Elizabeth didn't answer for a while, finally shrugging.

"You don't know?" Cat asked evenly.

"I don't know," Elizabeth repeated, raising her chin a bit as her pride kicked in.

Cat nodded slowly, her look considering. "Do you have any idea what you were headed for tonight?"

"What do you mean?" Elizabeth asked.

"Have you ever heard the term 'gang bang'?"

Elizabeth's eyes widened as she nodded.

"Well, you were going to be the entertainment tonight, sweetheart, the main course."

Elizabeth swallowed. She wasn't sure if she believed Cat or not. The two men that had taken her to that room had seemed intent on

161

having sex with her. Part of her was willing as long as she got the drugs she wanted—what was one or two more men she'd had sex with? It didn't seem to matter anymore. None of them did.

Cat narrowed her eyes at the younger woman, realizing she wasn't getting through to her. "It wasn't just those two, little girl," she said. "It was half the men in that house."

Elizabeth's head came up, her expression cynical now.

"Don't believe me?" Cat asked.

"No."

"Want me to take you back there so they can all get their piece of you before they beat you to within an inch of your life, if not just kill you so you can't report them?"

Again Elizabeth's eyes widened. "They wouldn't have," she said, shaking her head. Cat was just trying to scare her.

Cat nodded, giving a short, sarcastic laugh as she shook her head. "Tell that to the Latina we found last week who'd been gang raped and left for dead. She was ripped from front to back—she almost bled to death because they'd raped her so many times. Interestingly enough, she was found on the beach, just below that house. But hey, what do I know? I'll take you back there right now, and you can take your chances," Cat said, swinging the Blazer into a U-turn at the next light.

"No!" Elizabeth said, still not sure if she should believe Cat or not, but the mental picture Cat had just painted was enough to scare her.

Cat turned the vehicle around again.

Elizabeth was silent for a while. When she spoke again, her voice was very soft.

"I can't quit."

Cat looked over at her, seeing that Elizabeth was very solemn. Finally, she was seeing the scared young woman. For the moment, the brave facade had fallen.

"Do you only do coke?" Cat asked gently.

Elizabeth hesitated, then shook her head slowly.

"What else?"

"Meth," Elizabeth said, cowed.

Cat nodded, knowing this was going to be rough.

"Do you really want to quit, Elizabeth?"

Elizabeth blinked a couple of times, her face drawn and serious. She nodded, still looking scared.

"Well," Cat said, "there are a lot of good rehab centers here."

"No, I can't."

"Why?"

"My family will kill me. Or at least disown me."

"I doubt that. I think they'd help you if they knew for sure you needed it. Trust me, babe, they already suspect you're using."

"They do?" Elizabeth asked, surprised. She thought she'd been careful.

"Oh yeah. Your brother-in-law is the best narc in the country—did you think you could fool him forever?"

Elizabeth was silent, realizing she had thought she could. She'd been foolish.

"Still," Elizabeth said, "if I go into rehab now, what will that do to my aunt's campaign?"

Cat narrowed her eyes at the young woman. Elizabeth hadn't seemed to be worried about her aunt's campaign to become Attorney General when she was going to a drug house.

"What is it you think you want, Bet?"

Elizabeth noted the way Cat shortened her name, wondering at it—no one had ever called her that before. Then she realized there had been an edge to Cat's question. Narrowing her blue eyes, Elizabeth looked out the passenger window.

"I don't want anything," she said evenly.

Cat looked over at her, sensing correctly that Elizabeth had just yanked her facade back up. The walls were building again, and quickly. She could see Elizabeth taking slow, deep breaths, her spine straightening with every one.

Was this how it went? Whenever she felt like she might open up to someone, she used her well-constructed facade to put them off? Cat didn't know Elizabeth's story, other than what little she'd heard. According to everyone that knew her, Elizabeth was a spoiled young woman with too much time and money on her hands. She was given to creating scandals simply for the fun of it. And her family got her out of them every time. Was that why the scandals were getting more and more dangerous? Cat sensed there was a lot more going on here than just some spoiled brat getting her kicks.

Making a quick decision, Cat turned off and headed toward the beach. Once there, she parked the Blazer and turned to Elizabeth.

"Tell me why you do drugs," Cat said simply.

Elizabeth didn't look at her for a long moment, gazing out the passenger window instead. When she did look at Cat, her blue eyes were ice cold. The facade was very definitely in place once again.

"Because I like to party, that's why," she said lightly.

Cat narrowed her eyes at the girl. "Now try the truth."

"That is the truth."

"Are you hoping you'll get caught?"

"Why would I endeavor to hide my drug use if I was hoping to get caught?" Elizabeth asked condescendingly.

"You know what, little girl," Cat said, her eyes narrowing, her voice holding an edge of menace. "Don't even get bitchy with me. I'll drive your ass to your aunt's house and be done with you for good."

Elizabeth looked back at Cat for a long moment, surprised at her sudden change in attitude. She'd actually reminded Elizabeth of Midnight for a moment. Elizabeth wasn't sure what to say. The last thing she wanted at this point was to face her aunt and uncle.

Turning, Elizabeth got out of the Blazer, her hands shaking. Cat did the same, grabbing her cigarettes and lighter. Moving to the front of the car, Cat leaned against her bumper, taking out a cigarette and lighting it. She waited, knowing that Elizabeth was trying to decide her next move.

It took Elizabeth a full ten minutes. Finally she walked over, moving to lean against the front bumper of the Blazer as well.

"Can I have one?" she asked, gesturing to Cat's cigarettes.

Cat shook one out of the pack and flicked open her lighter, lighting it for Elizabeth. They smoked in silence for another few minutes. Elizabeth was the first to speak.

"Would you help me if I wanted to quit?" she asked cautiously.

Cat looked thoughtful for a moment, then nodded slowly. "It isn't going to be fun, you know."

Elizabeth nodded, looking reserved.

"Nick still staying at your apartment?" Cat asked.

"Yes."

Cat's lips twitched. It meant she'd need to take Elizabeth to her apartment. She couldn't risk Nick's father, the Assistant Chief of Police, coming by—for that matter, she couldn't risk the chief or Lieutenant Debenshire coming by either. The more she thought about it, the more Cat realized this wasn't going to go over well if they were found out. Cat was already risking her career by helping Elizabeth. What she should do, according to procedure, was arrest the girl and let County and her family deal with her.

Cat knew, however, that forcing someone to quit never worked. People had to want to quit, had to feel that it was in their best interest, for it to ever work. For some reason, she'd decided that Elizabeth really just needed someone on her side for a change. Her family loved her, sure, but it was pretty apparent that no one really liked her much—either that or they just weren't willing to deal with what they considered a great deal of self-indulgence on Elizabeth's part. And maybe that's all it was, but Cat didn't really think so. She hoped, for her sake, that she was right. If she was wrong, and Elizabeth was just using her to cause another scandal, Cat was going to be sorry she'd ever tried to help the girl.

Cat walked into her bedroom quietly. Elizabeth had basically been asleep for thirty-six hours. Cat knew it was withdrawal from the cocaine. She'd let Elizabeth sleep in her bed, since she knew she'd be doing it for a while. Cat had elected to use the couch; it was fairly safe to leave Elizabeth for the first day or so, as she'd be doing nothing but sleeping. Now she was watchful. People addicted to cocaine could have a number of withdrawal symptoms, not the least of which was depression. The last thing she needed was for the girl to try and hurt herself while in Cat's care. Cat was fairly sure that wouldn't be productive at all.

Moving to the bed, Cat stood watching Elizabeth sleep. She wasn't sure about Elizabeth's commitment to getting clean, but she was willing to give it a shot with her. Cat heard a knock on the front door. She walked into her living room and opened the door. Kana stood there.

"Hi," Cat said, looking contrite.

"So what's going on?" Kana asked, her sixth sense having told her Cat was avoiding her.

Cat had called Kana the night she'd brought Elizabeth back to the apartment. She'd told her that she was working on a project for the next few nights, so she'd be unable to see her. As usual, Kana's instincts had told her Cat was lying.

Cat looked back at Kana for a long moment, then blew her breath out in a sigh.

"Give me a minute, I'll come out," Cat said, walking over to her counter and picking up her cigarettes and lighter.

She went out to her balcony. Kana moved to lean against the low wall, her hands down on either side of her body. She waited silently for Cat to explain.

Cat lit a cigarette, taking a long draw and blowing the smoke out in a stream.

"I'm helping a friend dry out."

"Dry out?"

"Coke."

Kana narrowed her eyes. "Not exactly standard procedure for a narc, is it?"

Cat looked back at Kana, then shook her head. "No, it's not."

"So she's special," Kana concluded.

"Who said it's a she?"

"Is it a guy?"

Cat didn't answer for a long moment, then shook her head.

"So, who is she?" Kana asked, thinking it had to be someone important to Cat if she was willing to risk her career.

Cat hesitated, not wanting to tell Kana, since Kana was close to Midnight and Rick. She didn't know if swearing Kana to secrecy would work either.

"I can't," she said, shaking her head.

Kana narrowed her eyes again, her deductive mind going to work. "So I know her?"

"Why do you say that?" Cat asked, knowing she was dealing with a superior investigator here.

"Why else would you hesitate to tell me?"

Cat said nothing, realizing she should have just lied—she could have done that convincingly.

"Kana, look," Cat said, moving to look up at her. "I promised her I'd keep her confidence on this. Don't push me, okay?"

Kana nodded slowly, her look considering. "You don't trust me?"

"Can I?" Cat countered.

"With your life."

Cat nodded. "I just can't have you telling anyone, K. It'll cause more trouble than it will help, you know?"

Again Kana's eyes narrowed. "It's Elizabeth Endicott, isn't it?"

Cat's eyes widened, her mouth dropping open. "How did you come up with that?"

Kana grinned. "I know that the scuttlebutt has been that she's using, and I know that you work with Dave, who is married to Elizabeth's sister. And she's the only person I know that would be in this situation and wily enough to draw you in."

"Draw me in?" Cat asked quizzically.

"She's a user, Cat," Kana said, her tone very serious. "She'll use you, ruin your career, and then walk away."

"I don't think so," Cat said, shaking her head.

"You don't know her."

"No. But I do know that she's not getting any help from anywhere else."

Kana looked surprised. "Meaning?"

"Meaning," Cat said, taking another long draw off her cigarette, "that her family is so busy getting her out of trouble, they never bother to find out why she's doing it."

"You don't know what they've been through with that kid," Kana said, quickly jumping to her friend's defense.

Cat glanced back at Kana, her look measured. She didn't want to fight her about this. She realized that Elizabeth's family had done what they could with the girl. The problem was, getting her out of trouble wasn't solving whatever kept her going back to the drugs. Cat didn't know if she could do anything, but she was willing to try.

Finally Cat shrugged. "So if I get burned, I get burned."

Kana narrowed her eyes, not liking the idea that someone as callous as Elizabeth had any control over Cat's life, career, or future.

"She'll take you down, Cat. And I don't know that even I could help you then."

"I wasn't expecting anyone to help me," Cat replied calmly.

"Why do you want to do this?" Kana asked, her tone indicating that she thought Cat was crazy.

Cat considered her answer for a moment. "Because no one did it for my best friend growing up. She got into trouble—drugs, hooking, whatever it took. Everyone just said she was a wild child. They said that right up until the day she died from AIDS."

Kana looked back at Cat for a long moment, her eyes showing sympathy for what she had just said.

"Kana," Cat said, reaching out to touch her arm. "I'm not asking you to help me with her, I'm just asking you not to tell her family about this, okay? Let me try," she said earnestly. "Please?"

Kana pressed her lips together. She wanted to shake Cat and make her understand what she was doing. The last thing she wanted was for Elizabeth Endicott to screw up Cat's career. If Cat was caught trying to help a drug addict dry out instead of arresting her, she could easily be fired. And now Kana, a lieutenant, knew about it.

As if reading her thoughts, Cat looked up at her. "I didn't tell you any of this, Kana," she said stonily. "You didn't hear any of it. I'd swear to that in court if that's what it came down to, okay?"

"That's not what I'm worried about, babe," Kana said, her voice softening. "I don't want you getting used, okay?"

"I won't," Cat said sincerely.

"If you do, I'll break her neck personally," Kana said, her eyes narrowing dangerously.

She left a few minutes later, giving Cat a deep kiss and telling her to call if she needed her. Cat promised to come see Kana as soon as she felt Elizabeth was safe to be on her own again.

Cat walked back into the bedroom, looking down at Elizabeth again.

"You better not cross me, girl," she said quietly. "I'm risking my career and my girlfriend at this point."

It was four hours later when Elizabeth finally stirred. Cat was sitting at the foot of the bed, reading a book. When Elizabeth started moving around, Cat set the book aside and sat up. Elizabeth reached up and rubbed her eyes, moving to sit up and look around her. She saw Cat at the foot of the bed.

"How are you feeling?" Cat asked.

Elizabeth didn't answer right away, looking like she was trying to decide. Finally she shrugged sadly. Cat nodded, seeing that the feeling of hopelessness was setting in.

"Come on," she said, getting off the bed.

Elizabeth looked back at her suspiciously for a moment, then finally got out of bed and followed her. Cat led her to the living room, telling her to sit down on the couch. Cat made her tea.

"Sugar?" she asked, holding up the cup.

"And milk, please," Elizabeth said softly.

Cat nodded, fixing the drink and taking it over to her. Cat sat in the chair to the side of the couch, her look contemplative, but she said nothing. Elizabeth sipped the tea, glancing around at Cat's apartment. She hadn't noticed much before—it had been dark when they'd gotten to the house. The apartment was sparsely furnished, but still tastefully done. Not overwhelming, and certainly not as luxurious as Elizabeth's place, but nice.

Cat was watching her. Elizabeth wasn't sure what she was waiting for.

"So," Elizabeth said, breaking the silence. "What happens now?"

Cat's lips curled in a sardonic grin. "Well, once you're through with the withdrawals, you go back to life."

"That's it?"

"Well, hopefully you go back with a better idea of why you do what you do."

"And what good will that do me?" Elizabeth asked drily.

Cat shrugged. "I guess that depends on how honest you are."

"With you?" Elizabeth asked knowingly.

"With yourself."

"Well, if this is all on me, then what do I need you for?"

Cat grinned. "Well, for one thing, talking to yourself usually gets you the answers you're looking for, not always the right ones. Also, it makes people think you're crazy if you talk to yourself and answer yourself too," she added with a wink.

Elizabeth laughed softly.

"So where do I start?" she asked.

"Wherever you want."

"You said, why I do what I do. What did you mean by that? The drugs?"

Cat nodded. "That and all the other things you do, the wild child stuff."

Elizabeth grimaced, shaking her head. "It's really dumb, you know."

"What is?"

"Why I am like I am."

"Why is it dumb?"

Again Elizabeth grimaced. "Because it's so bloody cliché. I make myself sick."

Cat knew that part of Elizabeth's self-deprecation had to do with the withdrawals, but also that this was the time to get her to be honest with herself.

"Tell me," Cat said gently.

Elizabeth was quiet for a few minutes, sipping her tea. It was obvious she was trying to gather her thoughts. Cat waited patiently. When Elizabeth started to talk, it just tumbled out.

"When I was five or so, it became very obvious that Susan was the favorite child in the family. Susan, perfect little Susan, who never put a bloody foot wrong. She was smart, she was cute, she was so mild-mannered and sweet. She never cried, she never yelled, or made a fuss. Naturally everyone always asked me why I couldn't be like Susan." She made a disgusted face. "Who wanted to be like Susan? The little mousy thing, she was afraid of her own shadow. The problem was, if I didn't act like Susan they ignored me. So I did everything I could to be good like her. But I just couldn't do it. Eventually, however, I discovered the old trick of being loud. If I was loud, and stood in the middle of a store and screamed, suddenly not only did my parents pay attention to me, but so did everyone else. Unfortunately, eventually, they became immune to my screams.

"So I stepped up to breaking things. At first it was just dishes in the kitchen, or a glass. They came running, worried that I'd hurt myself. Suddenly I was the center of attention for a moment—they cared. Eventually, they stopped again. I guess I figured if I was bleeding all over their expensive Persian rugs, then they'd pay attention. So I moved up to Ming vases, Imari plates, Lladró statues, whatever it took." She shook her head, her lips curling in disgust. "They grew immune again and bought more insurance. Finally, I just started living for myself. I went out of my way to shock people, just to get something out of them. I no longer cared if my parents noticed or cared. They grew so used to everything I did, they merely shook their heads and walked away when I was in trouble." She took a deep breath, blowing it out sadly. "Have you ever read the story about the boy who cried wolf?"

Cat nodded, narrowing her eyes slightly, not liking the tone of the question.

"Well, I guess I did that once too often," Elizabeth said. "I guess I had them convinced that I just liked to make noise. Too well convinced," she said, pressing her lips together.

"What happened?" Cat asked softly.

Elizabeth put her tea down on the coffee table, lying down on the couch and looking up at the ceiling. She looked like she was near tears. Cat watched her for a long moment, then got off the chair, moving to sit on the floor next to Elizabeth's head. Reaching out, she touched her shoulder.

"What happened, Bet?" she asked again, her voice more gentle this time.

Elizabeth saw the look in Cat's eyes, and was surprised by it. Why did this woman care?

174

"Haven't you heard what a little drama queen I am?" she asked sharply.

Cat didn't reply, her look direct.

"Didn't they tell you how I make things up to get attention? How I fuck anything that wears pants so I can get attention? How I make my entire family look bad, just to get back at them?"

Cat's expression didn't change—she was waiting. "What happened, Bet?" she asked again, her tone just as soft as it had been before.

Elizabeth looked away, wiping irritably at the tears that had formed in her eyes at Cat's tone. No one had ever talked to her like that, no one that hadn't wanted something from her. Maybe that was it.

"What do you want from me?" she asked accusingly.

There was a flicker of amusement in Cat's eyes, then she shook her head slowly.

"You must want something," Elizabeth continued.

"Everyone does, right?"

Elizabeth didn't answer. She stared back at Cat for a long moment, easily reading the sympathy in her blue eyes. She didn't trust it.

"Everyone wants something," Elizabeth said, her tone far too world-weary for her age.

"From you," Cat finished the statement.

"Right," Elizabeth said sharply. "So what is it you want, Catalina?"

Cat didn't answer, merely returning Elizabeth's steady gaze.

"Tell me what happened, Bet," she said after a few moments, her tone indicating she hadn't been dissuaded in the slightest.

"Why?" Elizabeth asked, tears in her eyes again. She didn't bother hiding them this time.

"Because I think you need to," Cat said, her voice holding all the sincerity it possibly could.

Elizabeth swallowed convulsively, trying to rid herself of the lump in her throat. Her eyes turned to the ceiling again as she began talking. Like she was trying to distance herself from what she was saying.

"When I was sixteen, my father worked for this high-prestige bank in London. He had a man that worked with him who came to the house a lot. He was around his mid-thirties, and decent-looking. So, as usual, I had to cause a stir. So when he came over the first time I flirted with him, much to my father's dismay. I was only really flirty that first time, but after that, when he'd come to the house, he'd talk to me, say things like what a pretty girl I was, but always when my father wasn't in the room. At first I thought it was a game, how funny that he was flirting with me. If only my father knew!

"One day my parents were out, with Susan at some thing for her school. I was home alone. He came to the door. He said he had business to discuss with my father. I told him my father wasn't at home. He said he'd wait for him to return. I stupidly let him into the house, and told him he could wait in the sitting room…"

Her voice trailed off as she shook her head.

"What happened, Bet?" Cat asked again, reaching out to take Elizabeth's hand.

"He ended up raping me on the couch in the sitting room," Elizabeth said, disgusted. "I was so stupid to even let him in the house. I was stupid to flirt with him."

"He was scum for raping you."

Elizabeth made a face, disparaging. "Oh, he didn't rape me, you see? I encouraged him, I was always playing with fire, you see, and he took me up on my offer."

Cat's mouth dropped open. She couldn't believe that. "That's what he said, right?"

"No," Elizabeth said, her lips curling derisively. "That's what my father said when I told him what had happened."

"Holy shit," Cat said, feeling sick. "Did you tell your mother?"

"My father forbade me telling my mother. He said he would not allow me to spread slanderous lies about a colleague of his. He told me he knew that I'd been sleeping around, and that I was merely crying rape because I wanted attention as usual."

Cat shook her head, unable to believe that.

Elizabeth shrugged. "After that, I didn't bother to try and please them. If there was trouble I could get into, I did it. Why not be the slut my father thought I was? At least I'd have some fun doing it."

"When did the drugs start?" Cat asked carefully.

Elizabeth sighed. "About three years ago. I'd always smoked pot and drank. Someone had cocaine at a party, so I tried it. I actually smoke it more than I snort."

Cat nodded. Smoking cocaine was a better way to go undetected. No suspicious white powder under your nose, no chance of burning through the lining of your nose, or suspicious nose bleeds or sniffing all the time. All things that would alert any cop in her family.

Elizabeth moved to sit up, and Cat sat next to her on the couch. They were silent for a few minutes.

"You know what's really pathetic?" Elizabeth said wistfully.

"What?"

Elizabeth turned her head to look at her. "I really hate who I am now."

"So stop being what you hate."

"I don't know who to be anymore," Elizabeth said sadly. "I've become what I pretended to be for so long."

"Do you want to be different?"

Elizabeth nodded slowly.

"Then you're already taking a step in the right direction, Bet. You've realized that you don't like what you're doing. You're making a conscious effort to do something different now, something right."

"But what if I can't do it?" Elizabeth asked, tears in her voice suddenly.

"You can," Cat assured her.

Elizabeth shook her head. "I don't know... I just..." she said, the tears starting in earnest now.

Cat knew this was part of the withdrawals, combined with what Elizabeth had just relived. She didn't push; she merely pulled Elizabeth into her arms, letting her lean her head against her shoulder as she cried.

"Shh," Cat said. "It's okay, it'll be okay..."

Elizabeth lay against her and cried for a while, finally quieting. Cat sensed that she was getting tired again, so she moved carefully, taking her hand and pulling her up off the couch and leading her back to the bedroom. She put Elizabeth back into bed, covering her up. She picked up her book and sat at the foot of the bed again.

"Cat?" Elizabeth queried softly.

"Yeah?" Cat asked, looking over at her.

Elizabeth bit her lip, momentarily hesitant. "Will you stay in here with me?"

"Right here, Bet," Cat said, smiling gently.

Elizabeth nodded, looking very much like a little girl at that moment. Cat watched as she drifted off to sleep, and went back to reading her book.

It was hours later when Cat was jolted awake by a cry. It was Elizabeth. She was obviously having a bad dream, and thrashing about. Cat moved to her side, next to her on the bed, touching her shoulder gently.

"Bet?" she said. "Wake up."

Elizabeth woke with a startled cry, her eyes wide and scared.

"It's okay," Cat said soothingly. "It was a bad dream, it's okay."

Elizabeth was shaking, her lips trembling, her eyes terrified. Cat put her arms around her, pulling her close and holding her, much like one would a child. She smoothed her hand over Elizabeth's hair.

"It's okay, Bet, it's okay," she said softly. "No one's going to hurt you. It's okay."

Elizabeth relaxed in Cat's arms, pressing her face to her shoulder, one hand grasping a handful of Cat's shirt at the waist. After a while, Elizabeth started dozing off again. Cat moved carefully to try and get up. Elizabeth's hand tightened on the material she still held.

"Stay, please?" Elizabeth asked plaintively.

"Okay," Cat said, lying back down and putting her arms around Elizabeth again.

In the end, they both slept that way. Elizabeth woke the next morning feeling much better. She moved her head, looking up at Cat, and realized she'd just met her best friend.

Chapter 6

A couple of days later, Cat had a minor incident on a case. The guy she was working hadn't been taken in by her teasing, and had decided he wanted what he thought she was offering. When she'd danced just out of his reach, he'd tried to take it. She hadn't reacted fast enough, and he'd grabbed her by the throat, shoving her against a table. She had the abrasions on her back to show for it, and the bruises on her throat.

Christian and Mace, who'd been listening in on the tap, came to her rescue, without blowing her cover. Christian had burst into the room acting drunk off his ass, telling the guy that he had a deal that needed to be made at the door. The dealer had let go of Cat and walked out of the room to see to it. Money before sex any day. Christian went over to Cat, immediately seeing the bruises starting on her neck.

"You okay?" he asked, reaching up to touch her cheek.

She nodded, swallowing convulsively.

"Come on," Christian said, taking her arm and leading her out the back, while Mace distracted the dealer with a buy.

Christian had called it in to Dave, who'd told Cat to take the rest of the day off. Christian dropped her off at home, arranging for patrol to drive her Blazer to her apartment.

Later, Cat lay on her bed with her arm over her face. She was aching and tired, but she couldn't seem to sleep. She tossed and turned, trying to get comfortable, but the bruises on her back were bothering her. It was hot in her apartment, which wasn't helping. She wore a sports bra and the scantiest shorts she had to try and keep cool. She had the fan on full blast. Turning over onto her stomach, she settled again to try and sleep.

It was a half hour later when she heard a gasp from the door. Glancing over her shoulder, she saw Elizabeth standing there. She and Elizabeth had maintained communication after her getting-clean session. Elizabeth checked in with her on a regular basis, calling or coming over to talk. Cat welcomed her, knowing that Elizabeth needed someone to talk to, and actually enjoying her company. Elizabeth had a really good sense of humor, as well as a fun personality.

"You colored your hair," Cat commented, not having seen her since she'd been back from Vegas.

"Yes," Elizabeth said, grinning. "I thought I needed a change. What happened?" she asked, indicating Cat's back. She walked over to the bed, sitting down and touching the bruises.

Her touch was extremely gentle, but Cat flinched all the same.

"I'm sorry," Elizabeth said, grimacing.

"It's okay, Bet," Cat said, turning onto her side.

Elizabeth saw the marks on her throat then.

"Oh my God!" she exclaimed, her eyes widening dramatically.

"Relax," Cat said, holding up her hand to calm her.

Elizabeth nodded. "So what did happen?"

Cat shrugged. "Perp got a little too excited, ya know?"

Elizabeth grimaced, nodding. She couldn't fathom doing the dangerous job that most of her friends and family did. They were forever getting hurt, shot, stabbed. It was downright crazy, as far as Elizabeth was concerned.

"How did you get away?" she asked, curious in spite of herself.

"Oh, Blue and Mace took care of that part," Cat said, grinning. "The perks to having backup."

"Do you work with Blue regularly?"

"Often enough. Why?"

Elizabeth shrugged. "I've known him a long time," she said noncommittally.

Cat nodded. "And he used to date your sister, and you tried to date him while she was dating him."

Elizabeth looked at Cat, her eyes wide. "How do you know that?"

"Blue told me," Cat said, shrugging. "No big deal, Bet. It sounds to me like he was just as guilty as you were in that."

Elizabeth shook her head. "It was just another chance to scandalize everyone."

Cat nodded. "Although, he is rather irresistible," she said grinning.

"Oh yes he is!" Elizabeth agreed wholeheartedly.

"But definitely worth the trouble."

Elizabeth looked back at her for a long moment. "You didn't!"

"I did," Cat assured her, grinning.

"Stevie will kill you if she ever finds out, you know."

"She knows."

Elizabeth stared at her like she was the biggest liar in the western hemisphere. "You told her? And you're still breathing?"

Cat winked. "She was there, babe."

"You mean, you and she..." Elizabeth began, her eyes wide.

"And Blue," Cat finished.

"Oh my Lord!" Elizabeth exclaimed, shaking her head. "You must be nothing short of phenomenal sexually to have achieved that."

Cat shrugged. "They had fun, I had fun—that's what counts."

Elizabeth shook her head again, unable to believe what she was hearing. "But you're with Kana, aren't you?" she asked, having heard that along the way recently.

"I am now, but I wasn't then."

Elizabeth nodded, then canted her head to the side. "It's funny, but you don't look like a lesbian to me."

Cat laughed softly. "Well, I'm not," she said. "I'm bi—there's a difference."

"So you do both?" Elizabeth asked, intrigued.

Cat nodded.

"Hence, Blue," Elizabeth said, nodding to herself.

"Right," Cat said, nodding too.

"So," Elizabeth said, her eyes narrowed in askance. "Would you say sex is better with men or women?"

Cat thought about it for a moment. "I'd have to say women."

"Really?" Elizabeth looked surprised. "Why?"

Cat leaned back against the headboard carefully, not wanting to touch the bruises on her lower back. "Well, personally, I like to kiss," she said. "And I think women are so much better at it than men are."

"Hmm," Elizabeth said, looking thoughtful. "What's different about the way women kiss?"

"Think about the last time a guy kissed you. Didn't you sit there thinking, 'If he'd just do this or that it would be so much better'?"

Elizabeth thought about it, shaking her head. "I don't recall thinking that, but you're right, there are a lot of times when men's kissing leaves a lot to be desired." She shrugged. "I just figured that goes along with good sex, versus bad sex."

"True," Cat said, nodding. "But the thing about women is they tend to do those things that we women always want men to do. Since we're the ones that are more involved in the actual foreplay aspect of sex, we know what it takes to excite us. So women tend to do what women desire." She shrugged. "Women know what women want."

Again Elizabeth was contemplative.

"Well, I've been kissed by a couple of my girlfriends in London," she said. "And they did absolutely nothing for me."

"Okay," Cat said. "But were they family? Or were they just being outrageous?"

"Family?"

"Gay."

"Oh," Elizabeth said, shaking her head. "No, they weren't."

"That's the difference, honey. They weren't doing it to excite you, they were doing it to shock either you or people around you. It's not quite the same thing."

Elizabeth nodded, agreeing with that. Her friends were much like her, always striving to shock people into noticing them.

"I still don't know that a woman could excite me with a kiss though," Elizabeth said, sounding cynical. "I mean, women are still women, right? It's that whole same-sex barrier."

Cat shrugged, not looking concerned. "I tend to believe that all women are capable of being at least bisexual."

Now Elizabeth looked surprised. "Why do you say that?"

"Women need so much more than men require. And what women need, a lot of men can't provide, because it's not in them to do it."

"In terms of what?" Elizabeth asked, settling comfortably against the footrest of the bed. She was really enjoying this conversation. Cat had a way of thinking that was so unlike anyone she'd ever met before. It was endlessly interesting to learn her points of view, and Cat was always patient in explaining them.

"Women need emotional support, we need to be touched, whether it be emotionally or physically. Many of us need to be intellectually stimulated, and mentally stimulated in order to enjoy sex," she said, breaking into a wide grin. "Women need a reason to have sex—men just need a place."

Elizabeth laughed, nodding. It was true enough, in her experiences anyway.

"There are exceptions to that, though," Elizabeth pointed out, thinking of men like her uncle Rick and Joe, and Christian.

"There are exceptions to every rule, babe," Cat said. "That's human nature."

Elizabeth nodded in agreement. "So you think that because women need more, they're capable of getting that from other women?"

"I think it's all in how they've gotten it in the past and from who. But think about it, babe. Women get it from each other all the time—that's why you have girlfriends," Cat said, shrugging. "Sometimes it just becomes sexual too."

"Well, what about you?" Elizabeth said. "Why do you feel that you turned to women?"

"I didn't turn to women. I've always been attracted to women, since I was fifteen and had my first sexual experience with another girl."

"Oh," Elizabeth said, looking thoughtful. "But do you think that women who are, say, abused by men tend to turn to women?"

"Oh, definitely," Cat said. "They don't find women as threatening. They also get the love and support they've always craved."

Elizabeth nodded again. "So it's not really about sex at all, is it?"

"Most healthy relationships aren't, Bet."

Elizabeth looked back at her, surprised to realize that she'd never thought about it that way.

"So are all your relationships healthy?" she asked.

Cat laughed softly. "No, not all of them."

"What about this relationship with Kana?"

Cat thought about it, and nodded. "Yeah, I think it is."

"Do you love her?" Elizabeth asked, not sure why she wanted to know.

Cat looked contemplative for a moment, then shook her head. "I care a lot about her," she said. "But I happen to know she's still in love with her ex-girlfriend. I can't love someone that doesn't love me."

"Can't?"

"Won't."

Elizabeth nodded, thinking Cat really did have a handle on her love life. She seemed to know her boundaries, her needs, what she could give and what she'd accept in return.

"Have you ever been in love?" she asked.

Cat shook her head. "Nope. I care about people I see regularly, but I can't say I've ever been in love. You?"

"No," Elizabeth said. "Never anything like what my aunt and uncle have, or even what Susan seems to have found with Dave," she said, her tone melancholy.

"It'll happen," Cat said wisely. "It just has to be the right time, the right person, and the right situation."

"That's a lot of things that need to align," Elizabeth pointed out.

"True," Cat said, laughing. "That's why it doesn't happen a lot."

Elizabeth laughed softly, nodding. Then she gave Cat a pointed look.

"Now back to this kissing thing," she said with a wicked grin.

Cat laughed out loud at that. "Still not convinced, huh?"

"Nope."

"Want me to prove it to you?" Cat asked, her look challenging.

Elizabeth's eyes widened, even as she felt her pulse quicken at the thought. "I'm always game for a challenge," she said confidently.

Cat grinned, moving down to sit right in front of Elizabeth.

"Okay," she said, staring into her eyes. "I want you to think about the last time you got kissed. Think about it, and remember exactly what he did when he kissed you."

Elizabeth nodded, narrowing her eyes in thought. A guy in a club had kissed her the night before.

"Was he a good kisser?" Cat asked.

Elizabeth shrugged, making a gesture with her hand to say "so-so."

"Okay, think of what he did with his hands, how his lips felt, everything."

Elizabeth closed her eyes. He had put his hands to her waist, and his lips were strong, but more in a firm way, not so much in the way he kissed.

Before she knew what was happening, Cat's lips touched hers. The first thought was that Cat's lips were so much more soft and sensual than she'd expected. Cat's hand touched her cheek, her fingertips at where her jawline and ear met, pulling her face closer. Cat's other hand slid through her hair, guiding her head as the kiss intensified. Cat's lips became more insistent on hers, sucking just enough, parting to kiss over and over again. Within moments, Elizabeth found herself wrapping her arms around Cat's neck, wanting the kiss to continue.

When Cat pulled back to look down at her, Elizabeth found she was out of breath and feeling quite excited. Her eyes widened. The idea that this was a woman kissing her had never even gone through her head!

"Oh my Lord..."

Cat grinned. "See?"

Elizabeth nodded mutely. She did indeed see. And all she could think was, *Oh my Lord!*

"You win," she said, grinning as well.

Cat laughed. "I usually do."

Elizabeth laughed too. She had to hand it to Cat, the woman did not disappoint when she set out to make a point.

"You usually do what?" asked a voice from the doorway.

Cat and Elizabeth both turned to see Kana standing there.

"Win," Cat said, grinning as she stood up to greet Kana.

"Hey, Liz," Kana said as she walked over to Cat.

"Hey, Kana."

Kana's eyes searched Cat's person. Her fingers brushed the bruises on her throat, then she turned Cat around to check the bruises on her back, grimacing as she saw them.

"I know," Cat said, seeing Kana's expression. "They look bad."

"Yes, they do," Kana confirmed, touching Cat's cheek. "Are you okay?"

"I'm okay."

Kana leaned down, kissing Cat softly. Cat reached up, putting her hand to the back of Kana's neck. Kana pulled her closer as they continued to kiss. Elizabeth watched in fascination. It wasn't a long kiss, but definitely an intimate one. Now that she had a new perspective on women's kissing, it was interesting to watch.

"Well, I better get myself out of here," she said, standing up.

"You don't have to leave," Cat said, glancing up at Kana.

"No," Elizabeth said hurriedly. She smiled. "I have some things to do. I'll leave you two alone."

"You ever look into that restaurant and club idea?" Cat asked.

Elizabeth glanced back at her. "Actually, yes, I did," she said, surprised that Cat remembered.

They'd had a short conversation right before she'd left Cat's house that first time. Cat had told her that she needed to find herself something to do to keep her occupied so she didn't think about wanting to use anymore. Elizabeth hadn't been sure of what to do, other than shop. Cat had asked her if she'd ever had a dream to do something. Elizabeth had reluctantly admitted to wanting to open her own restaurant and night club. Cat had told her to go for it.

"And?" Cat said, giving her a pointed look.

"And," Elizabeth said, "I'm putting the few business courses I took in school to good use and looking for a location." She was inordinately happy that Cat cared enough about her to even ask. It felt so good to finally have a friend that cared about her, not how much money she had or who her parents were.

"Fantastic," Cat said, smiling brilliantly. "Let me know what you come up with."

"I'll do that," Elizabeth said, laughing softly. "See you soon."

Cat grinned. "See ya."

Elizabeth left the apartment with a lot on her mind. She had to admit that visiting with Cat always made her feel like she was really getting her life together. She finally had a friend who wasn't into the bar scene in a big way, didn't use drugs, wasn't always jetting off somewhere to attend the latest greatest party. Cat was a stable, caring, and very trusted friend, and Elizabeth honestly felt like she could tell her anything.

"So, what did you win?" Kana asked Cat, moving to sit on the bed, leaning against the headboard.

Cat grinned. "We were having a discussion on why women are better sexually than men."

Kana looked back at her openmouthed. "And why are women better?"

"Because we kiss better," Cat replied, smiling as she sat down, leaning back against Kana, careful not to bump her bruised back.

"So *how* did you win?"

Cat grinned mischievously.

"Oh, no, you didn't," Kana said, shaking her head and rolling her eyes.

"Uh-huh," Cat said, chuckling evilly.

Kana gave her a dismayed look. "Girl, you are crazy, do you know that?"

Cat raised her eyebrows, grinning.

"You kissed the chief's niece to prove that women kiss better than men?"

"Right," Cat said. "Although, I'm fairly sure that Bet's not going to go running to her aunt to report that fact, honey."

Kana gave a short, appalled laugh and shook her head again. "You're so bad. I should be jealous."

"Are you?" Cat asked with a knowing grin.

"Did you do anything but kiss her?"

"Nope."

"I'm getting the better end of the deal, so no, I'm not jealous," Kana said, leaning down to kiss the side of her head.

"Uh-huh."

"So what was all that about a restaurant?"

Cat shrugged. "We were talking about healthy hobbies for her to have, and she told me she had wanted to open a restaurant and club at one point. I told her to go for it."

"You did," Kana said, rolling her eyes.

"Why not?" Cat asked. "She's got a style all her own, and I'm sure she's been in enough restaurants and clubs to know what's been done, done, and overdone. Why shouldn't she give it a shot?" she asked, leaning her head back against Kana's shoulder, looking up at her.

Kana stared back at her for a long moment, then shook her head.

"You're going to fix the world, aren't you, babe?" she asked, ever surprised by Cat's desire to help people.

Cat winked at her. "One person at a time."

Kana observed as Cat smoked a third cigarette at lunch. Their food hadn't even come yet.

"Little bit on edge, little one?" Kana asked.

Cat glanced at her, then grinned. "Yeah, I guess so," she said. "Just feeling the need to cut loose a little bit."

Kana nodded wisely. "You got anything going tonight?"

"Nope."

"Let's go out then."

"Great!" Cat said, smiling.

Kana didn't go out often, and hadn't changed that practice while with Cat.

"What are the odds of getting you to go to The Flame?" Cat asked, giving her a sidelong look.

"Why?" Kana asked, narrowing her eyes.

Cat shrugged. "I'm in the mood to dance tonight, not fight."

Kana laughed. Whenever they went to Bourbon Street, Kana was consistently flirted with, hit on, eyed, and generally pawed. Kana knew most of the women that were regulars at the club, so they all felt comfortable flirting with her. Kana also had a few ex-girlfriends that were often at Bourbon Street, and Cat had had one too many run-ins with the exes.

Things had become physical a few times. Kana had stepped in once, and Cat had taken care of it herself otherwise. Cat zealously guarded her relationship with Kana, more so than she had with any other woman. But she was always possessive about people she was actually with. She felt others should respect that and not interfere, unless invited to do so.

"Fine, we'll go to The Flame then," Kana conceded.

"Thank you," Cat said, her look not so conciliatory.

Kana grinned unrepentantly.

That night, they arrived at the club just after 10 p.m. They found a table and greeted Cat's friends, who were always in evidence there. After the first meeting between Kana and her friends, Cat had asked them to hang back a bit. Kana didn't get comfortable around too many people, and there was still some residual unease between Kana and Sarah. So the girls held back and waited for Cat to come dance, which she did.

By midnight, she'd had a few drinks and was enjoying herself thoroughly. Kana and she had danced a few times, but Kana, as usual, left most of it up to her and her friends, and usually sat watching at the table. Cat was dancing, and looked toward where Kana sat. Only

Kana wasn't at the table. Cat quickly located her over by the bar, ordering another drink. Kana was easy to spot in the crowd; between her height, her long dark hair, and her overall presence that kept people out of her way, she stood out.

Cat watched as Kana turned and headed back to the table. Just as she was about to sit, Kana glanced up, and she froze. Her eyes were fixed on something across the room. Cat's eyes tracked her line of vision and located four women heading toward the table, skirting the dance floor. Looking back toward the table, Cat saw Kana straighten, her chin coming up in wariness.

The four women were closer now. One was tall with blond hair, thin and statuesque, and then there was a stockier-looking woman, obviously with the blonde, going by the proprietary hand on her arm. Another, the one in the lead, was tall with dark hair. That woman wore all black leather, a very butch, very dominatrix-looking outfit. The fourth woman was petite, much smaller than the other three. She had long dark hair and tanned skin and was absolutely gorgeous. This one was being led by the woman in black, reluctantly so.

Who were they? Cat wondered, edging closer to the table in case Kana needed some backup. They were obviously headed straight for her with a purpose in mind, and Kana's obvious wariness raised Cat's vigilance.

Kana couldn't believe what she was seeing. Her heart tried to tell her she was wrong, but her head told her she wasn't wrong at all. Palani. And she was obviously with some domme-looking woman. So she hadn't stopped seeing women... The thought rolled around in Kana's head as they made it to the table. Kana took in Jerry Castle, Palani's model friend, and Jane Ann, Jerry's girlfriend. Her eyes touched quickly on Palani, then went to the woman who was obviously holding Palani's invisible leash.

"You're Kana," the woman in black said.

Kana didn't reply, merely looking back at the woman, who, although she was tall, was still a head shorter than Kana.

The woman was obviously disconcerted. Kana wasn't sure if it was the size factor or the silence Kana held. Silence always drove people crazy—they wanted reaction, they wanted something, and when they didn't get it, it bugged them. Kana was a master of the use of silence.

The woman regained her composure. "I'm Nancy, and I just want you to know that Palani's with me now."

Kana's eyes reflected no emotion whatsoever. The only indication she gave that she'd heard the woman was the slight smirk on her lips. After a long moment, Kana tilted her head slightly to the side, her eyes dropping to Palani, who all but hid behind Nancy.

"I see your taste in women has changed," Kana said mildly, her eyes flicking back to Nancy appraisingly. "Drastically."

Nancy noted the disparaging look in Kana's casual once-over, and apparently took offense to it. She took a step forward, her manner threatening. Kana gave the woman a wintery grin, showing very white teeth.

"Oh, you just throw down, honey, make my night," she said.

Nancy had the temerity to look nervous then.

"Kana?" Cat queried, coming up from the side of the group, her expression alert, her manner authoritative. "Everything okay here?" She stepped to Kana's side, both possessive and challenging.

She'd heard what the woman had said to Kana. So she knew the beautiful girl behind the domme was Palani, Kana's ex-girlfriend. This was the one. Kana definitely wasn't a slouch in the taste department. Palani was beyond beautiful. And it was Palani's eyes that were narrowing now, staring straight at Cat. Then Palani looked up at Kana.

"And I see your taste for blondes hasn't changed at all," she practically spat.

Kana didn't reply for a moment, allowing a slow grin to spread across her features, showing that she'd noted Palani's obvious jealousy.

"The last brunette I had gave me heartburn."

Palani's eyes flared, and she turned and walked away. Kana looked to Nancy then, calculating.

"Looks like you have a sub to retrieve," she said, her eyes going to Palani's retreating back. With that Kana turned, taking Cat's hand and sitting down at the table, pulling Cat down on her lap.

Nancy turned and stalked after Palani. Jane Ann walked away too. Only Jerry remained for a long moment, her eyes narrowed at Kana. She'd seen the momentary flash of pain in Kana's eyes when she'd sat down. Palani and Jerry had had many conversations about Kana; Kana was used to hiding her true feelings behind perfect masks. Was that what she was doing now? Jerry was sure it was. After a long moment, in which Kana's eyes met Jerry's and held for a few beats, Jerry turned and left. Kana dropped her head to Cat's shoulder, blowing her breath out in a quiet sigh. Cat stared after the retreating women, feeling a sense of both relief and dread.

"I'm going to get us a drink," Cat said, turning to look down at Kana.

Kana nodded, not looking at her.

Cat proceeded to buy Kana drinks for the next hour and a half until last call. When the bar closed, she drove the Navigator back to Kana's house. Kana was swaying on her feet by that time. She'd had way too much to drink and knew it. Cat led Kana to her bedroom, sitting her down on her bed and kneeling to pull off her boots. Then she undid Kana's belt and pants, carefully removing her holstered gun from the back of her belt and setting it on the dresser. Then she pulled off her pants and took off her cover shirt, leaving her in only underwear and a black tank top.

Cat proceeded to push Kana back on the bed, pulling the covers over her. Leaning down, she kissed her cheek. Kana's eyes were already drooping slightly. Cat took the clothes, draping them over Kana's wardrobe next to her dresser. Then she turned off the light and walked out of the bedroom, heading down the hall.

Kana lay in her bed, her mind going in a thousand different directions.

Palani was with someone else! Palani was still seeing women! What happened to the baby? Was it already born? Yes, yeah, it was—it had been almost a year now since they'd broken up. Where did Cat go? Was she coming back to the bedroom? Why was Palani at the bar? It was calculated! Was it? Where was Cat? She was coming back, right? Of course she was—Cat always stood by her. *Why do you treat her like shit then? Why is Palani still seeing women?* The room was starting to spin, and Kana knew it wasn't a good sign. She didn't know how long she'd lain there, but she knew she felt really sick all of a sudden.

Getting up, she went into the bathroom and threw up. Now she felt worse. Sitting down on the floor, she closed her eyes again.

Why was Palani at the club? Did Matt know about her being gay now? Was this all some kind of game? Where was Cat? Did she leave? Why? Shit, shit, shit! Getting up off the floor, Kana made her way down the hall, feeling a little unbalanced from the alcohol still in her veins. The lights were all off. Getting to the kitchen, she turned on the light. On the counter was a quickly scribbled note.

"It's been fun. Take care." It was simply signed "Cat."

Kana stood at the counter for a long time, staring at the note. Finally she shook her head. What the fuck was she doing? Cat was the one that had brought her out of her emotional coma. The one she'd been put in by Palani's deceit. Seeing Palani had thrown her—she hadn't expected it—but did she want to lose Cat over that? No, she didn't.

Striding back down the hall, still a bit unsteady, Kana went back into her room. She threw on a pair of jeans, sitting down on the bed to pull on her boots. She left the house five minutes later.

Cat had taken a cab back to her apartment. She'd methodically undressed, washed off her makeup, and brushed out her long hair. There was a message on her answering machine, and she wondered if it would be Kana. She listened—it was Elizabeth, just asking how she was doing and telling her to call whenever she got back in. Climbing into bed, she lay on her side, staring off into space. She was forcing herself not to feel anything. She knew she'd done what she had to do in leaving Kana. She couldn't go on feeling like this.

The phone rang. She didn't answer it, and the machine picked up. Elizabeth's voice chimed in.

"It's just me," she said. "Guess you're staying with—"

Cat picked up the phone.

"I'm here," she said dully.

"Oh, you are," Elizabeth said. "I didn't wake you, did I?"

Cat glanced at the clock. It was 3 a.m., and Elizabeth was honestly asking that question?

"I wasn't asleep."

"Cat, what's wrong?" Elizabeth asked, hearing the dead tone in her friend's voice.

"Shitty night."

"What happened?"

"Nothing good," Cat said, her tone non-committal.

"Did you and Kana have a fight?"

"No," Cat said. "We just broke up."

"What?" Elizabeth exclaimed. "Why? When? What happened?"

"We went to the club, ran into her ex, she drank herself into a stupor, I took her home and put her to bed, and left," Cat rattled off, like it was a laundry list.

"Left the house."

"Left her."

"Oh…" Elizabeth said, her voice trailing off as she grimaced. "Are you okay?"

Cat was silent for a long moment, then sighed. "No," she said honestly. "But I will be. I can't go on playing the rebound girl forever, you know?"

"I know," Elizabeth said softly.

"I'm gonna try to get some sleep."

"Okay. Call me if you want to talk, okay?"

"Ten-four."

"Goodnight."

"Night," Cat replied, and hung up.

Kana walked into Cat's bedroom, looking down at her as she slept. Cat sensed her there and woke up. She immediately started to sit up, her hand moving toward the gun on her nightstand. The hand moved away just as quickly when she realized it was Kana.

"Jesus, K," she said, worried. "Tell me you didn't drive here."

Kana ignored the question, sitting down on the bed. She reached out and touched Cat's cheek. Cat's chin came up warily.

"I'm sorry, babe," Kana said. "I didn't mean to get so drunk, I just... I'm sorry."

"Kana, tell me you didn't fucking drive here," Cat said, her tone sharpening. She could tell Kana was still very drunk.

"I needed to talk to you," Kana said. "You left, I needed to talk to you."

"You're going to get yourself killed, Kana, damnit!" Cat exclaimed. "Or is that what you're going for now?"

"No..." Kana said, shaking her head. "Cat..." she began, and then it was like something clicked. And indeed it had. Kana's mind asked her, *What right do you have to keep doing this to her? Who the hell do you think you are?*

Without another word, Kana stood up, her eyes reflecting the pain of realization. The alcohol in her veins was making things seem more intense.

"I need to go," she said, starting to turn toward the door.

"Bullshit!" Cat grabbed Kana's hand and dragged her back down on the bed with all the strength she had.

Kana looked at her, her dark eyes pained. "I can't do this to you, it's not fair…"

"Kana, stay here tonight, okay?" Cat said, worried. "We'll talk in the morning. It'll be better then, okay?"

"No," Kana said, moving to stand again. "I need to leave you alone. I'm sorry."

Cat lunged for Kana's hand, pulling her back and moving to straddle her lap. "You're not driving like this, Kana," she said sternly. "I won't let you do it."

"Cat…" Kana said, shaking her head, her thoughts so confused.

"Please, K, just stay tonight."

"I can't, it's not fair to you. I can't."

"Damnit, getting yourself killed because of Palani and her bullshit isn't fair to me either, okay?" Cat growled.

Kana blinked as if she'd just been slapped. She looked back at Cat for a long moment, her lips quivering as she swallowed convulsively.

"Stay here, K," Cat said gently, leaning in to kiss her softly on the lips.

Kana's hands slid around her back then, pulling her closer. Cat slept in the nude, so she wasn't wearing a stitch of clothing. Cat pulled back to look at Kana, and Kana's lips reclaimed hers hungrily. Cat moaned, sliding her hands into Kana's hair. The kiss turned extremely passionate then, and Cat gave in to it, allowing it to happen.

As they kissed, Kana caressed her, making her writhe.

"I'm sorry," Kana murmured against her skin. "I'll make it up to you, little one, I promise you… I'm sorry…"

Cat's hands slid through Kana's hair, guiding her. Before long she was crying out in her release. Kana continued to kiss her skin, moving slowly, taking her time. Cat moved over her then, taking charge of the situation. In the end, she had Kana begging for release. As she brought her closer to it, Cat moved to Kana's ear.

"No more games, K. You're either with me, or without me. You need to choose, once and for all," she whispered harshly.

She brought Kana to release then, and Kana grasped at her, pulling her closer.

Afterward, Kana moved Cat to lie on her side, pulling her into her embrace and cuddling her close. Leaning down, Kana kissed Cat's temple.

"With you," she said simply.

Cat nodded, snuggling closer to her. She knew deep inside that she'd never have Kana's heart like Palani did, but she also knew that at this point Kana needed her. What was she to do? She was addicted to Kana, and she loved her. She didn't kid herself about that. She loved her for all that she was, but she honestly didn't think you could be in love with someone that wasn't in love with you. It didn't work that way. Only time would tell what would happen with them. Cat fell asleep that night thinking exactly that.

Things had been really good between them since that night at the bar. Kana seemed to be dedicating herself to the relationship now. Cat was enjoying it thoroughly, but she knew it wasn't forever. She didn't tell Kana that, but she just knew. Kana's reaction to seeing Palani with someone else had said it all.

Kana had finally told her the whole story about Palani. Cat had been surprised. She'd been shocked to hear that Kana had dated a woman that was not only bi-curious, but also married. Kana's comment had been that she just couldn't resist the extremely beautiful, intriguingly innocent model. With prompting, Kana had even shown Cat the pictures Palani had taken in Hawaii, the pictures that had made her doubly famous in the swimsuit edition of *Sports Illustrated*. She was beautiful, smiling with the sun setting behind her.

Kana also showed Cat the private picture Palani had reserved for Kana alone. It was stunning to say the least. She looked amazing in a black metallic bikini, her hair loose, her makeup perfect. But the look on her face was what made the picture incredible. She was looking straight at the camera, her eyes alight with love, and she was biting her lip. It was a very sexy picture, and even Cat couldn't help but be affected by it. Palani was beautiful, there was no question about that.

Palani lay in her bed in the apartment she was sharing with Jerry and Jane Anne. She couldn't believe she'd seen Kana. Kana never went to The Flame; she disparaged it as being a swinger bar. But she'd been there, with a woman no less.

Palani had been surprised by the blonde who'd come up to claim possession of Kana's hand. The girl was beautiful, very sexy, very intense, and very much another cop. Palani had been able to tell by the woman's presence, much like Kana's own. She hadn't wanted to see that Kana had moved on and actually gone back to the blondes she'd always preferred. Kana liked her women small, blonde, beautiful, and smart. Palani had qualified on all but one count.

"What is your problem?" Nancy asked, seeing the way Palani was curled up on the bed, staring into space.

Palani just shook her head. She didn't want to explain. It wasn't something Nancy would understand anyway. Kana's words had been biting, her look cold and distant. Palani knew she'd never forget the complete ice that had been in Kana's eyes and voice when she'd said, "The last brunette I had gave me heartburn." It had cut her to the core.

Palani was no fool. She knew Kana could have been much more vicious in her comments, and Kana had it in her, but it had still hurt so much.

She hadn't wanted to go out—she'd wanted to stay home. But Jerry and Jane Anne were determined to get her back into life again. They continually set her up with women they thought would help put Kana out of her mind. No one did—no one could. Kana was the only woman she loved or wanted. No other woman did anything for her.

"Talk about being single-minded..." Jane Anne had uttered disgustedly more than once.

To humor her friends, she'd tried it. Tried going out with other women. Nancy, a major dominatrix, had taken a liking to the petite Polynesian girl, and had come around a few times. Palani hadn't had the energy to tell her that she wasn't really interested. So Nancy mistook that for mutual interest. It was for that reason she'd felt cocky enough to confront Kana.

Palani had been sure that Kana wouldn't care. And apparently Kana hadn't, but she had taken Nancy down a peg or two with her confidence. Nancy had sensed Kana's commanding presence easily too. She hadn't been willing to test her. Not many people were, male or female. Kana had a look about her that stated very clearly not to mess with her. Like the decal on the windshield of her black Navigator, which read "Fear This" in electric blue. It was true—most people should fear Kana. If you made her mad, or trifled with someone she cared about, you could end up hurt. Kana didn't feel the need to conform to any particular rules. She did what she wanted to when she decided it was warranted.

Palani felt Nancy's hand on her back. She shrugged it off.

"Let's not get feisty tonight, huh?" Nancy said, leaning close.

"I'm really not in the mood tonight, okay?" Palani said mildly, hoping Nancy would take the hint and leave.

"You'll do what you're told," Nancy replied, slipping into her domme act.

"Not tonight."

"You little bitch…" Nancy said, moving to stand behind her.

Palani didn't see the belt that Nancy was sliding off and readying to hit her with.

"Do it and I'll kick your ass," said Jane Anne from the doorway.

Nancy glanced at Jane Anne uncertainly, then back to Palani, who was now lying on her back, looking at Nancy with narrowed eyes.

"Get out," Palani said.

"You heard her," Jane Anne said when Nancy didn't move.

Nancy nodded, turning and walking out of the room. Palani rolled back to her side, curling up in a ball and starting to cry. Jane Anne watched for a moment, then turned, looking at Jerry. She gestured with her head toward the room. Jerry walked down the hall and went into the bedroom, touching Jane Anne's hand as she did. They'd been trying to look out for Palani over the last few months.

Jerry sat down on the bed, touching Palani on the back. Palani cried harder.

"I hate this. I hate this…" she said, shaking her head. "I miss her so much, Jerry. I can't do this!" she cried, her voice hinging on hysterical.

"I know, I know…" Jerry said soothingly. She had no idea what to say or do. She just didn't want her friend to hurt anymore.

Kana and Cat had spent the weekend going out and cutting loose. Kana regretted it Sunday morning at 4 a.m., when she got a call from Tiny.

"We have a hit on one of our guys," Tiny said.

"Who?" Kana said tiredly, glancing at the clock.

"AJ," Tiny said with a grin.

"Shit… no way."

They'd been after AJ Perone for months. He'd shot two people in cold blood, reportedly because he felt like it. There was no motive, just a love of killing. Kana wanted this guy off the street as soon as possible.

"Where's he at?" she asked, sitting up and rubbing at her eyes. She and Cat had gone to bed not an hour before.

"Holed up in a house down in Chula."

"You got a warrant?"

"Would I have woke you if I hadn't?"

"No," Kana replied simply. "What time do you want to hit it?"

"Six. I'd like to catch the little bastard still asleep."

"True," Kana said, nodding. "Okay, call for some air support in case he runs."

Tiny grinned. "You got it, boss."

"Fuck you, Tiny," Kana said, grinning too.

"Not your type, K, remember?"

"I remember," she said, her eyes on Cat, who was awake now too.

"Meet me at the corner of Broadway and D at five thirty. I'll have the plan there."

"See you there."

They hung up a moment later. Kana lay back down, sighing deeply.

"That wasn't a raid I heard you agreeing to, was it?" Cat asked.

"Uh, yeah, it was, actually," Kana said, grinning.

"Uh, no," Cat said. "Call him back and tell him you can't go."

"Cat…"

"Bullshit, K," Cat said, looking worried. "You just went to sleep like an hour ago!" she exclaimed, shaking her head. "You're not up for this."

"Well, I will be," Kana said. "This is Perone, Cat. I need to get him."

"Let Tiny get him," Cat said, grabbing Kana's arm.

"I'm still his backup."

"You're his lieutenant, K."

Kana didn't reply, simply shook her head.

"Please, I'm serious," Cat said. "You're not up for this."

"Stop," Kana said, sitting up and putting her hand on Cat's lips to stop her talking. "I've done raids on even less sleep than this, okay? I'll be fine, babe, trust me."

"K…" Cat said, her face a mask of concern.

"Shhhhh…" Kana said, leaning forward and kissing her lips softly. "I'll be back by noon, and we can sleep the rest of the day, okay?"

In the end, Cat got up and made her coffee, strong Kona coffee. Kana drank it gratefully, leaning down to kiss her deeply.

"Go back to bed," she said as she picked up her gear bag. "I'll join you as soon as I can."

Cat smiled, reaching up to touch her cheek.

Kana left for the raid, and Cat went back to bed, feeling uneasy.

At the corner, Tiny laid out his plan for hitting the house. Kana agreed to it completely. She and Tiny would be on the entry team. They drove over to the house, stopping two doors down. Kana had just gotten out of her vehicle when she heard the helicopter. She glanced at her watch. It was 6:10.

"Fuck!" she yelled. That helicopter was going to give them away. Sure enough, she saw a blind being lifted in the house. "Damnit, Tiny!" she shouted. "We've been made!"

Grabbing her gun, Kana ran toward the house.

"Kana!" Tiny yelled, still strapping on his body armor. He finished hurriedly, glancing up as Kana kicked the door open. "Move in, damnit!" he yelled to the rest of his team. He didn't want Kana in there alone. He grabbed his gun, running toward the house as he pulled back on the slide. That's when he heard the blast. His heart stopped.

He sprinted to the house, frantic.

"Kana!" he screamed as he went through the door, shoving one of his team aside and moving past him. The sight he saw would haunt him for months to come. Kana was lying in a pool of her own blood.

"Sonofabitch! Call the paramedics, officer down!" Tiny yelled. He made his way through the house, his fury making him faster than he'd ever been.

Perone was headed out a window at the back, the Remington shotgun still in his hand.

"Freeze, Perone!" Tiny yelled.

Perone turned toward Tiny, bringing the gun up. Tiny fired five times, dead center.

Chapter 7

Three hours later, Dave stood at Cat's front door. He knocked, feeling sick at what he needed to do.

Cat answered, took one look at him, and strode into her kitchen, leaving the front door open. Dave walked in just in time to see her take an extremely long swig of tequila. She set the bottle down.

"What happened?" she asked.

"We need to go," Dave said, taking her arm.

"Shit, what happened?" Cat asked, walking with him all the same.

Dave grimaced. "She got hit with a shotgun blast."

Cat stopped dead in her tracks, her face going pale.

"Dave, is she dead?"

"No," Dave said, shaking his head. "But…" His voice trailed off as a lump rose in his throat.

Cat nodded, tears in her eyes instantly.

They arrived at the hospital just as most of Rogue Squadron did. Tiny was there with Jess. Spider and Tammy were already there, as was Randy. Kyle and Rhiannon arrived just after that, so everyone heard what Tiny told Kyle.

"We got to the scene, and air support was too early, or we were too late, I don't know," Tiny said, shaking his head. It was obvious he was distraught. "Either way, Kana yelled at me that we were made, and then she just grabbed her gun and took off toward the house."

"She wasn't wearing body armor?" Kyle asked.

"No," Tiny said. "She always gears up at the scene, but then that happened."

"When she gets better, Joe'll kick her ass for that one," Christian put, in his tone somber, even if his words were hopeful.

Kyle grinned slightly, nodding, appreciating that Christian was trying to give them all some semblance of hope.

"What happened next?" he asked Tiny.

"I was running toward the house when I heard the shotgun blast," Tiny said, looking sick. "I got there as fast as I could..." He shook his head. "But it was too late. She was lying in a pool of her own blood." He looked like he was going to be sick. "I yelled for the team to call for paramedics and went after Perone. I caught him trying to go through a back window. He still had the fucking shotgun in his hands. I yelled for him to freeze. He started to bring up the shotgun. I fired."

"Perone dead?" Kyle asked.

"More than—I fired five times," Tiny said, his eyes fiery.

"Good," Donovan said.

"IA didn't just hear that," Jess said evenly.

Tiny looked at his wife. He didn't care what happened—he was glad Perone was dead too. If Kana didn't make it, he was doubly glad.

"Good thing IA isn't here, right?" Jessica added, winking at her husband. It was her way of saying she was his wife right now, not Internal Affairs, the people that would look into the shooting of AJ Perone and determine if Tiny had been justified in using lethal force.

"Anyone get ahold of Midnight or Joe yet?" Tiny asked.

"Cassandra's working on it," Kyle said. "Dig in, everyone. It could be a long day."

Everyone moved to sit, stand, or lean on something in the waiting room. Rogue Squadron grouped around Cat, who hadn't spoken since they'd gotten to the hospital. She was holding it together—she hadn't even cried yet. Her team intended to be there when she broke down.

An hour later, Elizabeth arrived with Susan. Susan made her way to Dave, and Elizabeth walked over to Cat.

"Cat?" she queried, worry in her eyes.

"Hey, Bet," Cat said listlessly.

"Come on," Elizabeth said, reaching down to take Cat's hand. "You need to smoke."

Cat nodded, getting up. Elizabeth led Cat down the hall toward the open quad where smoking was permitted. Christian, Stevie, Donovan, Jeanie, Dave, and Susan all watched them walk away, glancing at each other and shrugging.

Out in the quad, Cat lit up with shaking hands, the one physical manifestation of her worry. Taking a long drag, she looked over at Elizabeth.

"Are you alright?" Elizabeth asked, her gaze critical.

Cat didn't answer for a long moment, taking another drag on her cigarette. "Alright isn't exactly how I am, no," she said, her voice tightly controlled.

Elizabeth nodded. She could tell Cat was holding on to her control with every ounce of her strength. The dam would have to burst at some point.

They stayed in the quad for a half hour, neither of them speaking. Just smoking and doing their best to forget why they were there.

Midnight was just walking offstage after making a speech when she saw Rick walk up. His face was grim.

"What is it?" Midnight asked, immediately worried.

"We need to go home," he said, turning and leading her to the car he had waiting to take them to the airport.

"God… Rick, what happened?"

"Kana's been shot," Rick said as they got in.

"What?" Midnight cried.

"She got caught by a shotgun blast."

"Oh, Jesus… How close was she?"

"Too close."

"Hurry," Midnight told the driver.

Midnight and Rick walked into the hospital two hours later. Everyone came to attention, crowding around Midnight as she got the report from Kyle.

"Damnit, she knows better than that," she said. "Have we gotten word yet on her status?"

Kyle shook his head. "She's been in surgery for going on nine hours."

Midnight shook her head, glancing around her. She saw Tiny's grim look, and went over to hug him.

"There's nothing you could have done," Midnight said. "Except maybe get shot yourself. Perone was determined to take someone out."

Tiny shook his head miserably.

Midnight glanced around, not seeing Cat. Finally she located her sitting in a chair at the other end of the room. She walked over, kneeling in front of the girl.

"How are you holding up?" she asked, noticing to her dismay that Cat wasn't even crying. It wasn't a good sign.

Cat looked at Midnight for a long moment, then nodded slowly. "I'm okay."

Midnight nodded, searching the younger woman's face. Cat was not okay, but she was holding on to her control with a steel-tight grip. Midnight stood up, turning around to see Rogue Squadron watching her. She walked over to Dave, and the rest of the group moved to stand around her.

"Keep an eye on her," Midnight told Dave.

Dave nodded, glancing at the rest of the group. They nodded too.

Joe waited for Jordan at the end of her show, pacing back and forth. Jordan came running off stage, grabbing a towel from an assistant.

"I gotta go," Joe said unceremoniously.

"Where?" she asked, surprised.

"Home. Kana's been shot."

"Oh my God," Jordan said, wide-eyed.

Joe took her hand and led her back toward her dressing room.

"I don't know how long I'll be gone," he said. "I called Mackie—he can be with you in twenty-four hours."

Jordan stopped, looking at him strangely.

"What?" he asked, impatient to get out of there and back to where he was needed right now.

"Joe, I'm going with you," Jordan said. "A member of your family's been shot. I'm not staying here and pretending everything's okay."

"Jordan, you've got shows…"

"I don't care. You're going to need moral support, and I'm going to be there."

Joe looked at her for a long moment, then nodded, walking over to hug her close.

"Thank you."

She snuggled into his embrace. Things had been strained recently, and she reveled in his embrace again.

Four hours later they were walking into the hospital, three hours after Midnight and Rick arrived. Joe walked straight over to Midnight, taking her into his arms and hugging her. He knew what she'd be going through at that point. He shook hands with Rick.

"Have we heard anything yet?" Joe asked, knowing they hadn't heard anything when Kyle called him five hours before.

"Nothing," Midnight said, shaking her head. "Joe, she's been under for twelve hours…" They both knew the longer someone was on the table for surgery, the worse it was.

Joe grimaced. Blowing his breath out, he glanced around at everyone.

"Kana's stronger than any of us," he said. "If anyone can make it through this, she can."

Jordan glanced at the faces of the people that stood around Joe. She saw the resolve strengthen in all of them. Whatever Joe said was what they'd believe—it had always been that way. If Joe or Midnight said something, it was law. She watched as Joe made the rounds, talking to everyone, even kneeling in front of Cat and talking to her for a few moments. He put his hand over Cat's, which were clasped tightly in her lap. Jordan saw Joe look up into her face then, his eyes searching. He said a few things, then stood up and walked over to where Jordan stood with Midnight, Rick, and Randy.

"She's going into shock," Joe told Midnight. "Her hands are ice cold."

Midnight glanced over at Cat, concern in her eyes. "She hasn't shed one tear yet that anyone's seen." She looked at Joe then. "What do you think we should do?"

Joe glanced back, seeing that Rogue Squadron was stationed around Cat in varying degrees of attention. Christian was leaning against the wall, behind her chair. Stevie was resting against the back of the chair next to her. Donovan was sitting in a chair to Cat's right, and Jeanie sat on the floor, next to Donovan's leg, closest to Cat. Dave and Susan were across from Cat, Susan on the couch, Dave on the floor in front of her, watching Cat closely behind sunglasses.

"Rogue Squadron's got her," Joe said. "Might just want to let Dave know about the possible shock. I'll go talk to the hospital maintenance about getting the heat turned up in that area." Joe grinned. "Warn them it's about to become summer again," he said with a wink.

It was another hour before the doctor finally walked out to talk to them.

"For Kana Sorbinno?" he called.

Midnight stepped forward, Rick at her back. Everyone else ranged out behind her.

"I'm Chief Chevalier. She's one of my people," Midnight said. "How is she?"

The doctor looked at her for a long moment, then sighed. "There was a great deal of damage. We worked on her for twelve and a half hours…" He shook his head, rubbing at his eyes tiredly. "She lost a lot of blood, and we weren't able to repair everything we wanted to—it was too risky to keep her on the table that long. Either way, I don't think it would have made a difference."

Midnight closed her eyes. *Oh God, he's about to tell me she's dead.*

"I wish I had better news," the doctor said, sounding like he truly did. "But I don't think she'll make it through the night. I'm very sorry. When she's brought down to recovery, we'll make sure you can get in to see her… to say goodbye."

Midnight was sure her heart had stopped beating. She reached blindly for Rick, her tears overwhelming her. Rick was there instantly, holding her and doing his best to keep his composure.

"This isn't happening," Midnight said, shaking her head, the tears that flowed down her cheeks clear in her voice. "This isn't happening."

"Midnight?" queried a voice to the side of them.

Midnight turned to see Palani standing in the corridor, her dark eyes glancing between the people standing around Midnight, searching for something. She'd heard that "a lieutenant for San Diego PD" had been shot, but they hadn't released a name. But she'd been feeling sick in the pit of her stomach all day. Kana was a sergeant, she'd reasoned with herself—it couldn't have been her. But when Midnight turned to look at her, Palani knew.

"Oh my God... It is Kana, isn't it?" Palani said, tears already starting to flow down her cheeks. "She was the officer shot..." Palani begged Midnight with her eyes to tell her she was wrong.

Midnight closed her eyes for a moment, then opened them, nodding.

Palani starting hyperventilating, her breath coming in ragged gasps as she walked toward Midnight.

"She's going to be okay, though, right?" Palani asked, a plea in her voice.

Midnight winced, glancing at Rick, then back at Palani, shaking her head slowly. "They don't think she's going to make it through the night," she said, as gently as humanly possible.

"No!" It was a primal cry that ripped from Palani's throat.

Midnight saw her wavering. "Tiny!" she yelled—he was closest.

Tiny lunged for Palani, catching her as she fainted. He picked her up easily and carried her over to one of the couches. Joe grabbed one of the nurses and asked for smelling salts. Midnight walked over, looking down at Palani.

"Maybe we should let her stay out," she said. "Might be easier for her for a while."

"Be easier for all of us," Rick said.

Midnight closed her eyes, nodding. When Palani did wake she was quiet, tears streaming down her cheeks. She glanced up and noticed the woman that had been with Kana at the club that night a month ago.

Cat was watching Palani, seeing the anguish on the girl's face. She felt caught in some kind of movie where she had no control over anything that happened. Her mind told her over and over again, *Kana's dying, she's dying, we're losing her.* If she'd only called Tiny back and told him that Kana shouldn't be on that raid… If only she'd stopped her… Damnit!

Cat got up and strode to the quad, pulling her cigarettes out and lighting up as the doors slid open. She stood leaning against the wall, her head back, her eyes closed as she smoked. Lifting her head, she let it drop back against the cement. She stayed there until she felt in control again. She refused to crumble here, because she had no idea whether she could stop once she started.

Elizabeth moved away from the door as Cat dropped her cigarette, stubbing it out with her foot. Cat walked back into the hospital and resumed her spot in the chair she'd been in all day.

It was another three hours before they were told they could go in and see Kana. Midnight gently suggested that Cat go in first. Cat looked back at her, then glanced at Palani. Finally she blew her breath out and nodded.

Walking into the hospital room was surreal. There were machines and tubes everywhere. Kana lay in the bed, her dark hair flowing around her. Her face was unmarked—she looked like she was sleeping. *She's not sleeping—she's dying,* Cat's mind reminded her.

She moved to the bed, taking Kana's hand. Allowing her tears to flow for the first time.

"Kana," she began softly. "I'm sorry I didn't stop you from going this morning. I'm so sorry..." Her voice trailed off as her emotions threatened to overwhelm her. "Kana, I love you. I didn't want to, I tried not to, but I do... I never said anything because I know I'm not what you wanted or needed. Kana, she's here—Palani's here. If you can hear me, K, that should make you happy. She's here." Cat leaned down, kissing Kana's lips softly. "I'm glad I got a chance to know you. I'm sorry it ended up this way. I'll never forget you."

Stepping back, she reached up, wiping her eyes. Swallowing convulsively, she turned to walk out of the room. Outside, she encountered Tiny waiting to go in. He looked at her, his eyes apologetic.

Cat hugged him. "You couldn't have stopped her, Tiny," she whispered. "Not even a Mack Truck can stop Kana when she wants something."

Tiny nodded, still looking bereaved.

He walked into the room, stepping over to Kana's side. He took her hand, reaching down to touch her cheek.

"Kana Akua Lee," he said, using both her middle names. "I am going to miss you more than you'll ever know. I'm sorry I wasn't faster. I'm sorry it wasn't me that got hit. I got the bastard though, K, just know that. He's not going to hurt anyone else ever. Tried and convicted in a fraction of a second," he whispered fiercely. Leaning down, he kissed her on the cheek. "I love you, my friend. Rest easy and know that you'll never be forgotten."

His tears flowed down his cheeks as he spoke. There were very few people he was this emotional over. Kana was like a sister to him, and he was losing her, and no matter what anyone said, he would always feel responsible.

Stepping back, he saluted her. Something he would only have done for Midnight before. Kana was his superior, and he was showing her a final piece of respect. He turned and left the room.

Rick and Midnight walked in next. Midnight stood staring down at Kana. Kana had been with her almost from the beginning. She had joined her when FORS was only two months old. Kana had been fiercely loyal from day one. She'd respected Midnight's fighting ability in the beginning, and come to respect Midnight as a leader after that. Midnight, too, had respected Kana. The Samoan woman had a way that made people pay attention to her. It was an admirable quality, one Kana honed into an extremely useful tool.

Kana had only been eighteen when she'd joined FORS. Midnight had watched Kana grow into an adult. She'd also watched as Kana struggled with her weight and became determined to trim down. She'd seen Kana's struggles with her sexuality and becoming who she was meant to be. The last two years, Kana had shown them all who she really was. She'd grown so much emotionally in the acceptance by her "family" of her sexuality. She'd felt so much a part of the group then, when before she'd felt like she was lying to all of them.

Midnight couldn't believe she was standing here to say goodbye. This just wasn't happening.

"I can't do this, Rick," she said, her voice filled with tears.

"I know," he said, his own voice choked with emotion.

"I can't bury another member," Midnight said, her voice breaking on the last word. "Not Kana. Not her. God…" She turned to Rick, burying her face in his shirt.

Rick held her against him, not sure what he could say to make this hurt less. There wasn't anything. Kana had been with Midnight longer than he had. She was one of the people in Midnight's life that was a solid presence. Dave, Tiny, Spider, and Kana were like the four walls that supported Midnight. They'd always been there for her. Losing Kana would rock that support. Rick had no idea what to say.

Midnight turned back to Kana, her tears falling unchecked. She held her hand, staring down at her face for the longest time.

"I'm so sorry, my friend," she said finally. "I have no idea what we'll do without you here. I wish you didn't have to go…" Her voice trailed off as her tears started again. "We love you, Kana, we love you," she said, feeling Rick's hands on her shoulders. She turned to him, crying again, doing the falling apart she couldn't do in front of everyone else. She had to be strong for the people left behind—she knew that. But she needed to cry now for what they were losing.

When Midnight quieted, Rick leaned over Kana, kissing her softly on the cheek.

"We'll miss you, Kana. Thank you for everything. Rest well." His words were simple, but the emotion behind them was very sincere.

Rick turned, ushering Midnight out of the room. He knew this was tearing her up inside, and he didn't want to put her through any more than was necessary. Seeing Kana looking so normal, without a mark on her face, made it harder to accept that she was going to die. False hope wasn't something Rick wanted Midnight buying into at this point. It would only crush her harder when Kana left them.

Dave went in next. Susan went with him but stayed back, allowing him the time with his friend. She looked on as Dave knelt next to the bed, his hand in Kana's. He reached up, stroking her hair.

223

"I don't know why this is happening, K," he said. "I don't know why you're being taken from us, but I know there's a purpose. Just know that we will miss you every day." He stood up, leaning down to kiss her cheek. "We love you, Kana. You'll never be forgotten."

Susan walked over then, reaching out to touch Kana's hand as Dave put his arm around her. Susan leaned down, kissing Kana's cheek. She was afraid to speak, her emotions were in such turmoil. She wasn't used to dealing with this kind of thing firsthand yet. In years past, she'd been left at home to watch the children. Now she was included, and it made her realize how draining it was, and how terribly sad.

As Dave and Susan turned to leave, Dave caught the slightest movement. He looked back at Kana and saw her grimace.

"Kana?" he said loudly.

Kana turned her head in response to his voice, grimacing again, in what looked like pain. Her hand grasped at the bed beneath her.

Dave strode to the door, putting his head out into the hall.

"Midnight!" he yelled. "She's waking up, and she looks like she's in pain. Get down here!"

Midnight went into action. "Tiny, get down there. Joe, go get a doctor or nurse or something. If she's in pain, I want her out of it, now!"

Tiny ran down the hallway, even as Midnight strode that way. The rest of the group moved with her, not wanting to get in the way but needing to know what was happening. Palani edged closer to the room, her eyes wide with terror. Cat hung back on the far side of the group, nearest the room.

Inside the room, Kana was indeed waking up and indeed in excruciating pain. The doctors obviously hadn't thought to give her pain meds, since they expected her to die without ever regaining consciousness. She was grasping at the sheets that she'd ripped from their place on the bed, panting in an effort to deal with the pain. Dave was standing next to the bed, her face in his hands, talking to her.

"Kana, stay with me. I know it hurts, but stay with me, babe," he said, glancing up at the monitors that displayed her heart rate and blood pressure. They were way up. Her blood pressure was 150 over 110, way over normal, and her heart rate was 110, up from a 70 resting rate. "You gotta ease up, K. Ease up, babe, breathe. Come on, babe... We're here—we're all here. We'll take care of you. Stay with me..."

Kana opened her eyes, looking into Dave's, her pain so evident that Dave visibly flinched. She let out a cry then, somewhere between rage and agony. Everyone heard it and flinched as well.

"It hurts, Dave," Kana said, her teeth gritted. "It hurts..." she said, panting with the effort.

"I know, babe, I know. They're coming right now. Just hold on, Kana. Hold on," he said, glancing at Midnight and shaking his head.

Midnight went out into the hall. "Get them down here now!" she roared, her voice all chief.

"Kana," Dave said, trying to think of something to distract her. "Look, babe, we need you to fight, here, okay? We need to you fight."

"Fight?" Kana asked, her voice still ragged.

"Yeah," Dave said, nodding. "They aren't giving you much of a chance, but we know you better than that. You gotta fight, babe. We need you here with us."

The nurse came in then, striding to the IV, bottle and needle in hand.

225

"Can you do that, K?" Dave asked, endeavoring to keep her distracted. "Please?"

Kana shook her head, closing her eyes as she gritted her teeth, letting out another scream of pain. "I can't," she said. "I can't…"

"Yes, you can—you can!" Dave yelled, wanting to get through to her.

The nurse stuck the needle into the IV, opening it up fully so the medicine would get into Kana's blood stream immediately.

"Kana?" Dave said, feeling the tension starting to leave her body. "Kana, fight for us. Please, we need you here…" he said, tears in his eyes now.

Kana closed her eyes, fading quickly. "I can't… Too tired…I don't want to fight anymore…" With that, she was out.

Dave looked at the monitors and saw them dropping too, but far too quickly.

"Midnight," he said gravely. "We're losing her."

"Nooooo!" Palani cried from the doorway. She knew that meant Kana wasn't going to fight to stay alive. Palani ran over to the bed, grabbing her hand.

"Kana, no!" she cried. "Please don't leave me! Please, Kana, please!" she said, her tears flowing and dropping on hers and Kana's clasped hands. "Please don't go, please don't go," she said, putting Kana's hand up to her face. "Kana, don't leave me, please—please!"

Dave watched in silence, then glanced at the monitors. His eyes widened. The numbers were climbing again. They'd dropped well past norms but were creeping back up.

"Midnight," he said, pointing at the screens.

"It's working!" Midnight said, stepping over to Palani. "Keep talking to her, Palani. She can hear you."

Palani's eyes widened, even as she nodded. "Kana? Kana, listen to me. I need you to stay here. I need you to fight. You need to stay with us, with me… please? Please, honey, please…" Palani continued to talk, and the numbers on the monitors continued to climb, leveling off at normal rates.

Everyone in the hallway breathed a sigh of relief. They were all so intent on watching the scene in the hospital room, no one saw Cat slip away to walk down the hallway. No one except Elizabeth.

Elizabeth watched as Cat went over to pick up her cigarettes and head out to the quad. She decided to leave her alone for a little while to sort out her feelings. What she didn't know was that Cat headed right out the other side of the quad and hailed a cab to take her home.

It took Elizabeth half an hour to figure out that Cat wasn't still in the quad. She did a cursory check of the area, then went to her car. Driving the Porsche out of the parking lot, the tires squealing, Elizabeth headed straight for Cat's apartment.

When she arrived, she went upstairs and unlocked the door with the spare key hidden under the doormat. Inside, Elizabeth looked around. There was music on, Evanescence's dark-toned debut album, *Fallen*. The song "Tourniquet" was playing, and the words to the first verse were haunting at best at this point:

"I tried to kill the pain

But only brought more

(So much more)

I lay dying

227

And I'm pouring, crimson regret, and betrayal"

"Cat?" Elizabeth called softly, walking toward the bedroom.

There was no answer. Cat wasn't in the bedroom. Elizabeth checked the bathroom, praying to God she wouldn't find her there. She wasn't there either. Walking back out into the living room, Elizabeth caught movement on the small balcony. Going outside, she saw Cat sitting in the only chair on the balcony, a bottle of tequila in one hand and a cigarette in the other.

Elizabeth stood staring down at Cat, searching for something to say to make things better. She couldn't think of anything. She'd heard what Joe had said about Cat going into shock, that she shouldn't be alone, things like that. She'd also heard that her aunt had instructed Rogue Squadron to keep an eye on Cat. That meant Midnight was worried about her too.

Cat looked up at Elizabeth, her face a passive mask.

"What are you doin' here, Bet?" she asked, her voice slightly slurred.

"I thought you might need some company," Elizabeth said, moving to squat down in front of the chair.

Cat gazed back at her for a long moment, her look considering. Finally she shrugged dismissively and lifted the tequila to her lips again.

"Cat..." Elizabeth said cautiously. She reached out, touching Cat's arm.

Cat snatched her arm away, as if Elizabeth had burned her. "Why are you here?" she asked again, her tone sharper now.

"Because you need me."

"No," Cat said, shaking her head.

"Yes," Elizabeth countered.

Cat looked away, grimacing in emotional pain.

"Please let me help you," Elizabeth went on doggedly, her voice gentle. "You've done so much for me. Please let me help you now."

It was all Cat could take. She'd been holding on by a thread all day, and now it snapped. She folded against Elizabeth, her tears flowing, her sobs loud and soulful. Elizabeth was shocked by the sudden change, but held on to Cat, hugging her, stroking her hair, even rocking her back and forth in an effort to soothe her.

Cat cried for what seemed like hours, holding on to Elizabeth as if for dear life. When she quieted, it became very obvious that she was exhausted. Elizabeth got her up and walked her into the bedroom. Sitting down on the bed, she pulled Cat down and drew the covers up over her. She stayed with her, watching her sleep.

"Where's Cat?" Dave asked when he came out of Kana's room, an hour after the incident.

Everyone started looking around.

"She was just here…" Spider said.

"I saw her near the room," Donovan put in.

"Shit, where is she?" Dave exclaimed. "Rogue Squadron, come with me," he said, walking down the hall.

Outside, he sent them off in different directions. He charged Stevie and Christian with checking Kana's house, while Donovan and Jeanie were to check The Flame and Bourbon Street, and Dave headed to Cat's apartment.

On the drive over, his cell phone rang. It was Midnight.

"Let me know if you find her," she said. "If I need to, I'll put out an APB for her."

"Thanks, Midnight," Dave said. "I'm headed to her place right now."

"Okay, keep us posted."

Dave hung up. He knew that Midnight was so used to crisis management that she covered all the bases. Cat was a part of the family, with Kana or not. She'd been welcomed in as a member of Rogue Squadron and had proven herself long before she'd gotten together with Kana. Their relationship had been a bonus as far as the rest of the group was concerned. Cat had helped heal what was hurt in Kana, and that counted for a lot with them too.

Driving up to the apartment, Dave noted Elizabeth's black Porsche parked at an odd angle. An angle that lent itself to the idea that the driver had been in a hurry. He also saw Cat's Blazer parked in her spot. Feeling the beginnings of relief, he dialed Midnight's number as he walked toward the apartment.

"Midnight, it's me. She's at her place, and Elizabeth apparently beat us all to the punch—she's here too."

"Elizabeth is there?" Midnight asked, surprised.

"Yeah. I'll brief you once I've got confirmation on it, but her Porsche is here."

"Okay, great, thanks," Midnight said, sounding relieved.

"Can you call the rest of my team and let them know I've found Cat?"

"You got it."

They hung up then.

Dave knocked on the door, but he could hear music coming from the apartment and figured they probably couldn't hear him. Trying the door, he found it unlocked. He walked inside, glancing around. He checked the balcony, noting the mostly empty bottle of tequila. He headed down the hallway to the bedroom, where he was greeted with the sight of his sister-in-law pointing a gun at him. She lowered it instantly.

"You even know how to shoot that?" he asked in a whisper, his eyebrow raised.

Elizabeth shrugged, grinning. "I'd learn quickly if I needed to," she whispered.

Dave's eyes fell on Cat, who was lying next to where Elizabeth was sitting up. Elizabeth's arm was up over Cat's head in a proprietary fashion. Dave wondered at that, but said nothing.

"Is she okay?"

"She cried for a long time," Elizabeth said. "But I think she'll be okay."

Dave nodded, hoping she was right.

"How's Kana?" Elizabeth asked.

"Her vitals are stable, but they're still not upgrading her condition. She's still listed as critical."

Elizabeth nodded. "Is Palani still with her?"

"Yeah, she seems to be the one thing Kana's responding to right now."

Elizabeth nodded. "See, that's the problem…"

"Problem?"

"For Cat. I know she wants Kana to be okay, but you've got to imagine how hard it is for her to stand by and watch someone else be

231

the one Kana responds to." She shrugged. "I mean, imagine if something happened to Susan, and the only person she responded to in her comatose state was Christian…"

Dave nodded, closing his eyes for a moment. He'd already thought about that, in terms of Kana and Cat, but having had it put in a such a graphic illustration pertaining to his own life made it even clearer.

"Would you stay with her here?" he asked Elizabeth.

"I had every intention of doing just that," Elizabeth said, a look of conviction in her eyes.

Dave grinned. "I can't think of any way to say this without sounding condescending, but I'm really proud of you, Liz. You've grown up a lot lately."

"Cat's the reason for that, Dave," Elizabeth said, glancing down at the woman sleeping beside her. "I owe her."

Dave nodded. "Well, if you need anything from any of us, give me a call, okay?"

"I'll do that. And please, let me know how Kana is doing."

"I will."

Dave left the apartment feeling both relieved and surprised. His sister-in-law was the last person he'd ever count on, and yet she'd been the one to be there when Cat had crumbled. Wonders never would cease.

Kana still hadn't regained full consciousness a week after she'd been shot. She'd stirred a few times, moving around, but never opened her eyes more than a slit, and then would be unconscious again. Palani stayed by her side the entire time. She also withstood the attitude of the nurse assigned to ICU. The woman was very obviously religious and didn't like Palani and Kana's lifestyle in the slightest. She frequently made comments under her breath, which Palani overheard, about them being "sick" and how "God would judge them." Palani ignored the woman, who also frequently tried to make her leave. Palani had been given permission to stay with Kana by Kana's doctor. Whenever the woman, Charlene, tried to kick her out, she always told her to go talk to Dr. Tillman.

One evening, Charlene was on her last round before going off for the night. Palani was sitting with her head down on the bed, her hand in Kana's. Charlene was also training another nurse, a much younger woman. Neither of them realized Palani was actually awake to hear their conversation.

"Isn't that the cop that was shot?" the younger nurse asked in a loud whisper.

"Yes," Charlene said, making a single word sound disgusted. "And that's her sex partner."

"What?" asked the younger nurse, sounding shocked.

"They're lesbians—don't you read the paper?" Charlene asked scornfully. "Absolutely sinful, this kind of thing. Why the good Lord chose to spare that one," Charlene spat, nodding her head toward Kana, "I'll never know. He's much more forgiving than I can find it in my good Christian heart to be."

That was all Palani could take. She sat up, her head coming up, her dark eyes blazing.

"Get out of here!" she yelled.

"Excuse me?" Charlene said, surprised. Palani had always been very docile.

"You heard me—get out, you horrid woman," Palani said, narrowing her eyes. "And take your narrowminded, evil thoughts with you."

Charlene stared openmouthed at Palani, drawing herself up sanctimoniously. "God will judge you," she said. "You and your lewd, evil ways."

With that she swept out, the younger nurse following her, wringing her hands nervously. Jenny Gaines didn't agree at all with what Charlene had said—the woman was quite mean-spirited. Jenny became a candy striper to help people, not to talk badly about them. Charlene had nothing nice to say about any of her patients. How could she care for them if she didn't care about them? All the same, she didn't stay in the room, not sure what to say to Palani.

As Charlene and Jenny headed down the hall, they passed Midnight on her way to visit Kana. Jenny turned to stare at the woman she was sure would be the next Attorney General for the state. She thought Midnight Chevalier was incredible. She had a great career, a handsome husband, and everything that came with it. Jenny suddenly remembered that Midnight was friends with the cop that had been shot. She knew, with a sense of dread, that Midnight Chevalier would hear about what Charlene had said. Jenny silently prayed that Palani would realize that Jenny had said nothing negative about Kana Sorbinno.

Midnight walked into the room and saw that Palani was clearly upset.

"What happened?" Midnight asked, walking toward the bed, her eyes on Kana.

Palani shook her head. "It's not Kana," she said. "It was that horrible nurse she has."

"Oh, the Bible banger?' Midnight asked, with a roll of her eyes.

"Midnight, she was so horrible a minute ago," Palani said, looking down at Kana. "She said she couldn't understand why God had spared Kana."

"Excuse me?" Midnight asked, her eyes narrowing dangerously.

"I told her to get out," Palani said, her lips curling in disgust.

"Good," Midnight said, nodding. "And I'll make sure she doesn't come back."

She turned on her heel and strode out of the room, down the hall to the administrator's office. One of the perks of being the Chief of Police was that first of all people recognized her, and secondly they responded when she spoke. Walking into the outer office, she stood waiting while the receptionist talked on the phone. Stepping closer, Midnight made her presence felt, her look telling the younger woman that she'd better cut the personal call short.

Hanging up, Sherry looked back at the woman whose face she knew well. Everyone knew who Midnight Chevalier was, especially if they watched the news at all.

"Chief Chevalier," she said, immediately intimidated. "What can I do for you?"

"You can get me in to see Mr. Deacon," Midnight said, her tone no-nonsense.

"Well, ma'am…" Sherry stammered—Ben Deacon wasn't the easiest man to work for, but she wasn't ready to lose her job just yet. "He's in a meeting right now."

Midnight canted her head to the side, her look telling the girl she knew she was lying.

"He's asked not to be disturbed," Sherry confided.

"Well, I'm feeling disturbed," Midnight said. "So it's only fair that he feels it too."

"But, ma'am, if I let you in there it'll mean my job."

"So tell someone you're going to the bathroom, and I'll just foist myself on him," Midnight said reasonably.

Sherry bit her lip, thinking that might just work. She buzzed the receptionist in the next office over.

"Hi, Jean," she said. "I'm going to the ladies' room. I'm going to transfer my calls to you for a few, okay? Thanks."

Sherry got up and winked at Midnight. "Thanks, Chief," she said. "Hope you win for AG."

"Thanks," Midnight said, smiling.

Midnight waited a few minutes, then knocked on Ben Deacon's office door. There was a moment of silence, then a surprised sounding "Yes?"

She opened the door, standing in the doorway. "Your receptionist was gone to the bathroom," she said. "So I just came on through. Hope you don't mind."

With that she walked in, kicking the door closed and moving to stand in front of Deacon's desk.

Ben Deacon was an older man, in his sixties, but he still ran the hospital with an iron fist. It had been his career, the medical field. He'd been a surgeon for years. When age had made his hands shake, he'd gone into administration, knowing that someone who knew medicine was better to run the hospital. He'd been right.

Ben looked the petite, copper-blond, cat-eyed Chief of Police over. He liked her—they'd talked a couple of times. The woman didn't pull any punches, but Ben understood that her concern was for her officer first and foremost.

"How are things, Chief?" he asked politely.

"Well, not so good, Ben," Midnight said, starting to pace in front of his desk.

"What's the problem?"

"Well, you have a nurse that apparently has a problem with my officer."

"What kind of problem? I wasn't aware that your officer had regained consciousness..." he said, trailing off as he began to worry that he was losing track of patients' status.

"She hasn't," Midnight said. "But her girlfriend is in there with her, and your nurse doesn't seem to feel that God should have spared Kana."

Ben closed his eyes for a moment, wincing. "I didn't realize that her nurse was a religious woman."

"'A zealot' would better describe her," Midnight said, her eyes sparkling with checked anger. "Either way, I thought nurses were supposed to be objective about their patients. Their background and financial or social status doesn't matter. They're relying on nurses to take care of them. Now that I hear that this woman feels that God made a mistake sparing Kana, how do I know she's taking the best care of her?"

Ben had been looking at lists, checking what nurse was assigned to Kana's ward.

"Charlene is one of the most experienced nurses on the ward," he assured Midnight.

"I don't care, Ben. Kana doesn't need any extra negativity in there. Can't you switch her out at least for a while?"

"I can't believe that your friend heard Charlene correctly, that she didn't think God should have spared your officer," Ben said, shaking his head. "She would know better than to say that in front of any patient's relative. I can't keep her from thinking it, but she knows to keep her mouth shut."

Midnight was ready to argue with him when there was a knock on the still open door.

"Sir?" Jenny said meekly from the door. "She did say that."

Ben looked over at Jenny, then at Midnight, who glanced back at the girl as well.

"Come in, Jenny," Ben said, motioning the girl forward. "Midnight Chevalier, this is Jenny Gaines. She's a student nurse."

Midnight extended her hand to the girl, smiling. "You heard Charlene?"

"Jenny is under Charlene's tutelage," Ben supplied when Jenny was too tongue-tied to answer.

"She says a lot of not so nice things about patients, sir," Jenny said, glancing at Ben and biting her lip in uncertainty.

Jenny and Sherry were friends and had run into each other in the hallway. Sherry had told Jenny that Midnight Chevalier, the Chief of Police, was in Deacon's office. Jenny had known it was time to tell someone about Charlene. She only hoped it wasn't going to cost her job.

"Does she say them in front of their relatives? Or in front of the patients themselves?" Deacon asked.

"No," Jenny said, shaking her head. "But I think she thought that girl in the officer's room was asleep."

Ben nodded, not looking pleased. "Regardless, it's apparent that Charlene has allowed her religious beliefs to cloud her judgment, and I won't allow it."

Midnight was silent, realizing she had to let Ben Deacon run his show. If this had been her department, Charlene would have been summoned, questioned, and then fired. But this wasn't her department.

"Chief Chevalier," Ben said, turning to Midnight. "I assure you Charlene will not return to your officer's room. I will assign a new nurse to her immediately. Thank you for bringing this to my attention," he said, walking around his desk to shake Midnight's hand. "Jenny, sit down. I'd like to talk to you," he said to the younger girl.

Midnight took that as her cue to leave. "Ben, can I see you outside for a moment?" she asked, nodding to the outer office.

"Certainly," Ben said. "I'll be right back, Jenny."

Jenny nodded, and was surprised when Midnight extended her hand to her again.

"Jenny, thank you for coming forward and telling the truth about Charlene. I appreciate your sympathy for your patients."

"Thank you, ma'am," Jenny said, smiling nervously.

Midnight pulled one of her cards out of her jacket pocket and handed it to the girl. "If you ever need anything, please don't hesitate to call me."

Jenny looked surprised, but nodded all the same. Midnight walked out of the office with Ben behind her. She turned to him as soon as he closed his door.

"Promise me you aren't going to run that girl through," she said.

"Through?" Ben asked, looking perplexed, then shook his head as understanding dawned. "Not to worry, Chief. I merely want to get a clearer picture of what Charlene has been saying and doing."

Midnight left Ben's office feeling more assured. She went back to Kana's room and assured Palani the problem had been taken care of. Midnight left an hour later. Palani was used to everyone's visits—it reminded her of how much Kana's extended family cared about her. They came routinely to see how she was, asking if there were any changes, celebrating even the slightest good news. They talked to her, often joking that this was a hell of a way to get a vacation or to take a rest.

Even Cat had returned after a few days. She'd walk into the room, her eyes searching Kana's face, then sit down. Palani would excuse herself and leave, wanting to give Cat some time alone, since it was obvious that she wouldn't talk to Kana if she was in the room. She was right—on Cat's third visit she'd walked back to the door, having forgotten her purse, and heard Cat talking to Kana. Cat's comments weren't joking. Nor were they angry or accusatory.

Palani had heard statements like "You have to get better, K," and "Everyone's here for you." Cat was being supportive. Palani had knocked politely before walking back into the room. She'd glanced at Cat, noting that there were no tears, almost no emotion at all. Palani hadn't been sure what that had meant.

Two hours after Midnight left, Palani was sitting reading a book when the door opened again. Looking up, she saw a new nurse. The woman smiled warmly at Palani, walking right over to her.

"Hi, I'm Geri," she said, extending her hand. "And you are?"

"Palani," she replied hesitantly.

"Beautiful name," Geri said, smiling, then nodded over to Kana. "And what about the strong, silent type here?"

"Her name is Kana," Palani said, her smile fond.

Geri nodded. "And she was the officer shot a week ago, right?"

"Right."

"Well, let me go ahead and do my job here," Geri said. "And you just go back to your book."

Palani smiled, nodding and sitting back in her chair. Geri checked Kana's vitals and the IVs in her arm.

"Everything looks good," Geri said. "Keep up the good work," she added, winking at Kana. "I'll be back in a few hours—no wild parties till I get back," she said to Palani, leaving the girl laughing softly.

Palani also found that she felt relieved. Geri's manner was totally different from Charlene's. Geri was warm, friendly, and didn't seem to have any problems with the nature of Kana and Palani's relationship.

It was another two days later when Palani noticed Kana shifting around again. She'd grimace, twitch her hands, and move her head around. Palani stood up, looking down into Kana's face.

"Kana?" she said softly. "Kana? I know you can hear me. Come on, babe, open your eyes."

Kana's head turned in her direction, and her eyes opened slightly. Palani bit her lip, trying not to get too excited.

"Come on, Kana, you can do it, open your eyes," she entreated softly.

Kana's eyes opened wider, and she looked around, then back at Palani. She started to sit up. Palani put her hands out to stop her.

"Don't, Kana. Don't move too much," Palani said, slightly alarmed.

Kana eased back against the pillows again, her eyes flicking around.

"Why?" she asked, her voice a hoarse whisper.

"Why?" Palani repeated, puzzled.

"Why...am I here?" Kana stammered.

"Oh," Palani said hesitantly. "You were shot."

Kana's eyes took on a faraway look as she tried to remember. The thought came to her.

"Perone," she said.

Palani nodded.

Kana nodded too, and closed her eyes. She was asleep again then. Palani sat back down, happy that Kana had finally awoken and was speaking and obviously remembering things. That was a very good sign.

Cat went back to work four days after Kana was shot. Everyone was very careful around her. It didn't take long for it to annoy her.

"Why is everyone treating me with kid gloves?" she asked Christian after that first week. "It's not like I was the one that was shot, remember?"

"True," Christian said, nodding, his face unreadable.

"So?" Cat asked after a long few moments when he said nothing else.

"So," Christian said, his lips twitching in a grin, "we want to make sure you're okay. Is that a bad thing?"

"No, but I'm fine, so you can all just relax, okay?" she said pointedly.

Christian looked back at her, his features schooled in a sarcastically obedient expression, his light blue eyes sparkling.

"Fine, huh?"

"Fine."

Christian nodded, looking unconvinced.

"She says she's fine?" Donovan asked, standing at his cutting board, chopping vegetables.

"That's what she says, man," Christian said.

"You believe her?" Jeanie asked, reaching over and plucking a carrot off the board and popping it in her mouth.

"No," Christian said. "But I tend to think if we push her too hard, she'll come back fighting."

"And that's the last thing we want," Stevie put in, gesturing with her shot glass.

"Is she coming today?" Dave asked, leaning against the dining room table.

"I don't know," Donovan said, shaking his head. "She knows everyone is coming over here... She never said if she was or not."

"Hopefully she will," Susan said, moving to sit in one of the chairs.

Dave went to help her. She'd been having backaches a lot lately. The doctor said it was totally normal, that the baby was putting some strain on her back. She'd been told to take it easy, and not to pick up the children in her charge at all.

Dave also caught the twinkle in his wife's eyes as she sat down.

"What did you do?" he asked, his eyes narrowed.

Susan smiled, shrugging. "I just sent in... I believe you call them 'a wringer.'"

Cat was sitting outside on her balcony smoking when Elizabeth walked out.

"What are you doing here?" Cat asked, grinning all the same.

"I could ask you the same question," Elizabeth replied, sitting down in the chair next to Cat's.

"Meaning?" Cat asked mildly, taking a long drag on her cigarette.

"Isn't it your boss's birthday today?"

"Isn't it your brother-in-law's birthday today?" Cat echoed, raising an eyebrow.

"Quite right," Elizabeth said, sounding very English. With that she stood up, taking Cat's hand and pulling her up out of the chair.

"What are you doing?" Cat asked.

"Going to my brother-in-law's birthday party," Elizabeth replied, leading the way out of the apartment.

Fortunately, Cat was dressed and had makeup on and her hair brushed—otherwise she probably would have argued. Instead she followed Elizabeth out to her Porsche with an indulgent grin on her lips. Elizabeth had turned out to be quite a good friend when she'd needed it. They'd become closer since Kana was shot.

Liz had a way of making her laugh when she needed to, and also a way of pushing her without being pushy. Like the birthday party for Dave. Cat had known about the party, but she had decided against going, even though she'd gotten dressed thinking she would. Everyone was driving her insane with their "concern," and she knew if she had to deal with it too much more, she'd scream.

Now here she was, sitting in Liz's black Porsche, being taken to the party. She sighed, reaching for another cigarette.

Chapter 8

Kana managed a few more minutes the next time she woke up. Palani was just coming back into the room when she saw Kana's eyes open. She walked over to the bed. It was obvious Kana was still groggy; her eyes stared up at the ceiling for a few moments then turned to Palani.

Kana went to move her right arm and found out how heavy it was with a cast. She glanced down at the cast, then looked back at Palani, askance clear in her eyes.

"You tried to block the shot," Palani said, saying it exactly as it had been explained to her by Joe.

Joe had said, "Kana probably tried to block the shot—it's a natural instinct." The doctors had confirmed that they'd removed buckshot from Kana's arm; one piece had broken a bone.

"It... hit my arm?" Kana said, perplexed. She knew she hurt much more than that. "How many times did he shoot me?" she asked, her voice still hoarse.

"You were shot with a shotgun," Palani said, realizing that Kana hadn't remembered that part.

"With a..." Kana began, her eyes widening. Then it all came back in a rush. "There was a helicopter... It was early... I knew he'd bolt... I ran in..." Her voice trailed off as she sucked her breath in. "Fuck, I was close," Kana said, her voice indicating sudden comprehension.

"Joe said probably about three and a half feet," Palani said, nodding.

Kana swallowed a few times, shaking her head. "I should be dead."

Palani looked at her for a long moment, her face solemn. "You almost did die, Kana," she said softly. "That very first night."

Kana stared back at her, her mind once again working to remember.

"The doctors said you wouldn't make it through the night," Palani said, her voice nearing tears. "But you woke up and were in so much pain…"

Kana was nodding; she vaguely remembered that.

"Dave talked to you. He told you that we needed you to fight, because the doctors weren't giving you much of a chance," Palani continued, tears in her eyes now. "But you said you couldn't, that you were too tired of fighting…" Her voice trailed off as she shook her head. "I was so scared, Kana. I couldn't let you go. I couldn't…"

Kana narrowed her eyes in thought, grasping for the memory. "I remember your voice… What were you saying?"

"I was begging you not to leave me," Palani said, her tears slipping down her cheeks now.

Kana nodded, reaching up to brush Palani's tears away with her thumb. "I didn't," she said simply.

Palani smiled softly, reaching up to take Kana's hand, which was still at her cheek. They were both silent for a while. Kana shifted in the bed, grimacing slightly.

"Are you hurting?" Palani asked immediately.

Kana canted her head to the side, her look more inward, as if trying to decide the answer to that question.

"Something's not right," she said.

"What's not right?" Palani asked, searching Kana's face.

Kana looked contemplative. She was searching herself internally to determine what wasn't right. In changing her entire lifestyle years before, she'd become very attuned to her own body. She knew when something wasn't right inside her. She was searching for the source of that.

Reaching her hand up, Kana pointed to her side, just below her rib cage.

"There," she said. "Something's not right there."

Palani nodded. She knew Kana knew her own body quite well. "I'll call the nurse," she said, reaching up to press the call button above Kana's head.

Geri got there right away.

"What's up?" Geri asked, her eyes going straight to Kana. She smiled. "Oh, you're awake."

Kana nodded, her dark eyes looking the nurse over.

"What's the problem?" Geri asked, her eyes skipping from Kana to Palani then back to Kana.

"She says there's something not right," Palani said.

Geri walked over to Kana. "Not right how?"

Kana looked thoughtful for a moment. "It's cold," she said, her hand hovering near the spot at her side again.

Geri canted her head to the side, shooting a look at Palani.

"Trust her," Palani said. "Kana knows her body."

Geri nodded in acceptance. "I'll get the doctor."

Twenty minutes later Dr. Jack Homme walked in, looking at Kana, then Palani. The entire hospital knew about the officer that had been shot. They also knew about Charlene being relieved of her duties because she'd been stupid enough to talk trash about the officer being gay in front of the officer's girlfriend. The last time Jack had seen Kana Sorbinno, she'd hovered near death on his surgical table for over twelve hours. She looked much stronger and much more intimidating now.

He took note of the incredibly beautiful dark-haired woman standing next to Kana Sorbinno. *Wow, they don't make ugly lesbians in this town, do they?* he thought. In fact, he was fairly sure he recognized Palani from the cover of the *Sports Illustrated* swimsuit edition. In fact, her picture was hanging in the lounge at the hospital—odd that no one had made that connection yet.

"How are we doing, Lieutenant?" Jack asked, his tone friendly.

"We?" Kana countered, raising an eyebrow at him. She'd seen him look at Palani. It amused her no end how men drooled over her; it always had.

"Yes," the doctor said, recalling himself and walking over to the bed. "My nurse tells me that you're complaining of a pain in your side?"

Kana nodded. "There's still buckshot in there," she said with certainty.

"Lieutenant, I spent over twelve hours searching your insides for buckshot," he said, his grin warm. "I was hoping I'd gotten it all."

"Well, ya didn't," Kana countered, grinning too.

"Where does it hurt?" he asked, lifting the covers away from her and moving her gown, exposing the bandages that still covered her surgical wounds.

"Here," Kana said, gesturing to the spot.

The doctor nodded, noting it was higher than the original cuts. "It might have shifted since you've awoken and moved around a bit. I'm going to press—tell me if it hurts."

Kana jumped as soon as his fingers pushed in slightly, sucking in her breath with a hiss of pain. Jack removed his fingers immediately, nodding.

"I'm going to get X-ray down here immediately, Lieutenant, but I'd hazard to say you're right on—there's still buckshot in there. Damnit," he muttered. "We'll need to do another surgery," he said, then looked at Kana. "I'd like to use a local if I can, rather than putting you under again so soon."

"Works for me," Kana said, having no desire to be put out again.

Ten minutes later the X-ray techs came in, their eyes on Palani and Kana. Kana got the distinct impression everyone was being very careful around them. She wondered at that, but said nothing.

One tech went to touch the area to ask if it was where they needed to X-ray. Kana's hand whipped out, grabbing his before he touched her.

"Let's not do that again, okay?" she said succinctly. "It hurts like hell. Just take the picture."

The tech's eyes widened, and he glanced at his companion. The other man shrugged, and nodded toward the machine they'd wheeled in. In minutes the X-rays were done, and the techs left.

An hour later they were ready to do the surgery. Palani asked if she could stay. The doctor said she could, but she'd need to gown up. Kana was moved to a surgical room, and Palani joined her, wearing a hospital gown, mask, and gloves. She moved to Kana's right side, taking her hand and watching what was happening. The doctor gave

Kana a shot to numb her side; she flinched slightly, turning her head to look at Palani. After the local anesthetic had taken effect, the doctor set to work. Kana kept her eyes on Palani. She saw her pale when the doctor cut into Kana's side.

"Look at me, babe," Kana said, knowing the sight of blood was probably freaking Palani out.

Palani shifted her eyes to Kana's. Kana winked, smiling slightly. Palani bit her lip, smiling too.

"You certainly lead me into new adventures," Palani said softly.

Kana chuckled softly. "Yeah, that's me."

"Got it," the doctor said after about twenty minutes. "Irrigate that area," he told the nurse assisting him. "I don't like the look of it…" he said, trailing off as he checked Kana's vital signs. "Lieutenant?" he queried. "I'm going to take a quick look around while I'm in here. Are you okay?"

Kana nodded, looking tired again already. Palani's eyes searched her face. Reaching out, she brushed Kana's hair back.

"Is it okay if she sleeps?" Palani asked the doctor.

"Sure," he said, grinning. "That's what I'm used to with my patients."

Kana smiled tiredly, her eyes only half open but still on Palani.

"Close your eyes, hon," Palani whispered. "Rest."

Kana nodded, closing her eyes. Palani's hand stroking hers soothed her to sleep.

A while later, as the doctor was closing the small incision he'd made to remove the buckshot, the nurse glanced at the monitors.

"Doctor, she's spiking a fever."

"Start antibiotics immediately," he ordered. "I knew that was a bad spot," he added, shaking his head. "It stayed in there too long."

"What's wrong?" Palani asked.

"She's got a fever," the doctor said. "Nothing major to be worried about—it probably means she's got an infection from that buckshot we just took out. Exposing the area to the air probably kicked in her natural defenses. The fever is trying to fight the infection."

Palani nodded. "But she'll be okay?"

"Yes," the doctor said. "She just needs antibiotics to fight the infection more effectively."

Palani nodded, sighing in relief.

Kana's fever skyrocketed after the surgery. Palani was beside herself with worry. The doctor assured her that the antibiotics just needed a chance to do their job. That night, Palani sat holding Kana's hand, watching her writhe, sweat beading on her forehead. She kept wiping Kana's skin with a cool rag, doing whatever she could think of to help.

At one point during the long, long night, Kana started muttering and talking in her delirious state. At first she made no sense at all. Then she talked about the shooting. "He's gonna run," Kana gritted out. "Need to stop him... Wait, just wait... No!" she cried out, her arms flying up to block the apparent shooting in her dreams.

Palani did her best to soothe her, worried that she'd hurt herself if she thrashed around too much. Later, Kana began talking again, moving her head from side to side. "Where's Cat?" she asked. Palani stood up, thinking Kana was honestly asking, but then Kana went on: "I need to tell her, I need to..." Kana's voice trailed off as she shifted around in bed, grimacing as she obviously caused herself pain.

Palani hit the call button. This had to stop.

"I need to tell her..." Kana said again, pausing for a gasping breath. "She needs to know... I can't do this... I can't..." she said, shaking her head. "I love her so much, I can't... I can't let her go... I can't..." Kana said, her voice becoming more hysterical.

Palani stared at Kana, feeling a sharp pain in her heart. She loved Cat? *Oh God!* Tears sprang to her eyes. That's when Geri walked in.

"What's wrong?" Geri asked, seeing the tears and also that Kana was thrashing around like a madwoman. She moved to Kana's side, checking the antibiotics, then Kana's blood pressure and pulse.

"I'm going to get her a sedative," the nurse said. "I'll be right back."

Palani nodded numbly, her eyes still on Kana. She closed her eyes slowly, feeling sick. The thoughts in her head hurt so much. Tears slid down her cheeks. She turned blindly and picked up her purse and book. She walked out of the hospital room and down the hall, then out of the building. In her car, she sat trying to breathe. Finally she got her emotions under control enough to drive. She went back to her apartment. Thankfully, Jerry and Jane Anne were out. She took a shower then crawled into bed, crying herself to sleep.

Two days later Cat went to visit Kana. She was relieved when they told her that Kana's fever had broken. She was surprised that Palani wasn't there, but figured the girl had just gone for coffee or something.

"Hey, K," Cat said, seeing Kana awake for the first time since she'd been shot.

"Hey," Kana said, her eyes shadowed.

253

They talked for a few minutes, the conversation very stilted. Cat finally left, unable to handle the strain.

"Hey," Tiny said as she started to walk past him in the corridor outside.

"Oh, hey, Tiny," Cat said, having been inside her own thoughts.

"How's she doing?"

Cat shrugged. "Seems okay to me."

Tiny nodded, not looking happy.

"Why?" Cat asked.

"Palani took off."

"Huh?" Cat asked, perplexed. "You mean, as in taking a break, or as in gone?"

"Gone," Tiny said. "Left, disappeared."

"Why the hell would she do that?"

"I don't know," Tiny said. "Kana's nurse said she was really upset the other night. The nurse went to get a sedative for Kana because she was thrashing around pretty bad. When she came back, Palani was gone. She never came back."

Cat curled her lips in thought. It didn't make sense. "K ask about her?"

"No," Tiny said, shaking his head. "But I could tell she was wondering where she was. You know K—her pride is stronger than any emotion she's ever had."

Cat nodded. Oh, she knew that for sure. "What's Palani's last name?"

"Ryker," Tiny replied. "Why?"

"Trust me," Cat said, giving him a wink.

Two hours later, she had tracked Palani Ryker down. She knocked on the door to Jerry and Jane Anne's apartment. Jane Anne answered, looking Cat over.

"I'm looking for Palani," Cat said, her tone all cop.

"And who are you?"

Cat narrowed her eyes at the taller woman. "Don't make me use force to find her."

"You think you can take me, little one?"

"I think you'll be sorry if I have to show you how well I can take you."

"Jane Anne," Jerry said from behind the tall woman. "She's that cop from the bar, remember? The one with Kana."

Jane Anne looked at Cat again, remembering her now. "What do you want?" she asked, her voice cooling considerably.

"I've already told you what I want," Cat gritted out. "Just get her, now."

"Jane Anne, let me handle this, please?" Jerry said, gently pushing her aside.

Cat looked at Jerry, her blue eyes icy. "Just get Palani, okay? I need to talk to her. It's about K, alright?"

"You going to warn her off your girl?" Jerry asked. "You don't need to bother—she won't bother Kana again."

Cat shook her head. "Just get her, okay?"

Jerry stared at Cat for a long moment, then shook her head, stepping aside and gesturing for her to come in. Cat walked in, looking around. It was an extremely nice apartment. She glanced at Jerry, waiting.

"She's down the hall, last room on the right," Jerry said, gesturing to the hallway.

"Thanks," Cat said, nodding.

Cat knocked on the door, and heard a quiet voice say, "Come in."

She opened the door and saw Palani lying on the bed. She was curled up in a ball, fully dressed.

"Palani?" she queried gently.

Palani looked at her, then sat up, her eyes wide as she hugged her knees to her chest.

"You're Cat," she said unnecessarily.

"I know," Cat couldn't resist saying, with a grin.

"What do you want?" Palani asked softly, feeling her stomach churning. This was the woman Kana loved now. Didn't she realize she'd won? Why was she here? To hurt her some more?

"I want to know why you left the hospital," Cat said, leaning against the door, her arms crossed in front of her chest.

Palani stared back at Cat, searching the other woman's face. Finally she shrugged. "Why does it matter?"

"It matters," Cat said, "because K needs you."

Palani looked pained. "She doesn't need me. I know that now."

"Now?"

"Yes," Palani said simply.

"What do you mean, now?" Cat asked. "What made you decide Kana didn't need you?"

"She told me."

"She told you she doesn't need you?" Cat asked disbelievingly.

"No," Palani said, her eyes dropping from Cat's.

"What *did* she tell you, Palani?" Cat asked, getting irritated.

Palani caught it, her eyes widening as she looked back at Cat. "She told me that she loves you, that she can't let you go."

Cat looked back at her for a long moment, then gave a short, sarcastic laugh, shaking her head.

"I don't know what you were smoking, Palani, but Kana doesn't love me. She can't—she's never gotten over you."

"She said it."

"I don't fucking care what she said," Cat said, becoming unaccountably angry. "She doesn't love me, and she does love you. And you need to march your ass back to her bedside before she gives up again. Because if she does that, I'm going to kick your pretty little ass all the way back to Hawaii. You got it?"

Palani jumped at the venom in Cat's voice. She stared back at the blond woman, unable to think of a reply. Finally she nodded, if nothing else to placate Cat.

"I mean it," Cat said. "So get up and let's go."

"But…"

"Now!" Cat yelled, her anger snapping.

Palani jumped off the bed and grabbed her purse, responding on a base level to Cat's command. Cat drove her back to the hospital in silence, dropping her at the front. Before Palani got out, Cat leaned over, taking her arm gently.

"Talk to her, Palani," Cat said softly. "I'm sure you heard her wrong."

Palani nodded, unable to understand Cat's motivations. She got out of the Blazer and watched as Cat drove away. Shrugging to herself, she walked inside.

At Kana's room, she took a deep breath, then opened the door. Kana was lying with her eyes closed. Palani walked over to the bed, reaching out and touching Kana's cheek. Kana's eyes opened immediately, searching Palani's.

"Why did you leave?" she asked.

Palani swallowed, trying to get past the lump in her throat. "I didn't think I belonged here anymore," she said softly.

"Why wouldn't you?" Kana asked, obviously perplexed.

Palani took a deep breath, blowing it out slowly. "While you had your fever, you said some things…"

"What did I say?" Kana asked, her eyes still searching Palani's.

Palani looked down at the blanket covering Kana. She picked at it nervously, not willing to meet Kana's eyes. "You said you loved Cat very much and that you couldn't let her go."

She didn't see the look of utter confusion on Kana's face, or the smile that started then. She was so intent on picking at the lint on the blanket, and trying to hold back tears, she didn't see anything. Kana's finger under her chin turned Palani's eyes up to hers.

"Babygirl," Kana said. "If I said that, I wasn't talking about Cat. I was talking about you."

"You were?" Palani asked, her eyes wide, her voice hopeful.

"You think I stay in this world for just anyone?" Kana asked, grinning. "Even when I have more holes in me than a piece of Swiss cheese," she said, shaking her head. "Only for you, babe. Just for you."

Palani cried, she was so happy. Kana shook her head, rolling her eyes heavenward, even as she held her arms out to Palani. "Dumbass," she said as Palani moved into her arms.

"Stop," Palani said, pouting prettily.

Kana shook her head again, grinning. "Next time, stick around long enough to ask for clarification, okay?"

"Okay," Palani said, biting her lip.

Kana kissed her forehead, hugging her as best she could from the hospital bed.

Cat lay in her bed, on her stomach, her arms outstretched above her head, her face buried in the crook of her arm. She wore a jog bra and sweats and hadn't bothered to cover up, even though it was only fifty-five degrees in the apartment, according to the thermostat. That was the first thing Elizabeth noticed when she walked in. Shivering, she went over to the thermostat and noted that the heater wasn't even on. She flipped the switch and set the thermostat to sixty-eight degrees.

Glancing around the apartment, Elizabeth noticed that the tequila bottle stood open on the counter. Her lips twitched at that, as she realized Cat must be upset again. The woman had a tendency to handle her hurts all alone. It was a nasty habit that Elizabeth intended to break. She put the top back on the tequila and put it away, then went to the bedroom.

She saw Cat lying on the bed, and stood in the doorway watching her for a few minutes. Finally she walked over. Cat sensed her there and turned her head slightly.

"Bet," she said by way of greeting.

"Cat," Elizabeth replied in kind.

Cat turned her head back to face the bed and was quiet again. Elizabeth scowled at her, though Cat didn't see it. Taking off her jacket and kicking off her boots, Elizabeth flopped down on the bed. Turning to her side, she faced Cat's motionless form. Reaching out, she brushed Cat's hair back off the side of her face.

"What happened?" Elizabeth asked gently.

Cat shook her head.

"Don't give me that," Elizabeth said. "I haven't seen you indulge in, what—a half bottle of tequila?—on a whim, Catalina. What happened?"

Cat turned her head, one blue eye peeking out from behind her arm. "I did my good fucking deed for the century," she said harshly.

Elizabeth nodded. "And what was that, love?" she asked softly.

Cat curled her lips in disgust. "Palani left the hospital. I got her back."

"And how did you do that?" Elizabeth asked, realizing there was a lot more to this story.

Cat didn't answer.

"Why did Palani leave? I thought she was determined to stay with Kana…" Elizabeth said.

Cat gave a short, sarcastic laugh. "That's the funny part, actually."

"What is?"

"She left because she thought Kana was in love with me," Cat said, giving another short bark of laughter that sounded anything but humorous.

"But you convinced her differently?" Elizabeth asked, grimacing at the way that sounded.

"Oh yeah," Cat said. "Then I dragged her ass back to the hospital."

Elizabeth took a deep breath, not sure what to say at that point.

"You know what really sucks?" Cat said. "What really pisses me off?"

"What?" Elizabeth asked quietly.

"When she said it, when Palani said that Kana said she loves me, that she can't let me go... I wanted to fucking believe it so much..." Her voice trailed off as she scrubbed her face against her bare arm. "Damnit," she muttered, feeling her throat constrict painfully.

Elizabeth winced at the sound of her voice. She touched Cat's head, stroking her hair. "Cat..."

"I can't even cry anymore," Cat said, her tone disgusted. "I'm out. I'm all out."

Elizabeth leaned in, putting her head against Cat's, commiserating with her the best way she could think of.

"Don't," Cat said petulantly, moving away slightly.

Elizabeth moved in again, resting her cheek against Cat's head.

"Don't," Cat said again, nudging her with her shoulder.

"I'm going to comfort you whether you like it or not," Elizabeth said firmly, a grin already on her lips.

Cat made a little noise in her throat, still sounding petulant.

"Catalina!" Elizabeth exclaimed. "You lie there and let me comfort you, or else..."

That garnered a grin out of Cat. She turned her head to look up at Elizabeth, whose head was just above hers. "Is that like 'You're going to have fun or I'll break every bone in your body'?"

"Yes," Elizabeth said, laughing softly. "Usually utilized on small children at Disneyland."

Cat laughed, shaking her head, tears in her eyes all the same. Elizabeth put her hand to Cat's cheek, her eyes reflecting her pain at seeing Cat upset. Their eyes caught and held, and it seemed inevitable that they'd kiss. And they did. Cat started to pull back as soon as she realized what they were doing; Elizabeth's hand moved to the back of her head, pulling her back.

Cat gave in for a full minute, her hands moving to cup Elizabeth's face. Elizabeth moaned softly, and the sound of it brought Cat back to reality. She pulled away, shaking her head.

"I can't do this," she said, breathing heavily.

"Why?" Elizabeth asked, surprised at Cat's sudden retreat.

Cat shook her head. "No, I can't. You're my friend, I can't…"

Elizabeth reached out, touching Cat's face, searching her eyes. "Cat, why can't you? Why can't we?"

"No," Cat said. "This isn't you—this isn't right." She sat up, pulling her knees to her chest.

"What do you mean?" Elizabeth asked, sitting up as well.

Cat looked at her, her face serious. "What part of 'straight' don't you get?"

"What?" Elizabeth asked, her face reflecting shock.

"You're straight, Bet. I know that. I don't need comforting that bad, not enough to use you," Cat said, her lips curling in self-disgust.

"But—"

"Just stop," Cat said, cutting her off angrily. Her anger was self-directed, but Elizabeth didn't know that.

Elizabeth's chin came up, her pride kicking in. "Fine," she said softly, trying to force back the tears that threatened to come up on her. In desperation to hide them, she got up and grabbed her boots and jacket. She walked out of the room without looking back. She didn't see the anguish on Cat's face.

"Good, Cat, real good," Cat said to herself. "Run off your last friend." The tears came then, and she lay back on the bed, letting them flow.

"Fuck!" she yelled to no one.

Geri walked into the hospital room and saw that Palani was once again by Kana's side. She smiled, glad that the girl was back. It had been obvious from Kana's slow recovery from the fever that she'd missed Palani. Geri found that she really liked these two. She knew exactly who Palani Ryker was, and she thought it was great that these two women had found each other and were apparently so in love.

"Kana?" Geri queried.

"Hmm?" Kana asked, looking at the nurse and smiling. "Hi, Geri, what's up?"

"There's a young lady out here that wants to see you."

"Who?" Kana asked, surprised. None of her friends would ask permission to see her.

"Her name is Elizabeth. She seems rather upset."

Kana glanced at Palani, who only shrugged.

"Let her in, Geri, thanks," Kana said.

Palani stood up as Elizabeth walked into the room. Elizabeth's anger was tangible.

"Elizabeth," Kana said curtly, her dark eyes searching the younger woman's face.

"I hope you're satisfied," Elizabeth said without preamble.

"With?" Kana asked, sensing that Elizabeth had a lot more to say.

"Yourself," Elizabeth spat, her blue eyes points of fire. "You've fucked Cat over pretty well. She can't even see her way out of the abyssal pit you've put her in."

Kana's head came up. She knew that what Elizabeth was saying was true, but also sensed something else altogether.

"When you get out of here," Elizabeth went on, "you stay away from her. Because I swear to you," she said, her hands clenching into fists at her side, "if you hurt her again, I'll personally..." She trailed off as she searched for the appropriate threat. "Hire someone to kill you," she finished, her voice as serious as the look on her face.

Kana nodded, not saying a word. Elizabeth stared back at her for a long moment, as if trying to drive her point home. Then she turned and stalked out of the room, doing her best to slam the door.

Palani looked at Kana, her eyes wide. Kana stared after Elizabeth, her eyes narrowing. Then she started to nod, as if confirming something to herself.

"What?" Palani asked, wondering why Kana wasn't more upset by the visit.

"She's right, I have fucked Cat over," Kana said, still nodding. "But," she went on, starting to grin, "that"—she pointed to the place where Elizabeth Endicott had stood threatening her—"was passion if I ever saw it."

"What?" Palani asked, not understanding what Kana was saying.

"Elizabeth has a thing for Cat," Kana explained, still grinning.

"Why do you say that?"

"For one thing, Elizabeth Endicott knows I can break her in half with little or no effort, so threatening me is the last thing she'd ever consider doing. Unless she's got something to defend, and that would be Cat."

"Maybe she's just worried about a friend…"

"No," Kana said. "Friends don't get that mad. That was passion, babe."

Palani furrowed her eyebrows, then nodded, seeing that Kana's mind was working now.

"What are you going to do?" she asked warily.

Kana shrugged, grinning. "Whatever I can."

"Kana…"

"Shh," Kana replied, reaching for her and pulling her down to kiss her softly on the lips.

Kana was finally released from the hospital a few days later. She slept most of the time. She was still in a lot of pain, and it bothered Palani no end that this was the case.

"Maybe you shouldn't have been released yet," Palani said worriedly on the third day, when Kana was still hissing in pain every time she moved too much.

"I was in the hospital for almost a month, babe," Kana said, settling herself gingerly against the pillows again. "I don't think you're legally allowed to stay after three weeks."

Palani looked shocked at that, then realized Kana was grinning. "You are so mean!" she exclaimed, laughing.

Kana chuckled. She was extremely happy to have Palani there with her still. She had begun to wonder when Palani would have to go home to Matthew and her baby. Palani hadn't mentioned either of them, so Kana hadn't either, not wanting to get into the conversation she wasn't sure she could handle just yet. Things were good between them, and she didn't want it spoiled just yet.

It was another two days before Kana felt strong enough mentally and physically to bring the subject up. They were lying on the bed, watching TV. Kana was on her side, the one that hadn't been injured in the shooting. Palani lay on her back next to her.

The show they were watching depicted a woman who was pregnant and thrilled about the baby she was expecting. Kana's hand rested lightly on Palani's ever flat stomach. She flexed her fingers, glancing down at Palani.

"Palani?" Kana said softly.

"Hmm?" Palani murmured, shifting her eyes up to Kana's.

Kana said nothing. The look in her eyes, combined with her hand on Palani's stomach, was enough to communicate what she was thinking about. Palani pressed her lips together, realizing it was time to talk about what had broken them apart. Picking up the remote, she turned off the TV and moved to sit up, turning to face Kana. Kana sat up carefully as well, feeling the need to keep the upper hand.

Palani searched for the words to explain everything. Finally she started to talk.

"Kana, the night I came here and told you I was pregnant…" She trailed off uncertainly when Kana closed her eyes for a moment, nodding. "I know I didn't handle things the right way."

"How else do you think you could have handled it?" Kana asked quietly.

"Well," Palani said, "I was still in shock. I had no idea how I could have gotten pregnant." The look in Kana's eyes changed to one of cynicism. "Kana, honestly," Palani said entreatingly. "I know it sounds crazy, but I didn't know how it was possible. I hadn't lied to you about Matthew—I didn't sleep with him."

"Then how did you get pregnant?" Kana asked, not sounding totally convinced, but not accusing either.

"Well, that was something that stayed a mystery for a while," Palani said, sighing. "Remember how you wanted me to go home every other night so that Matthew wouldn't get too irritated about the divorce when I had it lined up?"

"Yeah," Kana said, mystified.

"And remember I told you I was having to take Ambien most of those nights, or I wouldn't sleep at all?"

Kana nodded. She did remember that. Palani had said she couldn't sleep without Kana's arms around her. At the time Kana had been quite pleased that Palani missed her that much when she went home to Matthew.

"Okay, but what's that got to do with getting pregnant?" Kana asked.

"Well," Palani said, her eyes turning icy, "apparently Matthew decided that if I was pregnant, I wouldn't leave him…" Her lips curled in disgust.

"Oh my God," Kana said as she realized what Palani was saying. "He took advantage of you while you were asleep?"

"Apparently," Palani said. "He finally admitted it when I wouldn't let it go as to how it was possible that I got pregnant, since he and I weren't having sex." She narrowed her eyes in remembered anger. "He said that I should be happy about it, that I'd wanted a family. I was so furious I could have killed him."

Kana grimaced, shaking her head. "Babe... I'm sorry..."

"No," Palani said, shaking her head. "It's not your fault, Kana. I mean, who would have thought something like that? How else does someone who's married get pregnant other than sleeping with her husband?"

"But you promised me that you'd never lie to me about that," Kana said. "And you didn't."

"You didn't know that, though." Palani reached up to touch Kana's cheek. "I can't blame you for jumping to that conclusion— anyone would have."

"But I should have at least let you try and explain, babe..." Kana said, feeling disgust at herself for being so mistrusting.

"I wouldn't have been able to explain. I had no idea."

"When did he admit it?"

"When I was about four months pregnant."

"Nice," Kana said, narrowing her eyes. "Too late for you to abort even if you'd wanted to. Bastard."

"Well, once he admitted that to me, and even seemed rather proud of himself for doing it, I was through. It was bad enough that he'd done that to me, but his deceit had cost me you. I'd had it. I filed for divorce the next day."

"You did?" Kana asked, glancing at Palani's left ring finger. Of course she'd noticed that Palani wasn't wearing her wedding ring, but she'd assumed that she had just taken it off for when she was with her, not for good.

"Yes," Palani said. "Of course, that's when my family started in on me…"

"Where's the baby then?" Kana asked, not catching the change in Palani's voice.

Palani looked straight at her then, and Kana could see the pain in her eyes, could feel it, even before Palani spoke. "I lost the baby, Kana," she said softly.

"When?" Kana breathed.

"In the fifth month," Palani replied, closing her eyes for a moment, forcing back tears.

"What happened?" Kana asked, sensing it was something more than just a miscarriage.

Palani shook her head, her eyes downcast. "My family was very unhappy about me filing for divorce. They started calling constantly, reminding me that marriage wasn't always easy. Telling me that I should go to marriage counseling. Telling me what a good man Matthew was…" Her voice trailed off as her lips curled in disgust again.

Kana nodded, remaining silent, realizing there was more to the story.

"One day my brother Sampson arrived from Hawaii to talk some sense into me. For three days he wouldn't leave me alone, telling me over and over again how I was disgracing the family with this idea of divorce. He kept telling me what a good man Matthew was, how Matthew was the reason I was so successful. He kept talking about how I lived in this beautiful house because Matthew had helped my career. How if it wasn't for Matthew I'd be nothing but a pretty face working at some hotel in Hawaii still." She shook her head. "One day he followed me all the way upstairs, into my bedroom, talking at me. He started in again on how I had it so easy because of my husband, because of the man that loved me. That I owed Matthew the loyalty for the love he gave me…" Her eyes narrowed at a spot on the bed, as she remembered again the conversation and how angry she'd been. She shook her head. "I couldn't take anymore, Kana, I couldn't. I walked out of my bedroom, and still he was talking. So I finally turned to him and told him that everything I had was nothing, nothing at all, because I'd lost the one and only thing I'd ever loved because of Matthew and his treacherous trick to keep me. He asked me what I thought I'd lost. And I screamed at him that I'd lost the only woman I'd ever loved." There were tears in her eyes as she said it.

Kana winced, shaking her head and blowing her breath out in a disbelieving hiss. "You told a traditional Samoan male that?"

Palani nodded slowly, her eyes still downcast. Kana reached out, touching her under the chin, her eyes searching Palani's.

"I'm not going to like what you're going to tell me next, am I?" Kana said, already feeling sick inside.

Palani shook her head. "He backhanded me." She saw Kana take a sharp breath. "I was standing too close to the top of the stairs, and I stumbled backward."

Kana pulled Palani into her arms, holding her.

"He didn't mean to, Kana…" Palani said softly, her tears beginning in earnest.

Kana held her close, gritting her teeth at the pain, so heartsick that Palani had been hurt so badly and she hadn't been there to stop it.

"I'm so sorry, baby…" Kana breathed.

"It isn't your fault," Palani said, holding on to Kana's shoulders.

Kana shook her head, not replying. She knew that if she'd trusted Palani back then, and allowed her to explain everything, none of that would have happened. But she'd never fully trusted Palani. Not because of Palani herself, but because another woman had lied to her in the past. A married woman. That mistrust had been put onto Palani unfairly, and it had cost her dearly.

"I love you," Kana said, not knowing what else to say to take away the pain.

She had no idea how perfect that was. Palani had thought she'd never hear Kana say that to her again. Hearing it now filled her heart with more joy than she would have thought possible. She cried harder, because she was so happy. Looking up at Kana with tears streaming down her cheeks, she had no idea the picture she presented.

"I love you, Kana. I've missed you so much…" she said, her voice a fervent whisper.

Kana's hand smoothed away the tears on Palani's cheeks as she cupped her face gently. "I missed you too, baby," she said, her eyes reflecting love. Pulling Palani forward, she kissed her lips softly, deepening the kiss when she felt Palani sigh.

Unfortunately, Palani went to grasp Kana's waist, as she always did when they kissed. Kana jumped when her hand touched the still healing wounds at her side.

"Oh, Kana," Palani whispered worriedly.

"It's okay, baby," Kana said, smoothing the lines of worry from Palani's face. "It's just still a bit sensitive."

Palani bit her lip, deep concern in her eyes.

"Shh," Kana said, to quiet Palani's worried thoughts. Leaning in, she kissed her again, taking her hands and holding them. Palani realized Kana was keeping her from inadvertently hurting her again, and started to giggle. Kana began laughing too.

"Getting shot sucks," Kana said.

"Glad you realize that," Palani said matter-of-factly. "Make a mental note not to do it again, will you?" she added, her eyes narrowed at Kana comically.

"Will do, babygirl, will do," Kana said, pulling Palani into her arms again. She felt extremely happy. They'd lost a lot, but they'd found each other again, and that was what mattered. She knew she'd get shot all over again if she knew this would be the outcome. It was worth every twinge.

Cat was overdoing it. Everyone could see it, but no one could get her to slow down. She was in the office before everyone in the morning, and stayed late on the nights when they didn't have a raid. Christian also got it from a reliable source that Cat was out most nights too. It was becoming a chief concern for everyone in the unit. They were worried that Cat would either burn herself out or make a mistake during a raid and one of the team would get hurt. They'd just gotten Kana back on her feet; they were damned if they'd take a chance at losing another member of their family.

Stevie was the one to finally break the silence, one day right before a raid. She asked Cat directly if she felt she was overdoing it a bit.

"Why do you ask?" Cat replied defensively, her blue eyes closed off.

Stevie looked back at her, her emerald green eyes narrowing. "Because it might be my husband that gets shot when you can't hack it, that's why," she said, her voice tight with reined-in anger.

Cat's chin came up an inch as she caught the implication. She stared back at Stevie for a long moment, then nodded. Turning, she walked away, pulling the slide back on her gun. That day, it was Cat that took the punishment when she blocked a punch that was meant for Donovan. The force of the block threw her back into a wall. Donovan turned in time to grab the guy before he had a chance to do any further damage. Kevin moved to help Cat up off the floor. Cat stood up, nodding to Kevin for the assistance even as she shrugged off his hands. She then continued working the scene.

As they were readying to leave, Cat caught Stevie's eye.

"Happy? No one got shot," she said icily. "Least of all your man."

With that Cat turned and walked out of the house and to her vehicle. Starting it with a roar, she drove off, reaching for a cigarette as she did.

Stevie stared at Cat's retreating form in shock.

"Nice teamwork..." Christian muttered to his wife.

"Shut up," Stevie said, giving him a narrowed look.

She knew she'd said what everyone was thinking. She also knew Christian was kidding, but Cat's barb had struck home.

Cat's aggressive display to prove she wasn't overdoing it continued, garnering her a number of bruises and cuts and a sprained wrist. Everyone on the team found themselves at the end of a barbed comment or two when they made the mistake of telling her to slow down, or to be careful. She wasn't acting like herself at all, and it bothered everyone.

It bothered Cat too. She knew she was being a bitch, but she couldn't seem to help it. It was the only defense she had at this point to keep from breaking down. Elizabeth hadn't returned to Cat's apartment; she hadn't in fact called or talked to Cat at all since the night Cat had pushed her away. It bothered Cat much more than she wanted to admit, even to herself. She pushed herself harder, wanting nothing more than to fall into bed in the early hours of the morning and sleep like the dead until she dragged herself up to do it all again.

Kana heard about Cat's actions the weekend the Gang got together to celebrate her release from the hospital. She'd been out a week and a half by that time. During the course of the party, which Cat didn't attend, Kana heard comments about Cat pushing her limits beyond belief.

"What's going on?" Kana asked when she caught Dave, Donovan, and Christian talking about Cat again.

Dave glanced at the other two men. They both nodded, agreeing that they should tell Kana. Cat had been with her, after all—maybe she could talk some sense into the girl.

"Cat's been way overdoing it lately," Dave said, shaking his head.

"Overdoing it how?" Kana asked, her expression darkening.

"She's in the office before the sun is even up," Christian said.

"And she never leaves till long after the rest of us have packed it in," Donovan added.

"And I've heard when she's not working, she's out closing down the bar," Christian finished.

Kana's lips tightened in a grimace. Cat was indeed overdoing it. Kana knew she'd been totally remiss in not talking to her about everything that had happened. Palani had confided in Kana that it had been Cat who had prompted her return to the hospital after Kana's fever. She'd told her the whole story. Kana had known that she needed to talk to Cat about what had happened, she just hadn't worked up the right words yet.

"Do you think you could talk to her, K?" Dave asked, his concern for Cat obvious.

Kana looked pensive. "I think I'm about the last person she's gonna listen to at this point," she said, sounding chagrined at the thought.

Glancing around, Kana caught sight of Susan talking to Midnight.

"Susan," she called.

Susan turned her head, and came to stand next to Dave. "Yes?" she said, her English accent as sophisticated as ever.

"Where's your sister these days?" Kana asked without preamble.

Susan looked surprised by the question. "Elizabeth?"

Kana nodded.

"She's in England," Susan said, sounding as perplexed by the question as she looked.

"How long has she been there?"

Susan thought for a moment. "About two weeks, I'd say."

Kana nodded. "When's she coming back?"

"I'm not sure, really," Susan replied, a question in her tone.

Again Kana nodded. "Next time you talk to her—and make it soon—have her call me."

"Alright…" Susan said, still looking confused. She noticed, however, that Dave had started to nod.

Kana looked at Dave. "If she steps it up, let me know." She glanced down at Palani, who'd come over. "I'll intercede if it comes to that," Kana told Dave. He nodded, as did Christian and Donovan.

"Can I ask what that was about?" Midnight asked Kana a few minutes later on the back patio of the house.

Kana looked over at Midnight, her eyes gauging, then shrugged.

"I think your niece has a thing for Cat," she said. "And I tend to think Liz is the only person Cat will listen to at this point."

Midnight stared back at Kana, her eyes widening at first, then narrowing.

"I don't think I like the direction this is going," she said, shaking her head.

Kana's glance at Midnight was sharp, as was her tone when she asked, "Why's that? Gay friends are one thing, but you don't want one in the family?"

It was Midnight's turn to give Kana a scathing look. "As a matter of fact, I'm more concerned that my rebel without a clue niece will fuck Cat's career over with her antics, Kana."

Kana's mouth dropped open. She snapped it shut a moment later and shook her head. "I'm sorry," she said, sounding truly so. "I just thought…"

"I know, K," Midnight said, putting her hand on her friend's arm. "But believe me, I don't care if my niece likes women on Harleys who wear tutus as long as she's happy. I just don't want her doing anything to shock everyone and taking Cat out with her, you know?"

Kana nodded, quite embarrassed that she'd jumped to conclusions.

"I think Liz has done a lot more growing up lately than any of us give her credit for," she said.

"What makes you say that?" Midnight asked, surprised. Elizabeth had always been the one everyone rolled their eyes and shook their heads about. For Kana to be championing her, she must have made some kind of impression on the usually quite reserved woman.

"She came to see me in the hospital one night. And she basically told me that if I hurt Cat again, she'll hire someone to kill me," Kana said, grinning at the thought.

Midnight was shocked. "She said that?"

"Yep," Kana said. "And I don't think she'd do that if Cat didn't mean a lot to her. Why put herself out there like that?"

"True..." Midnight said, nodding, her eyes narrowed in thought. "But then why'd she take off for England in such a hurry?"

"I don't know. But it sounds like it was right after that night she threatened me, so..."

"So maybe something else happened we don't know about," Midnight said, finishing Kana's thought.

"Well, if Susan gets her to call me, I'll tell her to get her ass back here, that Cat needs her. Hopefully that'll take care of the problem."

"Hopefully," Midnight said.

***

Elizabeth called Kana the following day. She'd been out the whole night before, and had received a message from her sister upon returning to her London flat at eight in the morning. The message was simple.

"Kana wants you to contact her, Elizabeth," Susan had said, her sophisticated tone making her sound more uptight. "Do it, it's quite important."

Elizabeth had rolled her eyes at her sister's tone, but had called Kana all the same, having to contact Midnight to get the number.

"Kana, it's Elizabeth Endicott. My sister said you wanted me to call you."

"Do you care about Cat?" Kana asked without preamble.

Elizabeth was surprised. After a moment she nodded. "Yes, I care about her. Why? Has something happened?"

"Not yet," Kana said. "But if you don't get your ass back here soon, something could."

"What's going on, Kana?" Elizabeth asked, not liking the tone of this conversation at all.

"She's working herself into the ground, and getting herself pretty beat up in the process. She's burying herself, and I think you might know how to help her."

"Is it possible it's because of you?" Elizabeth couldn't help but snap.

"It's possible," Kana agreed evenly. "But I don't think she'll listen to me. I think she will listen to you."

"Why do you think that?"

"You know why I think that."

Elizabeth was silent. She knew she couldn't answer that. After a moment she sighed. She couldn't risk something happening to Cat if there was any chance she could help.

"I'll get back there as soon as I can," she said.

"Good," Kana said. "And Elizabeth?"

"Yes?" Elizabeth said, her mind already racing to figure out the fastest way to get back to San Diego.

"Thank you," Kana said somberly.

Elizabeth was surprised to hear the big woman expressing gratitude. She was fairly sure Kana had always written her off as a twit, like many of her aunt's friends had. Having Kana thank her now was surprising.

"Don't thank me yet," she said. "I have no idea what I'm going to say to Cat."

"You'll think of something," Kana said, grinning.

Elizabeth sighed. "I'll have to, won't I?"

Elizabeth walked into Cat's apartment at 9 p.m. that night. It had been a horrendously long day. She'd scheduled a flight that ended up getting delayed, so she'd been sitting in an airport or on a plane for over twenty hours. Between that, not getting any sleep the previous night, and the time difference, she was exhausted. She was also determined to talk to Cat before she rested.

She heard the stereo on in Cat's bedroom, so she walked down the hall. Cat was lying on her bed asleep, on her stomach, her arms to either side of her head, her face turned to the side. She wore navy blue sweats and a navy blue tank top. Elizabeth noted the Ace bandage on one wrist, and a number of bruises on her arms and back.

Kana hadn't been exaggerating about Cat getting herself beat up in the process of burying herself.

"Cat," Elizabeth said softly as she walked over to the bed.

She shrugged out of her coat, laying it aside on Cat's hope chest by the window. She wore a blue silk camisole top, a white denim miniskirt, and tan heeled ankle boots.

Cat stirred, turning her head to squint up at Elizabeth. Groaning, she moved to sit up, rubbing her eyes as she did.

The bathroom light was on, so Elizabeth could see her clearly. She sat down on the bed, only a foot away from Cat. Elizabeth scanned Cat's face. She had a cut lip, and a bruise on one cheek as well.

"Good Lord..." Elizabeth said, reaching up to touch the bruise.

Cat didn't move, looking back at Elizabeth. "I didn't think you were even talking to me anymore."

Elizabeth made a face, shaking her head. "Nonsense," she said, her English accent making her sound very proper. "I value our friendship much more than that, Catalina."

Cat said nothing, just stared back at Elizabeth for a long minute.

"I thought you were in England," she said eventually.

"I was this morning," Elizabeth said. "I just got back, and came here."

"Why?" Cat asked, her eyes narrowing slightly in suspicion.

"Because I needed to know something," Elizabeth said, her tone changing slightly.

"What did you need to know?"

Elizabeth gazed back at her for a moment, then without a word, she leaned in and kissed Cat's lips softly. Without pulling back, she kissed her again, reaching up to touch Cat's cheek. Cat tensed for a moment, not sure how to react. Elizabeth continued her exploration of Cat's lips undaunted, moving closer to her on the bed. She moved her other hand to Cat's shoulder, hesitantly at first. When Cat's hand slid into her hair, Elizabeth became much more sure of herself, and began to caress Cat's skin.

Cat deepened the kiss as she slid her other hand around Elizabeth's back, pulling her closer. Elizabeth groaned against her lips, her breath coming faster as a thrill went through her body. There was no hesitation then. Elizabeth's touch was tentative at first, but grew more sure as Cat expertly caressed her, making her body feel like it was on fire.

"Cat, please..." Elizabeth whispered desperately, not sure what she was asking for but wanting more.

Cat pushed her back, laying her down on the bed and moving over her, her lips moving from Elizabeth's, down her neck. Cat caressed her shoulders, her fingers brushing down, dangerously close to very hard nipples. Elizabeth groaned out loud, grasping at Cat's shirt. When Cat slid the straps of the camisole down, exposing her breasts, Elizabeth moaned softly. She cried out a moment later when Cat's mouth touched her.

"God, please..." she begged. "Please..."

Within minutes Elizabeth was beside herself with excitement. She was writhing under Cat's touch, tugging at Cat's shirt, wanting it off. Cat reached up, pulling off her shirt and tossing it aside, then did the same to Elizabeth's. She continued undressing them both. When they were naked, it wasn't long before Elizabeth was crying out in her release, saying Cat's name over and over again, her voice straining as waves of ecstasy washed over her. She was unable to believe the force of her orgasm—it was incredible. Cat knew exactly how to touch her, where and with just the right amount of pressure. What Cat had said about women knowing what women want was very, very true.

Afterward, Elizabeth lay panting in an effort to catch her breath. Cat's lips were pressed against her neck as she lay next to her. Cat stroked her skin softly. It felt so good, Elizabeth couldn't believe she'd ever doubted how this would feel with Cat.

"Is that what you needed to know?" Cat asked softly, her lips still against Elizabeth's skin.

"Yes," Elizabeth said, still breathless.

Cat grinned. "Even this doesn't make you gay, you know."

"What doesn't?" Elizabeth asked, furrowing her eyebrows.

"Enjoying sex with a woman."

Elizabeth was quiet for a long moment. "Well, perhaps that doesn't make me gay," she said amiably, "but I'm fairly sure being in love with you does."

Cat didn't move for a few moments, Elizabeth's words sinking in slowly. She lifted her head when they did, however, shocked.

"You what?" Cat asked disbelievingly.

"Love you," Elizabeth replied confidently.

Cat's mouth dropped open as she stared down at Elizabeth. She closed it and started to shake her head.

"Don't you dare," Elizabeth said, narrowing her eyes. "Don't you dare try and tell me I don't know how I feel about you. I know exactly how I feel. My heart has loved you for the longest time, and my soul belongs to you. I just needed to know if my body could too. And it does."

Cat blinked a few times, trying to assimilate what she was hearing. She'd purposely avoided her deeper feelings for Elizabeth all this time, because the girl was as straight as straight got. Regardless of Cat's theory about every woman being capable of being bisexual, she'd never thought Elizabeth was the type.

"Say something," Elizabeth begged, worry in her eyes now.

Cat stared down at her for a long moment, then a slow smile spread over her face. She laughed softly, shaking her head again. "You definitely know how to shock the hell out of someone."

Elizabeth laughed too. "I've become quite accomplished at that over the years," she said, then reached up to touch Cat's cheek. "But I'm not trying to shock you. I'm telling you the truth."

"That's what's so shocking, babe," Cat said. Leaning down, she kissed Elizabeth's lips. She pulled back, looking into her eyes. "And I love you."

It was Elizabeth's turn to be shocked, her eyes widening dramatically. "You do?"

"Thought you were alone, honey?"

Elizabeth said nothing for a moment. "I—Well, I didn't…" she stammered. "I thought you were still in love with Kana."

"I was never in love with Kana," Cat said. "I love her, and it hurt a lot, feeling like second best. But you were someone I was never going to have, so I never even considered it." She lowered her head, kissing Elizabeth's shoulder. "But I fell in love with the little girl that had to scream to be heard."

"And I fell in love with the first person who ever listened to me when I whispered," Elizabeth said, tears clouding her eyes.

Cat smiled fondly, leaning down to kiss Elizabeth's lips, deepening the kiss as they began to touch again. It was another couple of hours before they talked again.

"Cat?" Elizabeth queried. She was lying in Cat's arms, snuggled against her under the covers, her head resting against Cat's shoulder.

"Hmm?" Cat murmured tiredly.

"I know what I want to name the restaurant."

"Finally made a decision on that, huh?" Cat said, grinning. Elizabeth had been totally at a loss for a name for the restaurant that was due to open within a month.

"Yes," Elizabeth said, raising her head to look at Cat. "I want to name it Catalina's."

Cat was stunned, and it showed. "But babe, it's your restaurant. Why not your name?"

"Because if it wasn't for you, I would never have done this. Wait till you hear what I want to call the bar portion…" she said, trailing off mischievously.

"Oh shit," Cat said, rolling her eyes. "What?"

Elizabeth smiled. "Cat's Bet."

Cat's eyes widened, then she shook her head. "No, absolutely no."

"My bar, I can name it what I want," Elizabeth replied pertly.

"Brat," Cat replied, the beginnings of a grin on her lips.

"But your brat."

"Uh-huh," Cat said. "And how's your family going to feel about that?"

Elizabeth thought about it for a moment, then shrugged. "My mother accepted that Susan was seeing a narc."

"Honey," Cat said, "you're seeing a narc who's a woman."

"Ohhhh…" Elizabeth said. "I didn't think of it that way." Then she shrugged, looking wholly unconcerned. "I don't care what anyone thinks. I love you. If they don't like that, then bugger them."

Cat laughed. "If you say so."

"And I do."

"Then so be it," Cat said, making a gesture of finality.

Elizabeth laughed softly, then laid her head back against Cat's shoulder. She felt warm, safe, and extremely happy. She flexed her fingers, which rested on Cat's stomach, feeling Cat's arms tighten around her in response. They fell asleep lying close, touching each other fondly.

Cat and Elizabeth spent the next few days hanging out. Cat took Friday off, and they were able to spend the weekend just relaxing at the apartment and the beach. Elizabeth found that Cat was just as warm and fun to be with as ever, only now there was something deeper to their relationship. She quickly developed a sense for when Cat was tired. Elizabeth found herself encouraging Cat to sleep, while she made a point of ordering dinner, remembering Cat's favorites from the times they'd dined together.

One evening they were listening to the radio, and a song came on that Elizabeth liked.

"This song is good," she said, picking up the remote and turning it up.

The lyrics were interesting. Cat listened, raising an eyebrow at Elizabeth with a grin. The song talked about being together no matter what anyone else thought. It was a nice thought—it just wasn't realistic.

"Not quite as sure about us as you'd like to think," Cat observed when the song ended.

Elizabeth pressed her lips together in consternation, her eyes lowered.

Cat reached over, touching her under the chin. Elizabeth looked at her.

"It's okay if you're scared," Cat said. "Hell, I am too. You happen to be the niece of my chief, and the sister-in-law of my boss."

"They wouldn't do anything like fire you, Cat," Elizabeth said, shaking her head. "My aunt never mixes her personal business with the department."

Cat nodded, not looking totally convinced but not willing to argue with Elizabeth. What was the point? If she got fired, she got fired.

"So, tell me what you're worried about," Cat said, picking up her wine glass and taking a drink.

Elizabeth was quiet for a long moment, then sighed. "I don't know, really. I guess part of me is worried that my family won't accept it, that they'll be angry with me..." She shook her head. "I always tell myself I don't care what anyone thinks, but... I guess when it comes right down to it, I still want them to love me, you know?"

Cat nodded, looking like she did truly understand. "No one has to know about this, Bet," she said softly. "They already know we're friends, so it's not like they'll be surprised if we spend a lot of time together."

Elizabeth made a face, a kind of a grimace. "That's not fair to you, Cat. I'm with you—I don't want to hide it."

Cat gave her a pained look. "You can't have it both ways, babe," she said gently.

"I know," Elizabeth said, taking a deep breath and blowing it out. "That's why I'm going to let my family know exactly what's going on between us, and to hell with what they think."

Cat looked back at her for a long moment, shaking her head and rolling her eyes. "You do whatever you feel is best, Bet," she said. "Don't worry about me."

"Bugger that," Elizabeth said, making a face again. "I've spent my life thinking of me first. You're the first person I ever wanted to care about more than I care about myself. I'll be damned if anyone is going to make me become selfish again where you're concerned."

"Okay, okay, babe, I got it…" Cat said, grinning.

They spent the rest of the evening pointedly talking about other things.

However, on Monday morning, Cat was surprised when Elizabeth got up when Cat did for work.

"Where are you going?" Cat asked, raising an eyebrow at Elizabeth as she climbed out of bed.

"With you."

"To work?" Cat asked, shocked.

"Yes," Elizabeth said, giving her a challenging look.

"Okay…" Cat said, shaking her head as she walked into the bathroom to take a shower.

An hour later they left the apartment, driving toward the office.

"Just do me a favor," Cat said when they were halfway there.

"What's that?" Elizabeth asked, glancing over at Cat, who was smoking a cigarette with the driver's window open.

"Don't be too blatant, okay?" Cat said, her look pointed.

"You mean, openly affectionate?" Elizabeth clarified.

"Right. I do work there—it's not something I want to put in people's face."

"But your team knows, don't they? And Dave?"

Cat nodded. "Yeah, they know. But it's not something I run around advertising on a billboard, okay?"

"Got it."

Once in the office, Cat was happy to note that none of Rogue Squadron were in yet. She showed Elizabeth her desk, then pointed out who sat where. Elizabeth knew everyone in the squad with the exception of Kevin, since he was newer. Cat turned on her computer, then took a short walk with Elizabeth to get coffee. When they got back from the cafeteria, she asked Elizabeth what she planned to do with herself for the day.

"Well, I'm going to go upstairs and talk to my aunt for one thing," Elizabeth said, with a sparkle in her eyes.

"Oh Lord," Cat said, rolling her eyes.

Elizabeth laughed softly. "Stop that!" she said, making a face at Cat.

"Uh-huh," Cat said, sitting down at her desk. "Easy for you to say."

"Easy for who to say what?" Christian asked as he and Stevie walked into the office hand in hand.

"Nothing," Cat said, glancing around Elizabeth to smile at the two.

Christian's eyes were already on Elizabeth.

"Liz," he said, nodding curtly.

"Blue," Elizabeth replied, nodding in kind.

"Any trouble lately?" he asked, a jet black eyebrow raised.

"Nothing I can't handle," Elizabeth replied with a narrowed look.

Christian laughed. "Was there ever anything you couldn't handle, Liz?"

"Not bloody likely," Elizabeth replied, chuckling.

Christian looked at Cat then, narrowing his light blue eyes slightly, sensing a change but not commenting on it.

"Good to see you looking rested," he said.

She smiled. "Good to be rested."

Elizabeth turned back to Cat. "I'll be back later. Lunch?"

"If I'm still here," Cat said. "Hopefully no raids will go today, but I'll let you know, okay?"

"Okay."

With that, Elizabeth turned and left the office. Christian's eyes trailed after her, then went back to Cat. He got elbowed by his wife.

"Stay out of it," Stevie said quietly.

Christian only grinned evilly. He got swatted by his wife then.

Elizabeth knocked on her aunt's door.

"Come," Midnight called from within.

Elizabeth pushed open the door, peering inside. Midnight was alone.

"You're back," Midnight said, looking surprised, even as she stood, holding out her arms to her niece.

"Aunt Midnight, I've been back for four days," Elizabeth said, walking over to Midnight and hugging her.

Midnight had always been a source of awe for both Elizabeth and Susan, since they'd been at Midnight and Rick's wedding as little girls. Both had loved Midnight the minute they'd met her.

"You have?" Midnight replied, sounding slightly alarmed.

"Yes," Elizabeth said, moving to sit on the couch. Midnight walked over to join her.

"Uh," Midnight stammered, her look hesitant. "Have you seen Cat, by chance?"

Elizabeth's expression was pensive. "As a matter of a fact, I have. That's why I wanted to come see you."

"Okay…"

Elizabeth hesitated for a long moment, trying to figure out the best way to say what she needed to tell her aunt.

"Cat and I are together," she blurted out, grimacing afterward at how non-subtle that was.

Midnight nodded slowly. "As in a couple." It was a statement, not a question.

"Yes," Elizabeth confirmed, worry in her eyes.

Midnight caught the look and smiled at her niece. "Elizabeth, you know I just want you to be happy. If you're happy with Cat, then I'm happy for you."

"Really?" Elizabeth all but squeaked.

"Yes. I just…" Midnight trailed off as she wondered if she should say something.

"What?" Elizabeth asked, worried again.

"I just want to make sure you're with her for the right reasons, Liz," Midnight said, plunging ahead.

"What do you mean?" Elizabeth asked, her tone become slightly defensive.

Midnight reached out to touch her hands. "Well, tell me this. Why are you with her?"

Elizabeth was silent for a moment. She wasn't sure what Midnight was saying, but she knew she had to be honest.

"Aunt Midnight," she began, "Cat has been so good to me. She took care of me when I had no one to turn to. She listened to me when I needed someone to listen. In the end I fell in love with her for that."

Midnight nodded. She knew Elizabeth was referring to the drugs, but wasn't willing to give Cat's confidence up by telling Elizabeth that she knew.

"Aunt Midnight," Elizabeth said then, her eyes downcast, "I got into drugs. I'm not anymore! But it was Cat that helped me through getting off them. I would never have been brave enough to try it alone, and she was there with me the whole time. She took care of me... No one's ever taken such good care of me."

Midnight smiled sadly. It was a sad statement, but she was fairly sure it was true. For many years, Deborah, Elizabeth and Susan's mother, had been in a very unhappy marriage. She turned her children over to a nanny for the most part. Midnight was fairly sure growing up that way had jaded Elizabeth a great deal. It had certainly made Susan determined to love every child that came within ten feet of her. Elizabeth had gone in a totally different direction.

"Well," Midnight said, squeezing Elizabeth's hands, "it sounds to me like it was meant to be that you two found each other. I know

Cat's had a really hard time, with all that stuff with Kana, so maybe she really needed you too."

"You think so?" Elizabeth asked, her look wondrous. "She always seems so strong to me, like nothing can keep her down for long. She's a lot like you, Aunt Midnight."

"Well, that's not a bad thing, is it?" Midnight asked, grinning.

"No!" Elizabeth exclaimed before she saw Midnight's grin. She laughed then, happy she'd come to her aunt. If Midnight approved, Elizabeth didn't care who else did, not even her mother.

Unfortunately, that theory was put to the test a week later when Deborah called to tell her daughters that she'd be coming to town the next day. Elizabeth didn't know if it was just as Deborah said, that she was coming to town to support Midnight for her election and see Susan in her advance pregnancy, or if it was for a different reason. Either way, she worried all day long about the impending visit.

To add to that dread, Deborah had specifically asked Elizabeth to come and pick up her and Allison, one of Elizabeth's younger aunts, at the airport.

"Please come with me!" Elizabeth begged Cat that morning.

"Why?"

"Because!" Elizabeth said. "I need you there—please, Cat? Please?" she begged, grabbing Cat's hands.

Cat leaned back in her chair, extracting her hands from Elizabeth's so she could pick up her cigarettes and light another one. They were sitting on the balcony, drinking coffee and smoking.

"This isn't a chance for you to put me in Mom's face, is it?" Cat asked after a long while.

"No," Elizabeth said. "She knows you and I are friends—I told her about you when I was in England."

Cat curled her lips in contemplation. Finally she nodded. "Okay, I'll go."

Three hours later she was regretting that decision as they drove up to the airport.

"I'll wait here," she said as she parked at the curb and flashed her badge at airport security.

"Catalina…" Elizabeth said entreatingly.

"Babe, you got me here. Don't push it," Cat said, narrowing her eyes.

Elizabeth sighed, shaking her head. "Fine."

She waited at the gate for her mother and aunt, hugging them when they walked off the plane. Downstairs they chatted aimlessly while they waited for the bags. Elizabeth led them out to the curb, feeling her stomach tighten in nervousness. She wanted this to go well, she really did. She knew Cat was nervous too, because she was leaning against the side of the Blazer, smoking, when they walked out. Elizabeth raised an eyebrow at the butts littering the ground next to Cat's booted foot. Cat grinned, but said nothing as she went to open the back of the car.

"Mother," Elizabeth said, gesturing to Deborah, "this is Cat. Cat, this is my mother, Deborah, and my aunt Allison."

"Nice to meet you," Cat said, nodding to them both.

"And you as well," Deborah said politely, surreptitiously looking Cat over.

Deborah knew full well that this was the woman her daughter was seeing. Midnight had called her and told her about it. Midnight, as usual, was all for the union. Just as she had been when Dave and Susan had gotten together. Midnight assured her that Cat was a good person, and that Elizabeth was in very good hands. Deborah had, of course, been shocked. Her daughter? The one that had been dating men since she was fourteen? Her daughter was gay? No, not Elizabeth—that wasn't possible. She'd asked Midnight if she thought Elizabeth was merely trying to shock everyone again. Midnight had said that she didn't think so, that Elizabeth had been very sincere in her declaration of love for Cat. Deborah was still adjusting to the idea.

Seeing Catalina Roché wasn't helping that adjustment at all. The girl was beautiful! She wasn't what Deborah had pictured as a lesbian. Weren't lesbians more manly looking? She'd seen some over the years—they usually had short hair, didn't use makeup, and wore clothing that made them look more like men than women. But Catalina didn't look anything like that. She had long blond hair, held back from her face in a clip at the back of her head. She wore black leggings with brown knee-high boots, and a long brown suede shirt that fit her perfectly and showed that she had a very nicely shaped body.

She wore makeup—not overly so, but it was obvious makeup wasn't foreign to her. She had it exactly right, so you couldn't really see it, but it enhanced her bright blue eyes and high cheekbones. In truth, Catalina Roché looked like she could pass for a Debenshire, with her coloring and her bone structure. She nowhere near resembled what Deborah was expecting.

Deborah glanced at Allison. She, too, looked shocked.

They'd discussed it on the plane. Allison had asked Deborah what she thought about this union.

"Who ever knows what to think when my wild daughter does something outrageous?" Deborah had said.

"But what if Midnight is right, and she loves this woman?" Allison asked.

Deborah sighed and shook her head. "I guess I'll have to accept it. What choice do I have?"

Allison hadn't answered, merely nodding. Allison was in love with the idea of love. She'd been searching for the perfect relationship for years. Deborah sincerely hoped her youngest sister would find it soon.

In the car, Elizabeth sat up front with Cat, and Deborah and Allison sat in back. Cat ground her teeth, resisting the urge to smoke. Elizabeth's mother was every bit as polished and perfect as she'd heard she was. *I so don't fit into this group*, was all Cat could think, over and over again. She could see where Elizabeth got her sophisticated ways; her mother was the epitome of class.

"So, Cat, is it?" Deborah queried politely.

"Yes," Cat said, glancing over at Elizabeth, who tensed.

"You work for the department, don't you?" Deborah asked.

"Yes. I'm a narcotics officer," she said, grinning as she glanced at Elizabeth, remembering their conversation that first night after getting together.

Elizabeth laughed silently.

"Would you know my son-in-law then?" Deborah sounded slightly surprised.

"Uh," Cat stammered, then remembered. "Yes, Dave's my boss. Sorry, forgot for a minute that your other daughter is married to him."

"You work for Dave?" Deborah asked, sounding pleased for some reason.

"Yes," Cat said. "For about six months now."

"Hmm…" Deborah nodded. "Elizabeth talked a great deal about you while she was in England recently," she said, narrowing her eyes. "She never did mention that."

"I didn't really think about it, Mum," Elizabeth said, glancing back at her mother. "My whole world doesn't center around Susan," she added, her tone growing icy.

Cat reached across the seat and touched Elizabeth's hand. Elizabeth looked at her. Cat shook her head slightly, as if telling her this was not the time or the place to open that up. Elizabeth took a deep breath, expelling it slowly, and nodded.

Deborah watched the exchange, and said nothing. Cat certainly had a way of calming Elizabeth down. That was definitely a plus.

"So, Elizabeth tells me that you've been instrumental in her venture with this restaurant," Deborah said after a long few minutes. "She says you've also become her best friend."

"Mother," Elizabeth began, before Cat could answer, "there's something you need to know right now…" She caught Cat's grimace. "Stop it," Elizabeth said to Cat, giving her a narrowed look. "She needs to know."

"Now?" Cat asked cynically.

"Yes, now."

Cat shook her head, but didn't say anything else.

"Mum," Elizabeth began, taking a deep breath. "Cat and I are more than just friends. We're together... romantically."

Deborah said nothing, merely looking back at her daughter, her face reflecting shock, but not for the reason Elizabeth assumed.

"What I need to know," Elizabeth said contemptuously, "is whether or not you can handle that. Because if you can't—"

"Bet!" Cat put in warningly.

Elizabeth looked across at her.

"Chill," Cat said, her look pointed.

"Not to worry, Catalina," Deborah said, glowering at her daughter. "My daughter always speaks to me like this. Elizabeth, if you'd allow me to answer you before you start handing out ultimatums, you'd know that I just want you to be happy. If Catalina makes you happy, then I'm happy for you."

Elizabeth looked shocked for a moment, then glanced at Cat. Cat grinned, still looking out the windshield.

"Don't be smug," Elizabeth said, giving Cat a sour look. "It's not becoming at all."

"Neither is being a brat," Cat replied, chuckling. "But you carry it off pretty well."

Deborah and Allison were shocked to see Elizabeth stick her tongue out at Cat. Cat merely laughed, shaking her head.

Deborah noted quickly that Catalina was a good influence on Elizabeth. Cat neither gave in to Elizabeth's tendency toward drama nor put up with it. When Elizabeth would start raising a ruckus about something, such as the glasses she'd bought for the restaurant not being exactly perfect, Cat was the voice of reason and eventually out and out strength.

"The glasses are fine, Bet," Cat said reasonably.

"They aren't what I wanted!" Elizabeth raged. "I ordered Arctic Lights—this isn't Arctic Lights. I have no bloody idea what it is!"

Cat nodded, leaning back in her chair and glancing at Deborah, who made a point of looking around the interior of the restaurant.

Cat picked up the glass again, tipping it up and looking at the bottom.

"What brand did you order?" she asked Elizabeth.

"Mikasa. Why?" Elizabeth said, narrowing her eyes.

"It's Mikasa," Cat said, showing Elizabeth the bottom of the glass.

"That's not the point!"

Cat's eyes turned a bit icy as she sat up. "Lower your voice."

"Or what?" Elizabeth challenged, her blue eyes fiery.

"Want to find out?" Cat asked, moving to stand.

"No!" Elizabeth exclaimed quickly, reaching to touch Cat on the shoulder. "I'm sorry, Cat. Please," she whispered intently.

"Don't ever talk to me like the help, Bet," Cat said sternly.

"I'm sorry, Cat, I didn't mean to," Elizabeth said, touching Cat's cheek, smoothing her thumb over her cheekbone.

Cat nodded, not saying anything. Elizabeth's eyes searched Cat's face, clearly worried. Deborah had never seen her daughter called to task for her behavior. Nor had she ever seen her daughter concerned about her effect on someone else's feelings. Elizabeth was terrified at that moment, and it was evident. Cat hadn't raised her voice nor her hand to Elizabeth, and that meant that it wasn't fear of Cat that led to Elizabeth's concern. It was fear of losing this woman.

Later, in the Blazer on the way back to Elizabeth's apartment, where Deborah was staying, Elizabeth watched Cat from the passenger seat, searching her profile. Cat was smoking, having asked Deborah if she minded.

"You're not going to stay tonight, are you?" Elizabeth asked Cat knowingly.

Cat looked thoughtful for a moment. "I need to get back to my apartment and do some laundry."

"You can do it at mine," Elizabeth said softly.

"I need to check on the place, Bet. I don't have the security you have—the punks in the neighborhood could be cleaning me out as we speak."

"Well, if you'd just be reasonable and move into my apartment..." Elizabeth said, rolling her eyes heavenward.

"Don't start," Cat said, narrowing her eyes.

"It makes sense, Catalina," Elizabeth said entreatingly.

"Three thousand a month doesn't make sense to anyone, Elizabeth," Cat said, giving her a firm look.

"I'm paying it either way."

"And spending all your time at my place."

"My point exactly."

"Mine too," Cat said, grinning. "Give up your apartment and move into mine."

Elizabeth narrowed her eyes. "Give up yours and move into mine."

"Not at 3K a month, babe—not for you or anyone."

"I'll pay the rent!" Elizabeth exclaimed, exasperated.

Cat gave her a quelling look. "How many times do I have to remind you that you don't have to pay me to stay with you?"

"I'm not paying you to stay with me," Elizabeth said stridently. "I just want us to have a nice place to live."

"You're saying my apartment isn't nice?" Cat replied, raising an eyebrow.

"Oh Lord!" Elizabeth said, rolling her eyes. "I'm saying that my apartment has three bedrooms, yours has one."

"How many do we need?" Cat replied mildly.

Deborah smiled in the back seat. Cat certainly wasn't interested in the fact that Elizabeth was a multi-million-dollar heiress. She found it quite refreshing that Elizabeth had finally found someone that couldn't be bought. Maybe that's what her daughter had needed all along.

Deborah realized that Elizabeth was looking to her for assistance. She shook her head. "Time to compromise, love."

Elizabeth scowled, and noted that Cat was grinning. "Quit that!" she exclaimed, grinning herself.

The apartment issue had been ongoing. Cat refused to allow Elizabeth to pay her rent, so she wouldn't move into Elizabeth's apartment and let Elizabeth pay. She also refused to live in an apartment that cost as much as a house. Elizabeth had even suggested that she could buy them a house. Cat had resoundingly turned down that idea.

"Alright," Elizabeth said, looking stubborn. "How would we compromise on this?"

"You move into my apartment."

"Catalina!" Elizabeth said, scowling.

Cat laughed. "What?"

"Be reasonable."

"Fine," Cat said, nodding. "Find something decent for 2K a month—that I can afford."

"Oh, you're not paying our rent."

"Neither are you."

"We'll split it then."

"Fine."

"Fine."

"Can you find something for that amount?" Cat asked.

"I think there are smaller apartments in my complex for something around there…"

"Not around, babe—no more than 2K a month."

Elizabeth grinned. "I know, I know."

Cat narrowed her eyes. "And no making a deal with the manager to skim part of the rent either."

Elizabeth made a face.

"Keep doing that, and your face will stick like that," Cat said with a grin.

"It hasn't yet," Elizabeth replied pertly.

"Yet," Cat replied, reaching over and touching Elizabeth's hand, taking it and giving it a gentle squeeze. It was her way of telling her that everything was okay between them.

Deborah had never seen a more brilliant smile on her daughter's face. It was definitely going to be an adjustment, her daughter being gay, but Deborah knew that she owed Elizabeth her support, most of all. Elizabeth had been the troublesome child growing up. Wilson, Elizabeth's father, had absolutely no patience for what he considered impertinence. His response to it was to become even colder and more distant.

Deborah had known that Elizabeth was trying to get through to her father by being unruly. She had never known how to explain to her daughter that nothing would work to get through to Wilson. Nothing Deborah herself had done over the years had ever done it; there was no way a mere child was going to affect his busy schedule.

Deborah had never really had a chance to be a mother, even though her own mother had always been loving and kind. Living with Wilson had made Deborah cold and distant, just like him. She'd never realized how much Wilson's attitude had affected hers until she'd divorced him a few years before. By then it had been far too late to reach her wild daughter. Elizabeth had been beyond a simple hug. Deborah had been at a loss as to how to handle her, so she'd concentrated on getting closer to Susan.

She had seen in this short week with Elizabeth that it had hurt her younger daughter immeasurably that Susan had always seemed like the favorite. Deborah also comprehended easily why Elizabeth responded so well to Catalina. Catalina was in essence the loving but firm presence Elizabeth had craved for years.

A month later, Midnight Chevalier won the race for California Attorney General. The reception for her victory party was held at Elizabeth's new restaurant, Catalina's, the night before it opened officially to the public. Everyone was quite impressed with the combination of elegant and hip. As usual, Elizabeth's taste was exquisite, but her sense of style was evident everywhere. The food, made by the best chefs from Paris, Rome, and Switzerland, was fantastic, as was the service. The serving people were the best in the business, all dressed in perfectly tailored pants and crisp, white-collared shirts.

"Good job, babe," Cat said, standing just behind Elizabeth, her hands gentle on Elizabeth's waist.

"You think so?" Elizabeth asked, her eyes shining brightly as she turned to look at her.

"Definitely."

Elizabeth bit her lip, thrilled that everyone, especially Cat, thought the restaurant was nice. Reaching into the pocket of her jacket, Elizabeth pulled out a small box, handing it to Cat.

"What's this?" Cat asked, raising an eyebrow.

"It's a thank you."

"Bet…"

"Catalina, if it wasn't for you, I wouldn't be here tonight, celebrating the opening of my restaurant. Who knows where I'd be—maybe dead, maybe in some drug house," Elizabeth said sincerely as she stared back into Cat's eyes. "You're the reason I'm here, and I want to thank you for that. Please?" she said, her tone beseeching on the last. She knew how Cat felt about her buying her things. Cat's attitude was that she didn't need to buy her love, and she didn't want Elizabeth to ever try.

"Okay, babe, okay," Cat said soothingly, feeling bad that Elizabeth was so apprehensive about displeasing her.

She opened the small box, and nestled inside was a ring. The design was something she'd never seen before. It was a swirl, starting at the left edge of the ring with a black diamond baguette, graduating into a deep violet amethyst, to a deep, rich sapphire, a blue topaz, an emerald, a golden topaz, a surprisingly orange-colored stone, and lastly a rich red ruby baguette. The colors of the ring swirled around to culminate in the final stone, a perfectly cut round diamond. It was beautiful, and Cat was speechless.

"Bet…" she breathed, shaking her head as she looked at the ring, then grinned as it clicked in her head. "It's a rainbow," she said, identifying the internationally known symbol for the gay community.

Elizabeth bit her lip, nodding, her eyes shining. She pointed to the black diamond. "A transition from the dark," she said, moving her finger over the swirl of stones up to the diamond, "into the light."

Cat shook her head, smiling. "I don't know that that's how a lot of people would see it, but okay, honey," she said, leaning in to kiss Elizabeth softly. "Thank you. It's beautiful."

Elizabeth kissed her back. "You're very welcome."

Cat took the ring out of the box and put it on her right ring finger, reaching up to touch Elizabeth on the cheek again, smiling as she looked into her eyes. Then she looked back at the ring in amazement.

"What's the orange stone?" she asked. It was the only one she couldn't identify.

"It's a carnelian agate."

"Got me there," Cat said, winking.

Elizabeth laughed softly, feeling very happy.

"And what's going on here?" Kana asked, walking up with Palani next to her.

"Hi, Kana," Elizabeth said, turning to her with a smile. Cat said nothing, only glancing over at Kana.

They never had talked about all that had happened, and there was still a slight undercurrent between them that was easily felt.

"Palani," Kana said, glancing down at her girlfriend, "this is Elizabeth Endicott. Liz, this is Palani Ryker."

"Lovely to meet you," Elizabeth said. "Officially."

Kana looked mystified for a moment.

"I saw Palani at the hospital, Kana," Elizabeth explained.

"Oh," Kana said, nodding slowly, then looked at Cat. "And I understand you and Palani have already met," she said amiably.

"Yeah?" Cat asked, her look wry.

Kana nodded, narrowing her eyes slightly, sensing Cat's sarcasm and ignoring it—she wasn't about to argue with her. Cat had every right to be pissed at her, and Kana was going to allow her any jabs she felt the need to get in at that point.

"Elizabeth," Palani said, stepping into the silence that followed. "Why don't you and I go get a drink?" She took Elizabeth's hand and led her away.

Kana watched the two go, a grin tugging at her lips. Palani wanted Kana to talk to Cat; she felt that it was something that needed to be done. Kana didn't think now was the time, but obviously Palani did. Kana looked back at Cat, taking a deep breath and expelling it slowly, waiting.

Cat stared back at Kana, refusing to be the first to speak. After a long few minutes, Kana nodded slowly, accepting that she was going to have to make the first move.

"Cat," she began quietly, "I know I need to apologize, but I honestly can't think of a way to right now."

Cat's look was considering as she leaned back against the railing she stood next to. She looked fantastic, wearing a classic black jersey-style dress that clung to her body seductively and exposed a fair amount of beautifully shaped legs clad in sheer black silk. She wore metallic lizard high-heeled sandals with elegant little straps that crisscrossed her feet and circled her ankles. Her makeup, as usual, was perfect, with a rich auburn tint to her lips and just the right touches to make her bright blue eyes glow. She was a beautiful woman—there had never been any denying that.

"I'm not looking for any apologies, K," Cat said with a shrug.

Kana narrowed her eyes, then shook her head. "No, you wouldn't, would you?"

Cat said nothing, only looking back at Kana. After a few moments, she blew her breath out in a sigh and shook her head. "Look, it worked out in the end, right? You're with Palani again, I'm with Elizabeth. I understand you arranged that."

"I didn't arrange anything, Cat. I only told her that you needed her. The rest was all her doing."

"Okay," Cat said, a grin tugging at her lips. "And that's about all I did with Palani too, so we're even, right?"

Kana nodded, not looking even close to convinced. She knew it had cost Cat a lot more emotionally than she was letting on, but Cat wasn't the kind of woman that would bring that up. She was definitely an astounding woman, there was no doubt about that.

Later in the evening, Kana walked by Elizabeth, who was talking to Susan and Dave.

"Hope you realize what you've got," Kana said to her quietly when Dave and Susan moved off to talk to Erin and Kevin.

Elizabeth turned to look up at Kana, narrowing her eyes. "With?" she asked, already sure she knew what the big Samoan woman was referring to.

"Cat."

"I'm fully aware of what I've got," Elizabeth said. "And I'll do anything it takes to hold on to her."

Kana nodded. "Nice ring she's wearing," she said, nodding toward Cat, who was talking to Allison Debenshire. "From you?"

Elizabeth nodded. "If it wasn't for her, I wouldn't be here."

"So long as you realize that."

Elizabeth narrowed her eyes, pursing her lips, considering whether or not she wanted to comment on the fact that Kana herself was responsible for blatantly hurting Cat repeatedly. Kana grinned, sensing easily exactly what Elizabeth was thinking. She leaned down, her lips right next to Elizabeth's ear.

"I know it's tempting," Kana said, "but resist the urge, little girl." She pulled back and winked at Elizabeth, who was staring up at her openmouthed. Kana walked away chuckling to herself.

"What did you do?" Palani asked, putting her arm through Kana's.

"Nothing," Kana replied, almost managing to sound innocent.

Palani narrowed her eyes, then scowled up at Kana. "You better stop picking on Midnight's niece, Kana, or you might get yourself into some trouble."

"Midnight loves me—she wouldn't bust me," Kana said, laughing.

"I what?" Midnight asked, walking by at that point.

"Love me," Kana repeated with a grin.

"Well, yeah, I do," Midnight said with a wink. "But that doesn't mean I won't bust ya. What were you doing now?"

"Harassing your niece," Kana replied with a shrug.

"Which one?"

"The one dating my ex."

"Ah," Midnight said, nodding. "That one, huh?"

"Yup. How's Rick taking it?"

Midnight rolled her eyes. "I think he's convinced it's a phase."

Kana laughed, shaking her head. "He check the ring Cat's sporting, courtesy of his niece?"

"A ring?" Midnight asked, her look pointed.

"Uh-huh..." Kana said, grinning. "And there's a diamond involved."

"Oh boy," Midnight said, both in answer to what Kana and said and the fact that she'd just located Cat—and who should be standing in front of Cat, talking to her, but Rick. "I better go."

Cat had been talking to Allison Debenshire. Allison was surprisingly down to earth and seemed truly thrilled that Elizabeth had apparently found love. It was obvious Allison wasn't used to the idea that Elizabeth was in love with another woman, but she was doing her best to hide that. It had an endearing quality to it, so much so that Cat couldn't bring herself to be the blunt person she usually was when it came to her sexuality.

"So, did you know that Elizabeth was going to name the restaurant after you?" Allison asked, fidgeting nervously.

Cat nodded. "She talked to me about it. I wasn't really for the idea, but she was pretty determined."

"Why didn't you like the idea?" Allison asked, canting her head to the side. Her eyes, exactly the same shade as Elizabeth's, reflected honest curiosity.

"I just think she should have named it after herself. I mean, it's her restaurant, not mine..." Cat trailed off as she saw Rick Debenshire headed toward her, his look intent.

"But she said she would never have started the restaurant without your support," Allison said.

"I think she would have eventually," Cat said, dragging her attention back to Allison, even as she sensed Rick drawing closer.

Rick Debenshire had a presence you couldn't deny. He had a very intense way about him. His manner was direct, even if it was tempered with a generally gregarious personality. When Richard Joshua Debenshire wanted to be noticed, there was no ignoring him. Cat could feel him behind her even before he spoke. He had a rich, English-accented voice with the same hint of sophistication as Elizabeth's.

"Do you honestly believe that?" Rick asked.

Cat turned, searching his face, trying to determine what he was really asking. Finally she nodded.

"I think it was something she wanted for a long time, she just never took the time to try it."

Rick narrowed his eyes in thought, then shook his head. "I don't think she would have undertaken something of this magnitude," he said, gesturing around at the elegant interior of the restaurant. "Not without someone supporting her."

Cat shrugged slightly. "So maybe she would have turned to her family," she said, gesturing to Rick and then Allison.

"And we would have laughed our arses off," Rick replied, allowing a little of his own self-disgust to show.

Cat didn't reply, sensing that Rick was exercising a bit of his own guilt over ignoring Elizabeth's drug problem. She had no intention of contributing to it. Cat knew that he knew that denigrating any aspiration Elizabeth had brought to them would have destroyed her once and for all. She knew she didn't have to say it to him.

Rick was looking at her then—really looking at her, his eyes searching her face, his expression intently serious. "We all owe you a great deal, Catalina. You saw what none of us did."

Cat had no words to reply to him. She had no idea what to say. She was further shocked when Rick stepped closer, extending his hand. She took it, searching his eyes. She was absolutely stunned when he pulled her forward and hugged her. Glancing over his shoulder, she saw Midnight Chevalier-Debenshire standing just behind them, looking shocked as well. Then, as Rick stepped back, his look intent, Midnight walked up, grinning.

"And here I thought I needed to come rescue Cat," she said, putting her arm through Rick's and glancing up at him.

"What from? Me?" Rick asked, looking down at his wife, his grin showing very white teeth.

"Who else?"

Rick looked at Cat, then back at his wife. "Cat's part of the family now, love. I'm forbidden to do any evil."

"Like that's ever stopped you," Joe said from behind him.

"My thoughts exactly!" Midnight said, laughing as she glanced back at Joe, happy to note Randy was with him.

"Actually," Rick said, grinning at Cat mischievously, "being a member of this family tends to attract evil." He nodded at Joe. "Case in point."

Joe scowled at him. "Fuck you, Debenshire," he said with a grin.

"Boys…" Midnight said, giving both her husband and Joe a quelling look, then winked at Cat. Her eyes dropped to Cat's right hand. "Oh, is that the ring?" she asked, reaching out.

Cat grimaced, nodding as Midnight took her hand to examine the ring closer.

"Ring?" Rick asked, looking back at the two women, then leaning in to check out the ring too.

"Holy shit…" Joe said.

"Let me see," Randy said, moving in front of Joe. "Oh… that's beautiful."

"It is," Midnight said, nodding, then glanced at Rick, waiting to see if he got the significance of the rainbow-arranged stones. She knew the moment it clicked, and he looked at Midnight, raising an eyebrow. She gave him a look that told him not to say anything.

"From my niece?" Rick asked Cat.

Cat nodded. "She finally got away with buying me something."

"Trust me," Rick said with a wink, "it won't be the last thing she buys you."

"Over my dead body," Cat replied automatically, narrowing her eyes.

That had everyone laughing. Elizabeth walked up then, having noted the crowd gathering around Cat and wanting to make sure they weren't hassling her. She knew her family, littered with law enforcement ideals and morals that weren't as well adjusted to the idea that she was gay as she would have liked. She didn't want Cat suffering any attacks from them. She was shocked to hear them all laugh at the moment she joined them.

Stepping to Cat's side, she glanced at her uncle. He was smiling.

"He's being evil, isn't he?" Elizabeth asked Cat, her eyes on Rick.

"Me?" Rick asked, affronted.

"Yes, you, Richard," Elizabeth replied, grinning.

"I tell ya…" Rick said, shaking his head. He was assailed with a number of comments about his lack of innocence. It turned out to be a relaxing evening for them all.

When Kana and Palani got back to Kana's house, Kana was tired. She'd been back at work for three days, and it was exhausting her still. Palani had begged her to take it slow, but one look at the desk in her office and Kana was determined to get back to full time.

"I'm going to take a shower," Kana said.

"Are you okay?"

"Yeah. Just a bit sore. I want to soak before I try to go to bed."

"Okay," Palani said. "Do you want anything?"

"Nah," Kana said, grinning. "I think I had enough champagne tonight to last me a lifetime."

Palani laughed softly. It occurred to her then that Kana wouldn't have taken any medication if she'd known she'd be drinking. That was why she was sore. Palani got undressed, taking off her makeup and brushing out her long dark hair. She put on a short black-and-red silk Kimono-style wrap and went into the bathroom to check on Kana.

She was standing with her arms braced above her head on the tiles, the water running down her back. Every so often Kana would move just slightly to direct the hot water to a different spot. Palani stood admiring her physique. Kana had muscles and strength that Palani knew she herself could never achieve, so she respected Kana's body a great deal.

Kana was five foot, ten inches tall, and every inch was lean and powerful muscle, much different from the way she'd looked just a few years before. Kana had always been overweight and just plain bulky. She'd changed her life, learning to eat right, losing weight, and starting to go to the gym. Taking care with her personal appearance. She wore makeup now, but only the faintest amount. Her dark hair was thick, but silky and cut in a long, layered style that softened her features ever so slightly. Kana's face was the broad, chiseled face of a classic Samoan warrior woman. She had a strong jawline, high, broad cheekbones, and coal-black eyes framed with long lashes. Kana had a proud beauty—it certainly wasn't in any way delicate, but she was beautiful all the same. Palani had always thought so.

"Have I told you lately," Palani said from behind Kana, "how beautiful you are?"

Kana glanced over her shoulder, a grin in place. "Looking in the mirror again, babe?"

"Not funny at all, Kana Akua Lee," Palani said, making a face.

"Oh, that's becoming a nasty little habit, babygirl," Kana said with a scowl.

"What's that?" Palani asked brightly.

"You know what," Kana said, turning around and letting the water hit her neck and right shoulder as she looked at Palani. "I'm going to kick Tiny's ass for telling you my middle names."

"Who was Lee, anyway?"

It was a Polynesian custom for a woman to give her child two middle names. They would usually be the mother's maiden name and a token name, often the father's name or that of a dead relative they were honoring. So Akua would have been Kana's mother's maiden name, but Palani knew Lee wasn't Kana's father's name—it was too American, and Kana's father was full-blood Samoan.

"Lee was the doctor that delivered me," Kana said. "Apparently, I was not only breach, but I had the cord wrapped around my neck twice and was almost dead. This American doctor, Lee Camden, came in and assured my mother I'd be fine. He managed to deliver me, revive me, and give me to my mother in minutes. She named me after him for that."

Palani smiled. "Gave your mother trouble from day one, did you?"

"Don't start," Kana said, narrowing her dark eyes at Palani, who only laughed softly.

"Will you be done soon?" Palani asked.

"Yes, babe, soon," Kana said, moving to start washing her hair.

Palani nodded, then went back into the bedroom. She lay down on the bed, picking up the remote and turning the TV on.

"What is this?" Kana called from the bathroom at one point.

"What?" Palani asked, moving to the end of the bed so she could see the shower stall. Kana was holding up a bottle with a purple substance in it. "That's called a body scrub, K. Smell it—it smells good."

Kana opened the bottle and sniffed it, then looked back at Palani. "And?"

"And I thought you might like it," Palani said, shrugging. "It's called Moonlight Path. It's kind of a musk smell like you like... You don't like it?"

Kana sighed, shaking her head and looking up at the ceiling. "I like it, babe, I'm just not quite the Bed and Bath freak that you are."

"I am not a freak!" Palani said, laughing. "I just like to smell good for you. Is that a problem?"

"You trying to tell me something, babe?" Kana asked, her look pointed.

Palani laughed, shaking her head. "No, I love how you smell, K, I just thought you might like that stuff. If you don't, it's okay."

Kana made a face, then went back to her shower, making comments as she did.

"It's got scratchy things in it," she said at one point.

"That would be the scrubbing aspect, honey," Palani replied sweetly.

"Great, a few layers of skin later..." Kana muttered.

"I heard that!" Palani called, hearing Kana chuckle a moment later.

Palani was watching the news by the time Kana came to bed. She had dried her hair and donned her usual black tank top and sweats. She crawled under the covers, pulling Palani back against her as she did.

"All clean?" Palani asked.

"And scrubbed, and missing a great deal of skin," Kana replied, grinning.

Palani turned over, putting her face into Kana's neck and inhaling deeply. "Ohhh... and you smell wonderful..."

"Mmhmm," Kana said, closing her eyes and smiling. Her hands slid over the short silk Kimono. "And I so like this," she said, grinning as she touched bare skin.

"We need to discuss your sleeping attire, however," Palani said playfully.

"Oh, I see..." Kana began, leaning down to kiss Palani's lips, her arms tightening around her waist, pulling her closer and half over her body.

"Mmm..." Palani moaned softly. "I want to see just as much skin as you, K," she added, laughing softly.

They talked for a few minutes, discussing the party and Midnight's election.

"I didn't realize she's the first female Attorney General California's had," Palani said.

"Yep," Kana said. "If anyone could do it, it would have to be Midnight."

Palani smiled. "There's no end to the loyalty you have for her, is there?"

"Nope."

Palani nodded, biting at the inside of her lip. "Did you get things resolved with Cat?"

"Isn't that what you abandoned me to do?" Kana asked mildly.

"I didn't abandon you," Palani said, giving her a narrowed look. "I gave you and Cat some modicum of privacy to try and resolve some issues you two still had."

"Uh-huh," Kana said, looking unconvinced.

"So did you?"

Kana shrugged. "As best one can with someone like Cat."

"What does that mean?"

"It means that Cat is one of those people that doesn't wait for an apology," Kana said, her tone reflecting the grimace she made. "If you hurt her, she lets you know, and if you want to apologize, that's your decision. She sees her and I as even right now, for what I did in getting Elizabeth to come home from England to check on her."

"You don't sound like you feel that way."

"I don't," Kana said. "She went through a lot of shit because of me and for me, and it's not so easily fixed as she'd like to pretend."

Palani nodded. "But she is with Elizabeth now."

"I know. But that doesn't mean I won't be there for her if she needs me."

Again Palani nodded slowly, understanding that Kana meant that in a friendship way, not romantically.

"That ring Elizabeth gave her seemed pretty serious though, didn't it?" Palani asked.

"Fairly serious." Kana nodded. "But Cat isn't really one for serious, so I don't know that it got Liz anywhere."

"Speaking of rings..." Palani said, looking pointedly at Kana's left hand.

Kana rolled her eyes heavenward, looking like a kid who'd just gotten caught.

"Where is it?" Palani asked, referring to the platinum and black diamond ring she'd given Kana before they'd broken up. When Kana didn't answer, Palani's eyes widened. "You didn't throw it away..." she said, her voice trailing off in disbelief.

"Hell no," Kana said. "I know how much you paid for that ring—I wouldn't just throw it away. Besides, there was an emotional attachment there," she said, chagrin evident on her face.

"Good!" Palani exclaimed. "Now where is it?"

"In my top drawer," Kana said with a sigh.

Palani got up from the bed and walked over to Kana's dresser. When she opened the drawer, she saw the picture she'd given Kana the year before, the one taken by a professional photographer, capturing her at a very poignant moment when she'd been thinking of Kana. So she'd kept that too? *Good*, Palani thought. Picking up the black velvet box, she opened it and took out the ring. A platinum band inset with black diamond baguettes, it was intricately carved with Polynesian symbols.

Walking back to the bed, Palani slowly sat down next to Kana, her expression very serious. Kana was watching her, an amused grin on her lips. Palani took Kana's left hand, putting the ring on it slowly, looking straight into Kana's eyes.

"Marry me, Kana," she said softly.

"What?" Kana said, shocked.

Palani took Kana's hand, placing it on her cheek, her dark eyes staring down into Kana's. "I want this to be permanent, you and I here, together."

"We are permanent, babe," Kana said soothingly.

"I want more, Kana," Palani said, sliding her hand over Kana's arm, up her shoulder. "I want to belong to you, and you to me, officially."

Kana didn't reply for a long few moments, but her thoughts were clear on her face. Same-sex marriages were still fairly controversial, and Kana was the last person to participate in something that she felt was more for show than for sincere purposes.

"Babe," she began, her tone placating but firm. "You know I'm not into that kind of thing…"

"I know, Kana, I know," Palani said, nodding. "But it doesn't have to be like a regular wedding—it's more like a dedication of ourselves to each other…" She trailed off as she realized that Kana wasn't likely to give in on this.

Kana stared back at Palani for a long moment, trying to think of a way to say no gently. But then she really looked into Palani's eyes. It was obvious in the way she was grasping at Kana's shirt, the way her lower lip trembled, and the way she was blinking back tears of desperation, that Palani really wanted this.

"What are you afraid of, Palani?" Kana asked softly.

"I'm afraid I'll lose you again," Palani whispered. "That some other misunderstanding will have you sending me away again. If we're committed to each other, we'll have to talk, we'll have to work through things… won't we?"

Kana closed her eyes for a moment. Palani was right about that. If she was in a sanctified "marriage," she'd be less likely to allow her temper to run Palani off again. It had been her temper that had separated them before, and in the end she'd been wrong.

Kana sat up, pulling Palani into her arms and kissing her softly on the lips. "I'm not wearing a dress," she said simply.

Palani's eyes lit up so bright, it was almost painful to see. "Oh, Kana!" she cried, hugging her tight, pressing her lips against Kana's neck, whispering, "Thank you," over and over again.

After a few minutes, Palani raised her head, looking into Kana's eyes. "There's one more thing…"

"Oh Lord, what now?" Kana asked, rolling her eyes but grinning all the same.

Palani bit her lip, wincing. "I want to have a baby…" she said, trailing off as she saw Kana's look. It was somewhere between dumbfounded and annoyed.

"You want to have a baby."

"Yes," Palani replied determinedly. In truth, she was shocked Kana had agreed to the marriage so easily. She'd expected it to take days, weeks, even months to talk her into it.

"Why?"

"I want to be a mother, Kana. That was the one and only good thing about being pregnant before. I was going to be a mother…" Her voice trailed off as she thought about what she'd lost.

Kana took a deep breath, expelling it slowly. "Do you realize how hard that's going to be on not only you and me, but on the child as well?"

"Kana, we can't stop prejudice—it's as old as the world itself. We have a right to be parents, we have a right to want a baby. So we have to go about getting one differently than regular couples—so what? Lots of couples can't have babies and have to adopt. I want a baby, Kana, a child to raise with you. To love and cherish, and teach that love isn't about appearance, or money, or gender—it's about being connected to one person with your heart and your soul."

Again Kana was silent, mulling over what Palani had said. Thinking about the process, the effects, and how it would change their lives. Palani waited in silence, knowing that Kana wasn't one to make a rash decision on anything. She liked to look at something from all angles. She also knew that pushing Kana only made her push back. It was never wise.

Finally Kana sighed. "I'll agree to both, on two conditions."

Palani was so shocked, she couldn't think straight for a moment. Finally she nodded excitedly. "Okay, what conditions?" she asked, willing to do anything at this point.

"One," Kana said, holding up a finger and putting it to Palani's lips. "Does anyone in your family, other than Sampson, know about you?"

Palani bit her lip again, and shook her head slowly.

"Okay, that's the first condition," Kana said. "If we're going to do this, and have a baby too, your family needs to know, Palani. I can't start a life like this based on any kind of charade. They need to know who I am to you, and that we're going to bring a child into the world as its parents, their grandchild."

Palani nodded, understanding what Kana was saying. Kana knew how important family was to both of them, and she wouldn't allow Palani to go on lying to hers. Not if they were going to be committed to each other for life.

"I can't do it on the phone though, Kana."

"I figured that," Kana said. "We can go to Hawaii and do it together if you'd like."

Palani nodded, relieved. The thought of telling her parents and her brothers terrified her. She knew she could do it with Kana by her side.

"What's the second condition?" she asked.

"The second condition is about the baby. If you're going to get pregnant, I want to use sperm from one of my brothers," she said, grinning slightly. "Then at least the baby is still part Sorbinno."

"Will one of your brothers agree to that?"

Kana nodded. "Yeah. Nat's sworn he's never having kids of his own, so I'm betting he'll do it."

"I think that's a great idea," Palani said, excited at the prospect of the baby actually having both hers and Kana's genes

Kana smiled. "Good, then we're agreed."

Palani threw her arms around Kana's neck, kissing her deeply. She'd never believed it would be easy to convince her. She'd been determined, but she'd fully expected to have to beg, plead, harass, and downright threaten if it came down to it to get Kana to agree. Palani didn't think she could be happier.

Chapter 9

Kana sat on the lanai of her parents' home. It was very early morning, and the sun was just rising. She wore her black sweatpants and tank top. It was raining and chilly, but Kana didn't feel it at all. She was smoking and drinking fresh-ground Kona coffee, enjoying the rain and feeling very much at peace.

She and Palani had flown into Hawaii the night before. They'd gotten to Kana's family home at 10 p.m. Kana knew her family would be asleep, and also that her mother had set her and Palani up in the guest house down the long steps from the main house. So Kana had led Palani down to the guest house and they'd gone to bed. Palani had been shocked at the size of Kana's family home. Kana had only grinned in amusement at Palani's obvious surprise.

As was her normal habit, Kana awoke early, even earlier than normal given the three-hour time difference. She'd climbed carefully out of bed at 5 a.m., not wanting to wake Palani. She'd walked up to the main house, encountering many people along the way. Things started early on the coffee plantation; it was harvesting time for the coffee bean, or "coffee cherries," as they were accurately called. Kana had gone to the big kitchen and made a fresh pot of coffee.

She was on her third cup when her mother walked out onto the lanai.

"Kana," her mother said, walking over and hugging her daughter, kissing her on the cheek.

"Good morning, Ma," Kana said.

Aveolela—everyone called her Ave—sat down next to her daughter, looking her over. "You look very content."

Kana glanced over at her mother, grinning. "I am, Mama. Life is good right now."

Aveolela nodded, pleased. "Where is this girl you are committing to?"

"She's still asleep," Kana said. "I've always been an early riser, Ma."

"Growing up on a plantation does that."

Kana smiled as she took another sip of coffee. "It never tastes like this on the mainland."

"It's never as fresh on the mainland."

Kana nodded.

They were both silent for a long while, each looking out over the landscape. Kana's family home was situated high on one of Kona's many hills. The landscape below was lush and green and went down to the ocean's edge. The Sorbinno plantation was among the largest of the independent farmers' on Kona. Their family company was named Fire Mountain Coffee, out of respect for the volcano that provided the rich soil in which they farmed.

Ave reached over, touching her daughter's arm. "You are okay?" she asked, concern tinging her voice.

"Yes, Mama, I'm okay," Kana said. She knew her mother was referring to her being shot.

"We were told you almost died…"

Kana nodded seriously. "I did, but Palani pulled me back."

Ave said nothing, but looked surprised by that admission. Kana was the second-oldest of her nine children. She had never been one to be emotionally involved with people. It had shocked the entire family when, months before, Kana had come home devastated over a ruined relationship. She hadn't talked about what had happened, but it had been obvious she was heartsick. Now she was admitting that this girl had pulled her back from the brink of death?

"But you are okay?" her mother confirmed.

"It's taken some time," Kana said, nodding, "but I'm getting there."

Kana picked up her cigarettes, pulling one out and lighting it. Aveolela noticed the ring on Kana's left hand then. Reaching out, she took Kana's hand and pulled it over.

Kana grinned. "Palani gave it to me," she said, smiling fondly.

"It's very beautiful," Aveolela said, awed. "What kind of stone is that?"

"It's a black diamond. The metal is platinum."

"Very expensive."

"Palani has expensive tastes," Kana said affectionately.

"She has good taste. She chose you, right?"

Kana laughed softly. "I suppose. Personally, I think it was pure luck on my part."

"Why do you say that?"

"Wait until you meet her, Ma," Kana said. "You'll understand then."

Aveolela nodded, curious now as to what this young woman had that Kana was so enchanted with. She found out a little while later.

She and Kana were still sitting on the lanai; Kana had just gotten another cup of steaming coffee and was smoking another cigarette.

"Kana?" queried a soft voice from the doorway behind them.

Kana and Ave turned at the same time, but not before Ave saw the brilliant smile that crossed her daughter's face.

"Good morning, honey," Kana said, flicking her cigarette away and holding out her hand.

Palani took it, allowing Kana to gently pull her forward and down onto her lap.

"Mama, this is Palani," Kana said, her hand still in Palani's. "Palani, this is my mother, Aveolela Sorbinno."

Palani smiled shyly, keeping her eyes lowered out of respect for Kana's mother. "It is nice to meet you, Mrs. Sorbinno."

Aveolela noted that the girl kept her eyes lowered—it meant she'd most likely been raised in a traditional Samoan household.

"It is nice to meet you, Palani," she said, reaching out to take the girl's hand.

Palani raised her eyes then, looking into the smiling face and bright eyes of Kana's mother. She felt Kana squeeze her other hand gently.

Aveolela shook her head, looking slightly awed. "It is no wonder my daughter is so enchanted with you. You are very beautiful."

Palani bit her lip. "Thank you," she said modestly.

"Ah," Ave said, her tone one of discovery as her thumb brushed over the ring on Palani's index finger. "This is where your ring went, Kana."

Palani's eyes widened as she glanced back at Kana.

Kana was grinning, looking at her mother. "I gave it to her, Mama."

Ave nodded, smiling at Palani, realizing she'd worried the girl. "Kana had that ring for many years," she explained. "It was her piece of home."

Palani nodded, wondering why Kana hadn't told her the significance of the ring. She'd loved it simply because it was Kana's. Kana had given it to her when they'd been together the year before, when Palani had known she'd miss Kana terribly while on her photo shoot. It was when she knew she was in love with Kana and had finally confessed as much to her. It had been that ring that Jerry Castle had asked about one day while Palani was posing for the photographer. The brilliant smile that had lit Palani's face when she thought of Kana had been the picture that made her famous. It had also resulted in the picture Kana had of Palani biting her lip and looking extremely sultry.

"I got it replaced," Kana said, holding up her left hand with the platinum and black diamond ring on it.

"Oh," Ave said, smiling as she nodded.

"Mama," Kana said then, putting her arms around Palani. "You already know that Palani and I are going to commit to each other. I wanted to tell you also that we're going to have a baby."

"A baby?" Aveolela repeated, looking perplexed.

"Yes," Kana said, nodding indulgently. She knew her mother had no idea how this was going to happen.

"But how?" Ave asked.

"Artificial insemination, Ma," Kana said, knowing her mother was going to roll her eyes at such scientific means to do something natural.

Ave's face creased in the expected frown. "That's so medical, Kana."

"Yes, I know that," Kana said. "But my other option is to let a man touch my girl, and that's just not gonna happen."

Aveolela took a deep breath, nodding, as she struggled to understand.

"Mama," Kana said, putting her hand on the table next to Palani. "Think of it this way. If you wanted more children for whatever reason, would you want Papa to sleep with another woman to get her with child?" She knew her mother was beyond her child-bearing years.

"I'd kill him," Ave answered simply.

"My point exactly," Kana said, smiling.

Ave nodded in understanding then.

"The thing is," Kana went on, feeling Palani shifting uncomfortably and realizing that she was worried about what Kana's mother was going to think of all this, "we want to ask Nat to be the donor."

"Natano?" Ave asked, looking appalled. "Why him?"

Kana laughed, shaking her head. "Mama, stop that."

Ave put her hand on Palani's. "Natano is my laziest child."

"I thought he was a foreman at the mill now, Mama," Kana said.

"He is," Ave said, throwing up her hands. "We couldn't get him to harvest without falling asleep under one of the trees. This way he has an office to sleep in."

"Mama!" Kana said, laughing again.

Ave laughed too. It had been a long-time family joke that thirty-year-old Nat could sleep anywhere.

"His sleeping abilities notwithstanding, Ma," Kana said, "Nat's the healthiest of all the boys, and he's also the best looking."

"And the youngest."

"True," Kana said. "Plus he's said he never wants kids of his own, so I figure he'll be most likely to agree."

Ave rolled her eyes. "Natano with a child? The good Lord help us!"

Kana grinned.

"I never thought I'd have a grandchild from you, Kana," Ave said. "This will be such a pleasure."

Kana felt Palani relax then.

Later that morning, Kana took Palani out for a drive, showing her the plantation and where she'd grown up.

"Why didn't you ever tell me how successful your family is?" Palani asked.

Kana shrugged. "We never really talked about our families, babe."

"True. I guess I just always assumed..." Palani trailed off as she realized what she'd been about to say would sound insulting.

"That my family was low class?" Kana finished for her.

Palani pressed her lips together.

Kana grinned. "It's okay. You knew I was a gang leader, so you thought that meant I came from a low class, right?"

Palani nodded, looking embarrassed.

"Well, that's a lot of times true," Kana said. "And my family is far from rich. Then again, honey, Joe and Rick were both gang members, and they're both from lots of money."

Palani realized that was true. "It's bad to stereotype," she said solemnly.

"It is. But it's also natural," Kana said, reaching over to touch Palani on the cheek.

They spent a relaxing day driving around. Kana took Palani over to Kilauea, one of the two active volcanos on Hawaii. They walked down to the black-sand beach and stood watching the waves and the billowing steam rising up as the lava dropped into the ocean.

Later in the day, Palani persuaded Kana to take her to the one big shopping mall on the island, in Hilo. Kana indulged her, as she often did. Palani walked around the mall, looking at things as Kana trailed after her, often leaning against the wall outside a store, smoking. It was outside one such store that Kana heard something she hadn't heard in over twenty years.

"KanaLee?" a voice said from just beside her.

Kana turned and looked at the woman who had been the reason she'd left Hawaii in the first place. The woman who had been her best friend before she left the Sisters of Samoa and joined another gang. The woman who had eventually challenged Kana to a fight to prove who was the better fighter. When Kana had won, it was this woman who'd put the contract out on her life. The woman who'd been mortified by being beaten.

"Sohara," Kana said evenly as she moved off the wall, flicking her cigarette away. They stood ten feet apart. She didn't act surprised; she didn't give any indication of emotion at all.

"Then it is you, KanaLee?" Sohara said, clearly surprised.

"You weren't sure?"

"You look so different, it was hard to know for sure," Sohara said, her eyes searching Kana's face. "You stand the same way, though, and your walk hasn't changed either."

Kana nodded. "No point in changing what works."

Palani walked out of the store at that moment, glancing up at Kana and then at the woman she was talking to. She was big like Kana, not quite as tall but much heavier. She looked like Kana had years before.

"Kana?" Palani queried, sensing tension in her even though there was no outward appearance of it.

Kana glanced down at her.

"And who is this, KanaLee?" Sohara asked, a black eyebrow raising with interest.

"She's mine," Kana replied simply.

Sohara didn't look the least bit surprised, either by the fact that Kana was with a woman or that Kana's tone was still chilly. She grinned, in fact. "You never did share your toys well."

"I still don't."

Sohara stared back at Kana for a long moment, narrowing her eyes. "I'm not here to kill you, KanaLee."

"You couldn't if you tried, Sohara," Kana replied confidently, then shrugged. "Besides, no contract lasts that long."

Kana heard Palani draw in a sharp breath. "This is…" Palani started to say.

"Yes," Kana replied.

Sohara looked at Kana, still reeling at how different she was. She was trim and fit, yet she looked even more powerful than she had when she'd beaten Sohara over fifteen years before. Kana looked every bit the Samoan warrior woman, and Sohara easily sensed that she was more confident in her abilities now than she had been before leaving Hawaii. Kana's arms were down at her sides, slightly away from her body, her feet braced shoulder-width apart. A fighter's stance. Some things didn't change.

After a few tense moments, Sohara threw her head back and laughed.

"KanaLee," she said, shaking her head. "You haven't changed so very much." She gestured to Kana's stance. "You are still a warrior, aren't you?"

"Always will be."

Sohara nodded, then looked at Palani. "I am Sohara Monta," she said, stepping forward and politely extending her hand.

Palani didn't move until she saw Kana nod. She put her hand out to Sohara, surprised at the strength contained in the light grip.

"Palani Ryker," she said, her look direct.

Sohara caught the look, and knew that it indicated that this little woman was showing her that she wasn't intimidated by her. That had everything to do with Kana's presence. Sohara's lips twisted in a grin as she turned back to Kana.

"A feisty little one, eh?"

Kana shrugged. "She has problems with people that wanted me dead at some point."

Sohara chuckled. "I am sorry about that, KanaLee. Will you for-give me?"

Kana gazed back at Sohara for a long moment, her dark eyes unreadable. Finally she inclined her head in acceptance. It had been over fifteen years, and they'd been very young then. Sohara had always been a hot-head, and never had taken losing well.

"In the end, it worked out well for me," Kana said.

"Yes?"

"Yes, I joined a whole other gang."

Sohara nodded. "I heard you became a cop."

"Still am a cop."

Sohara nodded again. "I'm not in a gang anymore, though."

"I wouldn't have jurisdiction here anyway," Kana said, grinning for the first time.

"Would that matter to you, KanaLee?" Sohara asked, grinning too.

"Nope."

Sohara reached up and clapped Kana on the shoulder. "How is your family?"

"Come see for yourself. My family is having a party tomorrow night—come to the house."

"Will I be welcome there?"

"They don't know you were the reason I left, Sohara."

Sohara looked surprised by that, but she nodded. "I will come, and make apologies then."

"Don't open that can of worms," Kana warned. "Not at my engagement party."

"Engagement?" Sohara repeated, then looked at Palani again.

"Yes," Kana replied.

Sohara nodded. "I'll be there, my friend, and I'll wait to make my apologies to your family at a later time."

Kana nodded. "We'll see you then," she said, taking Palani's hand.

"See you then," Sohara replied, inclining her head to Kana and then Palani.

Back in the car, Palani looked over at Kana. "Why does she call you KanaLee?" she asked, running the names together as Sohara had.

Kana shrugged. "She always did, dropping my first middle name and opting for the second. Just the way she was—she said it rolled off the tongue better."

"And she was the one to put out the contract on you?"

"Yes. But she was also my best friend for five years before that, and part of my gang."

Palani was surprised at that, but only nodded. "Why was she so intent on apologizing to your family when they don't know about her threatening your life?"

"Sohara has a great deal of honor, babe, and the way she sees it, she cost my family years with me, so she feels like she needs to apologize for that."

Palani nodded, still looking surprised.

"Palani," Kana said, reaching over to touch her hand. "Honor is one of the few things that some gang members have to hold on to. Not all gang members have it, but the ones that do, hold on to it for dear life."

"Like you?" Palani asked softly.

Kana glanced over at her, then nodded slowly.

Kana's honor was going to be tested that night.

334

As she slid on her ankle boots, zipping up the sides, Kana glanced up and saw that Palani's hands were shaking as she put on her necklace. Kana straightened, walking over to assist her. Palani dropped her hands to her sides, letting Kana clasp the necklace. Once the task was accomplished, Kana wrapped her arms around Palani from behind, pulling her back against her. Palani reached back to touch Kana's thighs.

"You're nervous," Kana said simply.

"Very."

"I'll be there with you, babe," Kana said softly, kissing Palani's temple.

"And you're not nervous?" Palani asked, turning to face Kana.

"They won't have guns, will they?" Kana asked with a wink.

Palani laughed softly, shaking her head. "They own a hotel—I don't think that lends itself to guns."

"Then we should be fine."

"Did you wear your vest, just in case?"

"Damn," Kana said, snapping her fingers. "I should have thought of that."

They left the house twenty minutes later. Kana drove to the airport. It was an hour and ten minute flight to Honolulu. By the time they touched down, Palani was very nervous. Kana took her hand, leading her off the plane and to the car-rental agency. Kana had reserved a Navigator, knowing she'd need some kind of security; driving a vehicle like her own gave her that. She smoked all the way to Palani's parents' home. Outside the house, she got out of the vehicle and went around to open Palani's door, cigarette in hand. She glanced at Palani's family home. It was big, but not as big as Kana's family's. Palani only had two brothers. They didn't need as big a house.

Kana leaned against the door of the Navigator, taking a long draw on the cigarette, mentally clamping down on the nervousness that had gnawed at her constantly that evening. This was not the time to become a nervous wreck. She knew Palani needed her to hold it together. They had no idea how their news would be received. Kana fully expected to be ordered from their house.

In Samoan culture, Fa'a Samoa, the parents dictated who their children would marry. It was up to the parents to approve or disapprove of who their children chose. Kana realized that Palani's family, being a very traditional Samoan family, would expect to have full say in whether or not Kana was acceptable to them. It wasn't going to go over well that Palani was disgracing her family by denying convention and dating a woman, but to marry her? To have a child with her? That was going to go over like a lead zeppelin.

Dropping her cigarette, Kana stubbed it out with a booted foot. She wore black slacks and a black collared shirt. She also wore a black leather jacket that fell to her mid-thigh. Her long hair was unbound, flowing over her shoulders and down to the middle of her back in a dark, thick sheet. Her makeup was, as usual, subdued, but served to enhance her features. She looked like Pele herself, in the classic portrait of the proud fire goddess of Hawaii.

Palani watched as Kana closed her eyes, taking a slow, deep breath. She was centering herself, much as she did whenever she went into a raid, or any confrontation. It told Palani that Kana was indeed nervous, but she refused to show it.

"Let's go," Kana said, gesturing for Palani to precede her.

Palani climbed the stairs up to the front door. Knocking, she stood back. Glancing over her shoulder, she saw that Kana was looking over the landscape through the open window to the side of the front porch.

The door opened, and Palani was looking into the face of her mother.

Anone Malifa smiled, happy to see her daughter. "Palani!" she exclaimed, holding out her arms.

"Mother," Palani said, moving into her mother's arms, hugging her.

Anone's eyes went to the tall woman standing on the porch. Her stance was very proud, but her dark eyes were cast down respectfully. It was obvious that the woman was Samoan, just from her size, coloring, and features.

"Mother, I'd like you to meet Kana Sorbinno. Kana, this is my mother, Anone Malifa."

"Ms. Sorbinno," Anone said, stepping forward and extending her hand politely. "Please let me welcome you to my home."

"Thank you, ma'am," Kana said respectfully as she took Anone's hand, holding it gently as she stepped inside the house.

"Are you from the mainland too, Ms. Sorbinno?" Anone asked.

"That's where I live now, ma'am, yes," Kana said, "but I was born in Kona."

"Kana's family owns a large coffee plantation there," Palani supplied.

Anone looked back at Kana again, as if trying to reassess her. Kana glanced at Palani, then turned the glance into a gaze around the entryway of the house. The floor was marble, the walls wainscoted in bleached pine, the walls above painted a deep, rich blue.

"You said you needed to talk to your father and me, Palani," Anone said questioningly.

"Yes," Palani said. "Where is Papa?"

"Outside with your brothers. Let's go out there." Anone gestured toward the back of the house and turned to lead them—so she didn't see Kana tense at the mention of Palani's brothers.

Palani closed her eyes momentarily, shaking her head at Kana, even as they followed her mother back toward the lanai. Her eyes pleaded silently with Kana. Kana caught the look and nodded slightly, indicating that she understood what Palani was asking her. She wanted Kana to try and control her temper upon setting eyes on the brother that had hurt Palani.

Moments later they were on the lanai and Palani was making introductions again. Kana was introduced to Mika, Palani's father, Puna, one of her brothers, and then Sampson. Kana had shaken hands respectfully with Mika, as he was the matai, the head of the family. She inclined her head to Puna, as he was younger than her; it wasn't expected that she show him the same respect. When Palani introduced her to Sampson, Kana's eyes bored into his, with no show of respect at all. Sampson was taller than Kana by about five inches, but Kana felt no inferiority. He was younger than her by nine years, so the lack of respect wasn't an actual insult to the family, only to Sampson himself.

Sampson's eyes narrowed as he sensed something not only very different about this woman, but also very dangerous. He looked to his sister, who glanced away. He turned back to Kana, angrily this time. Who was this woman? It was obvious from the way she carried herself and showed the expected respect to his father that she practiced Fa'a Samoa. Yet she'd just witnessed his sister's disrespect of him, her older brother, in front of their father, in his family home, and she had not batted an eyelash.

She was the one, Sampson suddenly realized. The one that Palani had been referring to that day at the mansion in California. The woman she was in love with. This was what she wanted to talk to their parents about? No!

Sampson's thoughts played across his face as he and Kana stared each other down. Kana knew exactly when he realized who she was, and she started to grin, her dark eyes sparkling with barely contained malice.

"Sit, sit," Mika said, gesturing to the couch across from where he and Anone sat.

Kana waited for Palani to sit down, and then joined her. Palani edged closer, and Kana felt her tremble. She looked across at Mika and Anone to see if they'd noted their daughter moving closer. They hadn't, but Sampson had. His tension was almost tangible.

"Mama, Papa," Palani began softly. "Kana and I—"

"How dare you!" Sampson exploded, not able to stand even hearing the words "Kana and I" coming out of his sister's mouth. It sickened him.

Mika and Anone turned their heads toward their son, staring at him in shock. Sampson went on undaunted.

"How dare you bring this into our home," he raged, gesturing at Kana as if she were nothing but trash.

"Sampson!" Mika exclaimed. "Have you lost your mind? How dare you speak like that in front of a guest in this house?"

"Papa," Sampson began, his voice grating as he gritted his teeth. "She is Palani's lover, not a guest to be respected."

Anone glanced over at Kana, noting that her face remained totally calm. Kana's eyes met Anone's, even as Mika began to berate his son for saying such things about his sister. Anone's eyes widened slightly as she realized that Sampson was telling the truth. Kana had not dropped her eyes from Anone. Anone put her hand on Mika's to quiet him. Mika turned to look at his wife, and saw her nod slowly. Mika looked then at Kana, who met his eyes with an inclination of her head, her eyes lowered respectfully once again. All the same, Mika needed verbal confirmation of such an outrageous idea.

"Is this true, Palani?" he asked.

"Yes, Papa," she said, her eyes on the floor.

Mika nodded, taking a deep breath. Kana was sure the next words out of his mouth would be "Get out of my home!" She was truly surprised when he looked at his sons.

"Puna, Sampson, leave us."

"Papa!" Sampson objected immediately.

"Leave us," Mika repeated, his tone commanding.

Puna, who hadn't reacted at all to the news, grabbed his brother's shoulder and pulled him toward the door. Sampson threw a deadly look at Kana. She merely stared back at him, unmoved. Inside she was shaking from the adrenaline pumping through her veins. She knew she had to stay calm—this was not the time to lose it. Beating the crap out of Sampson in front of his parents definitely wouldn't earn their approval.

When the two men had left the lanai, closing the French doors behind them, Mika looked at Palani again, assessing.

He's trying to figure out what he did wrong, Kana thought, knowing full well that's how people thought when their children turned out to be gay. "Where did I go wrong?" was the battle cry of parents worldwide when their child came out to them.

"Papa," Palani began, her voice respectful but strong. "Kana isn't just my lover, like Sampson said. She and I are going to be committed to each other. Married, Papa."

Mika looked horrified, but Anone looked thoughtful.

"That isn't legal," Mika said. "It isn't sanctified by the church."

"No," Palani said, shaking her head. "But you have to understand, I love her. I want to be with her always."

Mika was silent, looking like he couldn't possibly believe this was really his daughter. His dark eyes went to Kana. Kana lifted her chin unconsciously, the idea of being looked over like some kind of possession warring with her sense of pride. She said nothing, however, waiting for what he'd say next.

When Mika shrugged, shaking his head as if trying to deny what he was hearing, Kana knew she needed to say something. She could feel Palani trembling next to her. It bothered her that she had to go through this. Kana wanted it either over or to make a difference in their thinking. Anything at this point.

"Mr. Malifa," Kana said respectfully, "I know that you don't understand this kind of relationship. And I'm not expecting you to understand it, or even accept it. What you need to know is that I love your daughter very much. She and I are meant to be together. You see, I'm a police officer in San Diego. Recently I was shot in the line of duty, and the doctors said I wouldn't live through the night, that there was no hope." She paused, reaching down to take Palani's hand, squeezing it reassuringly. "At some point during the night, I woke

341

up. I was in a great deal of pain, and my friends did everything they could to comfort me, but I was ready to let go of life." She looked down at Palani then, love reflected in her dark eyes. "I was already beyond hearing anyone. I was dying. Palani came into the room. She took my hand and begged me not to go, not to leave her." She looked over at Mika and Anone again. "She's the reason I'm still alive. And I promise you that if you give her into my care, I will protect her with my life."

Mika's mouth opened in surprise. Anone had tears in her eyes that she was doing her best to hold back. Palani wasn't doing as well. Tears slipped down her cheeks as she looked up at Kana.

Kana gazed down at Palani, shaking her head slightly as she reached up to brush away the tears. "Don't cry," she whispered softly.

All Palani wanted to do was lean into Kana and hold her, to shut out the world. But she knew that she couldn't do that, not right now. It would undo whatever good Kana had just done in making that speech. It was a brave thing to do, putting herself totally out in the open like she had—that was what had Palani crying. Knowing that Kana was setting aside her pride, to try and give Palani what she wanted, her parents' approval.

Anone witnessed the exchange and felt her heart go out to her daughter. She silently prayed that Mika was moved by it too. Anone had known how unhappy Palani had been with Matthew Ryker. She never smiled, except when she was in front of the cameras. It had been a battle with Mika to allow Palani to go into modeling, baring her skin to the world. But it had made Palani happy. Marrying Matthew, her manager, had seemed natural to everyone, but Anone had known that Palani was only doing it to make others happy. Now, she sensed that Kana made Palani happy—why else would she risk her family's wrath to bring her here, asking for their approval?

Mika was silent for a long few minutes. Then his eyes fell on Kana again.

"Please understand," he said, his tone conciliatory, "that this is quite a shock for us. Last year, Palani was married and pregnant with our first grandchild..." His voice trailed off as he shook his head. "Then the accident happened, and we don't hear from her all this time. Only to hear she divorced Matthew."

"Accident?" Kana repeated, raising an eyebrow.

"She miscarried the baby," Mika said, nodding.

Kana had to clamp her mouth shut to keep from informing them just how she'd lost the baby. She sensed Palani tense, and knew she was praying Kana wouldn't say anything.

"Now," Mika said, not noticing the tension in his daughter and Kana—Anone did, however. "Now she comes home telling us she's turning her back on convention and the church and is marrying another woman?"

"Daddy," Palani said hesitantly. "Kana was the reason I wanted to leave Matthew in the first place."

Kana mentally rolled her eyes, thinking, *Oh shit!*

"What?" Mika said, shocked.

"I met Kana when she was investigating the murder of one of the photographers I had worked with. We connected immediately, so I pursued it and found that she made me happy. I fell in love with her," Palani said, all but pleading with her father to understand.

"You cheated on your husband?"

"Papa… The only thing Matthew and I had in common was my career. Kana and I could talk about anything. She cared about me in a way I'd never known before. She took care of me, making me laugh, making me smile all the time. I love her. Matthew never made me happy."

"It's true, Mika," Anone put in, feeling the need to come to her daughter's aid. "She was never happy with Matthew. If she says she loves this woman, we need to give her a chance to be happy. That's what we've said we wanted for our children," she pointed out. "We can't take that back now, simply because what our daughter wants isn't something we understand."

Mika looked at his wife, seeing the plea in her eyes. He sighed then, turning back toward Kana. Then he glanced at his daughter. Palani was clasping Kana's hand so tight he could see white on her knuckles. Palani had always been the quiet one, meek to the point of being totally submissive to her father's wishes. Now she was taking a stand, begging him to accept it. His face softened, and he looked at Kana again.

"Can we have an opportunity to get to know you, Kana?" he asked, the use of her first name meaning he was past formality now.

"Of course," she said, nodding.

"And your family?" Anone asked.

"My family is having a party for us tomorrow evening," Kana said. "I'd be honored if you'd come."

Mika and Anone nodded. "Are you staying on Oahu tonight?" Anone asked.

"No," Palani said. "Kana has to get back to help with the party."

Palani's parents nodded, understanding that Kana needed to be with her family at that point.

The night of the party, Palani wore a sarong of deep, rich blues and teals. Her hair was swept up off her face and held in place with two teal sticks. She also had a hibiscus flower tucked behind her ear. Her dark eyes were accented with teal liner, her lips a rich burgundy, her cheek bones accented as well. She looked like the classic Samoan princess. Kana wore black pants, a deep blue silk collared shirt, and her black dress boots. She wore darker eye makeup than normal, which served to enhance her dark eyes. She wore her hair loose, as was her habit.

Her parents insisted on having a receiving line, because they wanted all of their friends and associates to meet Palani. Palani was nervous about meeting all these strangers, afraid many of them would be shocked by the fact that Kana was marrying a woman.

"Relax, babe," Kana said as she stood behind her. "My family has had six years to get used to the fact that I'm gay. Nothing is going to shock my parents' friends, or my family." She kissed Palani's neck softly. "Unless you count how shocked they'll be that I'm marrying such a beautiful girl."

Palani bit her lip, feeling a rush of affection for Kana. There was nothing Kana couldn't make better for her. Palani loved that about her.

Kana had been right. Just about every person that walked through the receiving line exclaimed at how beautiful Palani was, how lucky Kana was, and how happy they were that Kana had finally found her match. There wasn't a moment of uncomfortable silence, no looks, no stilted comments. Just happiness and acceptance. It was amazing to Palani.

What she didn't realize was that years before, when they'd come to accept Kana's sexual orientation, the Sorbinnos had told their friends in no uncertain terms that either they accepted Kana as she was or they were no longer welcome at the Sorbinno home. They had earned enough respect over the years from their friends to keep a great deal of them. As the oldest daughter, Kana was entitled to a great deal of respect of her own; with her parents behind her, she was accepted without question.

Palani kept her eyes lowered out of respect for all the members of Kana's family, acting as was the custom of a bride in the home of her intended. It impressed all that met her; she was indeed Fa'a Samoa. The first of the siblings that Palani met were two of Kana's sisters, the ones she hadn't already met. She already knew Lima, Kana's youngest sister, who was ten years old. Lima was a tiny little girl, obviously taking after their mother. She was very sweet and seemed fairly enchanted with Palani. Kana had explained that while Lima was very curious about Kana, she didn't really know her at all. "I've only been back about five times since Lima was born," she said with a grimace. "And that first time was right after she was born."

First was Fimalolo, the second-eldest sister at thirty-one. She was polite, but not overly friendly. She welcomed Palani to the family home and greeted Kana with a hug and a kiss on the cheek. After Fimalolo moved on in the line, Kana told Palani that her sister wasn't friendly to anyone, and not to worry about it at all.

Next was Pika, at twenty-five very outgoing and independent. She was much smaller than Kana, although still bigger than Palani, standing five feet, seven inches. Her features were much more delicate than Kana's as well. She didn't have the same strong, proud beauty.

"It's lovely to meet you, Palani," Pika said, smiling. Palani and she were nearly the same age, so Pika wasn't bound by the custom of showing respect to elders.

However, when Pika moved to Kana, she lowered her eyes and inclined her head to her sister.

"How are you, Pika?" Kana asked.

Pika lifted her head, grinning up at Kana. "Just great," she said brightly as she reached forward to hug her. Palani noted that as Kana and Pika hugged, Pika's face lit up. The girl obviously adored her older sister, although, Palani realized, Pika would have only been about ten when Kana had left home.

Pika moved on, chatting and giggling her way down the line.

The next person Palani met was Kana's brother Kalolo. He and his wife and three children walked up. Kalolo was thirty-five, so older than Palani. She showed him and his wife the proper respect and smiled warmly at the children, laughing softly when Kalolo's nine-year-old boy exclaimed how pretty Palani was.

"Thank you," she said, smiling. "And you are very handsome."

Young Tapali smiled brilliantly at the compliment.

Next up were Tao and Semo; Tao was thirty-three and Semo thirty-one. The two brothers talked business constantly, Kana had told Palani, so it wasn't a surprise that when they met Palani, Semo exclaimed, "Now that's the face we should put on our labels! We'd sell coffee by the truckload!"

"You aren't putting my girl's face on coffee, Semo," Kana warned him. "She's a world-famous model, not some has-been hack that needs a paycheck."

"But she'll be family now," Tao put in, grinning at Palani. "We would even pay you."

"Over my dead body," Kana said.

Semo and Tao looked at each other, nodding.

"Hey!" Kana said, noting that they didn't have a problem with that. Both men grinned mischievously as they headed up the line.

Kana shook her head, then looked down at Palani. "See? You will be the death of me," she said with a wink.

Palani opened her mouth to reply, when someone new spoke up.

"You should marry me instead," said a silky, smooth voice—a man's. He walked up, taking Palani's hand, lifting it gallantly to his lips and kissing it gently.

Palani's mouth dropped open. He was handsome, with smooth features but the strong jawline of a Samoan man. Very tall, at least six feet, five inches, and broad of shoulder with a tapered waist. His behavior was outrageous at such a gathering. Palani was sure Kana would be mad, but to her surprise she heard her chuckle.

"Back off, Natano," Kana said. "Or I'll shoot you where you stand."

Natano grinned unrepentantly. "Are you carrying tonight, sister?" he said, raising an eyebrow as she straightened and leaned down to kiss Kana's cheek.

"Lucky for you, I'm not," Kana replied, her smile warm. "Palani," she said then. "This is Natano—we call him Nat. He's my youngest brother."

Palani smiled brilliantly, pleased to meet the brother Kana wished to father their child. "It's very nice to meet you, Natano," she said, lowering her eyes as she inclined her head.

Nat's finger under her chin raised her eyes to his. "Your eyes are too beautiful to be lowered to anyone, Palani," he said smoothly.

"Natano," Kana warned, her tone still good-natured. "You keep touching my girl, and I'm going to call you out."

"You can't do that," Nat said.

"No? Why not?"

"Because I'm your favorite brother," Nat said, with a brilliant smile.

"That's easily changed, Natano."

"Natano, you're holding everyone up," came another voice from behind him.

Nat winked rakishly at Palani, then moved on. Up stepped a larger, older, and definitely more reserved man. Palani was surprised to see Kana lower her eyes this time.

"Akua," Kana said respectfully. "This is Palani Ryker. Palani, this is Akua, my oldest brother."

Palani lowered her eyes once again, inclining her head respectfully. She sensed that this was the brother to show the most respect to. He was the oldest child. He was the one to impress out of the siblings. Next to Kana's father, Akua was the most powerful man in the household.

Akua took Palani's hand, lifting it to his lips, kissing it softly. "It is good to welcome you into my family and our home, Palani," he said smoothly.

Palani lifted her head, looking at Akua. "I am honored to be here," she replied, her tone bordering on reverent.

Akua looked at his sister then. "Kana," he said, reaching out and hugging her. "It is good to have you home, and with such happy news."

"Thank you," Kana said seriously. "It's good to be home."

Akua moved on in the line, hugging his parents.

Kana told Palani later in the evening that Akua was very serious in his position as the eldest son. That he had also been the biggest antagonist about her being gay.

"He actually thought to hit me at one point," Kana said, looking amused. "That was before he figured out that I'd learned a lot while being a cop."

"What did you do?" Palani asked, wide-eyed.

"Took his ass down to the floor," Kana said, grinning.

"Kana, you didn't!" Palani exclaimed.

"Hey," Kana said. "I won't let dirtbags hit me, let alone my own flesh and blood."

"How did he react to that?" Palani asked, knowing exactly how her own brother would have—he'd have killed her.

Kana curled her lips in derision. "It took all four of my other brothers to get me off of him, and when he got up, he charged me. It took my father, four brothers, and three of the workers from the field to get us apart. It wasn't pretty."

Palani shook her head, but she understood Kana's reaction. Kana had the power and the means to fight back, and she had. Palani was fairly sure that Akua had probably learned a lesson. Kana was not so immersed in the culture that she'd allow herself to be hurt. She didn't respect anyone enough to allow them to hit her. Palani respected that about Kana—she was her own person.

Just when Palani was sure her parents had opted not to come to the party, they arrived. She was relieved to note that Sampson was not with them, though Puna had come. As they walked up, Kana glanced at Palani, seeing her smile brightly. Kana had known that it was very important for Palani's parents to approve of, if not understand, what she was doing. Kana was glad she'd invited them to the party—maybe this would be a chance for them to see what they needed to see.

Kana knew that many people outside the gay community felt that all gays were perverts and fetish freaks, believing that all gays ever thought of was perverted sex acts and how to get sex. It just wasn't true. Gay people thought no more about sex than a heterosexual did; the only difference was that when a gay person thought of sex, they equated it to someone of their own gender. That was all. Of course, as with any culture, there were always people with their own brand of kink. Heterosexuals had plenty of those, men that were into tying women up, women who were into playing the dominatrix, men into wearing women's clothes, women into auto-erotic asphyxiation. All kinds of kinky things went on in heterosexual lives, as many as there were in the gay community. But Kana knew that people like the Malifas need to see that for themselves.

Mika took his daughter into his arms and hugged her gently. Kana lowered her eyes as he moved to her.

"Welcome to my family home, Mr. Malifa. It is an honor to have you here," she said, the appropriate show of respect for her partner's father as well as an elder.

Mika inclined his head. "Thank you for inviting me into your home. It is an honor," he replied, the words appropriate and polite. He moved on then.

Kana glanced at Palani. She grimaced slightly, but said nothing. Her mother came to embrace Palani, hugging her tight. Then she turned to Kana.

Again Kana lowered her eyes respectfully. "Mrs. Malifa, thank you for coming. Welcome to my family's home."

Anone took Kana's hand, which made Kana look at her.

"Thank you for giving us this opportunity, Kana," she said sincerely. "And please, call me Anone."

There was no missing the sharp intake of breath from Kana just before she nodded. It was a great concession for an elder to allow a younger person to call them by their first name. It was even more shocking because of the situation they were involved in. Anone smiled sympathetically at the younger woman, understanding that this must be extremely difficult for Kana. It was obvious that Kana Sorbinno was a very proud, strong woman. Yet here she was having to pander to someone else's family and beg for acceptance. Anone suspected that acceptance wasn't something Kana was used to asking for, nor that she cared if she received it. Anone also guessed that Kana's pride was great, but that her love for Palani was greater. That was what motivated Anone to push for acceptance of this relationship. She wanted her daughter to find happiness.

Kana spent the better part of the evening introducing Palani to people who had been friends of her family for years. At one point, Sohara arrived. Kana and Sohara had a shot together and vowed silently to forgive and forget. Sohara seemed extremely relieved. Kana was at the point in her life where grudges just didn't hold water anymore. Sohara's death threat had been serious at the time, but things had changed, and so had they. It was a time to make amends and give forgiveness. Kana respected that Sohara was willing to ask for it, and for that reason she had no problem giving it to her.

Anone stood talking to Aveolela, her eyes trailing over to where her daughter stood with Kana. She noticed that they were holding hands, and smiled fondly. Aveolela noticed the smile and followed her line of sight.

"They seem well matched," Ave said softly.

Anone nodded slowly. "Your Kana seems to love my daughter a great deal,"

Ave nodded. "I believe that she does. She has never brought anyone home. And last year, when they broke up, Kana came home devastated by it. That is very unlike my daughter."

Anone looked at Ave for a long moment. "Kana is a very proud woman, isn't she?"

"Oh yes," Aveolela said. "Even as a child she was constantly striving to prove that she was just as good as the boys. Poor Kao, my husband, was always trying to leave her out of things because she was a girl. Kana would get right in there and do just as well as the boys, if not better. Whether it be picking, planting, plowing, whatever it took, Kana would do it."

Anone nodded, then looked askance at Ave, but she hesitated, not sure how to ask what she wanted to know.

Aveolela canted her head to the side, sensing the question before it was asked.

"You're wondering if Kana always wanted to be a boy?" Ave asked softly.

Anone's eyes widened, but she nodded slowly in response.

"No, Kana never wanted to be a boy," Ave said. "But the problem was, all of the little girls she went to school with were the size of your Palani. It left Kana out of both groups. She struggled to fit in for many years, and unfortunately turned to fighting as a means to prove her power." Ave grimaced, remembering well the sleepless nights she'd spent worrying that Kana wouldn't come home.

Kao and Aveolela had known of Kana's affiliation with the Sisters of Samoa, a renowned gang of girls that was considered to be very dangerous. When they confronted Kana about the group she ran with, Kana merely shrugged and said, "They're my friends." She never once showed any disrespect for her family, her home, or her parents, so there wasn't much they could do. Ave begged her on a number of occasions to quit the gang, but Kana simply stated that you couldn't quit a gang, unless you wanted to end up dead. It had terrified Aveolela.

The night Kana had come home with cuts and bruises all over her face, a knife wound, and what Ave was sure was a couple of cracked ribs, she knew she needed to get Kana away from the life she was living. Kana had stayed home for a few days and nights after that, recovering. She told her mother that she'd in fact won the fight that had caused her so much damage. When she went out a week later, she came home with a cut on her face and the news that she was leaving Hawaii. Ave sensed that Kana was afraid, and almost didn't want to ask why her fearless daughter was scared. But she did, and when Kana answered the question, Ave had wished she hadn't asked.

"There's a contract out on my life, Ma," Kana had said simply. "And if I don't get off of Hawaii, I'll probably be dead in a week."

That mobilized Aveolela. She wasn't losing one of her children to violence. She gave Kana as much money as she could get together, telling her that they would support her wherever she went. Kana had hugged her and thanked her, and left the house in the early hours of the morning. A week later she'd called them from San Diego, California, saying she had found an apartment and was looking for a job. Two months after that, she'd called with the surprising news that she was now working for a gang task force with the San Diego Police Department. Ave had been shocked but relieved. Kana had never asked for any more money from her parents. She'd called often to tell them how she was doing. She never visited enough, but seemed generally happy when she did, though there was never anyone special in her life. No man she was engaged to, no man she missed terribly while visiting home, nothing like that.

Thinking along those lines, Ave watched her daughter. "Kana came home about seven years ago," she said. "She spent a great deal of time out at the plantation, wandering the fields, or out on my lanai smoking and drinking coffee. We knew something was bothering her, that she was wrestling with some kind of decision. Finally she told us she needed to talk to us. She sat me and Kao down and told us that she'd made a discovery about herself, something that might bring shame to our family. She offered us the option of not speaking of it, and stated that she would never bring her personal life back home to shame us if that was what we wanted. It wasn't something Kao and I wanted to inflict on our daughter, so we told her to tell us what she'd discovered." Ave smiled sadly. "Kana said that she'd discovered that she preferred women to men, and that she was dating a woman in San Diego.

"Kao did not accept what she was telling us, sure that she was merely going through a phase in her life and trying to be honest with us about her discoveries. Akua, my eldest son, however, did not take the news well, screaming at Kana, telling her she was a disgrace. He became violent in his anger and attempted to slap Kana—she put him right down on the floor. Things were very tense for a while. Kana left shortly after that, and did not return to Hawaii until I called her a year later and begged her to come home. Kao and I had discussed it and knew that if we didn't want to lose our daughter, we needed to accept her as she was. Akua was told that he would accept Kana or he would not be welcome in the house when she was home. But things worked out, and now, Kana is happier than I've ever seen her. I honestly believe your daughter is responsible for that."

Anone had listened in fascination as Aveolela told the story. "I think that my daughter has never been happier either," she told her confidentially. "I only hope that I can convince Mika that she needs to follow her heart. He was so upset when she divorced Matthew, but he never understood that Matthew did not make Palani happy. Men do not understand these things as easily as we do," she said, smiling fondly. "They want to see their children prosperous and stable—we want to see them happy, and sometimes what makes them happy is something we can't understand."

Ave smiled. "I agree with you. We must see that our daughters are allowed their happiness."

"Yes, we must," Anone said, very happy to have an accomplice in this endeavor.

Later in the evening, Kana and Palani stole off together to a spot Kana had told her about. It was a place that Kana had often escaped to when she wanted to be alone, hidden in the trees, just high enough that they could look down at the ocean far below. On this particular night, the moon was hitting the ocean at just the right place. It was beautiful.

Kana leaned against a tree, pulling Palani back against her.

"How often did you come here?" Palani asked.

"All the time, it seemed like," Kana said, smiling as she looked out over the ocean, the breeze blowing her hair back.

"It's a beautiful spot," Palani said, sliding her hands over Kana's arms, which were wrapped around her waist.

"That's why I picked it," Kana said. "It was a place of peace. I could look out at the world, but hide from it too."

Palani turned to face her, looking up into Kana's eyes. "You hid a lot when you were young, didn't you?"

Kana glanced back at her, then nodded slowly. "I felt like I had to. I didn't belong anywhere."

Neither of them noticed the two people who had walked up quietly as they'd begun to talk. Nor did they notice them observing them and listening to their conversation.

"But you know where you belong now," Palani pointed out.

"Yes," Kana said, nodding. "I belong with you."

Palani smiled, her eyes shining. "And I with you."

"Which reminds me…" Kana said, her voice trailing off as she reached into her pocket and pulled out a small box. "This is for you."

"Kana…" Palani whispered softly.

"Open it, Palani," Kana said gently.

Palani took the box with shaking hands, opening it carefully.

"Oh, Kana," she murmured, awe in her voice. "It's so beautiful…"

The ring nestled inside was the perfect combination of their culture and the classic engagement ring. It was delicate petals of gold studded with tiny emeralds, then the intricately carved petals of a hibiscus flower in beautiful peach-colored coral, with a round diamond at its center. The hibiscus was detailed with tiny slivers of black. Hibiscus was the nationally known symbol for Hawaii as well as the state flower, and the coral was native to Hawaii as well.

"What are these?" Palani asked, pointing to the black lines.

"Black diamond baguettes," Kana said, smiling.

"Kana Akua Lee..." Palani said, doing her best to sound chastising, but the ring was beyond beautiful. It said everything about what they were to each other. They came from the same background, but were different in a way that made them a good combination.

Raising her eyes, Palani looked up at Kana. "It is so beautiful, Kana. Thank you so much," she said, her voice reflecting the awe she felt at receiving such a perfect gift.

Kana reached out, touching her face, smoothing her thumb over Palani's cheek. "I love you," she said. "You are everything I've ever wanted or needed, and I can't wait to spend the rest of my life making you happy."

There were tears in Palani's eyes as she gazed up at Kana. "I love you so much," she whispered.

Kana leaned down to kiss her softly, her hand still at Palani's cheek. They hugged then, holding each other for a few extra minutes.

When Palani pulled back, she looked up at Kana again. "Thank you for bringing me here, Kana," she said sincerely. "And thank you for making me be honest with my parents."

Kana nodded. "I knew that you needed to do this. I know your family means a great deal to you."

"They do," Palani agreed. "I only hope that they can accept us. If they can't, it will be very hard for me."

Kana nodded, looking serious. "You know that I'd never want to come between you and your family, Palani."

Palani nodded. "I know that you respect my family's place in my life, Kana, but if they cannot accept you, then they will no longer have a daughter."

"Palani…" Kana said grievously. "Don't say that."

"Kana, I have to live my own life. I love my family, but if they cannot understand that I need to be with you to be happy, then they cannot understand me. If it means not seeing them, then that is what it will mean. You are in my life forever, you are my soul mate, and I will not lose you again. Not for anyone."

Kana took a deep breath, blowing it out in a frustrated sigh, shaking her head, but she said nothing. She knew where Palani's mind was; she knew because she'd been there years before with her own family. Although then there had been no one that she felt so strongly for. It wasn't Kana's place to dictate what Palani would do with her family; she only hoped that somehow they could come to some kind of acceptance. There was hope with Anone—she seemed to genuinely want to understand—but Mika was the head of the household, and if he didn't approve, Anone couldn't either. Samoan culture dictated that the matai was the head of the household; Mika was the matai, and there was no getting around that.

Anone took her husband's hand, leading him away from the private spot where Kana and Palani had been talking. She knew it had been wrong to eavesdrop on them, but she wanted Mika to see that the two women genuinely cared about each other. She had hoped she wouldn't be very wrong that they'd be themselves in private, but she hadn't been. Mika had heard for himself what it would mean not to accept their daughter's choice. Anone knew his pride was telling him that his daughter must obey his wishes, but the fact was, Palani no longer belonged solely to their culture, and she could and would do what she chose to do. Anone didn't want to lose her only daughter.

"They love each other, Mika," Anone said. "It is the right thing to do to accept this union."

Mika was silent, his thoughts in turmoil. It frustrated him that his daughter had become so Americanized that she could divorce her husband without the family's consent. Now she had become involved in such a strange relationship and been so blatantly disrespectful to say that they would lose her if they didn't approve. Palani was a totally different person than she had been when she'd left Hawaii years before. Mika wasn't sure he liked the changes at all.

Nor was he sure what to think of Kana Sorbinno. On the one hand, she was very obviously Fa'a Samoa, in her ways of speaking, respectfulness of elders, and her own family. Yet she was gay? How was this possible?

Mika had spoken to Kao, asking him how he dealt with such a strange situation. Kao had simply shrugged.

"Kana has always gone her own way," he had said by way of explanation. "She shows me respect, and she shows her mother and her older brother respect as she should. It is not for me to say who she should love. As long as she continues to believe in the values I raised her with, she is still the child I fathered."

Mika was surprised by such a simple way of thinking, but he had to admit that it made sense. Palani had been respectful of her family, in telling them the truth about her feelings for Kana. Mika just wasn't sure how this kind of thing was supposed to be handled. What would their friends think? What would his own family think of such a thing? Kana had given Palani a ring that sounded like it was very expensive, so Kana was very serious about Palani. This was not a casual relationship of exploration. Palani had every intention of being with this woman as her partner. Mika just wasn't sure if he could handle it or not.

Later that evening, Kana and Palani sat by the fire pit with Kana's younger brother, Tao, and Pika and Sohara. The elder people had moved off to talk amongst themselves. The "young people" were laughing and having a good time. Palani was sitting in front of Kana, turned toward her, her arms around Kana's waist and her head against her shoulder. Kana had one arm around Palani and held a Guinness in her other hand. Tao had just made a comment about Nat's prowess in the prone position, and the comments about his abilities to sleep anywhere began in earnest.

Kana threw her head back, laughing as she shook her head. "No, no, that wasn't a pineapple tree, Natano, that was a truck."

That had everyone laughing. Anone, Aveolela, Mika, and Kao looked over from where they stood. Anone noticed how her daughter cuddled against Kana. As they watched, Kana glanced down at Palani, asking her a question, then brushed her lips against Palani's forehead. Palani said something, shaking her head, and Kana nodded, hugging her as she did. It was obvious they were close, they were so much at ease with each other. Kana was very attentive, constantly asking Palani if she was cold, did she want something to drink, something to eat? Anything? Anone found it very endearing that Kana took good care of Palani.

It was getting late. Kana looked down at Palani and noticed her eyelids were drooping.

"Getting tired, babe?" she asked softly.

"Mmhmm," Palani murmured sleepily.

"Do you want to turn in?"

Palani lifted her head, looking up at Kana. "Are you coming with me?"

Kana grinned. "I don't know that I can get away yet," she said, brushing her lips over Palani's forehead. "But I can walk you down to the guest house."

"No," Palani said, shaking her head. "I'll just wait for you to be ready to go to bed too."

"Okay, babe," Kana said, nodding as she gave her a hug.

It was another hour before Kana felt it would be acceptable for her to leave the party. By this time, Palani was asleep. Kana glanced down, smiling fondly at the woman resting against her.

Nat caught the look. "That much in love, are you?"

"And then some," Kana said, smiling at her youngest brother. "Have you thought about what we talked about?"

"About the donor thing?"

"Duh, Sorbinno," Kana said, rolling her eyes.

Nat grinned. "You get that from your cop friends, don't you?"

"What?"

"The calling people by their last name thing."

"Oh," Kana said, shrugging. "Didn't really think about it, but yeah, probably where I get it from. So are you in or not, Nat?"

"And you're sure you don't want me to do it the old-fashioned way?" Nat asked, grinning widely.

"Sure," Kana said. "As long as you don't mind being dead."

Nat laughed, holding up his hands. "Okay, okay, you win. The much less fun way it is, big sister."

Kana nodded. "Good. We'll get in touch with you when we know how this is all going to work. You'll need to come to San Diego, you know."

"Boy, that'll be rough on me," Nat said, smiling.

"Uh-huh," Kana said, rolling her eyes, but pleased that he'd agreed. She hadn't been sure that he would. God knew it would be just about that time that Natano would go Fa'a Samoa on her.

Kana moved to stand, picking Palani up in her arms as she did. Palani woke up, raising her head from Kana's shoulder.

"Time for bed?" she asked hopefully.

"Yes, babygirl, time for bed," Kana said, looking down at Palani with a smile.

"I need to go say goodnight to my parents."

"Okay, babe," Kana said, setting her down on her feet.

Palani took Kana's hand and led her over to where their parents stood. They made their goodnights, then headed for the guest house. Kana stopped halfway there, just where the path darkened. Her sixth sense was tingling. She'd let Palani's hand go, and Palani was just turning around to see why Kana had stopped when she was lifted off her feet. There was an arm around her waist, and it felt like a band of steel. Glancing back, she was horrified to see Sampson staring at Kana, with a nasty glint in his eyes.

"Put her down, Sampson," Kana said, her tone all cop.

Sampson sneered. "You don't tell me what to do with my sister, trash."

"Let me make this much clearer," Kana said, her tone dropping dangerously. "Put her down, or I'll kill you."

Sampson threw his head back, laughing sarcastically. "What do you think you can do to me, Kana Sorbinno? Dyke bitch?"

Kana's eyes narrowed. He'd just used a term she despised.

"If you even think about hurting her, Sampson, trust me, it will be one of the last thoughts you have."

"You think you can take me on, dyke?" Sampson asked, still holding Palani at an angle in front of him, his arm clamped around her waist.

"I think I'm about to show you I can take you on, little boy. Let's go," Kana said, canting her head to the side. "Or are you only tough with little girls?"

Sampson flung Palani away. Kana lunged for her, catching her before she hit the ground. Turning, she backhanded Sampson, Palani still held in her other arm. Lightning fast, Kana set Palani on her feet, telling her to stay back, and turned to Sampson again. He was staring at her with barely leashed fury.

"You're dead, you dyke bitch. You're dead."

"Bring it, little man," Kana said, gesturing to Sampson with her fingertips.

Sampson charged Kana. Unfortunately, she couldn't move, since Palani was behind her. He hit her full force in the midsection, and they both went down. Kana knew better than to end up under a Samoan. She twisted around in midair, and landed on her side with a grunt. She moved to get to her feet, but not before Sampson kicked her in the stomach. She heard Palani cry her name, but she knew she couldn't worry about that right now. Sampson was playing for keeps. If she lost, she might end up dead after all.

Rolling away from Sampson, she ended up on her feet again. She felt blood trickling down her arm, and realized she'd sliced it on a rock. She ignored that too. Sampson climbed to his feet, eyeing her warily. This woman was a better fighter than he'd figured her to be. He still had size and weight on her. He faked to the left, then stepped in to the right and slammed his fist into what should have been her face, but her arm came up, blocking him. Sampson was surprised to be caught in the midsection with a right jab. Stepping back, he surprised Kana by bringing his fist through, catching her on the chin. She jerked her head back, not in time to miss the connection, but quickly enough to keep it from doing a lot of damage.

In desperation, Sampson charged her again, slamming into her midsection. Unknowingly, he hit the side that was still healing from the gunshot. It caused Kana enough pain to stop her thinking for a moment, long enough for Sampson to land with her under him. He punched her in the face, hearing his sister scream over and over again. Then suddenly Palani was on him, yelling and clawing at his face. He threw her off, but when he did, he lost his perch on Kana. She took full advantage of that, bringing her booted foot up and putting it to his stomach, shoving him off of her.

Sampson landed on his back, and Kana rolled to a crouching position, coughing and trying to shake off the waves of nausea that were hitting her because of the pain in her side. Sampson jumped to his feet, ready to kick Kana as she crouched on the ground. That was when Kana's five brothers arrived on the run. They'd heard Palani's screams, and saw immediately what was going on.

Akua and Kalolo grabbed Sampson, hauling him away from Kana. Semo and Nat helped Kana to her feet as Tao moved to Palani to make sure she was okay. Kana stood up, spitting blood onto the ground.

"Kana!" Palani cried, breaking away from Tao and running to Kana's side. Kana's arm went around her protectively, even as she wiped her mouth with the back of her hand, her eyes on Sampson, her look dangerous.

"If you ever," Kana said, still panting from her exertions, "touch her again, I will personally kill you. Do you understand?"

"How dare you!" Sampson exclaimed. "How dare you threaten me. You are nothing, you have no respect, no honor, you are nothing but—"

"I'd shut up if I were you," Akua growled in his ear, his grip tightening on Sampson's arm, which Akua held behind him. "That's my sister you're talking to."

"Your sister is disgusting," Sampson spat.

"And you're not?" Kana asked, her eyes blazing.

"I am a true Samoan," Sampson said. "I respect my family. I don't sleep with members of my own sex."

"No," Palani said, her tone strong now, even as she trembled against Kana. "You just kill members of your family."

Kana glanced sharply at her, catching the angry glint in her eyes, which shone with tears.

"What is this?" Mika asked, having walked up during the argument.

Sampson said nothing. His glare at Palani was a barely veiled threat, however.

"What are you talking about, Palani?" Mika asked.

"Ask him," Palani said, nodding at Sampson.

"Sampson?" Mika queried, turning toward his son.

Sampson shook his head, not looking at his father.

"It was no accident, Father," Palani said. "My miscarriage, it wasn't an accident. Sampson was angry with me, because I admitted to loving a woman. He slapped me. I stumbled backward and fell down the stairs."

Kana's arm tightened around Palani as her tears started. "I told myself it was an accident, that he didn't mean to do it, but he did. He did…"

"Come on," Kana said, not willing to let Palani upset herself more.

Without a word, Kana walked her away toward the guest house. Once inside, Kana had to sit down, because her head was spinning.

"Kana!" Palani exclaimed, going to her knees in front of her, reaching up to touch her face, where blood was already trickling down from her cut lip.

Palani was crying, she was so upset at what had happened. "Kana, your side…"

"I'm okay, babe," Kana said wearily, feeling anything but. "I'm okay. Calm down, it's okay." She took Palani's shaking hands. "I'm okay, baby, it's okay…" she repeated, taking Palani in her arms and hugging her.

"No… no!" Palani said, her voice tearful. "He could have killed you, Kana. He could have killed you. I'm so sorry."

"Shh," Kana soothed. "It's okay, baby. I'm fine, everything's fine." She kissed Palani's forehead, smoothing her hair back, closing her eyes and doing her best not to throw up.

"Kana?" came a voice from the doorway. It was Anone.

"Hmm?" Kana murmured, suddenly too tired to think about appropriate respect and all that.

"Are you okay?" Anone asked, moving into the room. Mika stood in the doorway, looking extremely unhappy.

Kana nodded, not very convincingly.

Anone reached out, touching Kana's chin, seeing the darkening bruise there. Then her eyes trailed to Kana's arm.

"You're bleeding!"

Kana grimaced as Palani's head snapped up, fresh worry in her eyes.

Kana looked Palani directly in the eyes. "I'm okay, Palani. It's just a cut—it's nothing. It's okay."

Anone looked at the cut, realizing that Kana was making light of her injuries to keep Palani from worrying. Kana's hand smoothed over Palani's hair as she pulled her toward her again, hugging her close. Kana's eyes connected with Anone's over Palani's head, and it was as if they communicated telepathically. Kana was trying to keep Palani calm and wanted Anone to work with her on this. Anone nodded, as if Kana had actually spoken the words.

"Why has your son done this?" Aveolela asked as she walked into the room, her eyes on Kana.

"He was wrong to do this," Anone said, her words directed at Mika as well as Ave. "He felt he needed to defend the family, but he was wrong." She looked at Kana then. "I am very sorry for this, Kana. Sampson has gotten out of hand, and he will be called to task on it."

Kana nodded, not allowing herself to speak, knowing the words she'd use would be venomous.

"I will punish your son," came Kao's voice from the doorway as he strode into the room. "He has injured a member of my family with his anger and hate, and I will take retribution for it."

"No, Father," Kana said, her voice low but determined. She knew from the tone of her father's voice that he fully intended to beat Sampson beyond senseless, and Kana was fairly sure that would also involve her brothers. She couldn't allow that. Sampson was Palani's brother; even if he was a bigoted asshole, he was Palani's flesh and blood.

Even as she looked at her father, however, she saw Mika nodding in agreement with what Kao had said.

Mika turned to Anone. "Sampson has gone too far," he said. "And he's done so once too often now."

Kana knew that Mika meant Sampson's hitting Palani in San Diego. She set Palani back from her and moved to stand.

"Mr. Malifa," she began entreatingly, "I agree that Sampson went too far when he hit Palani in San Diego. He had no right, regardless of how he justifies it to himself. But this, tonight, this was what he felt he needed to do to protect his family. It's what we're taught, Fa'a Samoa—family comes first. He obviously feels, as you do, that Palani is making a mistake being with me. He was just more physical in his rejection of my presence."

"No man should strike a woman," Mika said, shaking his head.

"Because of my place in your daughter's life," Kana said, "I don't think Sampson sees me as a woman. He sees me as a threat to his family's good name. Isn't that how you feel?" Kana asked, no accusation in her voice, only resolve.

Mika was silent, even as Anone, Aveolela, and Kao all turned to look at him. He stared at Kana for a long moment. Palani stood and walked to Kana's side. Kana automatically curled her arm around her shoulders, pulling Palani into her uninjured side. Mika's eyes dropped to his daughter's face and softened. He'd seen how upset she'd been at Kana being hurt. She had been willing to throw Sampson to the wolves, telling her father about the miscarriage. Yet Kana wasn't willing to do that, and she'd been hurt too. It was obvious to Mika that Kana was indeed in pain, from the way she was standing, breathing shallowly. Yet she was defending Sampson's attack.

"It is how I felt, it's true," Mika said finally. "But I see how you conduct yourself, Kana Sorbinno, and you are not a disgrace to either your family or your name. And I do not feel that you will be one to my family either."

Kana stared in disbelief. She couldn't begin to think of a response. Finally she inclined her head to Mika. "Thank you, sir," she said solemnly.

Palani walked over to her father, hugging him. "Thank you, Papa," she whispered. He only hugged her tighter in response.

Anone and Aveolela smiled at each other, and Kao nodded his acceptance.

It was all about taking chances. Kana and Palani had taken a chance on their love, and in the end it had been worth everything.

You can find more information about the author and other books in the *WeHo* series here:

www.sherrylhancock.com

www.facebook.com/SherrylDHancock

www.vulpine-press.com/we-ho

Also by Sherryl D. Hancock:

The *MidKnight Blue* series. Dive into the world of Midnight Chevalier and as we follow her transformation from gang leader to cop from the very beginning.

www.vulpine-press.com/midknight-blue-series

The *Wild Irish Silence* series. Escape into the world of BJ Sparks and discover how he went from the small-town boy to the world-famous rock star.

www.vulpine-press.com/wild-irish-silence-series

CPSIA information can be obtained
at www.ICGtesting.com
Printed in the USA
LVHW031121141019
634125LV00001B/109/P